Chapter One

'There's a third lamb in here.' Mandy Hope looked over at the farmer. Mr Ruck crouched on his haunches on the cropped grass as he steadied the head of the Wensleydale ewe. Mandy was unsure how this information would go down. A pair of lambs was ideal – sheep had only two teats after all. Three was a bonus that not many farmers would appreciate. The two lambs that had already been born writhed in the grass next to the ewe.

But Mr Ruck grinned, his short white hair ruffling in the soft breeze that carried with it the clean scent of the moorland turf. 'The missus'll be delighted,' he said. 'This old ewe's one of her favourites. We'd almost given up on her this year, she's so late with her lambs.'

Mandy pictured Prudence Ruck in her mind. Mr and Mrs Ruck's daughter, Harriet, had been in Mandy's class at school and Mandy had often visited her friend at Quarry Cottage. Harriet's dark-haired, dark-eyed mother had always been creating something from the wool she and her husband produced.

'How is Prue?' Mandy asked as she nudged her arm a little deeper inside the sheep. So far, she had only found a head. There should have been two front feet as well. She

I

had to get them into the correct position before the lamb could be born.

'She's doing great,' Mr Ruck replied.

'Is she still knitting?' Mandy pressed her fingers forwards another inch. There was the left leg, tucked away along the side of the lamb's body.

'She is that,' the old farmer nodded. 'We've got a new outlet these days at Upper Welford. The unit there has been a great boon.'

Mandy thought back to the previous summer when she had visited the little row of artisanal shops that had been opened in the steading at Upper Welford Hall. She was glad it had boosted the business of many villagers. Jobs could be scarce around here, she knew.

Mandy's eye was caught by a movement near her elbow. One of the lambs that had already been born had staggered to its feet. It tottered across the grass, wobbling with knock-kneed determination towards its mother. Its tightly curled fleece was already almost dry, its rather large ears and bright eyes gave it a quizzical look. As she watched, it opened its mouth and let out a high-pitched bleat. The ewe lifted her head and gave the grumbling chuckle to her newborn lamb that Mandy loved so much.

She returned her thoughts to the invisible puzzle inside the ewe. Although she had brought the first leg forward, it wasn't in quite the right position. The elbow was now straight, but the carpal joint was still contracted. She left it for now. Pushing along the other side of the lamb, she felt for the second foot. There it was, right back against the compact little body. A tightening on her forearm told her the uterus was contracting. The ewe's head was back down and she grunted softly as she lay on her side and strained. Mandy waited until the pressure was past, then keeping the tiny cloven hoof away from the wall of the womb, she tugged it forward. As the next contraction began, she could feel two feet and one head pressing forwards.

Both of the lamb's toes were pointing downwards rather more than they should have been. Mandy held them safely within the birthing passage as the lamb surged towards her. The little hooves appeared first, followed by a re-assuringly twitchy nose. As the uterus contracted again and the sheep made a final grunting effort, the head appeared, followed in a rush by the rest of the tiny creature. Mandy removed the remainder of the amniotic sac from the small white face and to her pleasure, the lamb raised its head, shaking its rather large ears free. The ribcage lifted as the newborn took its first gasping breath.

Mr Ruck was looking at it with concern. 'Those front legs don't look quite right,' he said.

Instead of stretching out straight, the joints just above the little cloven hooves of both front legs were bent over. 'He has contracted tendons,' Mandy confirmed. 'It happens sometimes when there hasn't been much space. We'll need to wait and see how the little chap gets on when he stands up.'

She looked around at the surrounding moorland. It was unusual to be lambing a ewe up here on the high tops. It had been more common when her parents had first opened Animal Ark, the veterinary clinic that lay down in the valley.

Nowadays, most farmers brought their sheep into the practice for assistance, but Mr Ruck had flagged her down as she had been returning from an early morning call out.

'We won't be able to keep an eye on the little lad up here.' Mr Ruck seemed to have divined her thoughts. 'We'll take them down into the field beside the cottage. Could you wait while I give Prue a call, please? She'll bring the trailer up.'

'Of course,' Mandy said. 'If you could just hold onto Mum a moment longer while I have a last check inside.' Even though the ewe already had three lambs, it was vital to make sure there were no more, and that there were no problems with the uterus. Mandy lubricated her gloved hand one last time and bent to examine the ewe. Everything seemed fine. 'Yep, all fine,' she told the farmer. Pulling her hand out, she shifted up to the ewe's head and took over from Mr Ruck. There were no pens up here on the moor. If they let the wily animal go, it would be very difficult to catch her again.

Mr Ruck stood up, stretching his legs with a groan. 'I'll just take a wander over there,' he said, pointing. 'Get a better signal.' Pulling a mobile phone from his pocket, he strode off in the direction of the lane where Mandy's car was parked.

It was the most beautiful morning, Mandy thought. A soft breeze played across her face as the sun shone down from a clear sky. No matter how many times she assisted in a lambing, it never seemed to lose any magic for her. Three new little lives had begun today and she knew she'd helped it happen. She watched as lamb number three began to make his first tremulous efforts to rise. Despite the stiffness in his forelimbs, he was as determined to stand as his two siblings, who were already butting their heads against their mother's flank looking for milk. 'It's down here.' Mandy tried to guide them into position, but they pulled their heads away, shaking their ears at her. It would be easier when the ewe was home and standing up.

Mandy's gaze wandered over the moorland. It was so green under the huge curve of blue sky. Other ewes were scattered amongst the jutting grey rocks that littered the landscape. Their low voices called out, the piercing bleats of the youngsters answering as they gambolled in the sunshine. A few feet away, a pair of older lambs burrowed their heads underneath their mother for milk, tails whirling as they drank.

Near where she was kneeling, Mandy could see the yellow slippers of a patch of bird's-foot-trefoil bobbing in the wind. Her eyes followed the line of the dry-stone wall, which stretched across the dale. On the far side of the valley, the trees of Lamb's Wood wore the light green hue that came with the height of spring. Amongst the greenery, she could make out the dark roof of Wildacre, the cottage she had bought last autumn. It had seemed before Christmas that the renovations she wanted would never be complete, but now everything was coming together.

My own home!

Her eye was caught by movement further down the slope. A dark figure on a quad bike was riding across the field. She pulled her mobile from her pocket. Despite Mr Ruck's comment about signal, she seemed to have a couple of bars. With one hand still on the ewe's neck, she quickly typed in a message: 'Good morning handsome.'

In the distance, the quad bike came to a standstill. Despite being little more than a speck, she thought she could see the figure reaching into a pocket.

'Morning beautiful.' A kiss emoji. The message came winging back and the speck was on its way again. Mandy grinned. Jimmy Marsh, the wonderful man in her life, had no idea she was spying on him from afar. She hugged the information to herself.

'You're looking rather pleased.' Mandy turned her head as Gordon Ruck strode back up the hill.

'This has been a great start to the day,' Mandy replied. She felt a wave of happiness washing over her in a way that was becoming familiar. As well as Wildacre and Jimmy, she had Animal Ark and Hope Meadows. She had grown up in the shelter of Animal Ark, her parents' veterinary surgery, where she now worked alongside them as a vet. In the autumn, her wonderful adoptive parents had helped her to achieve her life-long dream of running a rescue centre. Hope Meadows was now filled with furry residents, all of whom needed Mandy's help. She couldn't help but feel very, very lucky.

'Prue's on her way,' Mr Ruck told her. Even as he spoke, Mandy saw the square shape of a Land Rover making its way up the narrow lane, towing a small silver trailer.

'I think that little chap's going to be okay.' Mandy nodded towards lamb number three, who was now standing on his toes. Though he couldn't straighten his legs completely, he was managing to totter forwards without falling. Had he been walking on his knees, she might have had to splint the legs to correct the deformity, but as he was managing to walk, a couple of days of running around outside would most likely sort him out. 'Keep an eye on him for a few days. If his legs don't straighten, then bring him in and we'll take another look.'

The Land Rover pulled up in the lane and Prue Ruck walked across the springy turf towards them.

'Morning, Mandy.' The dark hair and eyes were still as Mandy remembered from all those years ago when she had first visited her friend Harriet. There were a few more wrinkles, but Mrs Ruck barely seemed to have changed. Her face filled with delight as she regarded the ewe and her three lambs, which were all on their feet, gazing around with wide eyes. She bent down and put a hand on the mother sheep's flank. 'You're a good old lass,' she told the ewe. Mandy continued to hold the ewe's head as between them, they encouraged the sturdy animal to her feet. Prue took over and guided the long-legged sheep towards the trailer as Gordon Ruck assisted. Mandy walked behind, ensuring that the three lambs were following too.

'We can take it from here.' Prue turned to smile at Mandy as Gordon lifted the ramp to close the trailer on the four animals. 'Likely that little 'un will need an extra bottle or two, what with there being three of them. The old lass won't mind. Always been one of my favourites, she has. She was a pet lamb herself, years ago. My little Wendy.'

Mandy couldn't help but smile back. It was good to know that her patients would continue to receive good care.

'So how are you, Mandy? And how is poor James doing?' Mrs Ruck's eyes were kind.

A pang of sadness went through Mandy. It was nearly a year since James's husband, Paul, had died from the awful bone cancer that had riddled his body. Watching her best friend go through such grief had been the hardest thing she had ever experienced. 'He's doing . . . okay,' Mandy said. It was the truth. James would never be the same again, but he was managing.

'Well, give him our love, won't you?' said Mrs Ruck. 'I'll tell Harriet you were here. She's very busy at the moment, but she was saying just the other day that she'd like to see you two again.'

It would be nice to catch up with Harriet, Mandy thought. Behind Mrs Ruck, across the valley, a movement caught her eye. The tiny figure had climbed off the quad bike and was wielding a mallet to bang in a fence post. For a moment, Mandy was distracted, but pulled her mind and eyes back to Prudence. 'Thanks,' she told Mrs Ruck. 'Please give her my best.'

'Will do.' With a last nod, the older woman turned to get in the car alongside her husband. 'Best be getting along. I guess we'll see you at the Spring Show if not before,' she said. 'I've got a stall for my knitting.'

'That's great!' said Mandy. The Welford Spring Show was a highlight of the village year – and Mandy's too. A whole day outdoors, having fun, eating great food and being surrounded by beloved pets and livestock was something she could *always* enjoy. Mandy waited until the trailer had pulled away before returning to her own Toyota.

★ ★ ★

Morning surgery was in full swing at Animal Ark when Mandy returned. She was pleased to see Tango, the old ginger cat that her dad, Adam, had adopted, sitting on the reception desk. His golden eyes flickered as Helen, Animal Ark's veterinary nurse, typed in some information into the computer. Occasionally he reached out a paw to tap Helen's hand, as if reminding her he was there.

When Tango had first been brought from Hope Meadows, they had tried to keep him in the cottage. But he had been so persistent, following Adam out to Animal Ark every day and meowing loudly at the window until he was let in, that they had finally relented. He was now their official Practice Cat. He butted Mandy's face, purring loudly as she leaned down beside Helen to scan through the appointments.

'Just the one for you.' Helen pointed at the screen with a grin. 'Your dad is doing all the rest. He's really getting into the swing of all the dogs and cats.'

As time had gone by, Mandy had been taking over more of the farm work from her father. She had worked in a small-animal practice before her return to Animal Ark, but she loved going out to see the horses, cows and pigs that made up the majority of Animal Ark's larger patients. They rarely saw sheep outside of lambing time, but the spring flood of new births had been an added bonus for Mandy. Lambing was physically so much easier than calving and just as satisfying.

Adam seemed to be enjoying being in the clinic more as well. Emily Hope, Mandy's mother, had been unwell just before Christmas. Though she was better, following a series of injections of vitamin B12, and with iron supplements to help with her anaemia, she still seemed tired at times and was doing less work than she had before. It was good that she was listening to the doctor. Mandy knew that if she took the farm calls, her dad could be closer to her mum, which was a comfort to them both.

She peered at the screen, where Helen was pointing.

'Birch Fenwick,' she read. 'Dewclaw injury.'

Tango reached out his nose towards Helen's pointing finger and the nurse moved her hand to rub him behind his ear. 'I spoke to Dawn Fenwick,' Helen said as Tango began to purr loudly. 'Everything is going brilliantly. She's going to bring Flame in too.'

'How lovely.' Mandy was delighted to hear that the gorgeous golden lurcher she had rehomed back in January would be coming in with Birch, the tiny silver terrier. The pair had attached themselves to one another when both had been in Hope Meadows. It was great to hear that things were going well. A dewclaw injury was only minor, after all.

Forty minutes later, Mandy left Animal Ark, with Sky, her border collie trotting at her heels. Together, they walked into the field behind Animal Ark, towards Hope Meadows. Sky had been one of Mandy's first rescues at the centre, a shrinking dog, terrified of the world. Now, she was placid, loving and happy. Mandy stopped to fondle Sky and make a fuss of her before she went in to care for her current residents.

She opened the door and walked into the beautiful room with its huge window onto the fellside. It was half-term and Nicole Woodall, the shy teenager who helped Mandy out in the evenings and weekends during school time, was already halfway through cleaning out the cats. Mandy felt a surge of pleasure. Nicole was so willing, and more importantly, brilliant with the animals. She seemed instinctively to know when there was a problem. Mandy smiled. Despite being rather old, the second-hand cages she had bought were spotless and Nicole was engrossed in her favourite task of the moment.

'How are they?' Mandy asked, sliding down to sit on the floor beside the teenager. In her left hand, Nicole held a tiny black and white kitten. In the cage opposite, the kitten's two brothers, one ginger and one tabby, were snuggled against their mother. The little black and white cat had been brought in a fortnight earlier, heavily pregnant and desperately thin. She had given birth safely six days ago, but the kittens had not thrived at the beginning. Mandy had weighed them daily. By day three, it had become apparent that they were not growing. Since then, Mandy had been supplementing the mother's milk.

'They're doing wonderfully well.' Nicole had really come out of her shell since she'd been coming to Hope Meadows, Mandy thought. Mandy had met Nicole six months ago when she had been out riding with Molly Future at Six Oaks. Nicole worked as a stable hand for Molly and now, she split her time between there and Hope Meadows.

The girl's long blonde hair fell over her face as she leaned forwards to tend to the tiniest of the kittens. 'I've given them names,' she told Mandy, her eyes darting to Mandy's face, then returning to her minuscule charge. 'This is Button.' She cradled the tiny scrap of fur in one hand. With the other, she held a miniature feeding bottle. Button was suckling at the teat. Her teeny paws were flexing and relaxing in turn, kneading at Nicole's fingers. The small, domed head was still.

Mandy smiled at the ecstasy in the little face with its as-yet-unopened eyes. 'Why Button?' she asked.

'Because she's cute as a little button,' Nicole said. Button had let go of the teat. Her head was bumbling about as if searching for something, but Nicole smiled as she held the tiny body up and inspected the round tummy. 'I think you've had enough,' she told the kitten. She lifted a piece of damp cotton wool from a box. Turning the kitten over, she rubbed her underside, mimicking the action of the mother's tongue until the tiny animal passed urine. Nicole made sure the kitten was clean before she carried her back to her mother.

Mandy watched with pride. She had taught Nicole how to feed and handle the kittens and Nicole had picked it up perfectly.

I couldn't have asked for a better helper.

This thought was followed by Mandy's familiar stab of guilt that she wasn't able to pay Nicole for her help yet. She needed to find a way, she knew, but she'd been struggling to find funding for Hope Meadows altogether.

'Do the others have names as well?' she asked.

'Yes.' Nicole knelt at the door to the cage. 'That one's Jasper.' She pointed to the largest of the kittens, a ginger tom with a white chest who was squirming his way up his mother's flank. 'And that's Myler,' she said.

'Myler.' Mandy looked at the last of the kittens, the male tabby. 'It suits him,' she said with a grin.

Two hours later, she sat at the desk in the Hope Meadows reception area, gazing at the computer screen. All the bills for April had now been paid, but despite her best efforts, she was still going into the red by the end of every month. She chewed her thumb as she scrolled through the rows and columns of numbers, searching for inspiration.

What with the extra work of lambing time, and Emily being less well, she'd had no time to come up with any new fundraising plans. James and his assistant Sherrie were still sending contributions from James's café-cum-bookshop in York, but somehow it never seemed to be quite enough to keep everything ticking over.

'Mandy! Could you come here a second?' Nicole's voice floated through to reception. With a sigh, Mandy closed the lid of the computer and pushed her worries down.

Another day . . .

Chapter Two

The track that led to Wildacre no longer felt like a jungle safari. The plants had been trimmed back and the worst of the ruts filled in by the landscapers. Mandy's heart lifted as she drove towards her new home in the evening sunlight. The damaged parts of the weather-boarding had been replaced and the walls were freshly painted. The door was a lively shade of buttercup yellow. The plasterer's van stood in the little parking place in front of the house, so she drove round the side and pulled up next to the lean-to shed where the wood for the stove was stored.

Walking round to the front door with Sky at her heels, she stopped for a moment to admire the scenery. Like the track, the overgrown garden had been partially tamed. It was James who had pointed out last year that there would be a lovely view over the valley, and so it had proved. Between the tall trees, she could see right down to the river. Further away, the fell reached towards the sky, the dry-stone walls scaling the heights, as they had for hundreds of years.

The scent of new plaster met her as she opened the door.

'Hello.' The plasterer greeted her from the sitting room, in overalls covered with white, powdery plaster. 'Just finishing up,' he told her. Most of the work had been carried out a couple of weeks earlier, but then the electricians had been in to complete the rewiring. It was such a mundane thing, yet Mandy watched with her heart in her mouth as he smoothed the area below the light switch, his movements economical. 'And that's it.' He took a step back and regarded his handiwork with apparent satisfaction. Pulling off his gloves, he threw them into an empty bucket that was standing on the floor.

'It looks great.' Mandy gazed around, a grin spreading across her face. The ugly green wallpaper was gone, and the brick mantelpiece looked wonderful flanked by the new smooth plaster. The whole house already felt brighter.

I'll decorate as soon as it's dry.

She had already bought a warm shade of white paint called Sail White.

The plasterer tidied away his tools. 'I'll be off then,' he told her. 'Give me a shout if there's anything else you need.'

'Thanks,' Mandy said. When he had gone, she walked out of the sitting room and crossed into the kitchen. The late sunshine slanted in through the kitchen windows. The shutters had been cleaned and freshly painted, as had the cupboards and the walls. The ancient black wood stove and the shutters lent the room a slightly old-fashioned feel. Mandy had also spent ages stripping down the old oak table and it stood under the window, with the newly upholstered chairs either side. Once the cupboard doors were in place, this room would be finished. Rather than buying new doors, Mandy had sanded the old ones until her arm had ached, then she had painted them a smart shade of green. Bronze handles completed the effect. For now, they were leaning against the wall in the corner of the room, but soon it would all be done. Soon this place would be a real home.

'Evening!' There came a welcome shout, then the sound of the front door opening. Sky's tail began to beat against Mandy's leg and a moment later the collie rushed across the room as Simba, Jimmy Marsh's German Shepherd thundered in, followed at a more sedate speed by Zoe, his extremely pregnant husky. Jimmy followed close on their heels. He crossed the room and put a hand on Mandy's waist, kissing her warmly. Even after six months, his touch still left her breathless. When they pulled apart a moment later, both of them were smiling.

'Hello, you,' Mandy said, then bent to stroke Zoe and Simba, who having greeted Sky, were pressing against Mandy's legs as if she was the most wonderful person they had ever seen. 'And hello, you two.' Zoe licked her hand as Mandy scratched the soft fur behind the husky's ear. She followed Jimmy as he walked through into the sitting room.

'Wow, it's looking so good,' he told her after he had examined the new plasterwork from every angle.

'It is, isn't it?' Mandy agreed. Jimmy put an arm round her waist again and pulled her into a hug. 'It'll look even better when we've painted it,' he said. 'Shall we get those cupboard doors up?'

Moving back through to the kitchen, followed by the

dogs, Jimmy opened the toolbox that lay on the table. Lifting out a screwdriver and a box of screws, he set them on the side, then lifted up one of the brightly painted cupboard doors. 'You've made a great job of these,' he told her, looking up, his green eyes crinkling as he smiled.

Mandy waved away the dogs, who looked disappointed that there was no food coming as they trotted and flopped down on the rugs that lay by the door. Clearly they were quite aware of the fact that this was a kitchen, even if it wasn't quite finished yet.

Then she took the cupboard door from Jimmy and lined it up with the hinges, holding it so he could screw them into place. She glanced at him as he worked, and couldn't help smiling to see his eyes narrowed with concentration, his tongue slightly sticking out, almost like Tango's did when he was disturbed mid-wash.

Forty-five minutes later, the green cupboard doors were all in place and Mandy and Jimmy stood back together, admiring the completed kitchen in the warm evening glow.

Seeing they had finished, the three dogs stood up, yawning and stretching. Simba came over and looked at them, ears pricked, head on one side. Then with a small whine, she trotted out into the hall, then returned to gaze at them again. 'I think she wants some fresh air,' Mandy said.

'I think you're right,' Jimmy agreed. 'How about it?'

There was no need for jackets. With the three dogs trotting at their heels, they turned left out of the front door, through the yard at the side of the house and plunged into the woods. It was an old footpath, which Mandy recalled from her childhood. Years ago, she and James had walked here with Blackie, James's beloved Labrador. When she had returned to the cottage last year, it had been overgrown and almost unrecognisable, but she and Jimmy had reclaimed it, one Easter weekend, hacking away at the brambles until they had cleared a path to the open fell above Lamb's Wood.

There was just enough room for Mandy and Jimmy to walk side by side. The sun was low in the sky, sending shafts of golden light between the tree trunks, and the air was cool on her face. Sky and Simba had rushed on ahead. Mandy could hear them now and then as they crashed through the undergrowth. Occasionally their heads would appear, ears pricked, tongues lolling, then they would hare off again.

Zoe walked more sedately just in front of them, her swollen belly almost swinging with each stride. Now and then, she padded to Jimmy's side, looking up at him and licking his hand, then she moved on again.

They stopped when they reached the top of the woods to put on the dogs' leads. Mandy crouched down to rub Zoe's ear as Jimmy opened the gate that led out onto the open moor. 'She's starting to feel it,' Mandy said, looking up at Jimmy.

'She is,' he replied, holding out his hand to steady her as she stood back up. He was grinning. 'She's going to be the most wonderful mother.'

Mandy knew how excited he was about Zoe's first litter. He had paired Zoe with a champion sledding husky from Scotland. It had all been planned down to the last detail. If all went well, he was hoping this would only be the beginning. He wanted to breed his own little sled team, he had told her. Mandy grinned as she imagined them, racing along the tracks around Welford.

'Are we still on for the scan on Wednesday?' she asked as they stepped away from the gate and set off up the fell. Now that the husky was nearing her ninth and last week of pregnancy, it was time for her to have her first ultrasound scan. Mandy felt so honoured that Jimmy had involved her at every stage, asking her advice before conception, through the mating and then during the pregnancy itself. He had helped her so much over the past months with Wildacre, and in return she was determined that Zoe and the pups should have the very best care.

'Yes, we're all set,' Jimmy replied. They had reached the ridge that ran through an area of rough moorland. A green track meandered up the hill to their right and they turned onto it. With the three dogs close at their heels, they headed upwards. 'Oh, and I need to check, is it okay for Abi and Max to come along to the scan?' Jimmy added, cheerfully. 'They're just as excited as we are about Zoe. Also . . .' now, he spoke in a more tentative tone, and reached out to take her fingers in his own warm, slightly rough hand, '. . . if it's okay with you, I'd like to introduce you as my girlfriend.'

Mandy felt her stomach contract a little. Abi and Max were Jimmy's nine-year-old twins from his earlier marriage to Belle. At the beginning of their relationship, Jimmy had told her that he wanted to take things slowly between her and the children. She had appreciated his thoughtfulness, but in truth she hadn't wanted to rush in either. She had never been all that confident around children. They were like unruly baby animals, except they could talk, and they apparently took about eighteen years to be fully trained.

She forced herself to smile. 'Of course they can come,' she said, hoping her voice wouldn't betray her mixed feelings. 'It's important they remember to stay very quiet and calm,' she added. They were only a few years younger than Nicole, she reminded herself, though Nicole seemed so much more mature.

'They will,' he assured her. 'They're dying to see the puppies.'

Jimmy stopped beside her on the path. He gazed at her as if trying to divine her thoughts. 'I really want the children to share the experience of Zoe having puppies,' he said. 'And I think it's the perfect way for them to start spending time with you.' He squeezed her hand. 'And yes, that means I'm pretty deadly serious about you. I hope that's okay?'

Mandy felt a small shiver of happiness run through her, and now she found her smile came easily. 'Of course it is,' she replied. Leaning forward, she kissed him. 'It will be lovely to have them there.'

They walked on up the track. It really was a very beautiful evening. Down in the valley, the church clock began to strike seven. The tones hung in the evening air. In the distance, Mandy could hear sheep. At their feet, the dogs panted. Sky looked as if she was grinning as she glanced up at Mandy. They reached the cairn that marked the top of the rise and stopped. Below them, Welford's grey stone houses sent long shadows across the ground. Lamb's Wood, a few hundred feet below them looked green and inviting as spring worked its magic on the earth.

'I want to spend as much time with the children as I can at the moment.' Jimmy stood looking north, up towards the Beacon on Norland Fell. 'I don't think I told you – Belle and Dan are expecting a baby.' The sun shone on the side of his face, shadowing his eyes.

'That's lovely.' The words came automatically to Mandy, but a jolt of unease ran through her. She had no idea how Jimmy would feel. She knew Belle was remarried, to Sergeant Dan Jones from the police force in Walton, but Jimmy had never really talked about it much.

'It is lovely,' Jimmy said quickly. 'I'm thrilled for her. I'm just not sure how it'll affect the twins. I don't want them to feel pushed out by the new baby.'

Mandy felt puzzled for a moment. 'I'm sure Belle will love them all just the same,' she said.

Jimmy gave a tight smile. 'It's a bit more complicated than that when a new baby comes along,' he told her. Mandy found herself wondering exactly what he meant. Surely the only really important thing was that their mum still loved them? 'Belle's due date is in August. They've got time to get used to the idea. I'd like to give Abi and Max a really good summer. And now you're a big part of my life, I'd like you and them to know each other better.'

Mandy managed to smile. It was great that things were going so well that Jimmy wanted her to get to know his children better. She wanted to be in Jimmy's life, and she knew this was part of it.

But being part of Jimmy's plan for keeping the twins settled and ensuring they had a good summer made her feel a little bit twitchy. With this big change happening in their lives, this didn't seem like the best time to get to know them. What if they didn't like her? Wouldn't that make things worse?

Then her eyes fell on Zoe, who was sitting on the sloping grass with her tongue lolling happily as Sky bounded in circles around her.

It'll be okay, she thought. After all, the first event was going to be an ultrasound scan for Zoe. There were few places Mandy felt more at home than at Animal Ark and it would give them something to talk about.

We can count the puppies together. Maybe I'll show them the little hearts beating!

The thought was cheering, and she turned another genuine smile on Jimmy as he called the dogs over to begin the walk back down to Wildacre.

She told Helen all about her conversation with Jimmy the next morning. They were alone in the clinic, doing some much-needed prep in between appointments: Adam was out on a call and Emily, in keeping with her reduced workload, was having the morning off. Mandy's mum still seemed very lacking in energy, and Mandy was glad she'd had time to take her breakfast in bed before work.

'It's just that now it's so important to Jimmy that it all goes right with me and the twins,' Mandy said. 'What if I mess it up?'

There was sympathy in Helen's eyes. 'I do get it,' she said. 'But you've always known that Jimmy had children. There was always going to be baggage attached.' She looked round from the sink, where she was washing some surgical instruments and smiled over at Mandy. 'I think you're worrying over something that'll never happen.'

Mandy, across the room, slid a scalpel handle and some forceps into a sterilisation pack. 'You're probably right,' she admitted. This was what she loved about Helen. The nurse was always so practical.

'You know, I've seen Jimmy out with the twins a few times when I've been walking home,' Helen went on. 'He brings them round into the lane to feed Holly and Robin.'

'Really?' Mandy was surprised. She had never seen them there, but the mental image was lovely, and a little bit calming. Holly and Robin were two young donkeys she had rescued before Christmas last year, and the idea of the two nine-year-olds feeding them was very sweet.

Helen turned off the water and dried her hands. 'Abi and Max will love coming round to see you. You've got so many lovely animals here. And what about Zoe and her pups? Most people whose pets are having a litter must feel some worry, but Jimmy and the twins have their own exclusive vet. You're going to be the best stepmother in the world, with all that going for you.'

Stepmother. Mandy's eyes went wide and she almost dropped the next scalpel on her foot. She was about to deny that she was anyone's stepmother, when the door to the clinic opened and Helen rushed through to see who had arrived. Slipping the sealed surgical kit onto the autoclave shelf, Mandy let out a small sigh. It was going to be fine. Helen was right. How hard could it be to do a good job with two sweet, caring nine-year-olds in the room with her?

An hour later, she was finishing up with one of her rescue dogs in the paddock beside Animal Ark when two figures, one tall, one small arrived on the far side of the field. Mandy squinted into the bright spring sunshine and the figures resolved into Susan Collins, Mandy's friend, and her almost-four-year-old son, Jack.

The rescue dog, a handsome black Labrador called Brutus, looked over at them, then glanced up at Mandy as if to say, 'Is it okay?' Mandy smiled and gave him a scratch behind his ears, pleased that he had looked to her rather than barking. He had been quite reactive when he first arrived. Susan waved and stopped a few metres away with Jack as Mandy waved back and took the Lab inside the rescue centre. She returned a moment later with Sky trotting at her heels to find Susan and Jack feeding carrots to Holly and Robin.

When Jack had first visited the donkeys six months earlier, they had all been rather wary of each other, but now Jack was super-confident. He chatted away to the pair, holding out the pieces of carrot, his hand flat, as Mandy had taught him. Holly and Robin stood politely, their long, grey ears pricked as they took the titbits. Jack reached up to run his small hand down Holly's neck and the little jenny leaned her head on his shoulder, making him laugh as she sighed in his ear.

Mandy walked over to stand beside Susan. 'They're looking wonderful, as always,' Susan told her. Mandy nodded, pleased that her friend had noticed the donkeys' good health. Their eyes were bright, their fur clean and fluffy. 'He's convinced they're "his" donkeys.'

Mandy breathed in, relishing the freshness of the air. It was a wonderful fresh morning. 'I wish I could keep them here for him,' she said. 'I'm still looking for a home. They take up too much room to stay here forever.' They watched for a few moments longer. 'I need to take Sky out for a run,' Mandy told her friend. 'Will you and Jack come? You can come back afterwards for tea. I've got some lovely new rabbits for you to see.'

'That all sounds lovely,' Susan replied. 'Come on, Jack, we're going for a walk with Sky!'

Ten minutes later, they were on their way. There was a short track between a stone wall and a fence that led from the Hope Meadows paddock over to a small patch of woodland. Reaching it, Mandy let Sky off the lead. It was wonderful just how relaxed her beloved collie was with Jack. She leaned on the trunk of a silver birch tree. There was a slight breeze playing against her face. The leaves over her head were rustling and the dappled sun danced on the ground. Jack was laughing as he chased Sky. Susan was standing a little away from her, watching the pair of them. How peaceful it was, Mandy thought.

She watched as the lithe black and white body raced along the fence that bordered the land a few fields down from Animal Ark. There was a notice attached to the fence.

'Planning permission,' she read. 'Westbow Holdings Ltd.'

She moved a little closer to read the details. There was to be a small furniture factory where now there were ancient fir trees. She frowned. What a pity to cut them down. Would it disturb her animals, she wondered? Not that she expected perfect peace, but it would be bad for the whole neighbourhood if there was noise that set off the rescue dogs barking. Susan arrived at her side, puffing from her exertions, her hair tousled. 'Have you seen that?' Mandy nodded towards the notice.

Susan shook her head. 'A factory in Welford? No, I haven't heard anything about it,' she said with a shrug. Turning, they walked through the trees. Jack trotted ahead with Sky. Mandy's mind was still on the planning notice, but Susan grinned at her.

'Did you know I'd started online dating?' she said.

This revelation shoved the factory from Mandy's mind. She had been lucky enough to meet Jimmy in Welford, but she could see the appeal of trying to find a partner online. Her own life was busy enough – with working in the nursery and having Jack, Susan's chances of meeting new people were likely even more limited.

'No, I didn't! How's it going?' she asked.

Susan laughed. 'Up until last night,' she said, 'I would have said it was going well. I'd been chatting to a few people and finally selected this guy called Sam for a date. He sounded lovely, sweet and sensitive.'

They reached a shallow stream that ran through the

trees. Jack crouched on the edge, peering down at the water as it ran in a gully between rocks. Sky was sitting beside him, peering too.

'I'm guessing he wasn't quite so lovely, sweet and sensitive in real life,' Mandy hazarded.

'I should have worked it out when he asked me to drive,' Susan said. 'I took it as a good sign at first. Jack's . . .' she smiled ruefully and lowered her voice, so the little boy wouldn't hear her, '. . . his dad, Michael – he wasn't around for long, but he always had to drive everywhere. The one time I drove him, he clung onto the door handle the whole way.'

Mandy curled her lip. 'What an idiot.'

'Yup. But Sam, it turns out, just wanted free transport. He spent the first two hours telling me a sob story about his ex. When he started to tell me about the correct way to raise children, I finally picked up the car keys and told him that if he wanted a lift home, he'd better come now and come quietly!' She laughed again. 'I know it's not easy to take on a ready-made family,' she said. 'I would like someone else in my life, but Jack has to come first, so anyone else will have to fit around us. Their mind has to be open.'

Mandy sighed as her mind flitted to Abi and Max. Was her mind open enough? She certainly didn't have any set ideas on child rearing.

Ahead of them, Jack had stood up. Arms outstretched, he took a small step onto a stone in the smallest shallowest part of the stream. His heel slipped on the rock. Almost in slow motion, he teetered backwards, then fell full length into the glittering water with an enormous splash. His face was filled with shock. In a trice, Susan had scooped him up. For a moment, Mandy thought he wasn't going to cry, but after the most enormous intake of breath, he let out a howl. Susan, practical to the end, crouched beside him, hugging his little body to herself despite the mud, offering warmth and comfort until the spasm passed. She really was a wonderful mum, Mandy thought.

Chapter Three

Mandy glanced at her mobile. It was just after ten o'clock. Jimmy was due in at eleven with Zoe for her scan. She stood for a moment, a twinge of nervousness gripping her stomach. The twins were coming with him. She had met them before, but being introduced as 'Dad's girlfriend' made everything different. It felt almost as if they were right back at the beginning of their relationship and she had first-date nerves. She took a deep breath, squaring her shoulders, then opened the door and marched across the paddock to the rescue centre. She would use the time to do something productive.

Pulling up the lid of her laptop, she opened the Hope Meadows website and immediately relaxed a little. She had taken some photos of the rabbits she'd shown to Susan and Jack. How sweet they looked with their sad little faces and long floppy ears. She added them to the list of animals for immediate rehoming. They were in perfect health and didn't need any rehabilitation. There were some new photos of the kittens to add as well. Two of them had their eyes open now. It was still a while before they could be rehomed, but someone might easily fall in love with them in the meantime.

She opened the Hope Meadows e-mail inbox. There was a query about Holly and Robin. 'I was wondering,' the woman wrote, 'whether they would be suitable to be ridden?'

Poor little donkeys, Mandy thought. They weren't even a year old yet. She sent a polite reply, explaining that the young donkeys would not be ready to be ridden for three or four years. For a moment, she let her imagination run far into the future. She would love to break them in herself. But realistically, she had to hope they wouldn't still be with her in three years' time. They took up space in her field that she would need for other furry residents. They no longer needed specialist young-donkey food, but the bill for their feed and straw still added up.

The phone on the desk rang and Mandy jumped, then lifted the receiver. It was Helen. 'Jimmy's here with Zoe,' the nurse told her. Mandy felt a little stir of excitement mingling in with her nerves. It would be lovely to scan Zoe and see how the puppies were progressing. She was sure this was going to be fine.

Abi and Max were waiting in reception with Jimmy. She was struck again by how alike they were. Abi's hair had been cut into a rather severe-looking bob since the last time Mandy had seen them. They were dressed similarly, in jeans and T-shirts, though Abi's had a cartoon superhero Mandy didn't recognise on it and Max's had a cat fighting a triceratops. Mandy couldn't help wondering if it was meant to mean something.

Both had intense green eyes like Jimmy's. Both were staring at her.

'Hello, Mandy,' said Jimmy, with over-the-top cheerfulness.

'Hi,' Mandy said, managing what she hoped was a welcoming smile. For a fleeting moment, she wondered if she should hug them, but she was relieved when both returned her greeting without seeming to expect anything more. She bent, instead, to welcome Zoe, burying her hands and leaning her cheek against the soft fur, smelling the sweet scents of grass and damp earth. The husky's enthusiasm, as she wagged her tail and licked Mandy's hand, offered a temporary distraction from the awkwardness.

She straightened to find Max's eyes still on her. Abi was looking up at Jimmy. 'Will we be able to see the puppies' hearts, like we did with Mum's baby?' Mandy glanced back at Max. He was watching her still, his gaze wary. She wished he would look somewhere else.

'Maybe we will?' Jimmy looked at Mandy too. At least he was smiling.

'Hopefully,' she replied. A momentary worry gripped her. What if there were no heartbeats? She gave herself a shake. There was no reason to suspect any problems with Zoe's pregnancy. It was her first litter. She was two years old: fully mature, physically ready.

'Will we find out how many puppies she's going to have?' Abi was looking up at Jimmy again.

In turn, he looked at Mandy. 'Will we be able to tell?' he asked.

'It depends how many there are,' Mandy told Abi. 'If there are only one or two, we can probably count. If there are lots, we can get an idea, but we won't know for sure until she has them. Will you bring her through?' she asked Jimmy. It was better to get things under way, she thought. If Abi had any more questions, she could deal with them as they came up.

The ultrasound scanner was in a small area off the prep room. There were no windows and the light had a dimmer switch. Helen had already set the machine up so that everything was ready to go. Zoe was panting, Mandy noticed, which meant that she was either nervous or hot. It wasn't especially warm, though the husky's thick coat meant that she was always better prepared for winter weather than the warmer months. Still, it was likely Zoe might be anxious with the unusual situation. It was important everything was calm. The dim light in the ultrasound room was better than the bright glare that was sometimes necessary in the consulting rooms at least.

'I need her to lie down on her side,' Mandy told Jimmy. 'Then I'll shave some of the hair from her tummy. I need good contact with her skin to get a clear picture.' She was feeling less self-conscious, now that she could focus on Zoe.

'How long will the scan take?' Abi asked Jimmy. Mandy hesitated. She could answer, but she hadn't been asked, Jimmy had – would it be rude? Would she seem like she was butting in?

'I'm not sure,' Jimmy told her, 'but just be patient and we'll find out soon enough. Zoe needs us all to be quiet now, though. Okay?' He looked at Abi and then at Max. Max gave a solemn nod, Abi made a zipping motion across her mouth.

Mandy felt a rush of gratitude. Jimmy handled that well, and now she could get on with the scan.

Zoe is so good, she thought, as Jimmy asked the husky to lie down, then roll over, and she obeyed at once. 'Maybe you could gently steady her back leg,' she suggested to Abi, whose eyes widened as she did as Mandy said. Both children were kneeling close to Zoe's hind end, Jimmy was at the front, stroking the husky's head. Mandy showed Zoe the clippers, then switched them on to get her used to the noise, waiting for the husky to be completely settled again before she wielded them over the dog's abdomen. Once the skin was clear of hair, she put the clippers away and reached for the ultrasound handpiece.

The first puppy appeared on the screen almost immediately. Mandy shifted the probe slightly. 'Look,' she said, pointing to the screen. 'Can you see there? That's the first puppy's head.' She twisted the probe again. 'And there's his or her heart there,' she told them with a smile.

'Can you see it beating?' Jimmy asked the twins, who nodded, their eyes wide as they gazed at the black-and-white screen in the dim light.

Mandy moved the instrument. The white outline of another pup came into view within the black circle of the uterus. 'There's another,' she told them. Inside the uterine horn, the tiny pup was wiggling its legs. Pressing a few buttons, marking the edges of the skull on the screen, Mandy took some measurements. Both pups were a good size. She began to search again, following the uterus backwards towards the cervix, then forwards up the second horn. After twenty minutes, they had found five puppies. All of them seemed to be healthy.

'So she's going to have five altogether?' Jimmy looked

enchanted. He gazed from Mandy, to the screen, where Mandy had just completed the last measurement. His hand absently stroked the soft fur behind Zoe's ear as he turned his gleaming eyes back at Mandy.

'Well, without taking an X-ray, I can't be sure,' Mandy told him, 'but as far as I can tell, there seem to be five. All healthy,' she added.

'Hooray!' Abi let out a cheer, then clapped both hands over her mouth, remembering that she had to be quiet for Zoe's sake. Max's grin was as wide as Jimmy's. He stroked Zoe's leg as Mandy replaced the probe into its holder and began to wipe the gel from Zoe's abdomen. Max did look very much like Jimmy, she thought. She finished cleaning the husky, who stood up and shook herself, as soon as Jimmy released her.

'I think this calls for a celebration,' Jimmy said, standing up, and stretching after so long on his knees.

'Can we have pizza?' Abi piped up.

Jimmy grinned. 'Okay,' he said. 'And shall we invite Mandy?'

Pleased to have given so much pleasure, Mandy glanced at the twins, but Abi pouted. 'Do we have to?' she asked. Mandy felt her face reddening as embarrassment coursed through her. She was about to tell Jimmy that it was absolutely fine when he spoke calmly to Abi.

'That's not very polite to Mandy,' he told his daughter. 'She's my girlfriend and I would like her to come. She's also going to be looking after Zoe and the puppies for us, so I think she deserves some pizza, don't you?'

Abi didn't look thrilled, but she shrugged her agreement.

'Okay with you, Max?' Jimmy asked, the forced cheeriness back in his voice.

Max nodded too.

Mandy still wished she could disappear into a hole. *Hold back the stampede,* she thought, though she made herself smile. 'Thank you, that would be nice,' she said, hoping she sounded more enthusiastic than the twins had managed.

Jimmy smiled warmly at her. 'In that case, we'll see you later,' he said.

They made their way back out into the waiting room. Abi walked ahead, stopping at the door to wait. Max stood halfway between Abi and Jimmy, who had waited to walk beside Mandy. Both of the twins were staring again. Zoe's tail waved gently as she walked ahead of Jimmy on her lead. The husky and Jimmy were the only ones who seemed wholly at ease, Mandy thought. She had to work hard not to flinch as Jimmy reached in to kiss her goodbye. It was a long way from the warm kiss he would have given her had they been alone, but even so, Mandy felt the heat of the twins' eyes on them. 'They're fine,' Jimmy mouthed, noticing the direction of her uncomfortable gaze, then he grinned again as if amused. 'See you this evening,' he said. Mandy let out a sigh of relief when the door closed behind him.

'So how did it go?' Helen appeared from the front consulting room as soon as Jimmy and the twins had disappeared.

Not great, Mandy thought.

'Five pups, I think,' she said aloud. Despite the complications of the past few minutes, the scan itself had gone well. And Jimmy and the twins' delight had been a pleasure to see, even if Abi's affection was clearly reserved for Zoe.

'Nice litter size,' Helen said.

She was right, it was a good number, Mandy thought. With five puppies, it was unlikely they would be oversized, but it wasn't such a large number as to be overwhelming for a first-time mother.

'I was just going to the post office to post Gizmo Kramer's blood sample,' Helen told her, waving a brown-wrapped parcel. 'Is there anything you want from the shop?' The post office in Welford was attached to the little village shop where Mandy and James had bought ice creams when they were young.

Mandy thought for a moment. There was nothing in particular she needed, but it would be nice to get some fresh air and clear her head. Helen had been extra busy recently as well with Emily having been around less. 'Actually, I'd like a walk. Shall I go for you?' she asked.

Helen looked pleased. 'That would be amazing, if you're not busy,' she said. 'I was going to give the kennels a bit of a spring clean when I got back, but if I start now, I should be finished before lunch.'

'I'll give you a hand when I'm back,' Mandy said. She called Sky and together, they set off down the lane. It was another beautiful day. The hedgerows that lined the roadside were bordered with spring flowers. The air was sweet with the scent of growing things. Sky trotted ahead of her, exploring every inch of the grass, halting now and then when she smelled something especially interesting. She stopped dead as a leaf fluttered out from under the hedge, then chased it across the tarmac, pouncing with both front paws. She paused again, then leaped over it, body twisting to land her paws on top of it once more. Mandy smiled. Sky's life was so simple.

She doesn't have to worry about potential stepchildren.

Mandy called the collie to her and slipped the rope lead around her neck as they approached the junction with Main Street and turned left towards the village.

Outside the brightly painted door of the post office a young woman with black curly hair was struggling with a giant pushchair. As Mandy walked towards them, she could see that there were three babies, all strapped in side by side. The buggy was almost too wide to pass though the doorway. Mandy's eyes travelled back up to the woman's face. She seemed familiar, though for a moment, Mandy couldn't place her. 'Let me help.' Mandy bent to lift the wheels of the buggy over the door sill and something clicked in her head. 'Harriet?' she said as she straightened. 'Harriet Ruck?' How long had it been since she'd seen Harriet? More than ten years, she thought, though she'd seen Mr and Mrs Ruck a few days back. They had made no mention of babies that she could remember. Was it really her friend?

'Mandy Hope!' Harriet's face was pale and she had dark rings round her eyes, but she greeted Mandy with a grin. Mandy, meanwhile, was gazing at the three small faces that were looking out from the pushchair. Three babies, all at once; and she felt like Jimmy's twins were enough of a handful. 'Yup,' Harriet said, as if reading Mandy's mind. 'They're all mine. Triplets, two of them are identical – Giselle and Sophie – and this little poppet is Imogen.' Harriet leaned over to wipe away a small blotch of what looked like porridge from Imogen's smooth cheek with her thumb. 'Seven months old. And I . . .' she straightened up, '. . . am Harriet Fallon now.' She looked both proud and exhausted. Mandy found herself torn between admiration and sympathy.

Gemma Moss came out from behind the counter as Mandy, Harriet and the triplets manoeuvred their way into the post office. 'Hello Mandy,' she said. 'Hi Harriet.' She leaned over to admire the triplets. All three gazed up at her and gurgled. Sophie held out a tiny finger and Gemma met it with her own. Both laughed and then Gemma looked back up at Harriet. 'How are they doing?' she asked, adding, 'and how are you doing, more to the point? Are they sleeping yet?'

Harriet grinned again. 'Oh yes,' she replied. 'They do all sleep . . . just not necessarily at the same time.' Gemma and Mandy laughed, though Mandy's respect for her old friend was increasing all the time.

'Dad said you'd been up to the lambing, Mandy,' Harriet asked. 'And I hear you opened a rescue centre?'

'Yes,' Mandy replied. 'Hope Meadows, plus working with Mum and Dad at Animal Ark.'

'The lamb with the short tendons is almost normal now,' Harriet said, and Mandy smiled. 'They're doing well, all of them.'

'That's good to hear,' Mandy said. 'So what have you

been doing lately?' she asked, then cringed at her own question. 'I mean, before you had these three?'

Harriet seemed unfazed by the question. 'I was actually out of work for a little while before they were born,' she replied. 'Mike, my husband's a dentist, so we're managing, and I do two nights a week as a waitress in Walton, but I'd love to find something new. I used to work in a garden centre over towards Ripon when we lived there, but it closed down. Then Mike got a new job over here, and with this lot on the way . . .' she glanced fondly at Giselle, who was holding up her thumb and gazing at it as if it was the most amazing thing ever, then turned her eyes back to Mandy with a smile. 'I'm glad we came back here, but there's not much work. Bev in the Fox and Goose told me a couple of days ago that she'd heard something about a new place that's being set up. They were going to make furniture, she said.'

'Oh!' Mandy frowned. 'I might have seen something about that. There was a planning notice up in the spinney near Hope Meadows.' She stopped. It might not be ideal to have a workshop right beside Hope Meadows, but it would be great for Harriet if she could find work.

'That must be it,' Harriet said, then with a grin, 'So all I need now, is to be offered a job, AND find a local nursery with three free spaces that doesn't cost the earth!'

'You could talk to Susan Collins,' Mandy suggested. 'Welford nursery is very good, though I know nothing at all about how much it costs.'

She waited while Harriet bought some stamps from Gemma, then handed over the blood samples she had brought to be weighed.

'I'm off to the bus stop now,' Harriet said.

'I'll walk with you,' Mandy offered.

Together, Harriet and Mandy left the post office and crossed the road onto the green. Harriet turned the push-chair round to face them and they sat down on the bus stop bench, basking in the warmth of the spring sun.

'What a gorgeous dog.' Harriet watched as Sky lay down with her head on Mandy's feet. 'Is she one of your rescues?'

'She was.' Mandy leaned forward to stroke Sky. 'Harriet meet Sky, Sky, Harriet.' The collie sat up on hearing her name. She leaned her head into Mandy's fingers, half closing her eyes with pleasure as Mandy scratched behind her ear. When Mandy stopped, Sky sank back down again with a sigh. 'I've adopted her permanently.'

'How lovely.' Harriet looked wistful. 'I'd love to have a dog, but it's not practical just at the moment.' She held a hand out to Sky, who stood up and went over to investigate. 'She's got such soft fur,' Harriet said as she stroked the collie's ear. The three triplets were also watching Sky with interest. 'How would you three like a dog?' Harriet asked them. She received three grins and one happy shriek in response – Mandy counted a total of four teeth between the three babies.

'Would you like to come over to Hope Meadows some time?' Mandy offered. 'You'd all be welcome.' She gazed across the road to the quiet, grey church opposite. The graceful trees in the graveyard were moving gently in the breeze. Beyond the stone wall, the darker green trees of Longstone Edge Forest rose up the side of the fell.

'That would be great.' Harriet smiled as she too gazed

at the view. Then she got up and stretched as the bus rumbled into view. 'But right now, I have to get these three to the doctor's. They're due a health check. We'll all see you soon, won't we, girls? Wave goodbye to Mandy for me?'

One of the babies flailed an arm, and Mandy and Harriet both laughed.

'Good enough,' said Harriet, and waved herself as she wheeled the buggy towards the bus.

Mandy walked back up the lane with Sky a few minutes later. Harriet really had her hands full. Nine-year-old twins were daunting enough for Mandy, and she could barely imagine baby triplets!

She hadn't thought much about having a family of her own. She had been very focussed on becoming a vet, then on Hope Meadows. There had never been much space for children in her plans. What about Jimmy? she wondered. He had the twins. Would he want more children? They had never discussed it. She pushed the thought aside for now. She had enough to do, getting to know Abi and Max. That had to be her goal for the moment. She would make a special effort tonight, she decided.

In the meantime, she had work to do. Arriving back at the rescue centre, she walked into the cat kennel and opened the cage. She might not have any babies of her own, but she did have feline triplets that needed her attention.

'How are you, Mumma?' she asked the little black and white cat. She really should give her a proper name, she thought. Nicole had named the kittens, but not their mum. Button, the last of the three youngsters, had finally opened her eyes. To Mandy's pleasure, all three of them came over when she appeared. They were reaching the key age for socialisation, now they could see and hear, and it was important they met lots of different people. She would have to get Jack and Susan back over, maybe Roo Danjal, not to mention Adam and perhaps Grandad.

There was milk substitute already made up in the fridge. She fed the three tiny animals and lifted up Mumma for a check-over. There was no obvious reason for her lack of milk that Mandy could find. The little cat wasn't eating all that much, but she seemed generally well, although still rather thin. They had no idea what she had been through before she arrived. Next time Nicole was here, they could give her a more thorough examination, she thought.

Mandy's mobile rang in her pocket. She closed the kennel door, pulling herself upright before she answered.

'Hello?' A woman's crisp voice came down the line. 'Is that Hope Meadows rescue centre? I was wondering whether you had any nice cats that needed a new home?'

'We do have one or two,' Mandy replied, turning her back on the young litter and walking through into reception from the small side room. Mumma and her kittens were nowhere near ready, but there were two other adult cats who could be rehomed at any time.

'That's good.' The voice really was quite booming, Mandy thought. She half wanted to hold the phone away from her ear. 'My father is interested in getting a pet,' the voice informed her. 'I thought a rescue cat would be perfect.'

Mandy walked through into the main cat room with its rather old-fashioned wooden kennels. Either of her current residents would suit a quiet elderly owner perfectly. The younger of them, a black furry bundle called Pixie, was rubbing her face against the bars. The other, a tabby and white cat named Gull, was stretched out on her bed sleeping. 'Perhaps your father would like to come in and meet them,' she suggested.

'Excellent.' There was a brief pause. 'I'll tell my father to call in tomorrow morning. Ten thirty, if that's convenient?'

'That should be fine,' Mandy said, walking through to check the diary on the desk.

'Thank you.'

Mandy was about to explain a little more about the rehoming protocols, when there was a beep in her ear. The woman had hung up.

How odd. She hadn't even stopped to give Mandy any details. She frowned as she wrote 'an older man to meet Pixie/Gull' into the diary. *But does her father really want a cat, or does she just think he should?*

Chapter Four

Mandy paused for a moment outside the white-painted front door of Mistletoe Cottage, then knocked before she had time to change her mind. The door swung open. Jimmy grinned when he saw her face. 'They don't bite,' he said, his green eyes laughing. He pulled the door open wide and took her jacket. 'You can just come in next time, you don't have to knock,' he reminded her, as she followed him into the kitchen.

Abi and Max were sitting at the dark wooden table. Pencils and paper were strewn across it. Both looked up as Mandy walked in.

'Hello again,' Mandy said.

'Hi.' Max sent her a shy smile.

Abi met Mandy's gaze with seeming indifference, though she too said 'Hi.' Having done their duty, both of them bent their heads and returned to their tasks.

The kitchen was warm and the enticing scent of pizza filled the air. Jimmy broke the silence. 'So, Mandy, the twins are thinking up names for the puppies. Abi, why don't you show Mandy what you've done?'

Without looking up, Abi turned her piece of paper towards Mandy and pushed it across the table. Mandy leaned forward to look. 'These are singers,' Abi muttered, pointing to the first group of names on her list.

'*Taylor Swift, Katy Perry, Ed Sheeran . . .*' Mandy read, stifling a laugh at the idea of Jimmy striding across the fields calling for Taylor Swift. There were ten names in total, five male, five female: very thorough, Mandy thought.

'These are moorland plants,' Abi said.

This list was more to Mandy's taste. '*Heather,*' she read. '*Willowherb, Cottongrass.*'

'Each puppy has to have more than one word in its name,' Abi informed her, looking up at last. 'Our kennel name is going to be WildRun. A name can only have twenty-four letters.'

'I didn't know that,' Mandy said, quite impressed. 'I love the wild-flower names.'

Abi sent her a tentative smile. I'm making progress, Mandy thought, smiling back in return.

'I'm making a new list,' Abi said. 'Yorkshire cakes and biscuits, but I've run out. Were there definitely five puppies?'

'I'm fairly sure there were.' Mandy read though the third list. 'Yorkshire Parkin, Fat Rascal, Ginger Bread, Shortbread Thin, Tea Biscuit,' she read. She searched her memory. Dorothy Hope, Mandy's grandmother spent all her time baking. 'What about Treacle Toffee?' she suggested.

'That's not a cake or biscuit.' Abi's voice told Mandy not to argue the point. The girl pulled back the list, leaning over it as if to obscure Mandy's view. The brief moment of amity seemed to have passed and Mandy wondered what to say next.

Max came to her rescue. 'I've designed an obstacle course for the puppies.' He pushed his paper towards her. It showed an endearingly intricate design of cardboard boxes, hoops and tunnels for the puppies to run through.

'It's lovely,' Mandy said. *Totally impractical, but lovely,* she added, just to herself. She was trying to think of something else to say, when Jimmy asked her if she would chop some salad. With relief, she straightened up, crossed to the chopping board and grabbed a knife.

'Will you two clear your things and set the table, please?' Jimmy said. The twins scraped back their chairs and began to tidy away their pencils. Mandy finished chopping the cucumber and started on some tomatoes. She realised she had no idea how much the children would eat. Child portions were smaller usually, weren't they? But how much smaller? Had Jimmy passed her cucumber and tomatoes because that was what Abi and Max liked?

Don't panic, Mandy, it's just salad!

Abi dragged open a drawer and grabbed knives and forks. Max was pulling glasses and plates from the cupboard. Jimmy had taken two large pizzas from the oven. He sliced them into pieces, whilst Mandy put the salad in a bowl.

Setting the salad bowl in the centre of the table, she sat down in the seat where she normally sat when she visited Jimmy.

Max paused for a moment before setting down the last glass, but Abi was less reticent. 'That's Max's seat,' she said.

Her stomach clenching, Mandy stood up. 'Where should

I sit then?' she asked Abi, just as Jimmy said, 'It really doesn't matter, Abi.'

Abi frowned at him. 'But you said this is our home,' she objected. 'We should have our own chairs.'

'It is your home, but when we have visitors, it's polite to look after them.'

'I don't mind, really,' Mandy said, her face reddening with awkwardness. It seemed faintly ridiculous that there was so much fuss over a chair. After all, she came to Mistletoe Cottage at least as often as the twins did, maybe even more, and she didn't have her own chair.

They probably know that. It must be difficult to navigate when you're nine, she reminded herself, and sat down in the seat that Abi pointed out, beside Jimmy. It was a relief to serve herself some salad and grab a slice of pizza. It was spinach and ricotta and looked quite delicious. For a couple of minutes, there was peace, then Abi spoke.

'Did you know,' she asked Mandy, 'that Mum is like Zoe?' For a moment, Mandy was confused, but Max's next comment enlightened her.

'Mum's only having one baby,' he objected. 'Zoe's having five.'

'They're both going to get really fat, though,' Abi said. 'Mum said so.'

Mandy could feel herself growing hot again. Though under normal circumstances, she would have been delighted to hear about someone's pregnancy, she had no idea how to talk about Jimmy's ex-wife with his kids. *Their* kids.

'It's not fat when you're having a baby.' Jimmy seemed

to be taking the whole conversation in his stride. Mandy wished she could share his tranquillity. 'Besides,' he added, 'you should have seen how big Mummy was when she was having you!'

'How big?' Abi's eyes were wide. 'As big as Zoe?'

Jimmy laughed. 'Even bigger than that,' he told her.

'Tell me the story of the night we were born,' Abi begged him.

For the first time, Jimmy looked uncomfortable. Mandy tried to smile politely at him. She didn't want him to know that she would rather be pulling a rotten canine tooth from a Yorkie than hearing about the birth of Jimmy's children with his first wife.

He glanced at Mandy before turning his eyes to his daughter. 'Well,' he said. 'The first I knew of it was when I got a call from the hospital, telling me to come in. Mummy had already been in hospital for two days, but she managed to tell me that you two were on the way. It was a lovely summer's night,' Jimmy went on, glancing out of the window, then back to the twins, 'a bit like this one. I drove to the hospital as quickly as I could and even then I was only just in time. I ran into the room and the first thing I saw was your head starting to appear! You were born a couple of minutes later.' He smiled at the memory, his eyes crinkling with tenderness, and Mandy felt herself relax a little.

'The nurse handed you over to Mummy for a few minutes. Then your mum passed you to me, because Max was on the way. You and I had the most lovely cuddle while Max was being born.' He turned to his son. 'You, little monkey, were coming upside down,' he told Max, 'but

48

Mummy was very brave, and Abi and I held her hand until you finally appeared.'

Mummy was very brave . . . Mandy felt a shiver pass through her at Jimmy's words, knowing how much hurt and worry he must be hiding from the twins with that simple sentence. She couldn't exactly relate, but she'd presided over plenty of difficult animal births, and she could definitely empathise. She reached for his hand under the table and gave it a gentle squeeze.

'And then Mummy told me how happy she was to have the two most beautiful babies in the world and I told her I was the happiest man in the world to have you both.'

Mandy's smile froze a little as another wave of awkwardness hit her.

'Did you really say that?' Abi must have heard the story many times before, Mandy could tell, but she seemed to want to hear the last part again.

'Yes. Mummy and I really were the happiest people in the world, because we had the best babies in the world,' Jimmy assured her.

Max's face had taken on an anxious look. 'Will Mummy and Dan say that about the new baby?' he asked. Abi had just taken a new slice of pizza but stopped with the wedge halfway to her mouth.

'They'll say they have another baby to add to the best babies in the world crew!' Jimmy replied. 'Mummy has room in her heart to love every one of her babies more than enough.'

Abi took a mouthful of her pizza, chewed and swallowed, then said, 'I hope Mummy and Dan have a girl. I'd love to have a sister.'

'What about you Max?' Mandy asked. 'Would you like another sister?'

Max thought for a moment. 'I think I'd quite like a brother, though either would be okay.'

'Do you want to have a baby?' Abi directed the question straight at Mandy.

For a moment, Mandy wished she had an old-fashioned fan she could wave in front of her face to cool the heat that had rushed up to her cheeks. 'Um . . . no,' she replied, feeling almost faint with embarrassment. Would she have asked someone that when she was nine? Surely she had only been interested in puppies and kittens back then?

'Good! Daddy has us. He doesn't need any more babies.'

Mandy's mouth opened a little, and she forced it shut again.

Wow. At least I know where I stand.

Would it really be so awful for them if their dad were to have a new baby as well as their mum? What did it matter? She'd never thought about having children before, even with Simon, her ex.

'You should eat your pizza, Abi, before it gets cold.' Jimmy's voice was firm. He had let go of Mandy's hand, but he sent her an apologetic look.

This time Mandy couldn't bring herself to smile back. What was he thinking? Surely there would be a better time to get to know the twins? A time when their mum hadn't just announced she was going to have a baby in a few months?

But then, over Jimmy's shoulder, she caught a glimpse of Zoe, in her basket beside the sofa, snoring and twitching her ears. She suddenly felt a burst of jealousy, and stifled the urge to laugh. Maybe she could go and lie down in a darkened room, she thought. Just her, Zoe and Simba. They could come out when the twins had gone to bed.

The pizza was finished and they had all shared chocolate cake without any further difficult moments. 'Why don't we play Game of Life?' Jimmy suggested once the table was cleared. Max and Abi ran to the cupboard under the stairs to pull the colourful box out, and Mandy felt pleased too. She could remember playing Game of Life when she was much younger.

It didn't seem to have changed too much, Mandy thought, though she felt sure the version she'd played hadn't rewarded anyone for recycling rubbish or helping the homeless. She chose to pay the money and go to college. Before long, they were all spinning the coloured wheel and wending their way along the pathway, though Mandy was rather disappointed that the mountain pass had disappeared.

Max landed on a House Space and picked up the top two cards. He counted out his money, biting his lip as he concentrated. 'I'm going to buy the island holiday home,' he announced, as if this was the most wonderful news ever.

But Abi pouted. 'It's not fair,' she said to Jimmy. 'Max always ends up getting the island holiday home. It's not fair that he always gets to start. It's cheating.'

'He doesn't always get to start,' Jimmy objected. 'You have to take it in turns.'

'He started last time *and* this time,' Abi argued. 'It's not fair.' Mandy glanced from Jimmy to Abi, wondering what he would do. She couldn't help but feel glad she didn't have to get involved.

'I didn't start last time anyway,' Max put in. 'You did.'

'No, I did not.' Abi's bottom lip was sticking out so far it was the size of one of the pizzas they'd eaten earlier. 'It says in the rules that the youngest should start. Max is the youngest. He always starts.'

Mandy found herself studying her own house card. She had bought the windmill. It looked rather nice, she thought. Peaceful. Isolated.

'We're not going to get into a discussion about who started last time.' Jimmy's voice was steady.

'Well, I don't want to play any more.' Abi's voice wobbled.

'What about you join in with me as a team?' Jimmy suggested. 'That way Mandy and Max get to finish. Would that do?'

Abi agreed, though with such a show of reluctance that Mandy wondered whether it wouldn't have been better just to stop. Abi shifted around to sit beside Jimmy as if her arms and legs were made of lead and picked at the surface of the table. Whenever Max seemed to be doing well she sighed heavily and slumped lower in her chair.

She brightened up considerably when Jimmy won the game, and even bounced a little in her chair as she turned to him while he was packing up the pieces. 'Can we stay up for *Talent on TV*?' she asked. 'I'm sure Zoe would like to watch it,' she added, looking carefully at Jimmy's face.

Mandy watched him too. He had told her before that he didn't like TV talent shows.

'I suppose so,' Jimmy replied. His look was indulgent and for a moment, Mandy felt disappointed. She had half hoped that he would send the twins to bed.

Is that selfish of me?

She thought back to Helen's words. Jimmy came as a complete package. If she accepted him, she accepted he was a dad. And mostly he seemed to be a great dad. If he was willing for the twins to stay up late, then she would be fine with it too, though she had been hoping for a little time alone with him.

They finished the night with *Talent on TV*, which turned out to feature an opera singer from Wigan, a woman from Brixton who juggled knives, and a man from Llandudno who'd trained his ferrets to dance to 80s pop music.

Mandy curled up in the armchair where she knew Jimmy sat when he was alone. Zoe had sneaked up onto her knee at the beginning, and Mandy had done nothing to stop her, but her leg was now numb from the weight of the heavily pregnant dog. It wasn't surprising that Zoe was a little bit more clingy than usual, and besides, it was worth it for the fluffy cuddles.

Jimmy meanwhile was on the sofa, flanked by the twins. Now and then, he glanced over at Mandy and Zoe. He seemed quite satisfied to have them there, looking so comfortable.

Mandy stood up when the show was finished. 'I'd better get off,' she said.

The twins barely looked up, though both muttered 'Goodbye.'

Jimmy followed her to the door. 'Thanks for coming,' he said, in a low, happy murmur. 'It went really well, don't you think?'

Mandy's eyebrow twitched. Did he really believe that, she wondered, or was he just being kind?

He must have seen the doubt in her face. 'It'll get easier, you'll see. They'll learn to love you. Why wouldn't they?'

Because I'm just not good with children, she thought, *and the twins are so obviously unsettled about their new brother or sister* and *they probably want their dad all to themselves.* The thoughts ran through her head, one by one, but she squared her shoulders and smiled. When Jimmy leaned in for a kiss, it felt just as wonderful as ever, especially since she knew there weren't two extra pairs of green eyes watching.

Jimmy looked at her for a long moment. 'I'm free tomorrow night if you'd like to come round again,' he said. 'Abi and Max are going back to Belle's tomorrow. So just you and me.'

Mandy felt her heart lift.

'I'd love to,' she said.

As soon as the door closed behind her, she couldn't help but let out a large sigh of relief. The difficult part of the evening was over, and there was an evening alone with Jimmy on the horizon. Things were really looking up.

She really had been very lucky, she thought an hour later as she headed out from the cottage at Animal Ark to the field out the back where Hope Meadows stood. Although she had been adopted as a baby, her own childhood could not have been more stable. It must be hard for the twins, what with her and Dan and now the new baby.

She let out Hattie and Tablet, a pair of her rescue dogs. The late evening light sent long shadows through the trees as the two crossbreed dogs sniffed their way around the orchard. The blossom had fallen and scattered petals still dotted the ground. The brand-new buds that the blossom had left behind were a wonderful shade of lime green. The phone in her pocket buzzed and she pulled it out. It was James. She grinned as she pressed the button to answer the call.

'Hello,' the familiar voice came down the phone. 'How are things going?'

'Very well, thank you,' Mandy's eyes followed the taller of the dogs, whose name was Hattie, 'though I'm just recovering from my first big evening as a wicked stepmother.'

'Oh really?' James's voice was amused. He knew how she felt about children in general, and Jimmy's children, in particular. 'Did they burn you alive?' he said.

'If they could have fitted me in the oven, I think they might have done,' she replied, laughing. Hattie was crisscrossing the enclosure, while Tablet had just cocked his leg on a stump. 'We actually had pizza,' she added.

'You disappoint me,' James teased her. 'Really, though, it should be easy for you. You'd have no trouble at all if it was a crazy cow or a belligerent bull.'

'That's all very well,' Mandy retorted, 'but I can sedate those or put them in a cattle crush. I can't really do either of those things with Jimmy's twins.'

James laughed.

But she wasn't the only one who'd been out, she remembered. She had been rather surprised the last time she had spoken to James to hear he was meeting up with someone he'd met in his café. 'How did your date with Ian go?' she asked.

A sigh came down the line. 'It . . . didn't work out.'

Mandy waited for a moment to see if James would go into more detail, but there was only silence. 'Oh well.' She tried to keep her voice bright. 'There's no rush.'

'I know that.' The sharpness of James's words came as a slight shock and for a moment, she didn't know what to say, then his voice came down the line again. 'I'm sorry,' he told her. 'It's just – well, the wedding anniversary is coming round.'

Mandy felt a wave of sadness run through her. It had been such a wonderful day last year, when Paul and James had been married on Welford village green. No wonder her friend was finding it difficult.

'You should come down at the weekend,' she said, blinking away a thin film of tears. 'That's an order,' she added, when he didn't respond immediately. 'We'll have a day of fun. Distraction is the name of the game!'

James laughed. 'Yes, sir!' he said. 'Thank you, sir!' She could imagine him standing to attention and saluting.

They rang off a few minutes later. The sun had finally slipped over the horizon. Putting Hattie and Tablet back into their kennels, Mandy called to Sky, and they walked over to the cottage together underneath the stars.

Chapter Five

The phone in Rachel's pocket rang, just as Mandy was tying off the cervix during a bitch spay operation. Rachel Farmer had worked part time in Animal Ark for a number of years. Helen was having a rare day off, and Rachel was covering. She checked Mandy's patient before she pressed the button to take the call.

'Hello?' she said. 'Animal Ark and Hope Meadows.' Adam was out on call and Emily was off. Mandy's mobile had been redirected to the Animal Ark line while she was scrubbed up.

The ligature round the cervix seemed to be holding up well. Moving forward in the dog's abdomen, Mandy checked the ovaries. There was no sign of blood anywhere. It was time to stitch up. She tore open another packet of surgical suture.

'Okay, that's fine. I'll get her to call back as soon as she's finished operating.' Rachel was smiling as she ended the call. She looked up at Mandy. 'It was a man who's interested in Holly and Robin,' she said. 'Peter Warry. He sounded nice.'

Mandy hoped the man was as nice as Rachel thought. Though she was always glad when anyone took interest in her rescue animals, she was concerned that people would be interested in the donkeys as domestic pets or as sort-of-riding-ponies. Though they could be cared for as pets, whoever took them on would need masses of space and ideally experience breaking donkeys in. They'd also need a good deal of patience if they wanted children to ride the donkeys. It would be at least three years before Holly and Robin were old enough to take anyone at all.

She returned her full attention to the spay and inserted the final suture in the skin layer. The row of stitches looked neat and tidy. 'You can turn her off now,' she told Rachel, who had been monitoring the anaesthetic, but the receptionist had pre-empted her.

'Isoflo's off.' Rachel pulled the drapes away from the dog's head and smiled down at her sleepy face. Mandy was pleased too. The anaesthesia had gone as smoothly as the operation itself.

Rachel began to clean up the skin as Mandy pulled off her surgical gloves and went to the sink to rinse off the powder that clung to her fingers. Once the site was clear, Rachel rolled the spay patient onto her side. She was a slim black Staffie with a white chest. Her name was Anita. Mandy moved to the dog's broad head to check the position of her eyes to assess her level of anaesthesia. She was coming round nicely. 'How are you doing, Anita?' Mandy spoke to the dog quietly and ran her fingers repeatedly over the short fur below the Staffie's ear. That way, the dog would know she was there and wouldn't be shocked when she woke. Anita swallowed and with a swift motion, Mandy pulled out the breathing tube from her trachea.

'Can you give me a hand lifting her through?' she asked Rachel. Between them, they settled the Staffie into a kennel, covering her with a soft blanket, and closed the cage door quietly. Anita looked peaceful.

Leaving Rachel at the desk, Mandy walked into one of the consulting rooms and dialled Peter Warry's number.

As she talked to Mr Warry, Mandy's heart swelled with hope and relief. It turned out that he owned a smallholding just south of Northallerton where he already kept four alpacas, a llama and several cows, all of them rare breeds. And – Mandy crossed her fingers at Rachel as she gave her an enquiring look across the office – he seemed to be very knowledgeable about donkeys.

'I used to help look after a pair of retired donkeys when I was growing up,' he said. 'Poor things had spent most of their lives giving rides on the beach at Scarborough. We gave them a great retirement.'

Mandy couldn't help but squeeze her fist in a tiny gesture of victory. It didn't sound as if Mr Warry would be offering rides on Holly and Robin.

'So what are your plans?' she asked. 'Do you have plenty of space for them?' She sat down in the chair beside the computer and looked out of the window.

'I have the perfect field,' he told her. 'Not too much grass and there's a good solid shelter for them in case it's wet. I love having the cows and the alpacas,' he said, 'but I want to open the place up as a children's farm. I can't imagine anything more welcoming than a lovely pair of donkeys.'

Mandy could see Holly through the glass. The little jenny

was sniffing the ground under an apple tree filled with blossom. Robin trotted up to her, nudging her with his nose.

'Don't worry if they aren't used to children yet,' Mr Warry went on. 'That's something we'd work on before any paying customers were allowed anywhere near.'

Better and better, thought Mandy. She remembered Jack chattering away to the two young donkeys. 'They're already used to children,' she told Mr Warry, but I'm very glad to hear you'd make sure they were well settled before going ahead.'

'We would,' he assured her. He sounded wonderfully earnest. 'I'm planning to call the children's farm Rainbow Hill,' he said. 'I'll need a few more animals before we go ahead, but if we had your donkeys, it would be a great start.'

Mandy thought for a moment before she replied. 'There are a few things we'll have to do,' she told Mr Warry. 'I'll have to come over and see where they'd be living before they come to you, but in the first instance, you should probably come over and see them. Would you have time to come over at the weekend?'

'That would be lovely,' he replied. 'Sunday afternoon okay?'

'Perfect.' Mandy grinned with hope and relief as she tapped on the screen to end the phone call. She would miss Holly and Robin's sweet faces and deep liquid eyes looking up at her in the mornings, but she had to admit she wouldn't miss their feed bills, not one bit.

Back out in the waiting room, Rachel was busy watering

the plants. In the kennels, Anita still looked comfortable. Mandy decided to go into the cottage and let Sky out for a few minutes. There was nothing else pressing she had to do.

She found Emily sitting in the kitchen, drinking a cup of tea with Sky leaning against her leg. Mandy smiled at how relaxed they looked – until Sky saw Mandy and rushed over. Mandy bent to stroke her.

'Hello.' Mandy looked up at Emily as she buried her hands in Sky's thick fur. 'Have you been back long?'

'Just a few minutes.' Emily smiled, her old broad smile. Mandy was glad to see it. For ages, Emily had seemed so exhausted that Mandy had been really worried. It was great that her mum was taking the doctor's advice to rest seriously. She really did look better than she had for weeks. 'I'm going to have to love you and leave you, though,' Emily told her. 'I'm off to Walton to do some shopping. We've run out of Tango's special treats and now he's cross with me.'

Mandy laughed. It looked like it wasn't just Adam who was stuck under that fluffy ginger paw!

Emily stood up and pushed her chair in, then paused for a moment, moving her left foot from side to side. 'Sky's been sitting on my foot way too long,' she said with a laugh. 'It's gone quite numb.'

Mandy grinned. 'That's what you get for being so nice to her,' she said. 'See you later.'

Limping slightly, Emily walked over to the door and pulled her boots on. 'Bye love,' she called. Mandy followed her out of the door, then she and Sky walked round to the paddock. Holly and Robin were already waiting at the gate by the time she got there. Their ears were pricked forwards, their eyes bright. 'I think I might have a new home for you,' Mandy told them.

'Hello, I'm Oliver Chadwick. I'm here to see the person in charge of the rescue centre.' The polite voice was very clear.

Mandy stood up from the consulting room computer and walked through to the Animal Ark reception, just as Rachel replied, 'I'll just get Amanda for you.'

'Hello Mr Chadwick. I'm Amanda Hope.' Mandy was quite tall, but Mr Chadwick was still half a head taller. She looked up with interest into a pair of intelligent blue eyes. The man was about seventy, grey-haired and smartly dressed in very clean black trousers and a navy jersey. 'What can I do for you?'

Mr Chadwick gave a small smile. 'My daughter called yesterday,' he said. 'She wanted me to come over and choose a cat.'

Odd choice of words, Mandy thought. Mr Chadwick must be the father of the woman with the booming voice she had spoken to yesterday, and it seemed as if her instinct was right. For a moment, she wondered if she should ask straight out whether Mr Chadwick actually wanted a cat. She would hate to rehome one of her rescues to someone whose heart wasn't in it. But Mr Chadwick's eyes were kind. She decided, for the moment, to give him the benefit of the doubt. She would be able to tell more when she saw him with the cats.

'Come with me,' she told him and led him out of the clinic, crossing the path to Hope Meadows.

As always, she felt a thrill of pride as she led a new potential owner into Hope Meadows' reception. The huge glass window, with its wonderful view of the sheep-dotted moor was impressive enough for anyone. The little cat ward was slightly less impressive. The kennels she had bought second-hand were clean, but they were old-fashioned and made of wood. The inhabitants looked healthy, though. Not only that, but both of them stood up and came to the doors of their cages as Mandy led Mr Chadwick in. Mandy began to introduce them.

'This is Pixie.' She bent down and rubbed the cheek of the little black cat through the bars. 'And this is Gull.' The tabby and white cat purred as she reached out. Mr Chadwick's eyes were on Pixie.

'I'll look at that one,' he said, pointing at Pixie. Again, Mandy was struck by the hesitancy with which he seemed to be approaching the visit. But when she opened the cage, he bent obligingly to greet Pixie. He held out his hand, as if for a dog to sniff. Pixie just pushed her face against it. She too had started to purr and as she rubbed herself against Mr Chadwick's hand, he did unbend enough to give a small smile. He unclenched his fist and stroked Pixie's small head and the little cat closed her eyes and leaned towards him. 'It seems very friendly,' he commented.

'She is,' Mandy told him.

'What about the other one? Gull, was it?'

'He's a lovely cat too,' Mandy told him. She closed the door on Pixie and they moved over to Gull's cage. Mandy swung the rather heavy door open and Mr Chadwick leaned in. Gull, seeing his opportunity, made a rush up Mr Chadwick's arm and ended up standing on the man's shoulders.

Seeing the alarmed look on the Mr Chadwick's face, she quickly rescued him, taking Gull into her own arms. 'Sorry about that,' she said.

Despite a discreet glance down at his jersey, as if to inspect it for claw damage, Mr Chadwick still took the time to stroke Gull, though he made no attempt to take him back from Mandy. After a couple of minutes, he thanked her.

'I think I like Pixie best,' he told her. 'So what happens next?'

'Well, if you're sure you'd like to rehome . . .' Mandy left the statement in the air for a moment. When Mr Chadwick made no objection, she carried on, 'then I'll need to carry out a house check on your home to see if it's suitable.'

'And what does that entail?' he asked. He still sounded too polite, as if he was going through the motions.

'I need to check everything's safe and that you have as much information as possible before you agree to take Pixie on,' Mandy said. She looked up at Mr Chadwick again, trying to read his expression. He was smiling, but she had no idea what he was thinking.

'Would tomorrow afternoon do?' he asked.

'That would be fine.' Closing the door on the cats, Mandy walked back over to the reception desk. 'I'll just take some details,' she murmured.

Five minutes later, back in Animal Ark, Rachel looked at her, eyebrows raised. 'So how did it go?' she asked.

'He wants to take Pixie,' Mandy told her, 'subject to the house check of course.'

Rachel held up her hand and after a second's pause, Mandy returned the high-five that Rachel offered. 'Isn't it wonderful that so many people want to rehome your animals?' Rachel's voice held so much enthusiasm that Mandy couldn't bring herself to disagree. But somewhere, alarm bells were ringing in her head. There was something about Mr Chadwick's visit that struck her as off. He seemed lovely and he had been kind enough to the two cats. He just didn't have the enthusiasm she had come to expect from those who wanted to rehome an unwanted pet. She was going to have to ask him, she decided. Tomorrow, during the house visit, she would have to find out whether he really wanted a pet or not.

Chapter Six

'Sam Western called.' Mandy looked over at Rachel, her heart sinking a little. It wasn't that a call from Mr Western was unusual – there were so many animals attached to his extended farm that either he or Graham, his dairyman, called them out regularly. It was the way Rachel said it that set Mandy just a little on edge. Sam Western could be . . . difficult. 'He's asked to see you,' Rachel added, and Mandy's eyebrows shot up.

'Me? Not Mum or Dad?' It was true she had been doing a lot of the farm work recently, but her parents had both been going to Upper Welford Hall for years. 'Is it one of the cows I saw last week?'

'No.' Rachel tapped a few keys on the computer, then turned the screen to show Mandy. 'It's his bulldog Harley he's asking about. His skin's flared up again. You did a good job the last time, he told me.'

Mandy thought back to Harley's last visit to Animal Ark. She had noticed on previous occasions how stressed he became in the clinic. When he was upset, he panted and because of his shortened nose, he really did get very breathless. Mandy had examined him outside where it was cool and shady and had taken extra time to approach him slowly with plenty of rewards. Sam Western hadn't commented at the time, but Mandy knew that he loved his dogs more than he liked to let on.

'He'll be here in ten minutes,' Rachel told her.

'I'd better have a look at what I gave him last time,' Mandy said, peering at the computer screen. 'Seeing as he was so impressed.' Her voice was light, but she couldn't help but feel relieved.

Maybe he'll be reasonable, if he was pleased before.

It took only a couple of minutes for Mandy to reacquaint herself with Harley's history. Like most bulldogs, he'd had a lot of problems over the years, mostly to do with his skin. Mandy had talked Sam through the possibilities of exclusion diets to try to rule out food allergies. Then she had given him tablets that would get rid of any fleas and ticks. Though there was no official recommendation, Mandy knew there was some evidence the tablets could help to control mites as well. Bulldogs were prone to all kinds of skin problems.

'He's here!' Rachel murmured and Mandy straightened up.

Mr Western opened the door and strode into the waiting room. Years of truculent thinking had carved a deep cleft in the centre of his forehead. His white hair might have been cemented to his head, it was so smooth and regimented.

She and James had hated the farmer when they were children. He'd seemed impossibly ruthless. She had to admit that he wasn't quite the pantomime villain she'd thought him when she was little – his dairy at Upper

Welford Hall was run efficiently by Graham, whose care for the cows and calves was second to none. Running Wild, Jimmy's Outward Bound centre was set up in such a way that wildlife was protected. Gordon and Prue Ruck sold their woollen goods through the shops on his farm. Sam Western, for all his faults, had a big hand in the wellbeing of Welford and the surrounding area.

But part of her would never forget that he had once not cared so much about wildlife. He'd even tried to set up a fox hunt in Welford, before foxhunting was banned.

'Will you see Harley outside again, please?' The deep voice was matter-of-fact. There was nothing to suggest he was pleased to see Mandy, and perhaps that was fair enough. Mandy suddenly wondered what little Mandy and James must have looked like to Mr Western: this interfering boy and girl always sticking their noses into his business, when they'd only been a little bit older than Abi and Max.

But Mandy didn't need him to like her. It was enough that he recognised her actions were good for Harley. She nodded a greeting and followed him outside.

They examined the sturdy dog together out in the paddock. Mandy was pleased to see that the skin over Harley's back, which had been irritated and greasy before, was much clearer. 'I think you should continue with the tablets over the summer,' she told Sam. Harley had a new patch of dermatitis on his muzzle in one of the deepest of his skin folds. It looked painful. Mandy took a swab from the area as gently as she could.

Having completed the examination, Mandy stood up, gazing down at the quirky face of the bulldog with his wide, grinning muzzle raised towards her. 'It really would be helpful if we could begin to get Harley comfortable coming inside the practice,' she told Sam. It was good that for now they could reduce his stress by examining him outdoors. It would be better if he could learn that a trip to Animal Ark didn't have to be frightening. It was fine examining him outside on a sunny May afternoon. Not so good in the dim light of a winter's evening.

'How would we do that then?' Mr Western's voice was sceptical.

'If you could bring him now and then when he wasn't unwell, he might stop hating it so much,' Mandy said. 'We keep some hypo-allergenic treats in stock. Harley would be welcome to pop in during the day. Helen or I could take both of you around the practice. He knows something bad happens every time he comes. Give him a chance to learn that's not always the case.' She watched Mr Western's face, wondering whether he was calculating some kind of cost-benefit analysis in his head. She almost wanted to laugh.

'Maybe I could do that,' he conceded, and Mandy wondered whether he would come himself, or find someone else to do it for him. At least he had Harley's best interests at heart.

'Can I book a call out for tomorrow morning while I'm here?' Mr Western's voice had returned to its usual guttural practicality. 'Graham told me one of the cows might have slipped her calf. I won't be there myself. There's a land sale going through at present and it's very important I meet the client in person, but Graham asked if ten would be possible?'

Mandy knew they carried out routine fertility visits to Upper Welford, but the next one wasn't due for a couple of weeks. Graham was very observant in noticing when something went wrong. If he thought the cow had lost her calf, he was probably right. 'I'll put it in the book for tomorrow,' she promised. Harley was looking up at her, his stumpy tail wagging. She bent for one last ear scratch, smiling at how much the big dog seemed to be enjoying it.

When she stood back up, Sam Western was looking at her with what seemed almost like grudging respect. The effect was fleeting. A moment later, his normal expression had returned. With a tug on Harley's lead and a curt 'Come,' Sam Western strode off across the short grass and back to his car.

Mandy felt a weight lifting off her shoulders as she walked up the path to Mistletoe Cottage. It was Emily's evening for consultations, Adam was on call and Nicole had kindly offered to see to the animals in Hope Meadows.

Jimmy was waiting for her when she walked into the cottage with Sky. The worn carpets and antiquated furniture felt like home when she was alone with Jimmy and the dogs. She was excited about her move to Wildacre and all the renovations she was doing to make it her very own space, but it was wonderful to have this home-away-from-home to come to.

The delicious scents of tomato and spices wafted from the kitchen. She had bought Jimmy a vegetarian cookery book for Christmas and he had become quite adventurous trying out new recipes. He kissed her in the hallway as Zoe, Simba and Sky danced around their feet.

Released from Jimmy's embrace, Mandy walked through to the kitchen. The back door stood open; the sun was streaming in. 'I thought we could go for a walk,' Jimmy said, leaning over the stove and stirring the contents of a large pan. He replaced the lid and turned off the cooker, then turned to Mandy with a grin. 'I've made veggie curry, but it'll keep.'

'Sounds perfect,' Mandy told him. He closed and locked the back door, then called the dogs. Together, they crossed the garden and turned into the small lane that led downhill towards the river. On either side, white hawthorn flowers peeped out from amongst the small dark green leaves of the blackthorn. The tangled verges were filled with cow parsley. The scent of honeysuckle came to her on the breeze. Side by side, the three dogs panting ahead, they turned onto the track that ran alongside a smooth stretch of water. Ahead of them, the Beacon was bathed in golden evening sunshine.

There was a bench halfway along the track. Jimmy and she had met here, one difficult evening last summer, before they'd really known each other. He'd had Simba and Zoe with him, and she had been drawn into conversation almost against her will. She'd been so prickly, Mandy cringed at the memory. She'd been feeling patronised and under-valued after her move back to Welford, as if everybody refused to accept she wasn't a child anymore. When Jimmy had tried to joke about her various animal-saving crusades, she had taken it badly.

'The sand martins are nesting again,' Jimmy said as they walked down towards the long curve of the river, where the smooth water broke up, chattering over the stones. He pointed to the holes in the steep sandy bank on the far side of the water. As Mandy watched, a tiny bird emerged from one of the dark tunnels and flitted off across the water.

They sat down beside the river on the grass. It really was very warm. Mandy watched idly as first Simba, then Sky and finally Zoe entered the water, splashing in the shallows. 'Should we join them, do you think?' Jimmy's voice broke the companionable silence.

Mandy grinned. 'Let's do it!' She pulled off her shoes and socks and rolled up her trousers. She and James had paddled here as children. She could remember Blackie, James's Labrador, rushing into the water and coming out to shake, spraying the whole area with droplets.

The water was deliciously cool, the pebbles smooth beneath her toes.

Jimmy was beside her. 'Look!' He bent over, pointing at some tiny brown fish that flitted through the water, so close that they could almost have touched them.

'Simba!' Mandy giggled as the German Shepherd ran past her, splashing her with water.

'He wants you to play,' Jimmy laughed, as the black and tan dog spun back around and crouched in front of Mandy, his tongue lolling.

'Oh no, I don't feel like a swim today!' said Mandy, backing off. Sky ran and leaped at Simba. The two dogs rolled over in the water, play fighting and splashing everywhere. Zoe waddled over and sat between Jimmy and

Mandy, watching the other two. Her face almost looked indulgent, Mandy thought, as if she was already watching two pups playing.

They returned home, just as the sun was beginning to sink behind the distant curve of the moor that lay across the valley from Mistletoe Cottage. To Mandy's delight, Jimmy carried a table and chairs out into the garden and they ate veggie curry and warm garlic naan breads. In the distance, a nightjar began his churring song. From the hedge came the answering chirrup of a robin. The dogs were asleep on the grass. Sky's paws twitched as if she was dreaming.

Once the meal was finished and cleared away, they moved onto a bench in the lea of the hedge and Jimmy put an arm around her. Down in the village, the church clock began to strike eight. With a sigh, Mandy cuddled closer to Jimmy's side. 'This really feels a bit like the final scene in a movie,' she said, 'where everything has come right.'

Jimmy laughed softly, looking up at the sky, a deep blue speckled with one or two early stars. 'I hope it isn't our final scene,' he said. 'Isn't the next part where they live happily ever after?'

Mandy shook her head. 'They never show that part,' she said.

He was smiling. He looked as contented as she felt. 'Shall we head upstairs?' she asked, pulling herself upright. She wished the evening could last forever, but whatever time she went to bed, the morning feeds at Hope Meadows would wait for no woman.

★　★　★

She awoke beside him at seven. Jimmy looked so peaceful when he was asleep. She wished she could prolong the moment, but Sky was awake and pacing the floor by the foot of the bed. Climbing out of bed, Mandy made her way downstairs and let the dogs out, following them into the garden. There was still dew on the grass. A bumblebee wove its way across the lawn. Mandy stretched her arms up to the sky, enjoying the cool air on her skin.

When she went back into the kitchen, Jimmy was there, making toast.

'Morning.' He gave her a kiss, then turned back to the kettle. 'Coffee?' he asked.

'Yes, please.'

They sat down at the table. The back door was open. Outside, she could see the dogs exploring the early morning scents. It was going to be a lovely day.

A thought came into her head. 'Will you be about for the Spring Show?' she asked. 'I'm going to be the official vet this year.' Every year in May, there was an agricultural show and fair in the centre of Welford. Animal Ark had provided veterinary care for the animals for years, but this was the first time Mandy had been asked.

Jimmy wrinkled his nose, his face apologetic. 'I think I'm working that day,' he said. 'I'm really sorry. I meant to organise it so I made sure I had that day off, but then I forgot.'

'It's fine,' Mandy said. It couldn't be helped and usually it was she who had to cry off for work at the weekends.

'What about this weekend coming up?' he asked. 'Would it be all right if I brought Abi and Max over to see Holly and Robin? They'd love to come and visit.'

The twins. Mandy's good mood faded just a little. Not that she had forgotten them, but last night had been so wonderful with just her and Jimmy. She paused with her mug halfway to her mouth.

'I'm actually really busy,' she said. 'James is coming over. And there's someone coming to visit the donkeys . . .' she trailed off. Outside, a cloud passed over the sun.

Jimmy was looking at her. Could he read what was inside her head? 'You're going to have to get used to spending time with the children,' he said. His voice was still friendly, but the magic of the past few hours fled.

Mandy put down her mug. Her toast suddenly seemed far less appetising. 'It's not that,' she objected. 'I really am busy.' He was looking at her. Her conscience prickling, she added, 'It wasn't exactly a roaring success the other night, was it?' Across the table, Jimmy set his cup down. Trying to keep her voice steady, she rushed on. 'Obviously they want you to themselves at the moment. It's completely natural with Belle's new baby . . .'

But there never was going to be a good time, she thought, even if they waited. The baby was on the way and everything was going to change.

'I'm sure you're right.' Jimmy looked across at her, his mouth lifting at one side, as if he was trying to smile but couldn't quite manage. 'They probably do feel that way, but life doesn't always work out like that. It isn't neat and tidy.' He paused, took a small bite of toast, chewed it thoughtfully and swallowed. 'You're a part of my life now,' he said. 'We need to find a way for you to be part of their lives too.' He picked up his coffee cup and leaned back in his chair, cradling the drink between his hands as if warming them.

There was no real answer to that. It made sense, yet she was still uneasy. 'However much you want it, you can't force them to like me,' she pointed out. 'I can't force them to like me either.' The whole thing felt so unnatural. How could she expect them to take it in their stride when she, an adult, was finding it so difficult?

Jimmy grinned suddenly, as if pulling himself together. 'Come on, Mandy Hope,' he said, 'aren't you the woman who can tame wild deer and crazy dogs? If you can do that, you can tame my children surely?'

If only it was that easy, Mandy thought. Animals were far easier to understand. *And sedate*, she added to herself, thinking of her phone conversation with James. She smothered the smile that threatened to rise to her lips. She wasn't sure Jimmy would see the funny side.

'You can bring them over on Sunday afternoon,' she said. After all, James would be there. He was much better with children than she was.

Across the table, Jimmy looked pleased at her suggestion that they come over on Sunday. 'Thank you,' he said, reaching out a hand and squeezing hers. 'It will get easier.'

She squeezed his hand back, hoping he was right.

Chapter Seven

It had been a difficult morning for Mandy so far: three consultations, three dogs to vaccinate. All of them had growled the moment they had seen her. It had taken all her ingenuity and quite a bit of time to get them injected safely. Then she'd spent a good hour sedating a cat to treat an infected wound. Now she was on her way to Mr Chadwick's house.

Despite having slept on it, she still felt uneasy about his visit to Hope Meadows yesterday. He had been perfectly polite; she'd had no misgivings that he might mistreat the cats. But his lack of enthusiasm didn't sit right. It was almost as if he'd been going through the motions, trying to say the right things, but missing the target. Not that everyone who wanted to adopt had to love animals the way she did, but looking after pets could be hard. You had to really want to do it.

Mr Chadwick lived in a hamlet that lay in a small valley off the Kimbleton road. She drove carefully, peering at the satnav and at the small signs that indicated hidden turns off the lane, until she saw the one for his house, number 52. She turned in through a large iron gate and found herself heading up a long gravel drive to an enormous house built of weathered, grey stone, standing in a neatly trimmed garden. A large horse-chestnut tree stood to the side of the house and there was ivy trained up a trellis around the front door. Mandy rang the bell. For a moment her mind fancifully imagined a traditionally dressed maid coming to answer, but when the door opened, Mr Chadwick was standing there himself, smartly dressed as he had been when he came to visit Hope Meadows.

'Come in, please,' he said with a smile that didn't quite reach his eyes.

The house was immaculate. There were shelves full of neatly ordered books, cream walls, and pristine carpets. Even the ornaments on the drawing room mantelpiece were regimented. There was a grand piano, standing in state in the bay window. Other than what appeared to be a scattering of family photographs, it was almost like a show house, Mandy thought.

Wildacre has never been and will never be this clean, Mandy thought with a secret smile. *Even though the plaster just went on this week!*

Try as she might, it was hard to imagine Pixie running around burying her claws in the high-backed, crushed-velvet sofa or snoozing in front of the fire. Pulling a pen from her pocket, Mandy fixed her attention on working through the checklist she had brought. She was here to assess whether the house was an appropriate home for a cat, she reminded herself, not how inviting she found it herself.

In a theoretical sense it was perfect. The drawing room was perfectly safe and the kitchen had a door that was suitable for a cat-flap. There were no poisonous plants.

When Mr Chadwick opened the door onto the back garden, there was an enormous stretch of grass that backed onto a field. There were no main roads nearby. 'Your house is beautiful,' Mandy told him, once they had explored the whole of the downstairs. 'Is there somewhere we could go and have a chat, please?'

Together, they walked back through to the high-ceilinged drawing room that looked out towards the front of the house. Mandy found herself again wondering what was going on in her host's head as he trod the blue-carpeted hallway.

'Please do sit down,' Mr Chadwick urged, ushering her towards the wing-backed chair that stood near the window. Despite its upright appearance, it was unexpectedly comfortable. Mandy looked down at questions that made up the final page of her checklist. She had carried out so many house inspections now, that she barely needed to read them. One by one, she worked her way down the list. It was designed to find out how much the potential owner understood about their new pet, and to ensure they knew how to integrate him or her into their home. There were no searching questions about whether they really wanted a pet at all. Mr Chadwick answered them all perfectly.

'Do any of your neighbours have cats?' Mandy asked. It was the last question. Not that there were any close neighbours, she thought, remembering the road where she had driven in. The houses on either side had equally generous gardens.

'Mr and Mrs Chambers on the far side of the road have a cat,' Mr Chadwick told her, 'but it's mostly kept inside, I believe.'

There was sunlight slanting in through the window. Mandy could see motes of dust floating. Her checklist was complete. She searched for something more to say. Mr Chadwick hadn't asked any questions at all. Despite finding no specific obstacle to the match, she still had the unsettling sense that there was something she was missing.

Looking up, she was struck again by one of the photographs that hung on the wall beside her. The picture was of an attractive older woman, standing arm in arm with a girl who had a striking similarity to Mr Chadwick. Mandy had seen other pictures of them both, a laughing younger version of the mature lady in the kitchen, another with both of them, hanging in an alcove in the dining room.

Her eyes moved back down. Mr Chadwick met her gaze. For the first time, she caught a glimpse of sadness in his eyes. 'That's a lovely photograph,' she said.

'Thank you,' said Mr Chadwick. 'The younger one on the right is my daughter, Sophie. The other is . . . was, my wife Clara.' He pressed his mouth into a tight line and the muscles in his jaw clenched. Mandy wished she could say something to help, but had no idea what would be appropriate. 'I lost Clara two months ago,' Mr Chadwick said, when he could speak again. He took a deep breath, then cleared his throat. 'Sophie thinks a cat would be company for me. She says it will give me something else to think about.'

So that's *what this is about!*

'And . . . what about you?' Mandy's eyes searched his face, though her instincts were already telling her the answer. 'Do you feel as if a cat would give you company?'

His mouth quivered as a shudder passed through his

slim frame, then he smiled, though his face remained sad. 'I was a lucky man,' he said, his eyes on the photograph. 'We had thirty-two wonderful years together. She was beautiful . . . a beautiful person.' The bland politeness was gone, replaced with a melancholy certainty. He sighed. 'I know Sophie means well,' he said, 'but I don't want something else to think about. Not yet.'

For a moment, Mandy couldn't think of anything to say. James swum into her head. She had seen the same pain, the same bravery in his eyes. Platitudes were useless. She couldn't say that she knew how Mr Chadwick was feeling; she knew she didn't. 'She looks kind,' she said finally. It was inadequate, but what else was there? 'And your daughter is beautiful.'

Mr Chadwick's face softened as he looked at Sophie's picture. 'She's a very strong character,' he said. 'I was the same when I was younger.' He stood up and lifted another photograph down from the mantelpiece and handed it to Mandy. It showed a younger version of Sophie on her graduation day. 'Clara and I were so proud of her that day,' he told her, his voice warm with the memory. 'I know she's trying to do the right thing,' he said, 'but Clara and I never had any pets. We both loved the garden, and we loved to travel. A pet would have complicated things too much.'

Although she was sorry for him, Mandy was relieved that she understood the uneasiness she had felt earlier. She handed the photograph back and stood up. For a moment, she felt the urge to hug Mr Chadwick, but something in his expression stopped her. 'Thanks very much for your honesty,' she said with a nod. 'I'll cancel the application for now.'

He smiled as he led her out into the hallway. 'Well, thank you for yours,' he replied. 'It's unusual for someone so young to see things so clearly. And I'm sorry about Pixie,' he said, pulling open the front door. 'She really did seem like a lovely cat.'

Impulsively, Mandy reached out and put her arms around him, and after a moment of stiffness, he hugged her back. 'Don't worry about Pixie,' she said. 'I'm sure she'll find a good home with someone else.'

He stood with the door open as she walked down the path. He was still standing there as she closed the car door and drove away.

Although she knew it was the right decision, Mandy was disappointed that she wasn't going to be able to rehome Pixie. Not that one small cat made all that much difference, but the food bill for last month had been enormous. Still, it was better for both Pixie and Mr Chadwick to get the answer right.

She glanced at the clock on the dashboard. She needed to get back to Animal Ark before two, when afternoon surgery started. After that there were a couple of calls and she had to make up the spare room for James, who would be arriving at seven. There was just time for lunch. Despite her hurry, as she arrived back in Welford, on impulse she drove past Animal Ark and on up to Lilac Cottage where her grandparents lived.

Gran and Grandad were in the garden when she arrived. 'Hello love. We weren't expecting you.' Grandad looked up from his seedlings, a smile lighting up his face.

'I'll put the kettle on. It's almost lunchtime.' Gran put down the secateurs she was using and patted Mandy on the shoulder. She, too, looked delighted. Mandy followed them into the familiar kitchen.

'To what do we owe this honour?' Grandad pulled out a chair for Mandy, then sat down himself, gazing at her across the table as Gran took out cups from the cupboard.

Mandy thought for a moment. She hadn't really thought through what she wanted to say. 'I've just been out on a house inspection,' she said.

'Successful?' Grandad asked as Gran lifted the kettle, though it was obvious she was still listening as she poured the water onto the tea and moved everything over to the table.

'Not in terms of getting any animals adopted,' Mandy replied with a rueful smile as Gran sat down. 'The house was lovely, but something felt wrong. His wife died just a couple of months ago. They'd been together over thirty years. His daughter thought he should get a cat. He told me he's lonely, but he doesn't really want a pet.'

'Oh, are you talking about Oliver Chadwick? Poor man.' Gran pushed the newly poured tea across the table towards Mandy and held out a plate of cheese scones. There was sympathy in her slightly cloudy eyes. 'Clara was a lovely woman. He must be missing her, but he shouldn't get a pet unless he really wants to.'

Mandy shook her head as she took a scone and cut it in half, then reached for the butter. She shouldn't be surprised that Gran knew the Chadwicks – she'd lived in Welford so long that she seemed to know everyone who lived within a ten-mile radius of the village. 'That's what I thought,' she said, looking up. 'I felt so sorry for him, but I didn't really know how to help.'

Grandad reached a hand across the table, putting it over Mandy's and squeezing gently. 'It is sad,' he admitted, 'but sometimes there isn't much you can do.'

Gran's face was thoughtful. 'Perhaps he just needs to keep busy for a while. What about the indoor bowls club?' she asked. 'If you like, we could invite him to that.' She raised her eyebrows a little. 'Or there's the Pop-In Club. That's in Walton. Like a social club for over-sixties,' she explained when Mandy didn't immediately respond.

Tom Hope regarded his wife. 'We need to be careful,' he said. 'We don't want to overwhelm the poor man. But it's certainly an idea.' He looked across the table at Mandy.

'I think he'd be pleased,' Mandy said after only a moment's thought. 'How would it be if I call him tomorrow and give him your number. That way, he can make the first move if he wants to.'

Grandad looked pleased. Gran reached over and patted her hand. 'That's a very good idea.'

'Thanks, guys. By the way, these really are delicious.' Mandy took another bite of the new-baked scone. Gran looked gratified.

'They did turn out rather well,' she said.

Half an hour and several scones later, Gran reached out her arms and gave Mandy a hug as Grandad opened the door. 'You know you don't have to take on everyone's problems,' she told Mandy.

Mandy hugged her tightly back. 'I know,' she said, 'but

Mr Chadwick seemed so sad. I hoped you'd be able to come up with something.'

Gran's eyes were twinkling. 'I'm glad you came,' she said.

'Good to know we're not too old to help,' Grandad added, his grin mischievous.

Mandy wrapped her arms around him, then turned to hug her grandmother. 'You'll do a while yet,' she said.

'Mandy?' Emily put her head round the door of the spare bedroom. Mandy was making up the bed for James. She turned with a smile, but the happy feeling left her when she saw Emily's pale face.

'Are you okay, Mum?' she asked, dropping the pillow she was holding onto the bed.

Emily blinked painfully. 'Not really,' she admitted. 'I think I'm getting a migraine. It's as if there's something flickering in my left eye.'

'Do you think you should go to bed?' Mandy asked with a frown. She was starting to feel worried about her mum's frequent bouts of ill-health.

'I'm just going. It hurts when I move my eyes.' Emily managed a smile, but Mandy could see it was an effort. 'But I'm sorry, Mandy, there's a call in. Jack Spiller has a lamb with a broken leg. I know James is coming soon and I wouldn't normally ask but your dad's in the middle of surgery.'

Mandy walked across and gave Emily's hand a squeeze. 'You don't need to apologise,' she said. 'James won't mind. I'll send him a message. You go and lie down. James and I will make dinner when we get back.'

'Thank you.' Emily sounded so pathetically grateful that Mandy felt a stab of pain. Emily had always been so self-sufficient. She had been the one who looked out for everyone else.

'You should go back to the doctor's, Mum,' Mandy said.

Emily sighed. 'I know,' she said. 'My blood tests all came back normal last time. Dr Grace was lovely, but she said she couldn't find anything else. You know what it's like. Sometimes it takes ages for things to work.'

Mandy knew that only too well from her vet work. Sometimes there was nothing to do but wait and see.

'I'd better get off,' she said. She wished she could stay and help her mum, but the poor lamb couldn't wait either.

Climbing into the car, she typed a quick text to James. 'Going to Fordbeck Farm to see a lamb. Helen is in the clinic and will let you in if you arrive before I'm back. See you soon. Mandy x.'

Putting the car into gear, she turned down the lane towards the Fox and Goose, then headed onto the road that led up the fellside towards Black Tor. The lane rose steeply, emerging via a cattle grid onto the wide open moorland. A group of ewes lifted their heads to gaze curiously at the car. Two lambs skipped over the short grass under the late afternoon sky. *Poor Mum*, Mandy thought again. *She would love to see this. Maybe I'll bring her up here when she's feeling better.*

Jack Spiller was waiting for her in the farmhouse at Fordbeck. He opened the door in his boilersuit and grinned when he saw Mandy. 'I haven't seen you for a while,' he said.

Just then, another car pulled into the yard. 'Who's this now?' he asked, but Mandy recognised the driver.

'James!' she cried.

Jack Spiller laughed. 'I should have known when you arrived that this young man wouldn't be far behind,' he grinned. 'Never would see one of you without the other, back in the day.'

Mandy grinned. 'The dream team is back!'

James climbed out from behind the steering wheel of his Ford. 'Evening,' he said to them both, then looking at Mandy, 'I got your text message when I stopped for petrol. I thought I'd see if I could catch you.'

'Great! You're just in time to be my glamorous veterinary assistant!' Mandy laughed.

'No problem.' James grinned.

'So where's this lamb?' Mandy asked Jack and he led off across the smooth concrete and out into a paddock behind the house.

It wasn't a bad break. The lamb was surprisingly sprightly on its three good legs, but Mr Spiller had penned it with its mother, so it couldn't run far. It took only a moment to catch the woolly creature. James steadied the leg as Mandy applied a green padded splint and plenty of padded support bandages. The lamb bleated loudly as James set him back down in the pen, but Mandy was pleased to see he was already beginning to dot the newly bandaged leg on the floor. She grinned as he put his head down under the ewe, feeling for the teat. His tail started to whirl as her milk began to flow. 'You should bring him into the clinic in a couple of weeks,' she told Mr Spiller. 'We'll check how it's healing and change the bandage.'

They went inside and washed their hands, then James

followed Mandy back out to where their cars were parked. 'I'll follow you down,' he told her.

'Good.' Mandy nodded. 'Bye,' she waved to Mr Spiller and climbed into the driving seat of her SUV.

She could see James in the rear-view mirror as she drove out onto the narrow lane that led back down towards Welford. It was like a grown-up version of the old days when they would ride their bikes in convoy around the village.

Before her, the village spread out in the last rays of the evening sunshine. There were pink blossoms on the trees on the green and in the churchyard. The Fox and Goose already had a few cars parked outside. The beer garden would be full on a lovely day like this. She bumped over the cattle grid and was back between the high walls. James was still behind her. To her right, the turning for Mr Chadwick's hamlet led off through a small area of woodland. Mandy slowed down as she reached a bend in the road, and her heart began to race as she saw what was around the corner.

There was a grey van, half-tilted into the ditch, looking like it had just swerved off the road. Mandy slammed on the brakes and was relieved when James did the same, stopping a few yards behind her. Beside the van crouched a dark-skinned man wearing a turban. But what caught Mandy's eye was the bundle of brown fur huddled in the grass.

Chapter Eight

She was out of her car in an instant. 'Are you all right?' she asked the man. The brown bundle moved. A wing extended, flapped weakly and then was still again.

'I'm okay,' the man said, still looking down at what Mandy could now see was a tawny owl. 'It swooped out of nowhere and hit my windscreen,' he said, finally looking up. Mandy could see he was close to tears. Behind her she heard James's car door open and shut.

The owl stirred again, lifting its head. This time both wings moved, opening and flapping for a few moments. The bird managed to stutter a few yards along the grassy verge, then came to a halt, looking dazed. Its left wing hung down at its side. Mandy felt sick. If its wing was broken, she might have no option but to euthanise the beautiful creature.

'It came out of nowhere,' the man said again. He sounded shocked. He seemed oblivious to the state of his van, or anything else.

'It's a bad corner,' Mandy told him. It was difficult light too, she thought. The sun was dipping below the horizon and must have been in his eyes, maybe in the owl's too.

'I don't know what to do. I think it's injured.' He was shaking.

She laid a hand on his trembling shoulder. 'It'll be okay,' she told him. 'I'm a vet in Welford. We can take it to the clinic.'

'You're a vet?' For the first time, he looked up at her. He had huge brown eyes, which were full of worry.

James had taken off his jacket. 'Use this,' he said. Moving round behind the owl, he manoeuvred himself into position while Mandy shifted closer to the bird's head to prevent it from moving forwards. In a few moments, and with minimal disturbance, James had wrapped his coat around the speckled feathers and had lifted the bird into his arms.

The man was watching them, his eyes wide with relief. 'What's your name?' James asked.

'Raj,' the man replied, and held out a hand, then seemed to realise that James had his hands full of owl and awkwardly lowered it again. 'Raj Singh Bhuppal.'

'I'm James Hunter,' James told him with a reassuring smile. 'And this is Mandy Hope. She's a brilliant vet.'

Mandy could feel herself blushing, but she took pity on the man and shook his hand. Raj was looking less terrified already. James carried the bundled jacket over to Mandy's SUV. Turning the internal light on, Mandy helped him unwrap the owl. The owl tried to flap its wings again, so Mandy held it tightly. There was blood on the brown feathers just in front of the injured left wing. Parting them, Mandy could see a tear in the skin, just in front of the shoulder.

'We'll need to get it home to have a better look at that

wound,' she said. They would have to take some X-rays as well to see whether there were any broken bones. Owls were so reliant on flight for catching prey that they needed to be fully fit to survive in the wild.

'Do you have a box or anything in your car?' she asked James.

'I'm afraid not.' He shook his head.

'What about you?' she asked Raj.

'I'm so sorry,' he told her. 'I do food deliveries, but I'm finished for today. The van's empty.'

Mandy screwed up her face. 'In that case,' she said, 'one of us will have to hold it inside the jacket while the other drives down. We'll need to leave one of the cars,' she told James.

James frowned as he looked up and down the narrow lane in the gathering twilight. 'There really isn't anywhere to park,' he said. 'The road's too narrow and it's miles back up to the top of the moor where there's space.'

'I'll hold it.' For the first time, Raj's voice was decisive. 'My van isn't blocking the road, and it won't come to any harm. I'll come back later.'

Mandy was about to say she was sure they could manage, when James stepped in. 'Thanks very much,' he said. His voice was warm. 'That would be a great help. Just hold him firmly, but not too tight, right Mandy?' He handed over the injured bird, still swaddled in the light-weight jacket, then walked back to his own car. Raj opened the door and climbed into the passenger seat of Mandy's SUV, still clutching the precious bundle. The owl looked terrified but Raj held it perfectly and they reached Animal

Ark without incident. Sky sat in the back of the car, as good as gold.

Mandy was very pleased to see the lights were still on in the clinic. Evening surgery had run on and Rachel had just finished checking the inpatients.

'Would you mind staying a few minutes longer?' Mandy asked her, putting her head round the door. 'I need to anaesthetise an owl.'

'Of course.' Rachel closed the cage on the youngest of the animals, a puppy that had been terribly sick and had been on a drip for the past two days. 'I'll just wash my hands,' she said.

Mandy walked back into the prep room. Raj and James stood together in silence. Raj was still clinging onto James's jacket with the owl inside. 'I'm just going to set up theatre,' she told them as Raj handed her the owl.

'Okay, we're going to go and see to Raj's van,' James said. 'I'll be back in a bit.'

Mandy nodded as they left. She was thinking furiously. It would be best to leave the owl wrapped up, if possible. The less it flapped its wings, the less damage it would do. She and Rachel could mask it down, still swathed. It was really important not to cause any more stress than they had to. She would leave its head covered until the last minute.

She flicked a switch on the wall and the overhead suction unit droned into life. Pulling out a cushion and a heat pad from under the counter, she set them on the table and covered them with a disposable blanket. She grabbed a surgical kit and laid it on the side along with some suture material and a scalpel blade. Lastly, she set up the anaesthetic machine, slipping the corrugated tubing into place and attached the mask. It wasn't ideal, but it would have to do.

The swing doors opened, and Rachel appeared. Mandy switched on the oxygen. Between them, they unravelled the cloth from the owl's head. Rachel held the bundle gently on the well-padded cushion while Mandy applied the mask to the owl's face. Gradually, she added isoflurane to the oxygen. Within a few moments, the owl was still.

Between them, they unwrapped the slim body. Though she had been looking after injured birds for years, Mandy was still amazed by how little birds weighed compared to their animal counterparts. She turned down the gas a little. She didn't want the bird to wake, but it was equally important that it didn't go too deep.

Rachel had swung into action. She was already shaving around the wound. Once that was complete, she and Mandy checked the bird over for other injuries. So far as Mandy could tell, nothing was broken.

'I've the X-ray machine set up, just in case you needed it,' Rachel said. Mandy could have hugged her.

'We should do that,' she agreed.

The X-ray was clear. While Mandy scrubbed up, Rachel had checked over the rest of the body. There were no more wounds. She had wrapped the uninjured parts of the bird in bubble wrap to keep it warm, then cleaned out the messy wound on the shoulder. It must have been a stretching injury, Mandy decided as she inspected it under the bright overhead light. If she could suture the muscle well enough, the owl might make a full recovery. Slipping on a pair of surgical gloves, she picked up her scalpel and began to clean the wound, cutting away the dead tissue, then painstakingly began to stitch, pulling the ragged jigsaw back into shape.

By the time she had finished, there was only a neat line in the skin to show there had been a wound. Now she had to immobilise the limb. It was important to give support, but leave the owl with some movement. A few minutes later, she and Rachel stood admiring the neat wrap that encircled the wing. Mandy could only hope that when the owl was awake, it would tolerate the restraint. If it immediately pulled it off, they would have to rethink.

'We should move it over to Hope Meadows before it wakes up,' Mandy said.

For now, they would have to put it in a normal cage. It would be lovely to have a proper rehabilitation area for wild birds, she thought. Like everything else, it would cost more than she had just now.

Back out in the waiting room, she was surprised to see Raj sitting in one of the seats beside James. 'James called Mr Farmer from the garage out to collect the van,' he said, his eyes shining. He seemed far more relaxed than he had earlier. 'I wanted to see how the owl was before I went home. Is it going to be all right?' He stood up and walked towards Mandy, who was carrying the still-sleeping bird.

'The wing's not broken, just a nasty tear. I think it should be okay,' Mandy replied. 'We'll keep it in for a few days. It'll need antibiotics and pain relief and time to heal.'

Raj sighed and smiled. 'I'm so glad you came along,' he said. 'Where will you keep it?'

'I'm going to take it over to Hope Meadows, our rescue centre,' Mandy said. 'It's just next door and I run it.'

'I've heard of it, actually,' said Raj with a beaming smile. 'I didn't realise it was here in Welford. I always thought it was a great name.' Mandy glanced at James, a flicker of unease in her stomach. The name Hope Meadows had been chosen by Paul, James's husband. Would it stir sad memories?

But James looked pleased and proud. 'It is indeed an excellent name,' he said, sending Mandy a grin, telling her he was fine.

The three of them crossed the short pathway over to the rescue centre. Mandy's heart swelled with pride as she led Raj inside the attractive stone building with its huge glass windows, stretching to the roof, though the wonderful view of the fells was invisible in the darkness. She led them into the wildlife section and watched as James set up the cage with Raj's help. It was fantastic to have James here. He loved animals just as much as she did.

Raj seemed to be almost a kindred spirit. He was in no hurry to escape. Once the owl was in the cage, Mandy placed a towel over half of the door to give it some privacy. The three of them stood well back as the bird began to come round. Though it was bleary-eyed, it remained calm as it woke. After a few minutes, it was on its feet, clinging to the wooden handle they had provided as a perch.

'We should come out in an hour to offer it some food,' Mandy whispered. The worry now was whether the shy creature would eat. They tiptoed out, closing the door behind them with a click.

'How about a cup of tea?' Mandy offered. She still had to do the evening check of the rest of her furry Hope Meadows inhabitants, but they could wait a little while longer.

Sky and Tango were waiting for them in the house along with Seamus and Lily, James's beloved dogs. James must have brought them in while she was operating. The three dogs greeted them with their usual bouncing welcome, though Sky regarded Raj with some suspicion. She could often be a little hesitant around men she didn't know.

Tango had no such reservations. He made a beeline for Raj, tail aloft, and rubbed his face against Raj's leg. Raj leaned down. He seemed to enjoy the attention as Tango purred loudly, half closing his eyes and pressing his bony ginger face against the steady fingers that were stroking his ears.

Raj's phone rang just as Mandy set the mugs of tea down on the scrubbed pine table in the kitchen. He pulled his mobile from his pocket, pushed the chair out and wandered over to stand beside the darkened window as he listened. 'Thanks for letting me know,' he said a few moments later. He sighed as he ended the call and walked back over to the table.

'What's up?' James asked.

Raj gave a tight smile as he pulled out the chair and sat back down. 'The van's going to be out of action until tomorrow,' he said. 'They can't fix it tonight. I need to get home,' he said. 'I need to feed my cat.' A worried frown had appeared between his eyes.

'Where do you live?' James asked. 'I could give you a lift.'

But Raj still looked troubled. 'Halfway to York, I'm afraid,' he admitted. 'It's a good three-quarters of an hour away. I'll have to call a cab.' Tango had returned to his side, but Raj looked distracted as he reached down to stroke the ancient cat again.

'No need,' James said. 'I'll take you. It's really no trouble, I do that drive all the time. What about you, Mandy?' he asked. 'Will you come?' James was so easy-going, Mandy thought. The tension had left Raj's face already.

'If you don't mind,' Mandy looked from James to Raj, then back again, 'I should stay here and do my evening rounds.' She smiled at Raj. 'It's not just your cat that needs feeding,' she said with a grin.

The three of them finished their tea. Mandy was tired after her long day, but James and Raj kept the conversation going. It seemed that Raj sold all kinds of international food from his van, everything from biscotti imported from Italy to specialist Indian sweets made in Bradford.

'I want to thank you for everything you've done,' Raj said to Mandy as they stood up. 'For keeping me calm, as much as our poor owl friend! Do you have a website that takes donations? It's the least I can do now I've brought you a new patient.'

Mandy was about to say that there was no need, when she stopped herself. It wasn't true, she thought. There was every need and Raj was very kind. 'That would be wonderful,' she said. 'I'll give you our bank details.'

'Great. And you will let me know how the owl gets on?' Raj added. Mandy assured him that she would.

Chapter Nine

Mandy woke to the sound of the alarm and jumped out of bed. She was going to make a lovely breakfast for James. Washed and clothed, she ran down the stairs with Sky at her heels and into the kitchen. Adam was standing beside the fridge, but looked round when he heard the door open.

'Mandy.' He sounded relieved to see her, but worried all the same. 'I was about to come and wake you. I know James is here, but your mum's really not feeling well. She needs to stay in bed.' Adam looked exhausted too as if he'd been up half the night, Mandy thought, but she hadn't heard the phone; it hadn't been work that had disturbed him. 'I'm really sorry, but could you possibly get surgery?' Adam asked.

For a moment, Mandy fought the sinking feeling in her stomach. She'd promised James she'd spend the day with him and she hated having to let him down when he was feeling low.

'I'm sorry,' her dad said again with a grimace. 'I'd do it myself, but I'd arranged to go to Hare Hills to castrate three colts.' Mandy nodded – she hadn't even seen a colt castration since she came back to Welford, let alone tackling three by herself, but that wasn't what was making her queasy.

'Is Mum okay? Is it still a migraine?' She frowned, looking again at Adam's haunted eyes. Emily was supposed to be getting better: she had been better. Now she seemed to be sliding backwards.

'I don't know.' Adam seemed to have stuck somewhere halfway through making tea. The kettle was boiling and he was clutching two mugs to his chest, one in each hand. 'The doctor did say she'd be a bit up and down until her iron levels were right back up, and she's had migraines before, years ago, but . . .' he trailed off. Mandy could see he was as worried as she was. Yet the doctors had done so many tests when Emily was first ill that it was difficult to know where they could go next.

James wouldn't mind, Mandy knew. He had always loved Emily, but Mandy felt a stab of guilt that she had brought him here to cheer him up and now she had to go out without him. 'Of course I'll take the surgery,' she told Adam. She walked over and took the mugs from his hands. 'Do you need to get going?' she asked. 'I can make breakfast for James and Mum.'

Adam smiled at her, suddenly looking more like himself. 'Thanks, love,' he said. 'The oven's on and there are some croissants in the bread bin. I'll be back this afternoon, so you and James can have some time.'

Mandy opened the croissants and put them in the oven, then set the table. She would take Mum breakfast in bed, then she and James would have time for theirs. They could take the dogs out for a few minutes before she had to begin.

By the time James clattered down the stairs, closely attended by Seamus and Lily, breakfast was ready. Emily didn't look any worse than yesterday when Mandy carried her breakfast upstairs, but she didn't look better either. After the dogs had been out for a quick run in the garden, Mandy and James sat down at the kitchen table.

'So what do we have planned today?' James asked, picking up a croissant and putting it on his plate.

Mandy sent him a rueful smile. 'I'm afraid I've got to work,' she said. 'Mum's not well and Dad's out on a call already.'

'Oh?' It was James's turn to look worried. 'What's wrong with Emily? Does she need a doctor?' he asked. Emily had been in bed by the time they came in last night. Mandy had been so caught up with the lamb and Raj and the owl, that she had forgotten to tell him.

'It's just a migraine,' Mandy told him, though she didn't feel as light inside as she was making it sound.

James looked relieved. 'Your poor mum,' he said. 'I hope she feels better soon. And don't worry about working. I can go over to see Mum and Dad.'

Mandy smiled. 'Good idea. I'm sure they'll be pleased to see you.'

It was lovely to get outside and feel the breeze on her face after spending all morning inside Animal Ark. Mandy glanced at her phone. It was twenty past one. She had agreed to meet James back at the cottage at two. There would just be time to check in at Hope Meadows before lunch. She also realised, with a jolt, that she hadn't texted Jimmy since yesterday morning. She sent him a quick message, explaining what had happened with the owl last night, and that she was having to cover for Emily today. She felt guilty as she sent it off. Being busy so often made her feel like a bad girlfriend. Jimmy's reply came shooting back:

So sorry to hear about Emily. Give her my love. You know James won't mind if you need to work a bit. Can't wait to meet the owl! Love you xxx

Mandy instantly felt a little calmer, grateful to have someone as supportive as Jimmy. She walked into the cat room to be greeted by Nicole, who had just finished feeding the three kittens.

'How is everything?' Mandy asked.

Nicole's hair was sticking up as if she had been in a rush, but she sounded calm as she answered. 'I've done all the morning feeds,' she said, 'and cleaned out the cats and the small furries. The dogs have all been out except Brutus. Aren't Myler, Button and Jasper getting big?' She grinned as she glanced down into the kennel.

'They are,' Mandy agreed. The three kittens were already lying fast asleep, huddled into Mumma's flank. They made a lovely group. Mandy had to resist taking yet another photograph of them.

'I'm afraid the catch on the kennel at the end is broken again,' Nicole told her.

Mandy sighed. Though the second-hand cages had seemed a bargain, and although they were perfectly safe, there always seemed to be something going wrong. She'd have to fix the faulty catch, she thought. Almost all the kennels were full.

It often seemed that way in the spring. It was just long enough after Christmas for the novelty of new animals to have worn off and the rescue centres started to fill up with unwanted pets. Mandy pursed her lips. The running costs would be astronomical if she couldn't find homes for some of her rescues. It was a pity that Mr Chadwick had recognised he didn't want to adopt. Even as she had the thought, Pixie's small heart-shaped face appeared, and she rubbed affectionately at the bars of her kennel. Sometimes, even now, Mandy wished she could keep them all. There was no way she would ever send an animal to a home where the owner was less than one hundred per cent behind the idea.

Emily was sitting up in the kitchen by the time Mandy got back to the cottage. She looked so much better, that Mandy felt a flood of relief.

'How would you like some of my quesadillas?' she asked her mum.

Emily smiled. 'That would be lovely,' she said. 'I'll chop the salad.'

James arrived back at two as planned. He bounded in with Seamus and Lily and made his way over to give Emily a hug. 'Feeling better?' he asked her.

'Much.' Even Emily's voice sounded stronger, Mandy

thought. For a moment, she toyed with the idea of taking Mum up the road towards Black Tor to see the lambs, but she had invited James over. They should spend some time alone together. They tucked into the quesadillas with the dogs sitting hopefully at their feet.

The phone in Mandy's pocket buzzed. It was an unknown number. Half hoping it might be someone who wanted to adopt, she clicked on the button.

'Hope Meadows Rescue Centre.'

'Hello.' The man's voice on the other end of the line was brusque. 'I'm looking for Amanda Hope. I'm outside Wildacre at Lamb's Wood, delivering some paint, and I need someone to sign for it.'

Oh no!

Mandy could feel her face growing hot. The sitting room paint! She had quite forgotten that today was delivery day. 'I'm so sorry, I forgot,' she told the man. 'I'll be there in five minutes.'

She turned to James. 'I'm really sorry,' she said. 'I arranged ages ago for them to deliver paint and they're at Wildacre right now. I have to dash up and sign for it, but after that I really will be all yours.'

But James grinned. 'I've got a better idea,' he said. 'Why don't I come with you? I'd love to see the house. You can show me what you've been doing and we can make a start on the painting.'

'If you're sure?' Mandy looked at James, who smiled back and nodded with genuine enthusiasm.

'Would it be okay for me to leave the dogs here?' Mandy asked Emily. 'They can go out into one of the big kennels if necessary.' The dogs really couldn't come when they were painting, and she didn't want to burden her mum.

'Of course they can,' Emily said. 'They're no trouble. And,' she added in a firm voice, 'I really am very much better. Your dad and I can manage everything between us. Hope Meadows as well, if you divert your calls. We can call you on James's number if there's anything urgent.'

Mandy looked at Emily in delight. It would be lovely to have a few uninterrupted hours with James. 'Thanks, Mum,' she said. She clicked a few buttons on her mobile to divert the incoming calls. Now they really were free. With a quick last car-scratch for Sky and a hug for Emily, she followed James out to the car.

The sitting room was going to look fantastic when it was finished, Mandy thought. She slipped the head of her paintbrush inside a plastic bag to stop it drying out and set it down on the plastic sheeting that was protecting the floor.

'Coffee?' she asked James.

'That'd be great.' He looked down from where he was perched at the top of a stepladder. 'I'll just finish this corner and I'll come through,' he said and turned back to the job in hand.

Mandy switched on the kettle and leaned on the bench that faced the window. Every time she went in the kitchen, it gave her a lift. It reminded her of a shady forest with its soft green cupboards and rustic oak table. There was no need to light the wood-burning stove at this time of year, but its unpolished simplicity gave the room a homely feel. The clatter of James's feet descending the ladder heralded his entrance.

'Wow, Mandy! It's looking amazing,' he said.

The kettle was boiling. Mandy filled the two mugs and stirred them before joining James at the table.

'So how's it going with Jimmy and the twins?' James asked, taking the mug from Mandy and taking a grateful sip.

Mandy chuckled. 'Jimmy's great but the twins are still terrifying,' she admitted. 'If you're here tomorrow afternoon, you'll meet them,' she said. Peter Warry was also coming to see Holly and Robin in the evening, she remembered. It was going to be busy.

'That'll be nice,' James said.

'Glad you think so.' She grinned. 'I'm hoping they're so distracted by the animals that they forget I'm a wicked stepmother.'

James laughed. 'You worry too much. Forget all about trying to be a stepmother or how they'll react to "Dad's new girlfriend",' he advised. 'Just be yourself: a fun friend. You've so much going for you with all the animals and the rescue centre. Remember what Animal Ark was to us as kids?'

Mandy chortled and nodded. It was easy for James to say *stop worrying*, he was always the calm one. But he was probably right. She looked out of the window. Between the trees, the river was visible down in the valley. How lovely it had been the evening she'd been down there with Jimmy. 'It'll be easier with you there,' she said.

'Being myself, I mean.' She and James had been friends for so long that it sometimes felt as though he was a part of her.

'How about you?' she asked. 'How are things going?' She hesitated to ask directly about the unsuccessful date with the mysterious Ian, but James seemed to guess what she was asking.

'Do you mean my disaster date with Inebriated Ian?' His mouth quirked upwards at one side. 'It wasn't one of the finest evenings of my life,' he said.

'Inebriated Ian?' Mandy grinned at the description. 'That good?'

James shrugged, then lifted his mug to take a sip of coffee before answering. 'We were meant to be going for dinner,' he said, setting his drink back on the table. 'We'd been chatting online and he'd always been fun. He turned up to the restaurant half wasted. I understand being nervous on a first date, but it's better to arrive at least partially sober.'

Mandy found herself smiling. James had the knack of making even the most awkward things sound funny.

James let out a long breath, wrinkling his nose. 'Somehow he "forgot" about our dinner plans and he'd already had his. I had to order, though. He wouldn't hear of my going hungry.' He rolled his eyes and grinned. 'Just as the waiter arrived with my Pad Thai, he stood up to go to the toilet, staggered to the side and knocked the plate flying. Next thing I knew, I was wearing noodles on my head and tamarind sauce in my ears.'

Mandy burst out laughing.

'Quite a way to start your very first date, with a food fight,' she said. James laughed too.

'Yes,' he said. 'I won't be seeing him again.' For a moment, James's face fell and Mandy wondered if he was thinking about Paul and his wedding day. Then James pushed back his chair and stood up. 'Time to get on,' he said.

They finished painting, just as dusk was falling over the trees across the valley. Mandy looked around the room, feeling her heart lift. The warm Sail White paint contrasted with the muted red of the brick fireplace. A toasty carpet, some friendly pictures and a few pieces of comfy furniture would complete the effect.

After dinner with the Hopes – Adam's signature chilli, which was so hot it brought tears to Mandy's eyes – they went out to Hope Meadows. James was keen to see the owl they had rescued the night before. The bird was sitting on its perch, its wide eyes calm. It was eating well. Mandy was glad; it could be hard to tempt birds of prey in captivity. As they watched, it tried to stretch its wings, but the bandage that was restraining its left wing hampered its movements and it gave up and stared at Mandy and James. It was dark outside the window and Mandy had not turned on the overhead light, but they could see the creature clearly in the light from the open door. It should be swooping through the air outside, Mandy thought, not cooped up here in a kennel, poor thing.

James took out his phone and without turning on the overhead light, he managed to get a lovely clear photograph of the owl. 'I'll send this to Raj,' he said, peering at the screen with obvious pleasure.

Mandy felt a prickle of guilt. 'Oops, I was meant to update him this morning, but it went clean out of my head. Can you apologise for me when you send it?'

It had been a long day, what with the calls in the morning and the painting in the afternoon. As they walked back into the cottage, Mandy remembered that her phone was still redirected to the Animal Ark line. Pulling out her mobile, she removed the diversion. Mum would have told her if anyone had called, she thought, but when she checked the list of received calls, she was surprised to see Jimmy's number.

Emily was still downstairs in the sitting room. Mandy was glad she hadn't gone to bed. 'Did Jimmy call when we were outside?' she asked, trying not to frown. It was unlike Emily to forget something like that. What if it was something important?

A look of guilt crept over Emily's face. 'I'm so sorry, I forgot to tell you,' she said. 'I meant to do it, but it slipped my mind.' She looked so remorseful that Mandy wished she hadn't asked. It probably wasn't anything anyway. Jimmy would have phoned back, wouldn't he?

'It doesn't matter, Mum,' Mandy assured Emily. 'I'll call him back tomorrow morning.' It was too late to do it tonight, but she sent Jimmy a quick text. He'd find it in the morning if he was already asleep. Mandy hugged Emily, then together with James, they made their way upstairs. Mandy was only in bed a moment, before she fell into a deep and restful sleep.

Chapter Ten

Mandy's phone rang on Sunday morning when she was halfway through breakfast.

'Back in a minute,' she mouthed across the table to James. Pushing out her chair, she rushed into the hall. 'Hi Jimmy. Sorry I didn't get back to you last night.' She felt a little out of breath as she spoke. He was due to visit the donkeys this afternoon with the twins. He'd phoned late last night and now again first thing. Was something wrong?

'It's fine,' Jimmy assured her. 'We found something when we were out last night with the dogs. I know we're coming round later, but I thought you'd like to see it.' Even down the phone, she could tell he was smiling.

Mysterious . . . Mandy thought. 'What is it you found?' she asked.

'You'll have to come and see,' he told her.

Mandy heard Abi's voice in the background. 'Dad, look!'

'I'll have to hang up,' Jimmy told her. 'Will you come?'

Mandy didn't know whether to be exasperated or excited. 'James is staying with me,' she reminded him.

'He can come too.' Jimmy still sounded eager. Whatever it was, it must be something fun, Mandy decided.

'Well, okay. We'll be there in about an hour,' she said

after a moment's calculation. That would give them time to finish breakfast and have a quick look at the animals.

'So he didn't give you any idea what it was?' James asked as they drove towards Mistletoe Cottage almost an hour later.

'No,' Mandy said. 'He honestly didn't. I don't *think* it's anything bad, though.'

James grinned. 'I love a good mystery.'

Jimmy opened the door before they had even had a chance to ring the doorbell. 'Come in,' he urged them. 'In the kitchen.' He seemed almost *too* enthusiastic.

A large cardboard box stood on one of the chairs. Abi and Max were peering in through a small gap in the lid. They were still in their pyjamas. Both of them looked up as Mandy and James came in.

'Come and look.' Mandy had never seen Abi's eyes so wide. The girl had a breathless air, as if sharing whatever was in the box was a wonderful treat. Max's eyes had only briefly flicked upwards on their arrival as he sent them a grin. He seemed unable to take his eyes off whatever was inside.

Mandy walked over to the chair and peered in through the gap. In the corner a tiny shape was huddled. Reddish brown fur and a tufty tail curled upwards.

It was a baby red squirrel. Mandy felt herself become still. She too found it difficult to take her eyes off the tiny creature, but not just because it was hypnotically cute. Mandy's brain was suddenly whirring at a hundred miles an hour.

Red squirrels were a protected species. If the twins had

found a baby one, that meant there must be at least two more in the area. And that was wonderful, but . . .

'What do you think?' Abi asked, interrupting her train of thought. 'We found it in the grass last night when we were out with Zoe and Simba.'

'We think it must have fallen from its drey.' Max's voice was earnest.

'It was in shock,' Jimmy added. 'We brought it home to recover. Isn't it great?'

Their eyes were expectant as they looked at her. They wanted to share this with her, were offering it as a treat.

Mandy's heart sank. Didn't Jimmy know not to remove a wild animal from its habitat without very good reason, Mandy wondered? He must know that. When she looked back to Jimmy, his expression was guarded.

'Abi and Max wanted to take care of it,' he said. 'We were worried about the little thing. They've done a good job of looking after it. It's much better this morning.' Though he was trying to keep his tone light, a touch of defensiveness had slipped in.

He knew it was the wrong thing to do, Mandy thought, her heart sinking even further. Max and Abi were still gazing at her, wreathed in smiles, hoping she would add her praise.

James was standing very still beside her. Dragging her eyes away from Jimmy, Mandy glanced at him. It wasn't just that it was important to leave wild animals where they were; red squirrels were endangered. To remove them was breaking the law. James knew it as well as she did, but when she looked back at the children, they were still waiting for a reply.

She dredged up a smile, trying to take the sting from her

words. 'It looks . . . comfortable,' she said. 'But, you guys, red squirrels are endangered. There are hardly any left in England so it's really, really important not to disturb them even if you find a baby one by itself.' She paused for a moment. The excited expressions were slipping. 'You should have called me if you thought it was injured or unwell,' she said. 'Not brought it home, even if you were worried.'

'We did phone you,' Jimmy objected. 'Your mum said she'd get you to ring right back.'

Why hadn't they just asked Emily, Mandy wondered. Had Jimmy not wanted to trouble her? He knew Mandy was worried about her mum. She felt her own guilt rising. If she hadn't put the phones through . . .

'You should have asked Mum or left it where it was and called again,' she said to Jimmy, then spoke to the twins. 'We're going to have to take it back,' she told them. 'Straight away, I'm afraid. It was actually illegal to remove it from wherever you found it.' She tried to keep her voice brisk, but it was the wrong thing to say. The effect was immediate. Hurt appeared in the two sets of green eyes. She looked round towards James, whose expression was grave.

So much for being a fun friend . . .

Mandy looked at Jimmy, pleading with her eyes for him to understand.

He sighed. 'Mandy's right,' he said. 'We should take it back.'

Mandy smiled, glad of his intervention, but he was looking at her with an odd expression. What was it he wanted? Was she supposed to tell them they'd done a good job taking care of the squirrel? They'd done the exact opposite. If the mother wouldn't take it, then the little creature would die. However much they wanted to, the twins couldn't look after it. What could she say? She wanted to please them, but she couldn't lie.

'You made a lovely little nest,' she conceded, 'but you should still have left it where you found it and we need to take it straight back.' Despite her efforts, the twins' expressions, which only a moment ago had been welcoming, had begun to close. Two bottom lips began to wobble.

'It *is* a lovely nest you've made.' James had dropped to his knees beside the box and having peered in, was now smiling warmly up at the twins. 'Mandy's right. We have to take them back, but I can see you've done your best to make them comfortable. You must love animals very much.' He looked out of the back door to the garden, where Zoe was panting in the sun and Simba was dawdling round, sniffing at the flowerbeds. 'Before we go, do you think you could introduce me to your dogs?' he asked. 'Are they friendly? I have two dogs myself, but they're much smaller.'

'They're very friendly,' Abi told him in a wavering voice.

'Zoe's going to have puppies.' Max smiled at James as James got up from where he had been kneeling beside the box.

'Wow, can we go and see them now?' said James. The twins led him out into the garden, obligingly.

How did he do it? Mandy wondered. How was he so easy and natural with them? There was no step-parent tension, obviously, but James had always been much better with children than she was. For a moment, she felt tears pricking behind her eyes. She blinked them away. She wasn't going to cry, but it was depressing to feel so awkward.

She felt worse when she turned to speak to Jimmy. She wanted his comfort, but there was anger in his eyes.

'Mandy,' he said. 'Come on.' His voice was chilly. 'Couldn't you have been a bit more sensitive, told them what a good job they'd done?'

Mandy frowned. Did he expect her to lie? She felt her own irritation rising. 'I told them they'd made a nice nest,' Mandy pointed out. 'But I couldn't tell them they'd done a good job. You know perfectly well you shouldn't take wild animals home. You shouldn't move them at all unless they're hurt and then you should check with a vet. Seb Conway would have told you the same thing if you'd asked him.'

'I did try to call you.' Mandy could see Jimmy's jaw muscles clenching.

For a moment Mandy felt guilty again, but she pulled herself together. Jimmy had put her in an impossible situation. He shouldn't have allowed it to happen. 'I'm sorry if I upset them,' she said, 'but I don't understand why you brought the squirrel home. You know it's wrong. I wasn't telling them off, but I'm not going to encourage them. I won't lie to them.'

'I don't expect you to lie,' Jimmy protested. He glanced again towards the door. Outside in the sunshine, James and the twins were chasing Simba. 'But you told them they'd broken the law. Even if it's true, there was no need to scare them. The squirrel looked dazed, they wanted to bring it home and I let them. If you want to lecture me for doing something illegal then go ahead, but leave them out of it.'

Mandy found her fists clenching. Drawing in a long breath, she let it out slowly, making herself relax. 'I'm sorry,' she said again. 'You're right, maybe I shouldn't have said about it being illegal, but I won't lie to them and tell them they did a good job. I just can't. It's not right.'

Jimmy's face drew into a frown. For a moment, she wondered if Jimmy was going to ask her to leave. What was it Susan had said about her awful date? That when he'd started to tell her about the correct way to raise children, she'd taken him home? Wasn't that what she was doing to Jimmy? But what else should she do when his actions might harm a wild animal? 'I can't tell them they did the right thing when they didn't. It's just who I am,' she said finally.

For a long moment, they gazed at one another and then the doorway darkened as James walked in, hand in hand with Abi and Max. The three of them walked straight up and stood in front of Mandy.

'We're ready to take the squirrel back now,' Max told her. 'James has explained how important it is not to take wild animals away from their homes.'

'James said we looked after it really well and it's good that it's so much better this morning,' added Abi.

Both of them seemed so much calmer that Mandy couldn't help but feel relieved. She glanced at James, who sent her an encouraging smile. How did he do it? she wondered. He seemed to have got the message over without upsetting them.

'May I carry the box?' James smiled as he looked from Max to Abi.

'Okay, if you're really careful,' Abi replied.

James bent down and lifted the carton with care. 'We

should try to be quiet,' he whispered. 'It's important not to disturb it.'

Max put his finger on his lips and Abi nodded.

'Thanks James,' said Jimmy, warmly.

In a line, they walked outside. 'It'll be quicker to take the Jeep,' Jimmy said, unlocking the door of the SUV. Abi and Max jumped into the back and James handed the box onto their laps, then climbed in behind them. Mandy was left to take the front, but Jimmy didn't smile at her as she clambered in.

'Where are we going?' James whispered to Abi.

'The little fir wood in the valley,' Abi told him quietly.

Mandy frowned. Which little fir wood did Abi mean? Most of the woodland here was deciduous. To her surprise, Jimmy drove the short distance down the lane, then turned onto Main Street, passing the village green, then up the lane that led towards Animal Ark. He pulled up at the side of the road beside a bungalow. One of Mandy's clients, Liz Butler, lived there with her Bernese Mountain Dog, Emma. James got out of the car and Abi and Max led him through a gateway and up the track that threaded its way towards the little paddock beside Hope Meadows. The little trail led out onto the path she had walked along not so long ago with Susan Collins. A few minutes later, they were standing in amongst the ancient fir trees that stood in a group close to the fence.

They stopped beside a tall Scots pine. 'This is where we found him,' Max said.

'Poor little squirrel,' James said, putting his arms around Abi and Max's shoulders. 'Hopefully, if we leave him here, his mum will come and find him.'

Very gently between them, they tilted the box and let the lithe red-brown body out onto the clumpy grass. For a moment, it quivered there and then it made a scurrying rush across the ground, disappearing towards a mass of coppiced silver birch trunks.

On the far side of the clearing, something white caught Mandy's eye. 'Planning permission,' she read. 'Westbow Holdings Ltd.'

A cold feeling ran through her. This was the woodland where the factory was to be built.

The worry about the twins and the argument with Jimmy thrust themselves to the back of her mind. If someone was building a factory here, they would destroy the squirrels' home. It wouldn't matter that the twins had moved the young animal if builders came and tore its habitat apart. Staring at the notice, it struck her how little information there was on it – no contact number, not even an e-mail address. For a moment she felt helpless, but then she pulled herself together. If the squirrels were in danger, then it was her job to find out what she had to do to help.

At her side, the twins were whispering, their eyes fixed on the tree cover overhead. James and Jimmy were searching too. Mandy looked upwards. There was no sign of a drey, or that there had ever been any squirrel here. The dark green spiky branches looked black against the brightness of the blue sky.

Chapter Eleven

It was Friday morning again. Mandy slid the litter tray back into Pixie's kennel. It had taken even longer than usual to clean out the cats because the catch on Gull's cage had broken. It wasn't difficult to mend the catches, but it was a fiddly job. It was also time-consuming. Mandy had more than enough to do already. She knew she needed to upgrade to new kennels, but there was no way she could afford it yet.

She looked in on the rabbits, who were curled up together in a corner. The tawny owl, whom she'd named Frank, was alert but clearly quite nervous still. Mandy tried to keep her distance as she fed him and cleaned the cage. She didn't want him getting used to human contact.

All that was left, was to check on Mumma and her kittens. The little family were growing well with their supplemented milk. When she opened the cage door, Mumma seemed to remain calm. She was learning to trust, Mandy thought. All three fluffy babies started mewing. She reached out a hand to stroke each of them and was rewarded with three tiny purrs starting up.

Other than the kittens, it hadn't been a good week in general. After the squirrel had been released, Jimmy and the twins had come back to Hope Meadows to see the donkeys, but it hadn't been a great success. James had been a hit, as had Holly and Robin, but it was obvious the twins didn't want to be near Mandy.

Jimmy had been polite, but Mandy had felt a distance between them that hadn't been there before. Mandy found herself wondering how they could bridge it again. She would *always* put animals first, no matter what. But Jimmy would always put his children first. That was as it should be, but would this cause them to clash again in future? Were different priorities a long-term issue? Mandy just didn't know. Sunday evening hadn't gone as planned either. Peter Warry, who should have come for a visit to see Holly and Robin, had phoned to say there was an emergency and he couldn't make it. He'd invited her over to see Rainbow Hill the next weekend, so she could check out where the donkeys would live. She was looking forward to it, but still it was disappointing to put Holly and Robin's new life on hold for another week.

When Mandy had returned to the house Emily had been in bed again. Other than James's visit, the weekend had been a washout.

The following week hadn't been much better. There had been an awful lot of night calls recently. This had been her first spring in general practice and it had been tough. Despite being tired, Mandy had phoned the council on Monday morning to find out more about the planning permission for the new factory. If there were red squirrels on the land, it was important that they were protected. But the overbearing man she had spoken to would only tell her that the land had been passed for development. That meant all the checks were complete, he told her. When she had asked for contact details for Westbow, the company listed on the planning sign, he had refused to provide an e-mail address or telephone number. Mandy had written to the PO box address he'd grudgingly supplied, but she had heard nothing back. She'd been out walking with Sky on the land again and spotted a quick flash of red, but it was gone too quickly for her to take a picture, and when she got closer, she couldn't find any evidence of squirrels.

By now, all three kittens were on Mandy's knee. Mumma was looking much better, Mandy thought. It was time for her daily weigh-in. She gave the kittens a last stroke as she set them back inside the warm box inside the kennel. Then she lifted Mumma and carried her through into the examination room. The scales were on a table and Mandy held the little cat in her arms as she pressed the button to switch them on. Taking her time, she lowered Mumma towards the cradle. As she released the slim body, a volley of barking rang through the wall from the dog kennel. Mumma's eyes opened wide. She scrabbled wildly at the scales, jumped off the table, and the cradle fell to the floor with a crash.

Mandy dropped to the floor and coaxed the frightened cat back into her arms. She held Mumma close stroking her silky fur and speaking softly. Once she was calm, Mandy carried her back into the cat room, and slipped her into her kennel.

By the time she got through to the dogs, there was nothing to see. Brutus stood wagging his tail at her. Tablet and Hattie stood up and stretched as if they had been lying down for ages. The other three dogs stood at their doors, peering out. There was no obvious cause for the disturbance. With a sigh, Mandy went back through into the examination room to inspect the damage. The scales were comprehensively smashed.

For a moment, Mandy felt like throwing something at the wall in frustration. The scales had been expensive. She used them every day. Putting the pieces in the bin, she walked across to the clinic. Just before Christmas last year, everything had gone wrong. She and Jimmy had fallen out, Emily had been unwell and she'd been faced with the prospect of closing Hope Meadows, but the New Year had brought several months of peace. Emily had improved, and spring had breathed new life into the village as always. Now with summer on its way, Mandy felt her world should be filled with sunshine. Instead, her problems seemed to be piling up. At least her vet work was going well, she thought.

Helen smiled as Mandy came in. 'Morning! You'll be pleased to hear it's a quiet day,' she said. As spring wore on, Animal Ark always became less busy. With June approaching and the animals out to grass, the rush of calvings and lambings had slowed to a trickle, though they were still busy with early morning visits to dairy cows at milking time.

'Where are Mum and Dad?' Mandy asked.

'They're in the cottage,' Helen told her.

Emily and Adam were sitting at the kitchen table when she went in.

'Is everything okay?' Emily asked. She always knew when there was something wrong. Even after so many years, Mandy was still amazed.

'The cat scales are broken,' Mandy admitted. For a moment, she toyed with the idea of pouring out all her frustrations: about the factory being built where red squirrels were nesting, and her frustration with the kennelling and about Mr Chadwick and Mr Warry and the failed adoptions, and worst of all, Jimmy's coolness, but she looked into Emily's tired eyes and bit her tongue.

'Well' Adam looked up from the newspaper he was reading with a smile. 'Why don't you go through to York and buy some more? You've had a lot extra to do lately. I'm sure we can manage.'

She really ought not to, Mandy thought. If she was tired from night work, her mum must be worse. But the sun was shining outside the window and York was only an hour away. Hadn't Helen just said it was quiet? They could always contact her if the situation changed.

'Thank you,' she said. 'I'll keep my phone on,' she added.

The drive was tedious. Mandy got stuck behind several tractors, a horsebox and finally, a large lorry. Usually, she wouldn't mind such obstacles; they were part of country life, after all. But today, it felt like fate was trying to stop her from getting to York and sorting out even just one of the things that had gone askew in her life. The thought of all the things she had to worry about weighed heavily on her mind.

A three-hour round trip and all I'll have sorted is the scales. They would have new kennels at the veterinary supply centre too. But they were so expensive, it was pointless even thinking about them.

Then, as Mandy descended towards the city, a thought struck her. The council planning offices were in York. Maybe she could pay a visit whilst she was here?

It would be good to get that *issue taken care of . . .*

It was not easy to find a parking space near the council offices. Eventually, she found a spot in the car park in Queen Street and headed round on foot to the graceful stone buildings that housed the planning department. It took her several minutes to find the right door and by the time she had walked halfway round the building, she was beginning to feel warm. Inside, the air was a little cooler. There was a queue at the reception desk and Mandy's heart sank.

How long is this going to take?

The man at the front seemed to be getting frustrated. He had a piece of paper, which he was showing to the receptionist, his finger jabbing at the text. 'This is what I'm talking about,' he said. His voice was angry.

Mandy reached into her pocket and pulled out her mobile. There were three bars on the signal. If she was needed, Helen could call her.

'I need to know when it's going ahead.' In spite of herself, Mandy's eyes were drawn away from her phone. If she was feeling warm, it was nothing to the way the man at the front of the queue was looking. His face was scarlet and a trickle of sweat ran down from his forehead. He looked almost as if he was going to burst into tears. There were three people ahead of Mandy in the queue. Two of them seemed to be fascinated with the pattern of the tiles on the shiny floor. The third had his eyes closed.

'There's nothing I can do.' The woman behind the desk had a nasal voice. 'You'll have to go to the orange zone. I don't deal with dates.'

Mandy wondered for a moment whether the man would explode, but he seemed to deflate instead. Picking up his paper, he trudged off towards a distant door at the far end of the hallway.

The queue shuffled forwards a few inches. More questions. More nasal deflections. Pink Zone. Green Zone. Blue.

Mandy had worked out her strategy by the time she reached the front of the queue. She would be super-polite, she decided. It must be boring for the nasal woman to stand there all day directing people. 'Hello . . . Wendy.' Mandy managed a bright smile as she looked up from the name badge on the woman's lapel. Wendy had mousey hair, tied up in a messy bun and a green jacket over a pink blouse with a fussy bow. Bright blue beads completed the garish effect. Mandy found herself speculating on whether Wendy had an item of clothing for each of the colour-zoned sections she seemed so keen on. 'I wonder if you can help me. I'd like to see some plans for a furniture factory that's going to be built in Welford, please.' If she was polite enough, perhaps she would get some help here and not be zoned.

Wendy had her head on one side. She looked as if she

was considering. Mandy rushed on. 'I was hoping you might be able to give me some details first. It's a company called Westbow and I want to contact them about their plans. I've written to them, but I'd much prefer it if I could phone.'

'Where did you say it was again?'

Mandy wasn't sure how anyone could ask a question with so little interest.

'Welford Village,' she replied. 'It's north west of here, up beyond Walton. The company's Westbow Holdings. I need to get in touch with them.'

'Purple zone.'

Mandy waited for a moment for some sign of interest in the blank expression opposite. Perhaps if she gave Wendy some time, she would come up with more information. She dredged for another smile, but only achieved a grimace. Wendy's mouth widened into a stubborn line and she turned her eyes to the computer screen on the desk in front of her. 'Welford Village. Purple zone,' she said, her eyes fixed on the monitor.

The words held a finality that Mandy found it hard to ignore. 'Where is the purple zone, please?' Mandy asked.

For a moment, she wondered if Wendy was going to blank her altogether, but without looking up, Wendy snapped, 'Down the stairs. Follow the corridor round to the right. Take the fourth turning on the left.'

Mandy was glad that her memory was good. By the time she had walked downstairs and found her way through the maze of passages it would have been easy to become disoriented, but she found the purple zone on the first attempt. All she had to do now was locate the factory plans. She walked round several displays, searching hard, but couldn't find any reference to the mysterious Westbow Holdings. Perhaps Wendy had sent her to the wrong place. Perhaps on purpose.

'Can I help you?' The dark-skinned man who had watched her weave three times round the room was approaching. His name was Devan, according to his badge. He raised his eyebrows at Mandy with a smile.

'I'm trying to find out about a company called Westbow Holdings,' Mandy explained again

'And there are no details out?' he asked. When Mandy shook her head, he walked over to consult his computer.

'I'm ever so sorry,' he said, having worked his way through several screens of information. 'It looks like the consulting period for that project is over. Permission has been granted, it says here.' He turned the monitor and pointed to the entry on the screen.

It was odd that she hadn't heard anything about it, Mandy thought. The area was so close to her parents' land. Perhaps there had been a letter and it'd been misfiled or binned by Adam or Emily without anyone looking closer – and if she was honest with herself, she suspected she wouldn't have given it a second thought either if it hadn't been for the squirrels. 'Wouldn't they have to tell us?' she asked.

Devan shrugged, his face sympathetic. 'Impossible to say, I'm afraid,' he told her. 'For permission to be passed, all the rules should have been followed. There aren't any details on contact requirements.'

'Well, can you find out who owns the company?' Mandy asked.

'I'm really sorry.' From his face, Mandy could see that Devan was telling the truth, 'but I can't tell you that.'

'Well, can you see whether a wildlife survey was carried out?' Mandy asked. 'It's in a protected area. I think there are red squirrels living there.'

Devan looked again at his computer screen. He seemed to be scrolling through all kinds of records, though Mandy couldn't make out what. Finally, he looked up and shook his head. 'I'm sorry,' he said again. 'Those should be on here, but I can't find them. There's a glitch. I can't see inside the Westbow folder.' Mandy felt frustration building up inside her. This was all such a big mess! How could a computer error be getting in the way of protecting endangered wildlife? She was about to say something to that effect when she saw Devan's face. He looked so downcast at his failure to help, that Mandy felt sorry for him. She sighed to herself. It wasn't his fault if the system was impenetrable. She would have to persevere with writing or try to find out if anyone else in the village could throw any light on the mystery.

'Thanks anyway,' she muttered.

Mandy felt better as she escaped into the sunshine. Even in her gloom, she hoped the weather would hold – the Spring Show next Saturday would be wonderful if it was bathed in sunshine like this.

She would buy the scales next, she decided. Andersen's

medical and veterinary equipment warehouse was not far away. The shop windows she passed were bright with outrageous colour schemes. Mandy looked down at her own well-worn jeans and utilitarian blue jumper, both slightly stained from the morning feeding and cleaning. She couldn't remember the last time she went shopping for clothes and she suddenly felt quite scruffy and drab on the smart city streets. But really, she reflected, it all came back to time and money. She didn't have enough of either to be worrying about what she looked like.

The equipment warehouse was chilly after the afternoon warmth. Mandy hunted up and down the aisles for the scales she needed but couldn't find them. She flagged down a passing sales assistant and asked where the cat scales were.

An apologetic frown crossed the assistant's face. 'Oh, I'm so sorry,' he said. 'I'm afraid we just sold our last set. We can order some in for you, but they won't be here for a few days.'

Mandy sighed. *Looks like nothing's getting sorted this trip.* 'Okay, can I order them, please?'

Chapter Twelve

There was a fine drizzle falling when Mandy arrived at Rainbow Hill on Sunday morning. She jumped out of the car onto the cobblestones of an attractive yard. Purple and white petunias filled three white-painted wooden tubs and there was an old stone water trough in the corner that was filled with clean water.

One of the farmhouse doors opened and a smartly dressed man with friendly eyes appeared.

'Amanda Hope?'

Mandy smiled and nodded. 'I am. Peter Warry, I presume?'

'In the flesh.' He held out his hand. 'Sorry about last weekend. My mother was taken ill. She's on the mend now, but I really couldn't get away to visit your donkeys.'

'Oh, I completely understand,' Mandy said, thinking of Emily as she shook his hand. She looked around the yard again. It was the kind of steading that she loved the most. An old grey tractor stood in the barn under an attractive stone archway. Two goats, one black, one white stood with their feet on the bars of their pen, watching with interest. There was clean straw under their feet and plenty of hay in the rack on the wall.

'Those two'll be going out into the paddock later,' Mr Warry told her. 'I brought them in for worming yesterday.' Both goats looked well cared for. Their feet were in good shape, their eyes bright. As if unable to resist, Mr Warry walked over and stroked one and then the other. The animals seemed completely unafraid. 'I make sure they're handled plenty,' he told her. 'My nieces and nephews are often round.'

'That's good,' Mandy replied, holding out her hand. The black goat reached through the bars and nibbled her fingers.

'So, you'll want to see where Holly and Robin will live if they come here.' Although Mr Warry seemed serious, there was so much warmth in his eyes that Mandy already felt certain he would look after the little donkeys. 'If we bring them inside, they'll be in there,' he showed her a pen that looked very like the one the goats were in, 'but mostly they'll be outside in the old orchard.' They walked over to a metal gate in the side wall of the yard. The steading had been built in a hollow and on three sides was bounded by hills, but on the fourth side the land fell away. Many years ago, someone had planted an orchard. The gnarled trees in the gently sloping field reminded Mandy of those behind Animal Ark. Holly and Robin would feel very much at home, she thought. Beyond the trees, despite the misty rain, she could see right across the Vale of Mowbray to the Pennine hills beyond.

'I've put a few toys in,' Mr Warry pointed to a thick knotted rope that was tied securely to one of the trees and a large blue plastic barrel that would roll around if pushed, 'to give you an idea, but those'll be changed now and then. I know how easily donkeys get bored.'

'And what about shelter?' The trees would give them some protection from the wind, Mandy thought, but not from rain or snow. It could be wild up here on the edge of the North York Moors.

'That's over here,' Mr Warry assured her. Mandy followed him as he rounded the corner of the outer wall of the yard. A sturdy wooden structure stood in the lee of the wall. It was enclosed on three sides, with a wide doorway on the fourth. 'Better protection from the wind round here,' he explained. It seemed as if he'd thought of everything.

'It's great,' Mandy told him. They walked back out of the shelter. The soft rain had stopped. Across the valley, a ray of sunshine broke through the clouds.

'Would you like to see Dora the llama, and the cattle?' Peter Warry seemed so proud of his smallholding, Mandy thought. It would be lovely if he made a success of his children's farm. 'Dora's just over there,' Mr Warry pointed and Mandy smiled. The llama's long nose was poking over a tall wooden fence. 'She's in with the Belties at the moment,' Mr Warry said, 'but I'm going next week to see another young llama called Cupcake. Dora seems to like the cows, but it'd be better for her to have another llama for company.'

They walked to the gate of the enclosure and Dora came to meet them, batting her long eyelashes at Mandy and snuffling at Mr Warry as if to find out if he had any treats. 'I've nothing for you today,' he told the llama. Reaching up his hand, he scratched her neck and she seemed quite content. Across the field, three Belted Galloway cattle watched them for a moment, then put their heads down and started to crop the grass.

'As well as the Belties, I've a pair of dairy shorthorns,' Mr Warry said. 'Also, some sheep. Dorset Horn and Black Welsh Mountain.' He showed her the remaining animals. In every pen, there was clean water, adequate space and food and safe wooden fencing that would keep predators out, as well as the animals in. In front of the farmhouse itself, there was a duck pond. Several chickens were wandering in the garden, scraping at the ground. It was idyllic, and Mandy had a very good feeling about it.

She drove back to Hope Meadows feeling very pleased. It would be great to have a permanent home for Holly and Robin. Nicole was waiting for her in the rescue centre. Mandy was surprised to find none of the cages had been cleaned yet. Nicole was usually faster at chores than Mandy herself!

'Is everything okay?' Mandy asked. She opened the door of Brutus's kennel and the Labrador greeted her, his tail thudding on the wall.

'Everything's fine,' Nicole told her. 'I was just tidying the big cupboard behind the desk a bit.' There was a moment's pause. Mandy was waiting until Brutus calmed down before she put his lead on. She frowned. Why would Nicole clean out the cupboard? What an odd thing to do. Brutus was over-excited still, rushing backwards and forwards. Nicole raised her voice to make herself heard over the racket his paws were making. 'I was having a look round. Do we have any official stationery yet? You know, with the Hope Meadows logo?'

Mandy felt even more confused. Whatever could Nicole want with writing paper? 'We don't have any proper stationery,' she replied, glancing up at Nicole, who looked quite pink. Brutus remembered himself and sat down at her feet, his tail brushing the floor. Mandy reached down and attached his lead then lifted her eyes to speak to Nicole. 'But we do have some stickers to add to the top of letters. They're in the little cupboard to the right side of the reception area. Top shelf. Did you need them for something?'

'No,' Nicole's reply came a little too quickly. 'I just wondered, that's all.'

'Can you bring Tablet?' Mandy asked. Nicole's face cleared into a sweet smile. The little brown crossbreed was her current favourite.

Out in the paddock, the two dogs rushed around, sniffing in the corners, chasing one another. Brutus really had come a long way, Mandy thought. He had been nervous and likely to snap when he'd arrived, but now he seemed relaxed.

Nicole turned to her. 'When you go on a house visit like this morning,' she said, 'do you take some kind of checklist with you?'

'Yes.' Mandy took a sidelong glance at Nicole. She looked much the same as usual. Why on earth was she interested in the Hope Meadows admin all of a sudden, Mandy wondered? They were busy enough without having to worry about non-essentials. One day she would be able to afford some permanent staff and then it would be different, but for now, she needed Nicole to help with the animals. But Nicole didn't enlighten her and within a few minutes everything seemed to have returned to normal.

After a quick lunch with her parents, she called to Sky. 'Just going for a walk,' she told Emily, who was lingering over a cup of tea. With Sky trotting at her heel, she walked up the short track to the woodland where the twins had found the squirrel. She still hadn't heard anything back from Westbow. Even if she had, she had no evidence that there were red squirrels there. The little animals were notoriously shy and hard to spot, but if she looked carefully, she might find other signs. She let Sky trot off by herself for a bit as she pulled out her phone and searched. She needed to be ready to snap a photo in an instant. She found an area of tightly packed Sitka spruce. After scanning the high branches, she pushed through into the centre to look for chewed pine cones. Not that it was possible to differentiate between red and grey squirrels that way, but if she could find where they were feeding, it might help her to find their nest. She found one that looked like it *might* have been chewed a little, but she knew she wouldn't be able to present it as evidence. She pushed her way back out from under the spruce trees and continued to pick her way through the undergrowth. Despite exploring for a good forty minutes, she found nothing. Even if she did discover evidence, would the council listen to her, she wondered? Though Devan had tried to help, it didn't seem like the system was set up to be at all transparent.

She found the path again and glanced around. She could hear Sky but couldn't see her. 'Sky,' she called. There was movement in the trees and Sky rushed up and sat down right in front of her. Mandy bent down and buried her hands in the soft fur at the sides of the dog's face. With a tiny whine, Sky reached up and licked Mandy's ear, then looked around as if she wanted to explore some more. 'You're right,' Mandy told her. 'We need to take a different approach.' Sky regarded her, head on one side as if listening intently. 'I think we should put up a notice in the post office to see if anyone can help. What do you think?'

Sky whined again, then gave a little bark. Mandy hugged her before standing up. Together, they made their way back down to the cottage.

An hour and a half later, Mandy and Sky turned out of the post office and walked across the green towards the little grocery store on the corner of High Street. Mandy had pinned up a notice about the red squirrels and the planning permission, asking whether anyone who had legal or planning experience could help. It was a long shot, but the post office was one of the hubs of the village. Perhaps she would find someone who had more information. She had also written a second letter and posted it to Westbow for good measure.

When she came out of the grocery clutching a bag of tagliatelle, she saw Harriet Fallon standing in a small group of villagers outside the door of the post office. Mandy raised her hand to wave at Harriet. Harriet looked straight at her but didn't wave back. In fact, she looked a bit upset.

Mandy crossed the road. 'Is everything okay, Harriet?' As she approached, she saw that Mrs Ponsonby was part of the group, holding Fancy, her Pekinese. Sally Benster, the mother of Mandy's old schoolmate, Tania, was there too, as well as William Hastings, who Mandy had known since he was a small child a few years below her at school. They all looked a bit grim as well.

'I'm not sure,' Harriet replied, turning to face Mandy. Her mouth was set in a thin line. 'I just saw your notice in the post office. Are you trying to stop the factory from being built?'

Mandy stared at her. 'Not exactly,' she said. 'It's just that someone found a baby red squirrel on the site where it's going to be. I'm trying to find out if they're breeding there. If they are, it's illegal for the building to go ahead.'

'A likely story,' muttered William, whilst Harriet bent over her buggy to straighten the triplets' hats.

'I've nothing against the factory itself,' Mandy went on. 'It's just red squirrels are really rare. It would be awful if these ones were put in danger.'

Harriet straightened up and, for the first time, looked directly at Mandy. 'I know how much you love animals,' she said, 'and so do I, but wild animals can look after themselves. Once the builders move in, they can find somewhere else to live. People do need jobs, you know.' Her face reddened as she spoke. Mandy didn't know what to say. The factory obviously meant more to Harriet than she'd realised.

'That's right,' Mrs Ponsonby added. 'We need to think about what's best for the village.' Mandy wasn't sure why Mrs Ponsonby was so concerned with the employment opportunities in Welford since she hadn't had a job since before Mandy was born, but she felt that now wasn't a good time to point that out.

'My Tania's hoping for a job there,' said Sally Benster. 'She's working on the far side of York right now, but she wants to come home. My niece can't find a job at all. It would be selfish to stop it.'

'I'm afraid they won't find somewhere else,' Mandy explained. She very much wanted them to understand. 'There aren't many places here they can breed. They've almost been wiped out. If there are places where they can live, it's important they aren't destroyed. Wouldn't that be more selfish?'

'You can't put some squirrels above people!' William spluttered. 'Lots of my friends need jobs. It's easy to be high and mighty when you have a comfortable line of work.'

Mandy was beginning to feel overwhelmed. To her dismay, another three villagers came out of the Fox and Goose and joined in the discussion. Mandy wanted badly to make sure the squirrels were safe, but she felt apprehensive. She had spent a long period last year worrying about ill-feeling towards Hope Meadows when a young man had started a campaign against her. She'd had no idea her notice would cause trouble.

'Hello Mandy.' Mandy turned when she heard yet another voice hailing her. It was Mr Chadwick and for a moment, Mandy wondered whether he was going to lay into her as well. 'What's going on?' he asked. He held up his hands when they all started to talk at once, but then listened as they listed their grievances one by one.

'I'm sure Mandy doesn't want to stop the factory being built,' he said, once he had caught up with the conversation. 'Do you, Mandy? She just wants to make sure the squirrels are safe.' Mandy sent him a grateful glance. It was a relief to feel that someone understood. Mr Chadwick's presence seemed to calm the group. 'I think we should stop arguing about who's right,' he added, 'and try to find a better way. There must be somewhere else the factory can go.'

Mrs Benster looked for a second as if she was going to argue, but she looked at Mr Chadwick's face and thought twice. He was an imposing figure, Mandy thought, though his expression was benevolent.

One by one, the crowd of people melted away and Mandy was left alone with Mr Chadwick. 'I don't know about the legal aspects, I'm afraid,' he told her, 'but I'll try to find out if anyone knows anything more about the situation.' He smiled.

'Thanks, that's really kind of you,' she told him. He gave a brisk nod, his expression satisfied.

'Let me know if there's anything more I can do in the meantime,' he said. 'Good luck with your search.' With a final smile, he turned towards the shop and disappeared inside. Mandy looked down at Sky, who had been sitting politely at her heel through all the kerfuffle. 'Come on,' she said. 'Time to go home.'

Chapter Thirteen

Mandy was only just back when her mobile rang. Pulling it out of her pocket, she checked the screen. It was Jimmy.

'Hi love. Abi and Max are here for the night,' he told her. 'Would you like to come round? To make up for the squirrel thing?'

Mandy's smile faded. Why should she 'make up' for anything? The twins had been in the wrong to take the squirrel home. It was up to Jimmy to make that clear.

Did she really want to go over and 'make up' for the mistake she didn't make in the first place?

'I'm actually really busy,' she told him. 'The rescue centre's full. It'll take me ages to get through the evening feeds.' It was the truth at least, even if it wasn't the whole truth. 'And I was going to go up to Wildacre afterwards,' she added, thinking of this on the spot. It would be lovely to hide away in her perfect home-to-be after the day she'd had . . .

There was silence on the line, then Jimmy's voice again. 'I know it's difficult,' he said, 'but it's important to me.' There was another pause. Mandy could feel her face reddening. Jimmy could always tell what she was really feeling – most of the time it was wonderful, but right now it was just irritating.

'If you're busy with Hope Meadows, couldn't we come over to you?' he asked finally. 'We can help.' His voice was patient. Mandy rolled her eyes.

'Okay, if you think they'd enjoy it.' She tried to sound genuinely happy about it. However hard it was to get on with the kids, Jimmy was obviously making an effort and she should too. None of this was the twins' fault.

'We'll be there in half an hour,' he told her, sounding pleased. Mandy wished she felt more enthusiastic.

With a sigh, she put the phone back in her pocket. She hadn't expected to be entertaining anyone this evening. Had she known the twins were coming, she would have bought some biscuits. There wasn't time to go back to the shop before they arrived. She opened the cupboards and then the sparsely-stocked fridge. Not that long ago, there would have been plenty of snacks. She felt a little guilty about how much of the household organising Emily normally did, and how obvious it was when she wasn't able to keep it all up. There were plenty of staples, but nothing very appealing. There wasn't time to bake anything either. Eventually, she decided to cut up some carrots. There was a tub of hummus and one of tzatziki in the fridge. They could dip the carrot sticks.

As she finished cutting the carrots, Mandy heard a car pull up outside. Rinsing her fingers under the tap, she shook the water off and went to open the door.

'Hello you.' Jimmy smiled at her as he ushered Abi and Max in and then hugged her. He didn't seem remotely self-conscious in front of them. Despite their slightly strained phone conversation, Mandy felt her heart lift a little as she hugged him back. 'I've brought you this,' Jimmy told her as they parted, holding out a small object in camouflage colours. Mandy recognised it. It was the wild-life camera he had used last year to catch the criminal who had attacked Hope Meadows and broken into Wildacre. 'I thought you could use it to look for squirrels,' he said.

'That's a great idea! Thanks, Jimmy.' She wanted to reward his thoughtfulness with a kiss, but settled for squeezing his hand, not sure if kissing in front of the twins was the right thing to do. 'Hello Abi, hello Max.' She tried a grin. If Jimmy was making an effort, then she would do the same. But the twins only lifted their eyes briefly as they muttered their greetings. Jimmy sent her a reassuring smile and a wave of determination filled her. Between them, they would make this evening work. She would take them to see the kittens first, she thought, then to Holly and Robin afterwards. She knew the twins loved the little grey donkeys with their long ears and inquisitive faces.

The twins were delighted with the kittens and on Mandy's suggestion, quickly slid down onto the floor for a cuddle. Mandy lifted Jasper first. 'This is Jasper,' she told them. The kitten let out a piercing mew.

'Can I hold him?' Abi gasped when she saw the little ginger and white cat. Mandy put the tiny animal into Abi's hands. Abi seemed quite confident and very soon Jasper was gazing up at her with his wide orange eyes. 'This is

Myler.' She handed over the tabby to Max. She could hear both kittens purring as the twins stroked them. They had grown so much in the past few weeks. Soon she would start to wean them, but for now, Mandy was still giving supplementary milk. 'And this one is Button.' She placed the black and white kitten in Jimmy's hands. He seemed just as enamoured as Abi and Max. 'Would you like to give them some milk?' she asked. 'Their mum wasn't well when she came in. She's much better now, but I'm still topping up their food.'

Their eyes widened. Even Jimmy looked excited. 'Can we really?' Max asked.

'Yes please,' Abi added.

For the first time since they'd arrived, Mandy found her smile easily. 'Of course you can,' she said. 'Do you think you can look after them while I make up the bottles?' She addressed her question to the twins, rather than Jimmy.

'Yes!' Max and Abi nodded their heads. They seemed to take the responsibility seriously and Mandy felt a rush of relief. Wasn't this what Helen and James had said? Having access to all the animals in the rescue centre would make things easier with the children. It was easier than trying to find something to say across a table. And while they were feeding the kittens, she could get on with doing her evening rounds.

She quickly measured out the milk powder and water and separated the liquid into three bottles.

'I need to take the dogs out. You'll be okay here, won't you?' she asked when she went back. Jimmy nodded at Mandy, then returned his gaze to Abi and Max, who seemed enraptured. How happy he looked, Mandy thought. It was all going to be okay.

When her tasks were complete, Mandy returned to the kitten room. The kittens had finished their milk. Abi and Max had swapped, and Abi was now petting Myler while Max observed Jasper, who looked half asleep.

'Shall we go inside for a snack?' Mandy asked, wondering whether they would prefer to stay with the little cats, but both twins handed over the kittens, looking content. 'Can we come back to see them another day?' Jimmy whispered as they made their way back outside to the paddock.

'Of course,' Mandy whispered back.

Mandy led Jimmy and the twins back into the cottage to wash their hands. While they were at the sink, she took the carrot sticks and dips on the table and put the kettle on.

'What would you like to drink?' she asked Jimmy.

'Coffee, please,' he replied.

'And what for the children?' Mandy asked. She only had water or milk, she realised, unless they liked hot drinks.

'Milk would be fine,' Jimmy told her.

Abi and Max were not impressed.

'Do we really have to eat those?' Abi asked, pointing to the plate with the chunks of carrot and the two bowls of dip.

'Don't be cheeky, Abi. Look they're lovely.' Jimmy reached out and took one of the sticks, dipping it in the hummus before putting it in his mouth and crunching.

'I'm not really hungry,' Max told Mandy, his face apologetic.

'Come on, guys,' Jimmy said, taking another of the sticks. 'Mandy's made the effort to chop these for you. You could at least give them a try.' He dipped his stick in tzatziki this time.

'It really doesn't matter,' Mandy said. 'Don't worry if you aren't hungry.' She ignored Abi, who was gazing at the glass of milk with a look of disdain.

'Would you like to bring some of the carrot sticks to the donkeys?' she asked a few minutes later.

'Yes!' said Max, but Mandy suspected his enthusiasm was more for getting rid of the carrot sticks than for the donkeys themselves. She would have to put most of them back into the fridge and use them later. Even Jimmy had given up chomping after only a few mouthfuls.

'Come on then,' Mandy said as she beckoned them over to put their boots back on. She was still doing her best to keep up the enthusiasm. Max was warming up to her a little, but it didn't seem as if Abi was ever going to like her.

Hopefully Holly and Robin would buy her some more points with Abi, Mandy thought as the girl walked out in front of her. She lifted Holly's pink headcollar from the hook and gave it to Max. She handed Robin's blue one to Abi and was pleased to find that the twins remembered all her instructions about how to approach. After only a few minutes, Holly and Robin were tied up to the fence together, and Abi was stroking Robin's cheek with an unguarded smile.

Mandy brought out the brushes and began to show the twins how to groom the rather shaggy grey coats. 'You can start with this,' she said, holding out the rubber currycomb to Abi. 'They're losing their winter coat at the moment. Give Robin a good brush over his back.' Abi took the currycomb. 'And you can start with this,' Mandy handed over a softer body brush to Max. 'That one's for the more sensitive areas where the hair is shorter. Holly likes her face being brushed and her legs, but she's not so keen on her ears being touched. Make sure you do them, but be gentle so she doesn't get scared.' Max nodded, his face serious as ever. Abi was already running the rubber comb over Robin's shoulders. His coat really was coming out in clumps and for a few minutes, the air was filled with donkey hair and the twins' chatter as they cooed and fussed over their fluffy charges.

'So, have you heard anything more from Mr Warry?' Jimmy asked, his voice quiet. Mandy had told him on the phone about her visit.

'He's coming round one evening this week to see them,' Mandy told him, 'then all being well, he'll collect them at the beginning of next week.'

'Collect who?' Abi's voice piped up. Mandy hadn't realised she had been listening. The girl had stopped her brushing and was gazing at Mandy with interest.

'Holly and Robin,' Mandy said with a smile. 'I've found a lovely new home for them. They're going to go and live on a children's farm, so it's great that you two are helping. It's really important they're used to kids.' She glanced round at Jimmy. Surely this was a good angle to take with the twins? They would be happy to know they had helped the little animals, wouldn't they?

Jimmy looked pleased, but to Mandy's dismay, when

she looked back at Abi, the girl was glaring at her. 'You're getting rid of the donkeys?' It sounded like an accusation.

Now Max had stopped his grooming too. He wasn't looking at Mandy, but his hand had halted in mid-air and he was obviously listening. 'I'm not getting rid of them.' Mandy tried to explain. 'I've found a new home for them. That's what the rescue centre is for. I can't keep all the animals for ever. There isn't space.' She found herself hoping the girl would understand, but Abi was scowling.

'Don't you love them?' Was Abi trying to be deliberately difficult, Mandy wondered. But then when she was younger, hadn't she wanted to keep all the animals she rescued? She had grown up with Mum and Dad's rules about not keeping them and she had become used to it, but it had been a difficult lesson.

'I do love them,' she said, meeting Abi's stubborn gaze as best she could. 'Very much. But it's best for them that they get a new home.'

'Best for them, or best for you?'

Mandy's heart sank. Of course, from Holly and Robin's point of view, they had a great home here. Mandy's aim was to help as many animals as she could. Part of that task was to ensure every new home she found was as good, if not better than the care she could give here at Hope Meadows, but she wasn't sure whether that would cut any ice.

'I can give them a good home here for a little while,' she said. 'But their new owner will be able to look after them just as well. They'll get lots of attention, I've been out to see where they'll be living and it's lovely. I've spoken a lot to Mr Warry who's taking them. He's really nice. I can't keep them forever, no matter how much I'd like to. I need the space in case there are other animals that need help.' She glanced again at Jimmy, who sent her an encouraging look. It was a bit like the squirrels again, she realised. Sometimes the most appealing thing wasn't the same as the right thing to do.

Please understand, she thought. *And Jimmy, it wouldn't hurt to weigh in right about now either . . .*

But Abi had put down her brush and stuck out her bottom lip. 'I don't want them to go,' she said. Mandy's heart sank. She was trying to do the right thing, but Abi was going to see her as the bad guy again.

'You understand, don't you, Max?' Mandy asked, hoping against hope that Max would say something positive.

'I do see,' he said, his voice earnest as ever. 'But it does seem sad to get to know them when they're going away so soon. Will it really help if we brush them?'

'It really will,' Mandy assured him and was pleased when he picked up the currycomb that Abi had dropped and set to with brushing Holly's soft coat. 'And Rainbow Hill isn't too far away. I'm sure when the farm's ready for visitors we can go and see them.'

After a few moments, Abi picked up the body brush and made a start on brushing Robin's legs, but Mandy suspected the damage was done.

'Thanks very much for all the effort you've gone to,' Jimmy whispered as he hugged her half an hour later.

'Thank you. The kittens were lovely,' Max said as he stood at the gate, waiting to go home.

Abi stood a few feet away with her back to them.

'Say thank you to Mandy,' Jimmy told her.

For a moment, Mandy thought the girl would refuse, but without turning round, she muttered, 'Thank you.' Jimmy's smile was apologetic. Mandy just shrugged and shook her head. It wasn't his fault. Not that it was exactly Abi's either, she reasoned as the three of them got into the car. It was an impossible situation for all of them, and it certainly made sense that Abi wasn't the biggest fan of things changing suddenly, after Jimmy and Belle's break-up.

Despite Jimmy's whispered words, she found herself hoping that he would back off a little on his plans to get her familiar with the twins for now. Though Max was polite enough, he was hardly gushing with enthusiasm, and Abi obviously didn't want to get to know Mandy at the moment. Surely the adults should respect their feelings? There would be time later when they could get to know each other. She waved as the car drove off, but only Jimmy was looking. With a feeling of resignation, she walked back inside.

Her eyes fell on the wildlife camera Jimmy had left. Feeling that a quick walk would do her good, Mandy picked it up, slipped Sky's lead on and headed towards the little fir wood.

I need to find my proof before everybody *turns against me.*

Chapter Fourteen

'So where are you and Seb planning to go on holiday?' Monday morning surgery had been fully booked. Emily was still in the adjoining consulting room with her own client, but Mandy's last client of the day had cancelled, so she was leaning against the wall beside the desk while Helen worked at the computer.

'We're thinking about Portugal,' Helen replied.

Mandy was about to ask where in Portugal when a loud crash from the consulting room made both of them jump.

Helen jumped down from her stool, but Mandy had already reached the closed door. Before opening it, she knocked. If one of Emily's feline patients was doing the wall of death round the shelves, the last thing she wanted to do was let it escape.

A worried voice called out, 'Come in.' Mandy shoved the door open. To her horror, her mum was spread-eagled on the tiled floor. Several metal bowls lay scattered around the room and a kidney bowl full of water was upended underneath the table. Roo Dhanjal was crouching at Mum's side, with her two cats still in their baskets by the door.

Mandy rushed over and knelt down next to Roo and

grabbed her mum's hand. Emily's face was deathly pale. Her eyes were open but confused.

'What happened?' Mandy raised her eyes to Roo.

Roo looked stricken. 'One minute she was fine, then she went white as a sheet. She grabbed at the shelf, but she went down before I could do anything.'

Mandy's eyes dropped again to her mum's face. Though she was still white, she was at least breathing regularly. Her head was bleeding. As Mandy watched, a trickle of blood ran from the side of her forehead onto her hair and dripped onto the floor. Helen too had come into the room. She reached for the pack of gauze swabs that lay on the side. Bending, she pressed the swabs gently onto the wound. Emily stirred. The hand Mandy was clutching moved, the fingers squeezing Mandy's tightly.

'Mandy?' Emily's voice was shaking. For a moment her expression was so bewildered that she seemed like a stranger.

'I'm here, Mum.'

To Mandy's relief, Emily's eyes cleared a little and she looked up. 'Did I fall?' she said, then frowned as she saw Helen and Roo.

'It's okay, Mum.' Emily's hand was still in hers. She didn't want to let go. 'Can you call an ambulance, please?' she asked Helen.

Emily's eyes widened and she shook her head, dislodging the swabs. 'I don't need an ambulance,' she objected. 'I'll be fine in a minute.' Blood began to seep from the wound again.

Helen put another bundle of swabs on Emily's head,

then looked at Mandy, eyebrows raised, waiting for a decision.

'I don't want an ambulance,' Emily insisted, trying to sit up. Mandy supported her until she seemed steadier, then between them, they helped her into a chair. 'See, I'm fine,' she said. 'They did say I'd be up and down.'

'I don't think they meant this!' Mandy said. She was gripping her mother's hand. It felt incredibly warm. She tested her forehead, and that was hot too. 'I want to go with her,' she told Helen. 'If anyone calls, you can give Dad a shout. Roo,' she looked at her friend, 'could you bring the cats back tomorrow, please, and I'll see to them. I need to take Mum to hospital.'

'Of course I will.' Roo pressed her lips together. She still looked concerned for Emily, but she lifted up her cats in their carriers and nodded to Mandy. 'I hope you feel better soon,' she told Emily, then with a final glance, she left.

Helen was still standing beside the door. 'Will you take her yourself, or did you want an ambulance?' she asked Mandy. Mandy glanced at Emily.

'Will you take me?' Emily pleaded. 'I don't want to go in an ambulance.' She looked scared, Mandy thought.

'Yes of course.' Mandy felt relieved that her mum was agreeing to go at all.

'I'm sorry to be such an inconvenience.' Emily's mouth quivered.

Mandy managed a smile. 'Mum, you've never been an inconvenience to anyone in your life,' she said.

Emily closed her eyes for a moment, then opened them again. 'I'll be fine in a minute,' she said again.

Mandy put an arm around her shoulders. 'I'll go and bring the car round to the door,' she said. 'Helen will stay with you. I'll only be a minute.' Helen took her place at Emily's side, crouching down beside the chair.

By the time Mandy brought the car round, Emily seemed to have rallied a little. She still seemed shaky as she made her way to the car, but some colour had returned to her face in the form of two red spots in the centres of her cheeks.

'Where are you taking me?' she asked Mandy after they had been driving for a few minutes.

'Northallerton,' Mandy replied. She had considered taking Mum to the minor injuries unit in Ripon, but if Emily needed a CT scan, then Northallerton was the right place. Emily made no objection.

There were a lot of people waiting at the hospital. Having given in Emily's details at the desk, Mandy helped her mum to a seat, but they were only there a few moments before a nurse wearing dark blue scrubs appeared and scanned the waiting room.

'Emily Hope?' he called and smiled as Mandy waved a hand. Mandy steadied her mum as she stood up. It was alarming to see her so weak, Mandy thought. They made it to a cubicle and the nurse helped Emily onto a trolley.

'There were an awful lot of people here before me,' Emily objected. 'I had migraine. I only fainted.'

'Well, you're at the top of my triage list,' the nurse told her. He had taken Emily's hand and was smiling, but his words gave Mandy a nasty feeling in her stomach. Being top of the list was not good news, and she knew Emily knew it too – hopefully she was reassured, and not frightened. Mandy was very glad they had come to the hospital. 'I'm going to take a quick look at you,' the nurse explained, 'then the doctor will come and see you in a few minutes.' He fetched a machine to measure Emily's blood pressure and heart rate. Mandy watched the numbers on the screen. Both were fine.

Within fifteen minutes, the doctor came. Her white coat was clean but crumpled and she had a stethoscope slung round her neck. Mandy listened as Emily recounted her symptoms.

'I don't think I've ever really got rid of my migraine,' she said. 'My left eye's still blurry. It's worse when I've been working hard.' Mandy frowned, dismayed, and her unease only deepened as Emily explained that her left foot had gradually become numb, right to the knee. The only time Mum had mentioned numbness had been the day she'd told Sky she'd been sitting on her foot too long.

That was the same day Peter Warry first phoned, Mandy realised. *What else haven't you told us, Mum?*

The doctor seemed efficient. She examined the wound on Emily's head and pronounced that it didn't need stitching, but she ordered a CT scan and blood samples. 'We'll take a spinal fluid sample as well, so all our bases are covered,' she said. 'You'll have to wait a little while. Once we've got the results, I'll come back, okay?'

Despite the bright lights and the bustle of the department all round them, Emily seemed to drift off into sleep. Mandy checked with the nurse that her mum was okay, then sat back in her orange plastic seat and watched the back and forth of doctors, nurses and auxiliary staff as they went about their business. She called home to check in and update her dad. He sounded anxious, but said he and Helen were managing in the clinic and not to worry. She told him the same, and hoped she sounded confident.

Within an hour, the tests had all been done. Back in the cubicle, Emily went to sleep again. Three hours later the doctor returned, looking more crumpled than ever. Mandy reached out and squeezed Emily's hand to rouse her.

'The blood tests were all clear,' the doctor said, 'as was the CT. Most of the spinal fluid results won't be back till tomorrow.' She had lifted the information sheet on its clipboard and was looking at it. 'Have you had migraines before?' she asked, lifting her eyes from the page to look at Emily.

Mandy glanced from her to her mum. 'Not often,' Emily replied, 'and it was years ago. Do you think that's all it is? Did you check vitamin B12? I was anaemic a few months ago, but I've been taking iron. Was that all normal?'

'B12 and haemoglobin were both fine,' the doctor assured her. 'It's difficult to say exactly what's causing it.' She flipped over the top sheet to study the readings taken by the nurse, then looked up again. 'We can keep you in overnight if you prefer, just to be on the safe side, but either way, we'll have to refer you for further tests. I'm going to recommend you have an MRI and I want to get a neurologist to look at you.'

'Today?' Emily looked as if she was going to start objecting that she was fine again.

The doctor smiled and shook her head. Her certainty was reassuring. 'Not today,' she said. 'You'll be seen as an outpatient. It shouldn't be long. In the meantime, you can go home so long as there's someone who can be with you over the next twenty-four hours.'

She glanced over at Mandy, who nodded. 'Not a problem,' she told the doctor.

'Well, in that case,' she said to Emily, 'good luck with the investigation and I hope you feel much better soon.'

'Thank you very much,' Emily had a look of relief on her face. She sat up, turned on the trolley, put her feet down and waited for a moment before standing up.

'I feel much better already,' she told Mandy. She did look better, Mandy thought. She had slept quite a long time. She must have been exhausted.

Adam came out as soon as he heard the car arriving. He gave a sympathetic smile when he saw Emily with her bandaged head and pulled her into a big hug.

'That doesn't look too bad,' he said. 'From what Helen told me, I was sure they'd keep you in. Come inside, you.' He held out an arm and supported Emily as she walked slowly to the sitting room. Despite it being May, the fire was burning brightly, and he settled Emily into one of the comfortable chairs. 'The kettle's on,' he said. 'I'll just get you a cup of tea.'

'What did the doctor say?' he asked Mandy, as soon as they were outside the door.

'She's going to get her referred for more tests,' Mandy

told him. 'She said an MRI and that she wanted her to see a neurologist. Has Mum had migraines before? I don't remember.'

'She did a few times when she was much younger,' Adam said, 'but not recently. Is that what she thinks it is?'

'I don't know,' Mandy admitted. 'The doctor asked her that and I wondered.' There was no point in trying to guess what was in the doctor's mind, she realised. If she'd thought it urgent, she would have kept Emily in. They would just have to wait for the referral. 'The doctor said the neurologist's appointment wouldn't be too long,' she added.

Adam sighed and started cutting up some sandwiches he'd apparently made while they were on the way back. 'Well, at least one of us should be able to stay here this evening,' he said, as the kettle finished boiling and Mandy made Emily's tea. 'And if a lot of emergency cases come up at once, we'll call on Gran and Grandad.'

Between them, they carried the tea and sandwiches through to Emily and sat down together for a quick lunch. The sandwiches were thickly sliced with cheese and tomato. Mandy was so hungry after her long wait in A&E that she tucked into several, all washed down with strong tea. Emily only ate a little. She was still pale.

Once they had eaten, Adam took Mandy back out of Emily's earshot. 'We're going to have to be very organised with the cases,' he said. 'I'll continue mostly with the small animals, if that's okay?'

'Of course it is,' Mandy assured him. Though he was trying to appear calm, she could tell the ground was shifting under his feet. He wanted to be in and around the clinic, in case Emily needed him. So, she would do the farm work, and be around for Emily when she could. 'I can ask Nicole to do some extra shifts in Hope Meadows,' she said. 'I'm sure she'd help out for Mum's sake.' Emily had looked after Nicole one day when she'd fallen off her bike on the way to Animal Ark. Nicole had also told Mandy that if she needed extra help in an emergency, all she needed to do was ask.

'Gran and Grandad'll help out in Hope Meadows too,' Adam told Mandy. 'Dad loves helping.'

'I'll give them a call,' Mandy said, reaching out and giving Dad's hand a squeeze. She would check with them whether they would be around this evening as well, just in case. A few moments later, she was speaking to Gran.

'We'll be around tonight,' Gran assured her. 'Just give us a shout if you need anything. I'll talk to your grandad. We'll work out a timetable for the rescue centre. Give my love to your mum and dad, won't you?'

Mandy put down the phone feeling a little easier in her mind. Gran really was wonderful. She and Grandad would help. Helen would chip in too, as would Rachel. And perhaps even if Wildacre was ready she would hold off on the move, just until Emily had a clean bill of health from the neurologist. It would be easier for everyone if she stayed in easy reach.

Hopefully, by the summer, all Emily's tests would be done, and they would have some answers at last. She didn't want to think beyond that point at the moment. Mum would be fine. It would all be all right again.

Chapter Fifteen

'How's your mum this morning?' Gran and Grandad had turned up bright and early, just as they had promised.

'She seems okay,' Mandy told her grandfather. 'She was up and having breakfast when I came out. She said she'd slept well.'

'I'll pop in and see her in a few minutes,' Gran said, holding out a Tupperware container. 'I brought her some biscuits to cheer her up.' She lifted the lid and showed Mandy the shortbread inside. Despite having just eaten breakfast, the sweet aroma made Mandy's mouth water. Gran's baking was enough to brighten anyone's day.

'So where would you like us to start?' Grandad asked. 'If you need to get on with your vet work, we can manage here.' He stood straight-backed, his eyes bright.

I'm so lucky, Mandy thought. *This wonderful, extended, adopted family. They never let me down.*

'I don't need to go just yet,' she said. 'Surgery doesn't start for another forty minutes and it wasn't looking too busy. Dad said I could get on out here.'

'Shall we make a start cleaning out the cages?' Grandad suggested.

'That would be great,' Mandy said. 'If you could do that, I can get the morning feeds sorted out.' Most of the feeding was routine, but one of the dogs was on special food for arthritis, an older cat needed a kidney diet and of course there was Mumma, who needed encouragement. Gran would love to help giving milk to the kittens later.

'I'll start with the dogs.' Tom Hope squared his shoulders.

'And I'll sort out the rabbits,' Dorothy said with a smile that lifted Mandy's heart.

An hour later, the three of them were sitting in the reception room, facing the huge glass window that looked out onto the fellside. Grandad was holding Myler, Gran had Button and Mandy was feeding Jasper.

'What a sweetie,' Gran said as she looked down at Button. The kitten had her eyes closed in ecstasy as she suckled. Her tiny paws were kneading Gran's arm. Mandy smiled. The kittens had brought so much pleasure to her and Nicole. It was lovely to share them with her grandparents. Grandad seemed smitten as well.

'Did you manage to get any more information about your planning permission?' Grandad asked, looking up. 'We saw your notice in the post office.'

'There's been a lot of chatter about it in the village,' Gran added.

Mandy could tell from Dorothy Hope's face that this wasn't a good thing. She sighed before replying. 'Lots of people think I'm meddling,' she admitted. 'There was a whole crowd of them outside the Fox and Goose a few days ago, telling me I should stop.'

Her grandfather sent her a sympathetic smile. 'We did hear,' he admitted.

'Did Oliver Chadwick tell you?' Mandy asked. 'He came to my rescue. I was very grateful.' She looked down at Jasper, who had finished his milk and seemed to have fallen asleep in her arms. How sweet he was with his fluffy little face. It looked like he was going to be long-haired.

'Yes,' Tom Hope nodded. Myler had finished too. Now he had clawed his way up and was exploring her grandfather's shoulders. 'Oliver told us you were getting a lot of flak,' Grandad went on. 'He said you were standing up for the squirrels.' Catching movement from the corner of his eye, he twisted round and grabbed Myler, who was teetering on the edge of the chairback. He turned to Mandy with a grin. 'He seemed impressed by your moral fibre.'

Mandy couldn't help but feel pleased with Mr Chadwick's assessment. 'I was glad he came,' she said. 'Everyone else seemed to think I should stop.' She looked over at Gran. Button had finally finished her milk. Mandy stood up and Gran and Grandad did the same, following her into the cat room. They put the kittens back in with Mumma, then stood and watched as the mother cat began to lick them clean.

'We don't think you should stop,' Gran said, returning to the topic of the squirrels. 'Endangered animals need someone on their side. People do need jobs, but there are lots of other places they could build.'

'I went to the council offices in York,' Mandy told them. 'It's so difficult to find anything out. The man in the department was trying to help, but he couldn't find any information about surveys. You'd think the public would be able to find out what's going on in their area.' She sighed. What should happen and what did happen were often a long way apart.

'Maybe you could contact Natural England,' Tom Hope suggested.

Mandy stood very still for a moment. She'd been so caught up with Mum and Jimmy, Abi and Max that she hadn't even thought to do that. Natural England was the government authority that oversaw protection of endangered species. If anyone could help, it would be them.

'That's a great idea,' she said, then glanced at the clock. It was just after nine. 'I could call them now. Are you okay here?' she asked.

'Of course. We can get on and take Tablet and Hattie out, then the other three,' Grandad told her.

'Great, thanks. Leave Brutus for now, I'll take him out to work with Sky later,' said Mandy as she went through to reception.

'Christine Harford, Natural England, how can I help you?' The voice on the other end of the line sounded friendly. Mandy found herself pouring out everything about the squirrels and Westbow and her frustration that she couldn't find the information she needed.

'You were quite right to call,' Christine assured her when

she had finished. 'There are too many of these companies taking shortcuts. The legislation's in place for a reason. So many people seem to think it's optional.'

She sounds even more cross than me!

Mandy warmed to Ms Harford instantly and was delighted when she said, 'I'm just going to access the planning records. We have the authority to do that. It's ridiculous they didn't give you the information in York.'

Mandy thought back to Devan and his abortive attempt to find the information. It hadn't been for want of trying.

'Okay, I have the names here,' Christine Harford interrupted her musing. 'Westbow has two listed owners, Mrs Marissa Bowie and Mr Sam Western. Does that help?'

Mandy all but gasped when she heard Sam Western's name. Was it possible he was behind all this? He had mentioned it, she realised, thinking back to the day she had seen Harley. He'd told her he had a land sale meeting, but she had assumed he was buying some new land. He'd done enough of that before. He owned several of the farms adjacent to the original Welford Hall land.

Marissa Bowie? Mandy trawled through her memory, but the name meant nothing to her. 'I know Mr Western,' she said slowly, 'but not Mrs Bowie.'

'Well, that might help. If you know Mr Western.' Christine sounded positive, but Mandy wasn't so sure. Since her return, she had begun to think she'd misunderstood Sam Western. She had a certain respect for the positive impact his business had on Welford and the farmers who lived nearby. And sure enough, this factory itself was no bad thing, it would bring jobs to the area . . .

But something told her that if anything small, red and fluffy threatened his business plan, he wouldn't let it go without a fight.

Ms Harford was speaking again. 'We'll see what we can do about finding the survey documents,' she said. 'We should be able to access them one way or another. In the meantime, if you know Mr Western, perhaps you could approach him directly? He'll likely have all the documentation to hand.'

Mandy was standing in front of the huge glass window in the Hope Meadows reception. Outside the window the sky was threatening rain, but still sheep grazed peacefully on the fellside. What if she drove to Upper Welford Hall and just asked?

That Mandy Hope, prying into my business yet again, she could imagine him thinking.

No, Sam wasn't likely to give her the information. He hadn't put his name on the planning permission notice and he must have heard about Mandy's notice in the post office; gossip spread fast in Welford. 'I'm not sure Sam Western will want to help,' she said, 'but if I see him, I can ask.' What harm would it do? she thought, stifling a sigh. She ought to give him the benefit of the doubt. Maybe he had done everything by the book. She probably wouldn't run into him anyway. Hopefully it wouldn't take Natural England too long to get the information.

'Don't ask him if you feel you'd put yourself at risk.' Had the woman picked up the uneasiness in her voice? Mandy wondered. Not that she was at risk from Sam Western. Not any physical risk anyway, though as a client of Animal Ark, he could probably cause some trouble. 'If we need to, we can ask the National Wildlife Crime Unit to get involved,' Christine went on. Mandy made a mental note to Google the crime unit.

'Thank you so much for your help,' she said. 'I'll call you back if I find out anything more.'

'Thank you,' Christine replied. 'We'll find out what we can and get back to you.'

Mandy hoped it wouldn't take too long.

After the call, Mandy had checked out the National Wildlife Crime Unit, and she'd also Googled Marissa Bowie. She hadn't been able to find a phone number or e-mail address – the best she could do was a Twitter account that hadn't been updated in a few weeks and a Facebook page that was locked down except for a few photos – Ms Bowie seemed to be a middle-aged lady with iron grey hair. Mandy didn't recognise her face.

As she drove round on her calls, Mandy thought about Sam Western. When she was younger, she had never hesitated in going up against him when an animal needed help. She wasn't exactly afraid of him, but the situation was more complicated now. She was his vet. She wanted to believe everything was above board, but her instincts had kicked in. He must know she had been asking around about the development. If he'd nothing to hide, wouldn't he have come forward?

Should she go to Upper Welford Hall and bang on his door? She had been debating the point all day in her head.

She had no idea when building would start, but if permission had already been granted, as Devan had said, there was nothing to stop them starting right now. As she drove back through the village on her way home for dinner, she saw Sam Western's Jaguar parked outside the Fox and Goose.

That has to be a sign . . .

Pulling in behind it, she sat for a moment, staring at the spotless emerald green paint on the immaculate bonnet. Then taking a deep breath, she opened the door of her SUV and walked into the bar.

It took her eyes a moment to adjust to the dim light, but when she could see again, there he was, sitting alone at the bar with a pint of ale. The deep cleft in his craggy forehead deepened as she walked towards him, but other than that, his expression didn't change.

'Good afternoon.' His tone was conversational. 'Can I buy you a drink?'

Mandy couldn't help but be taken aback. She had been prepared for him to jump in about her notice in the post office. Was it really possible he hadn't seen it?

'No thanks.' Her words were automatic, though she regretted them almost immediately. Would it have been more civilised to accept? The bar was a business, not a public meeting room. She saw Bev Parsons, co-owner of the Fox and Goose glance at her, then her eyes slid away. Mandy wondered whether she was listening as she stood there, refilling snack jars.

Mandy set her feet more firmly on the floor. 'I came in to ask you about Westbow Holdings,' she said.

with Harley is anything   .
re are very lucky. How   ired,
To Mandy's amazement,   dy's
d brought out a cheque-   lown
opened it and started

said,

trying to *bribe* her?

he could feel her face   you

But if he thought giving   rying
t that the habitat of a   who
e could think again. Was   was
the council as well? She   , she
ficulty he'd had opening   quir-
ncil in Sam Western's   are
ng's been done by the   build
s calmly as Sam Western
ou do a wildlife survey?'   that
ny voice was still steady and he was smiling,
thought she caught a flicker of anger, deep

s of mine found a young squirrel by the
ins through it,' Mandy said. 'That could
t only living there, but they're breeding as

rything by the book.' Sam's eyes flickered.
n't always seen eye to eye about wildlife,
ly grey squirrels living on that site. Are
iend wasn't mistaken?' Before she could
n, 'I know you're doing good work with

your rescue centre. If your work
to go by, the animals in your ca
would it be if I made a donation?'
he reached into his jacket pocket ar
book, laid it down on the bar,
searching for a pen.

Mandy's jaw dropped. Was he
'I don't want your money.' S
reddening, the anger rising.

Actually, she thought, *I really do*
it to her would make her forge
protected species was in danger, h
that how he'd got his way around
thought back to Devan and the di
the file. Were people at the co
pocket? 'When you say everythi
book,' she forced herself to speak a
had, though it was an effort, 'did y
Devan had specifically looked for one. H
it.

And now, for the first time, Sam's ange
to break through his carefully construct
should be ashamed to ask me that,' he sai
louder and for the first time, several of t
the bar looked up. 'I said I've done everyt
and I have. This is an important projec
People here need jobs. Why are you getti
what people need?'

Mandy concentrated on him, trying
of interest that was running through th

If she had hoped for a reaction, she didn't get one.

Sam Western merely raised one eyebrow and murmured, 'Oh yes?' as he lifted his pint and took a sip. Mandy's mouth felt dry. She wished again she hadn't turned down the offer of a drink.

'I understand you're co-owner of Westbow,' she said, 'and that you're thinking of building a factory.'

'That's right.' He seemed perfectly at ease still. 'Are you sure you won't have a drink?'

Mandy shook her head. 'Thank you, no. I've been trying to get in touch,' she said. She glanced again at Bev who was still polishing the glass with a studied air. There was no way to stop her hearing. Turning back to Sam, she launched in. 'I have reason to believe there are red squirrels living on that land,' she said. 'Red squirrels are endangered. If I'm right, then it would be illegal to build there.'

'What makes you think there are red squirrels on that land?' His gravelly voice was still steady and he was smiling, though Mandy thought she caught a flicker of anger, deep within his eyes.

'Some friends of mine found a young squirrel by the footpath that runs through it,' Mandy said. 'That could mean they're not only living there, but they're breeding as well.'

'I've done everything by the book.' Sam's eyes flickered. 'You and I haven't always seen eye to eye about wildlife, but there are only grey squirrels living on that site. Are you sure your friend wasn't mistaken?' Before she could reply, he went on, 'I know you're doing good work with your rescue centre. If your work with Harley is anything to go by, the animals in your care are very lucky. How would it be if I made a donation?' To Mandy's amazement, he reached into his jacket pocket and brought out a cheque-book, laid it down on the bar, opened it and started searching for a pen.

Mandy's jaw dropped. Was he trying to *bribe* her?

'I don't want your money.' She could feel her face reddening, the anger rising.

Actually, she thought, *I really do.* But if he thought giving it to her would make her forget that the habitat of a protected species was in danger, he could think again. Was that how he'd got his way around the council as well? She thought back to Devan and the difficulty he'd had opening the file. Were people at the council in Sam Western's pocket? 'When you say everything's been done by the book,' she forced herself to speak as calmly as Sam Western had, though it was an effort, 'did you do a wildlife survey?' Devan had specifically looked for one. He hadn't found it.

And now, for the first time, Sam's anger was beginning to break through his carefully constructed façade. 'You should be ashamed to ask me that,' he said. His voice was louder and for the first time, several of the customers in the bar looked up. 'I said I've done everything by the book and I have. This is an important project for the village. People here need jobs. Why are you getting in the way of what people need?'

Mandy concentrated on him, trying to ignore the stir of interest that was running through the bar. Her hand was trembling. She closed her fingers to form a fist. 'The only thing I want is to protect an endangered species. If you really are working within the law, then will you please show a copy of the survey either to me or to Natural England.'

'What have Natural England got to do with anything?' Sam demanded, his eyes flashing. He seemed to have forgotten all about the other customers.

'Is this to do with your notice in the post office?' Mandy looked round in surprise. It was Bev who had spoken. She had moved over and was looking at them with her hand on one of the beer taps.

'Yes,' Mandy replied. She had begun to feel as if she was in some kind of pantomime. 'I'm pretty sure there are red squirrels on the land where Mr Western here is going to build his factory. They're endangered. I'm just trying to find out whether the land has been checked properly. It's a legal requirement.'

'I take it that the wildlife camera I found belongs to you?' Sam Western's voice had dropped to a dangerous murmur. 'If it is, you were trespassing. It was off the public right of way. Have you been trespassing on my land? If I find you have, I'll call the police.'

For a moment, Mandy felt sick. Would he call the police? If she tried to go down the legal route, would he retaliate? He had the money to fight any case he chose to begin.

Another voice came from behind her. 'Why would you interfere in the new factory?' Mandy turned and recognised one of her small-animal clients, Danny Tickner, whose daughter, Ashley, was school leaving age. 'Mr Western employs a lot of people round here. If he says he's done everything by the book, why wouldn't you believe him?'

'My brother sells wooden toys from one of the shops at Upper Welford. Lots of people work for him. Leave him alone.' That was Ian Cooper, another client. Would they all desert Animal Ark if she pushed her case through? Would Sam withdraw his custom? What would Mum and Dad say? She felt sicker than ever. 'I'm sure Mandy doesn't want to stop the building.' Gary Parsons came up beside Bev and put an arm round her. He looked at Mandy with concerned eyes. Mandy sent him a grateful look, but nobody else seemed to be listening.

'I'm going to go now.' She held up her hands. 'I'm sorry I came in. Sorry.' The last word was directed to Gary and Bev. Neither of them looked angry, to Mandy's relief, but Sam Western was glaring daggers into his pint. She was breathing fast. Her intervention had done no good at all and now Sam knew that she had involved Natural England. What would he do now? She couldn't help feeling that she had just kicked over a hornet's nest.

Chapter Sixteen

Saturday dawned bright and clear. Today was the day of the Spring Show in Welford. Mandy had visited almost every year as a child, but this year would be the first time she attended the show to vet the entrants. She'd been looking forward to it for months, but now it was here, with all her worries weighing down on her, Mandy just felt flat. Instead of a day of excitement, it felt like a whole day away from all the urgent things she had to do, and also a whole day amongst potentially hostile villagers.

What fun . . .

She could have happily burrowed under her duvet and stayed there with Sky all day, but Mandy forced herself to get up and dress. She rushed through the Hope Meadows morning routine alone: she'd given Nicole the morning off, since she was taking her horse, Braveheart, to compete in the dressage class at the show.

A little while later, Mandy pulled her SUV into the parking space that was reserved for the official veterinary surgeon. The village green was already swarming with activity. Cheerfully decorated stalls had been put up the night before and a maypole had been erected close to the war memorial. For now, its brightly coloured ribbons were fluttering in the breeze, but later the dancers would weave them into patterns as they danced.

Mandy made her way over to the animal lines, which were in a field beside the churchyard. Many of the farm stock had arrived already. Graham, the dairyman from Upper Welford Hall was washing a long-legged Holstein heifer. Bert Burnley from Riverside was combing the tail of a muscular Charolais bull. Sweet scents of grass and hay mingled with the aroma of sheep and goats. There were all kinds of animals: sheep and cattle were ranged beside llamas and woolly Mangalitza pigs. Mandy had always been amazed by the enthusiasm the show generated. Greetings rang out as the farmers called to one another over the clamour of bleating lambs and rumbling ewes. On the far side of the field, a number of horse-boxes were arriving and parking in the shade of the tall trees that lined the meadow. Behind all the activity, the fellside was bathed in early morning sunshine. Later, runners would scale the heights of Black Tor, then make their way over to the Beacon with its ancient Celtic cross, but for now, there were only sheep dotting the hillside. To her relief, the farmers hailed her with friendly greetings, rather than the hostility she had been fearing.

Mandy worked her way through the lines. It was important to check that the animals were healthy. She was pleased to see Mr Thomas from Ainthrop with two of his ewes.

'Hello.' She smiled at him and was amused when he politely doffed the drop brim tweed hat he was wearing. Despite looking about a hundred years old, Mr Thomas always seemed to dress like an immaculate 1940s gentleman.

'Good morning, Miss Hope.' The voice and mannerisms matched the image too. 'Aren't they lovely?' He gestured at the pen beside him.

Mandy looked down at the two woolly Portland sheep he had brought. The pair gazed back at her, their yellow eyes alight with wary interest. They looked clean and healthy in the deep straw. Mandy turned back and smiled at Mr Thomas. 'Daffodil not here today?' she asked. She had visited Daffodil back in the late autumn when the ewe had been lame.

'Not today.' Mr Thomas had a twinkle in his eye. 'She's at home being looked after. She's expecting.' Mandy raised her eyebrows. Lambing was pretty much over for this year. Mr Thomas seemed to read her mind. 'Portlands were the first breed in Britain that could have lambs at any time of year,' he explained.

'How lovely!' she exclaimed. Mr Thomas looked so pleased with his news. 'Do keep me posted on how she gets on,' she said.

'Of course I will. You'll be the first to know.'

'These two look like they're in good shape,' she told him as she examined his charges.

'I'm so glad you think so.' Mr Thomas beamed. 'Don't you think they'd make lovely Calendar Girls?' he said. 'I'm hoping they make the front cover.'

Mandy laughed. Every year at the show there was a calendar competition for sheep. It was always fiercely contested. 'Well, good luck,' she told the old man. Polite till the last, he nodded at her as she moved on.

Alongside the other animals, there were several llamas

in the lines. Mandy had read in the *Dales News* that there was a whole new class this year for llama agility. She had wondered whether it was a mistake, but she had consulted her computer and had been amazed to discover videos of the curious creatures being led up and down steps, kicking balls and even reversing out of tightly spaced lines. She was looking forward to seeing Welford's version.

They were fascinating creatures, she thought as she slid up the side of one of the tall animals to check its head. They looked so alert with their long ears and huge eyes. Their luxuriant eyelashes gave them a bashful look.

'Hello again,' said a voice, and Mandy looked up to see Peter Warry strolling up to her.

'Hello Mr Warry! I thought I recognised Dora,' said Mandy, and they shook hands warmly.

Beside her, Dora twisted her head to snuffle in her ear, then stuck out a long tongue and licked her hair. With a slight laugh, Mandy reached up and gently pushed away the soft muzzle.

'Sorry about that,' Mr Warry said with a grin. 'Dora's a friendly old thing. She does love licking people's hair for some reason.'

'Are you entering the agility competition?' Mandy asked. Dora breathed in her ear, making her want to laugh.

'We are indeed.' Mr Warry reached out and scratched Dora's furry rump and she turned away from Mandy to cast her enquiring gaze over him instead. 'Not that we'll win, but it's all good fun.'

He did seem very pleasant, Mandy thought. It was

obvious he was fond of Dora and as well as being friendly, the llama looked in good shape.

'We'll need to arrange a new date for me to come and see Holly and Robin . . . if that's okay still?'

'Absolutely,' Mandy replied.

She glanced round just as another livestock trailer was turning into the field. The lettering on the side said, *West Mitling Safari Park*. 'There's Polly Cormac,' Peter Warry said when he saw it. 'I must go and have a word. Polly's a bit like you,' he went on. 'She takes all kinds of exotic rescue animals when they're unwanted or have been mistreated.'

'Is she bringing exotic animals to the show?' Mandy wondered. She hadn't had much experience with species outside of regular pets, native wildlife and livestock.

'Oh, Polly has non-exotic animals too,' Peter explained. 'I think she's bringing her pygmy goats today. Would you like to meet her?'

'I really would,' Mandy said, as a tiny blonde lady jumped down from the trailer. She was wearing a patched jumper and frayed jeans and when she turned, Mandy saw she had bright blue eyes.

'Polly!' Peter Warry hailed her.

Polly waved and trotted over.

'Polly, I'd like you to meet Mandy Hope, she's one of the vets at Animal Ark and she's on duty at the show today. Mandy, this is my friend, Polly. She owns West Mitling Safari Park.'

Polly smiled and stuck her hand out. 'Lovely to meet you! Although don't let the goats hear you say I run the park, Peter. They're very much under the impression that they're in charge!'

Mandy laughed, feeling herself warming to Polly already. 'You've brought your goats today?'

'I have,' Polly said. 'Well, five of them at least. I have ten more back at the park. These are my calmest so they're my park ambassadors. Although calm is a relative term – they're a handful pretty much all of the time . . .'

Mandy laughed again. 'I'll have to do a health check, but I can come back and see them last, so they have time to settle from the journey, if you like.'

A comical grimace passed over Polly's face. 'That's probably for the best and I'm sorry in advance!'

Two hours later, all the animals had arrived, and Mandy's examinations were complete. Polly's goats did indeed prove to be as much of a handful as she had warned, but with a little help, Mandy was able to quickly examine them and Sporty, Posh, Scary, Baby and Ginger were happily playing in the sunshine. For now, unless there was an announcement, she was free to enjoy the rest of the fair. She had a fleeting moment of disappointment. It would have been nice to walk around with someone.

She made her way past the show ring, which was being prepared for the llama agility. A small pond had been set up for them to walk through. Mandy knew that later it would be used as the water jump in the gymkhana. There were steps up and down, a tunnel made of bent hoops and a number of wooden structures: squares to stand in and zig-zag pathways. She was looking forward to watching, especially now she knew Mr Warry would be taking part.

Back over on the village green, the stalls were alive with people. The sweet scent of candyfloss filled the air as Mandy walked between the brightly coloured awnings. There were plenty of local goods on sale. Mandy recognised one of the women from Welford Hall cheese shop standing behind a large array of Yorkshire cheeses. Prudence Ruck was there, selling hand-woven rugs and various knitted goods. It wasn't the right time of year for mittens, but Mandy couldn't resist buying a gorgeous red and white Argyll knit pair. She could always give them to someone for Christmas, she thought. To her dismay, Prudence was quite distant with her. Mandy supposed Harriet had been telling her mother about how Mandy was ruining her job prospects.

Heart sinking, Mandy walked on. She had never felt set against so many villagers at once before and it hurt. She stopped in front of some hand-carved house signs, not really registering what was on them, when a voice from behind her said, 'One of those would look amazing on Wildacre's gate.'

She turned and looked up into the green, smiling eyes of Jimmy. For a moment she quite forgot the coolness between them over the squirrel, and she grinned.

'You made it!' she said. She thought about hugging him, but then she remembered the tension with the twins over the squirrel and the donkeys and shifted awkwardly.

She shook herself and found her smile again. It was hard to bear a grudge against Jimmy at the worst of times, let alone when all around them were the lovely sights and smells of springtime in Welford in full swing.

She reached out and took his hand. 'Let's go.'

Gran and Grandad were running the cake stall. Gran was serene as ever as she took payment for some fruit scones. Grandad was grinning roguishly as he persuaded Mrs Ponsonby to try a piece of Gran's carrot cake. As ever, Mrs Ponsonby was carrying her beloved Pekinese, Fancy. She was also wearing a rather unlikely hat, which seemed to be shaped like a two-tiered wedding cake, complete with icing roses and purple ribbons.

'Go on,' Mandy heard her grandfather say. 'It was baked fresh this morning.'

With an almost theatrical nod of thanks, which emphasised the unusual height of her hat, Mrs Ponsonby handed over her payment and received a large slice of the delicious-looking cake.

'Here, Fancy.'

Mandy and Jimmy turned away to cover their laughter as Mrs Ponsonby, pillar of the community, held out her gran's delectable cake for the little dog to eat. Gran's face was a picture, but Grandad chuckled. 'Good to know your baking's still appreciated in the upper echelons of Welford's society,' he said in a loud stage whisper and Mandy laughed again.

Mrs Ponsonby turned and spotted Mandy standing there. Her face instantly clouded. 'Ah Mandy, you're here. I'm pleased the show wasn't disrupting the wildlife too much for your taste.' She swept away from the stall, trailing crumbs as they fell from Fancy's mouth.

'What was that about?' asked Jimmy, looking perplexed.

Mandy sighed. 'I'm Welford's public enemy number one at the moment.'

She explained to him about the sign in the post office and the scene it had caused.

'But that's ridiculous!' exclaimed Jimmy. 'It's not your fault if something shady is going on. I'll back you up. I'll tell everyone I saw the squirrel too!'

Mandy felt a rush of warmth at his indignance on her behalf.

It feels like a while since we were both properly on the same side.

But she knew she couldn't let him. 'Jimmy, Sam owns the land you work on. You don't want to publicly accuse him of lawbreaking,' Mandy pointed out.

'She's right,' said Grandad. 'Besides, our Mandy has been taking on Sam Western since she could walk and talk!'

'Hello there.' Mandy turned to see Mr Chadwick behind her.

'Oliver, great to see you.' That was her gran's voice.

Mr Chadwick waved. 'Hello again Dorothy.' How different he sounded, Mandy thought as he greeted her grandparents. 'Tom.' He nodded at her grandad. Mr Chadwick looked different as well. His sad expression had been replaced with a grin. He was wearing a fur hat with teddy bear ears and, somewhat unexpectedly, he was clutching an inflatable shark under his arm.

'We thought you'd gone,' Grandad said.

'Have you come back for more cake?' Gran asked. She was smiling warmly.

Mr Chadwick shrugged and looked round at the wooden toys on the next stall and the open-topped cart opposite, which was filled with enormous swirly lollipops. 'I couldn't possibly go home yet,' he told them. 'I won this shark on the ball-in-bucket and the hat from the hook-a-duck stall. In a few minutes I'm going to dance round the maypole and I'm definitely staying for the llama agility. He looked almost sheepish as he turned back. 'Do you need any more help?' he asked Gran.

'I think we can manage,' Dorothy Hope replied with a laugh.

Waving goodbye, Mr Chadwick passed on down the line.

Gran, who had finished tidying the stall, offered Mandy and Jimmy a large plate of chocolate chip cookies.

'How much are they?' Jimmy asked.

'Seventy pence each,' Gran replied. Jimmy handed over the money and Mandy grabbed a cookie happily. The takings from the cake stall and various other activities went to local charitable causes each year. This year the proceeds would go towards buying a specially equipped minibus for the care home where Robbie Grimshaw, the previous owner of Wildacre, now lived.

'So, have you been seeing much of Mr Chadwick?' Mandy had been itching to ask. They seemed to be well acquainted from the way they had all greeted each other.

'We have, actually,' said Grandad.

'We're very glad you put him in touch,' added Gran, who had put Mandy's money away into a box and was bustling round the stall, moving cakes an inch here and there.

'He seemed so different,' Mandy said.

'Yes, he's really coming out of his shell,' said her grandmother. 'He's already volunteered to drive the minibus for the Rowans once it's bought. And he's been helping out with the Pop-In Club, driving some of the older members home.'

Mandy felt a rush of warmth run through her. Even if Mr Chadwick hadn't rehomed Pixie, her visit to his house and the discussion they'd had seemed to have sparked something good.

'Are you going to go and watch the Welly Wang?' Grandad asked, holding out the printed programme to Mandy. 'I think it's starting in a few minutes.'

'Ooh, I love a Welly Wang,' said Jimmy, taking the paper.

'I bet you're good at it too,' said Mandy. 'But I'll have you know it won't be an easy win. I'm a pretty good Wanger myself, you know. And last year there was a major upset – you know Liz Butler, who lives in the bungalow near Hope Meadows? She managed *twenty-nine meters*! To be honest, having seen Liz control that enormous Bernese Mountain Dog of hers, I wasn't that surprised.'

In the end Jared Boone, the farm manager at Upper Welford Hall and Jimmy's closest friend in Welford took the cup, and Jimmy and Mandy both clapped so hard for him their palms ached. There was a hair-raising moment when his rather wildly thrown boot appeared to veer off course. For a second, it looked as if it might unseat Mrs Ponsonby's wedding-cake hat, but it curved back at the last minute, falling between the lines at just under thirty metres. Despite her best efforts, Liz conceded defeat with a handshake and a grin.

Nicole and Braveheart gave the most beautiful dressage demonstration. Mandy had never seen a more beautiful collected canter and Nicole rode out of the show ring to the sound of enthusiastic applause.

The highlight of the afternoon was undoubtedly the llama agility. Mandy and Jimmy stood together by the sidelines with plastic cups of sweet tea, grinning like loons as the llamas did their very best to navigate the course. Dora, with gentle encouragement from Peter Warry came a very creditable third, having failed to make her way under the hoops, despite her owner's persuasion. Mandy had been delighted to see how calm Mr Warry was, and how gentle and patient. Dora looked properly proud as she stood in line waiting for her prize and licked the judge's hair as he pinned the rosette to her halter.

'I have to go,' Jimmy said, as the excitement of the llama event drew to a close and the crowd began to disperse. 'Gotta pick up the twins. But this was wonderful. We should come every year.'

'It's a date,' Mandy grinned. She leaned up and kissed him. She wished with all her heart things could always feel this easy. When it was just her and Jimmy, it was just *right*. But they needed to be able to handle all the other things: work, family, life.

We can't exist in a bubble.

Mandy took a deep breath. 'Jimmy, about the other day. I'm sorry if I wasn't tactful enough. I can work on that.

But the one thing I can't change is that the animals come first. They always will with me.'

He smiled down at her. 'I know, and that's one of the things I love about you. It's just,' his eyes broke away from hers, 'sometimes you're so laser-focussed that you seem to forget that you care about us humans too. I'm an adult, I can take it. But the kids need to hear it. Especially right now.' He looked back at her and hugged her close. 'Let's just agree: I messed up by moving the squirrel, but you could have been a bit gentler with the twins. Right?'

Mandy nodded. 'Okay, but I . . . I don't know how to be different.'

Jimmy kissed her again. 'I'll help you. We'll get there, I know we will.' He squeezed her hand before heading off into the crowd of summer dresses and farmer's tweeds.

Chapter Seventeen

Mandy was just finishing up in the clinic on Monday, when Harriet walked in. Mandy was pleasantly surprised to see her, but a bit thrown – she didn't have the triplets with her, and she didn't have a pet who could need treatment.

It had been an exhausting day already. She had been woken at five in the morning by Mrs Waterstone at Woodbridge. Her patient had been a cow with staggers – life-threatening magnesium deficiency – and Mandy had dashed from her bed and up to the farm as quickly as she could. She had saved the cow, but then there had been another call out, this time to a cow that had gone down due to calcium deficiency. That patient had also rallied, but there had been no time to return to bed. Lunch had been three bites of a sandwich between a hoof-trimming session at Baildon Farm and afternoon surgery. Adam had been out at a colic most of the afternoon. It really had been crazily busy.

'Could I have a word with you?' Harriet asked Mandy.

'Of course.' Mandy checked with Helen that she had time, then led Harriet into the house.

'Would you like a cup of tea?' she asked Harriet. Harriet

seemed ill at ease, standing by the kitchen door. She seemed wary of meeting Mandy's eye. 'Where are the triplets?' Mandy asked, trying to find a topic her friend would find easy. She didn't know what Harriet wanted to talk about, but she was willing to listen.

Harriet smiled, her face relaxing at the mention of the triplets. 'They're at Mum and Dad's,' she said.

'They'll be knitting before they can walk,' Mandy joked, thinking of Prudence Ruck and her wool, and was rewarded with a small smile.

'I will have that tea,' she said. Mandy motioned for her to sit down as she put the kettle on.

'I heard you ran into a bit of trouble with Sam Western in the Fox and Goose yesterday,' Harriet said, once Mandy had set a mug down in front of her.

Mandy flushed and grimaced. 'You could say that.'

'You remember I said I sometimes work in Walton?'

She'd said so outside the post office, the first day Mandy had met the triplets. Mandy nodded. 'Well, it's quite a fancy place I work,' Harriet said. 'Sam Western's in there quite often.'

Mandy lifted her mug and took a sip of tea. She had no idea where Harriet was going with this, but she didn't want to interrupt.

'I was sorry to hear that you'd got into trouble with Sam,' Harriet went on. She put her hands around her cup as if looking for comfort, then she lifted her gaze and looked Mandy in the eye. 'I know I was angry before about the factory, but I know you. I know you're only thinking of the animals. I should too.'

She pulled herself up straight and took a deep breath before going on. 'So, I wanted you to know,' she said, 'that Sam Western sometimes brings members of the council to the restaurant. Dad used to help them out all the time, so I know their faces. Sam Western always picks up the bills.' She frowned down at her tea, then looked up again. 'They seem to get through an awful lot of food and wine. Sam always requests a little table near the back. It's very discreet.'

Mandy stared at Harriet. Sam Western had offered her money in the Fox and Goose and now Harriet had told her that he had been wining and dining members of the council. 'Do you think he's been bribing them?' she asked.

Harriet shook her head and pursed her mouth. 'I can't say,' she admitted. 'I've no proof of anything, not even that they were there, because Sam doesn't use his real name. I don't think he recognises me. It's probably no help, but I just wanted you to know.'

Mandy's mind was reeling. 'That's really interesting, Harriet, thank you.'

Although it's yet another thing I know is wrong, but I can't prove . . .

They finished their tea together. 'How would you like to come round here with the triplets?' Mandy suggested. Harriet had looked down, ever since she'd admitted she had no proof about Sam. 'I could show you the animals,' she said. They could all have tea in the garden.

Harriet seemed pleased with the offer. 'That would be lovely,' she said.

* * *

As Mandy was heading back to Hope Meadows to check on Holly and Robin, her thoughts about squirrels and Sam Western were interrupted by the buzz of her phone in her jeans pocket. She sighed. Was there yet another call? She wanted to get everything at Hope Meadows checked out so she could get back for dinner with Adam and Emily. But the muscles in her shoulders relaxed as she checked the screen: it was Jimmy.

'Jimmy! Hi.' She couldn't keep the relief out of her voice.

'Hello. Do you have a moment?' The politely worded question caught her by surprise. He was trying to sound calm, but there was an edge to his tone.

'What's up?' Mandy closed her eyes for a moment, leaning against the fence and breathing slowly. Was it something with the twins? she wondered.

'It's Zoe. I think the puppies are on the way.' Mandy allowed herself a smile at the nervousness in his voice and at the loveliness of the news.

'That's great,' she said. 'I'm at home. I need to go in and check, but I should be able to come . . . If you'd like me to,' she added.

He laughed. 'Of course I'd like you to,' he said. 'You love Zoe as much as I do.'

It was true, Mandy thought. Though Sky was her very own, she loved Simba and Zoe as if they were hers as well. 'I'll just pop in and see Mum,' she told him, 'and check there's nothing else in.'

'Okay, I'll see you soon,' he said, sounding pleased. 'I have to call Rachel. There's a big group coming to Running

Wild tomorrow. I can't get out of it and she said she'd look after Zoe if I was stuck.'

'Of course.' Mandy couldn't help but smile at his earnestness. He really was going to make sure this litter was well looked after. The call ended, and she slid the phone back into her pocket.

Emily was sitting at the table when Mandy walked into the kitchen. Adam was at the stove. 'I'm making macaroni cheese,' he said, looking round with a grin. It smelled delicious.

Emily had some colour in her cheeks and her eyes had some of their old sparkle. 'I've been feeling much better this afternoon,' she said, when Mandy asked how she was. 'I've been out for some fresh air with your gran and we baked flapjacks.'

'That's good,' Mandy said. It was lovely to see Emily looking more like herself. The cut on her head was healing well, though the bruising round it had reached peak purple.

'Would it be okay for me to go to Jimmy's?' she asked. Not that she really had to check, but with Mum unwell, she wanted to be sure she didn't leave Adam in the lurch.

Emily smiled. 'Yes of course,' she said.

Adam, who was stirring the pan with fierce concentration, turned round. He stuck out his bottom lip, trying to look aggrieved. 'My macaroni cheese not good enough for you?' he demanded.

Mandy laughed with an exaggerated eye-roll. 'I'm sure

your macaroni's good enough for the pope himself,' she said, 'but Jimmy thinks Zoe's whelping.'

Adam became serious in an instant. 'If you need any help, just give me a shout,' he told her. 'Helen's on call too.' He paused for a moment, then grinned. 'Maybe we'll give the pope a ring. He can come and eat your portion.'

'Why don't you take Jimmy some flapjack?' Emily suggested.

'I'll do that.' Mandy walked over and gave her mum a hug.

When she arrived at Mistletoe Cottage, Simba and Jimmy met her at the door.

Jimmy took her jacket as she stepped inside and hung it on the pegs beside the door. 'How is she?' she asked as she walked along the hallway. Jimmy had prepared a quiet box for Zoe under the stairs, but when she peeped into the cosy cupboard, it was empty.

'She seems okay. She's decided to have them where her bed usually is.' Jimmy took Mandy's hand and led her to the sitting room. The curtains were half closed and the room was pleasantly dim as they put their heads round the door. Zoe was standing in the whelping box to the side of the fireplace. Jimmy had lined the box with towels and there were newspapers all round. As Mandy watched, the husky turned around twice, lay down and then stood up again. She was panting, her mouth wide. 'Her temperature dropped this morning,' Jimmy told Mandy, 'but the mucus plug has only just come away.'

Zoe certainly looked as if she was going into labour, Mandy thought. Still panting, she lay down again, then stood back up. Mandy reached out and gave Jimmy's hand a squeeze. 'We should give her some space,' she said. 'It could be a while before the puppies begin to arrive.'

Jimmy had bought some ready-made cannelloni, which he put in the oven to warm up. He chopped some tomatoes and cucumber and set two plates on the table. Mandy was grateful that he was being so thoughtful even while he was worried. She was starving after her long day. They tiptoed through to peek at Zoe several times while the food was warming up. When it was ready, they ate quickly, then went back through. Jimmy had moved the two armchairs into the corner of the room that was furthest away from Zoe's nest. Mandy watched to check that the husky was not disturbed by their presence. She was still very restless, but she seemed happy to be there in the room with them.

'We had a lovely time on Sunday,' Jimmy said, keeping his voice low. 'The twins loved Myler, Jasper and Button. Maybe we could come and see them again sometime?'

Mandy kept her eyes on Zoe while she thought. She was sure it was true that the children had enjoyed seeing the kittens, but the rest of the visit hadn't gone so well, especially at the end with the donkeys. 'Did they get over their worries about the donkeys and their new home?' she asked.

'I think they did.' Jimmy seemed to take the question in his stride. 'I explained it again to them. Told them the kittens would also need a new home sometime and that you couldn't keep all the animals, or you wouldn't be able to help any more.'

Zoe stood up, turned round and round three times, then lay back down with a whimper.

'Thanks.' It was good to know he'd tried – although it would've been nice if he'd said so at the time. She paused, her mind whirring. 'You're all very welcome at Hope Meadows,' she said eventually. 'Abi and Max . . .' she took a deep breath searching for the right words. 'I just feel as if we're trying to push them into . . . well, into liking me. If they'd rather keep me at arm's length for now, don't you think it would be better?'

Jimmy put his hand over hers where it was lying on the arm of the chair. He too seemed thoughtful. 'I get what you mean,' he said. 'You can't make them like you. But I think we need to take the lead. I won't push them into doing anything they really don't want, but we have to carry on trying. It's not as if you're a monster.' He managed a grin. 'They've just got to get used to you.' *And me to them*, Mandy added in her head. 'Trust me.' Jimmy patted her hand, then gripped it for a moment. 'It takes time,' he said.

'Okay.' She would keep trying for his sake, she thought. They were his children. She thought of Susan and her anger when her date had tried to tell her how to parent. Like it or not, she had to take his lead, as he had said.

'There's one thing I did want to say.' Jimmy was holding her hand still. His eyes were serious in the dim light. 'I'm sorry about the whole squirrel thing. You were right, we should never have picked it up . . . I should have told them we couldn't bring it home,' he amended, 'and I'm sorry I let them think you were to blame.'

'Oh!' Mandy hadn't expected his apology. Warmth

rushed through her. She really would make the effort with the twins he was asking for. However difficult she found it, Jimmy was worth it.

Darkness had fallen outside the window and the only light in the room was coming from the slightly open door into the hallway. It was ages since they had last spoken. All their attention was on Zoe. 'I think this might be it,' Mandy whispered.

Jimmy's grip tightened on her fingers. Zoe was no longer panting. For the past thirty minutes, she had been lying in her bed, straining in earnest. Now she lifted her tail, turned her head and started to lick herself. This was the moment of truth, Mandy thought. They sat together in the semi-darkness as Zoe continued to strain and lick. Then Mandy heard it: the snuffling squeal of a newborn puppy.

She heard Jimmy's gasp of delight. Together, they stood up and tiptoed over to the nest. There it was, a tiny squirming shape in the half-dark. Mandy felt Jimmy's hand as he reached for hers. He squeezed her fingers tightly. Mandy could feel tears pricking the back of her eyelids. She had seen so many baby animals in her life. Even long before she had qualified, she had loved to help her parents with birthing animals, but the magic never seemed to fade. The tiny pink nose snuffled towards its mother, and the plump body wriggled, already unmistakably husky-coloured with a pale stomach and dark grey colouring around its eyes and back.

Letting go of Mandy's hand, Jimmy knelt down at Zoe's head and caressed her ear. 'Good girl,' he said. 'Beautiful girl.' For only a second, Zoe reached up and put her muzzle against his face, then she turned back again to lick her puppy. Jimmy pushed himself onto his haunches, then gradually stood up. 'Good girl,' he whispered again. For a moment, he seemed unable to take his eyes off the scene. He reached out his arms and gave Mandy a hug, his face still turned as if to watch. Then letting out a long breath, he made his way back to the chair in the corner.

'I can hardly believe it's happening,' he told Mandy in a low voice, once they were back in their chairs. 'It feels like so long since I took her to be bred. I was beginning to feel this day would never come.' He sighed again and smiled, teeth white in the darkness. For Mandy, the tension of the past few hours fled. She had been strung up, waiting for Zoe to give birth, but now the first pup was here, it wouldn't be long before the rest made their appearance.

A wave of tiredness ran through her. She had forgotten, in all the excitement, just how long today had been. She glanced at the clock on the wall. It was nearly midnight. She had been up for almost nineteen hours. No wonder she was flagging. 'Would you like to try some of Mum's flapjack?' she asked. 'I think I need a coffee.'

They tiptoed over to check Zoe twice more within the next hour. The first puppy was doing well. It had made its way round to Zoe's teats and had already begun to suckle, but as yet, there was no sign of any other puppies. Mandy was feeling twitchy. Most long-nosed breeds gave birth quite quickly, once they'd begun.

Mandy got to her feet. She would check again, she thought. Zoe was panting hard. She stood up, arched her back and let out a tiny groan. Her tail lifted as she strained. She lay back down and heaved again. For the first time, her head had begun to droop as if she was exhausted. 'I want to examine her properly this time,' Mandy said. It was important not to disturb Zoe unless it was essential, but Mandy was starting to suspect that a puppy was stuck. She needed to do a vaginal examination.

Jimmy had followed her over. Together, they knelt down beside the agitated husky. 'Can you hold onto her head, please?' Mandy asked Jimmy. His hands were gentle as he reached out to cradle Zoe's muzzle. Despite her exhaustion, Zoe reached up and licked his face and he bent to put his cheek against hers. He straightened and lifted his trusting gaze to Mandy. 'Ready now,' he said.

She pulled on vinyl gloves and smeared lubricant onto her fingers. Shuffling up behind Zoe, she explored the birth canal. There was no sign of any obstruction, but nor was there any sign of another puppy or even of a sac or waters breaking. She sat back on her heels for a moment, just gazing, waiting for her head to clear. She didn't want to worry Jimmy, but she felt sure something should be happening by now.

'I think we should take her in to Animal Ark,' she said, looking across at him, trying for a reassuring smile. 'I'd like to do an X-ray.' There was the tiniest tremor in her voice. Despite all her experience, it was hard to remain objective when it was Zoe. Was she jumping in too fast? The textbook description was seared across her brain. It could be up to two hours between puppies. That was the guidance she would give to an owner, but her instincts were twisting. Zoe should have had another puppy by now.

'If you think we should, then that's what we'll do.' Jimmy smiled. He seemed to have absolute faith in her. 'What do we need to take?'

'Not much,' Mandy replied. 'We've got most things in the clinic.' Between them, they carried the few things Zoe and the puppies would need out to the car.

Chapter Eighteen

Zoe was panting in earnest by the time they reached Animal Ark. Mandy opened the back door of the car. When Zoe sat up, her whole face was filled with tension. It had been the right decision, Mandy thought. Adam's car was missing. He must be out on a call. For a moment, Mandy wished he was there to help her, and for an even briefer second, she wondered if she should wake Emily, but she gave herself a shake. She was being ridiculous, she thought. This was something she should be able to manage without them.

'I'm just going to give Helen a shout,' Mandy said to Jimmy. Zoe looked limp as he led her in. If they had to do a caesarean, she didn't want any more delays. She left Jimmy comforting Zoe and her puppy in the prep room and walked through to switch on the X-ray machine. It was important now that they should get a move on. The birth canal had been empty when she had examined Zoe back at Mistletoe Cottage. If there were no obstructions, she could give the husky a microdose of oxytocin to try to stimulate contractions, but it was essential to check that the remaining puppies weren't too big, or in the wrong position. It only took a few minutes to get the X-ray ready. The newborn pup would need to be kept comfortable while they were working with

Zoe, so she put a heat pad in a box and lined it with towels. Jimmy had brought a soft toy that smelled of Zoe and she put that in too. Mandy opened the door to the prep room, walked across and bent down to stroke Zoe's soft fur. Despite her obvious exhaustion, Zoe reached up and licked Mandy's ear. 'Come on through,' she said, speaking half to Zoe and half to Jimmy. She took the squirming puppy, carried it through and laid it in the already-warm box. Its tummy seemed to be full. Hopefully the little thing would sleep for now. Between them, they lifted Zoe onto the table. While Jimmy kept Zoe steady, Mandy slid the lead apron over her shoulders and got out the protective gloves.

'If you can lie her down on her right side,' she said. In a moment, Jimmy had done as she asked. Mandy flicked a switch and the top of the table moved. She lined Zoe's abdomen up with the dark cross that showed where the X-ray would be centred.

'What now?' Jimmy's face looked calm, but his voice wavered slightly as he looked down at Zoe.

'I'll hold her and take the picture,' Mandy told him, 'if you can wait outside. Then we'll get it developed and we can decide what to do next.'

He looked uneasy, but nodded as Mandy slipped into place, lying her arm over Zoe's neck and grasping Zoe's lower paws to stop her from getting up. He sidled out of the room, shutting the door quietly behind him. Ensuring that Zoe's abdomen was still correctly lined up with the plate, Mandy hooked the floor pad towards her with a foot. With her toe hovering over the switch, she pressed once and listened for the whirr that meant the machine was ready, then pressed the pad a second time. There was a clicking noise as the picture was taken and the whirring came to a halt.

'Good girl,' Mandy whispered to Zoe, letting the still-panting animal sit up. 'You can come back in now,' she called to Jimmy. 'If you can just hold her there,' she said. Zoe could wait on the table until she was sure the picture was good enough. Jimmy did as she asked. Mandy's heart was racing as she pulled out the large X-ray plate and took it through to the developer.

It was a lovely clear picture, she thought as she gazed at the computer screen a few moments later. She had lined up the image perfectly. There were four puppies, as she had seen on the ultrasound. None of them was too big. They seemed to be lying normally. She moved and clicked with the mouse, measuring the skulls and Zoe's pelvis. Walking back into the X-ray room, she helped Jimmy lift Zoe down from the table and led him through to show him the picture.

'Wow!' Jimmy seemed impressed with the clarity of the image. 'I hadn't realised you would see the puppies so clearly.'

'You can see they don't look too big,' she said, showing him the measurements she had made of the pelvis and the puppies. 'I want to give her a tiny dose of oxytocin to help her uterus contract. Once she's had that, it shouldn't take too much longer.'

Jimmy smiled, his eyes grateful. 'I'm so glad you're here,' he said.

Mandy couldn't help but heave a small sigh of relief that she could inject Zoe, rather than rushing her into theatre. It would be better for Zoe if she could have the puppies without an operation.

I'll give her some calcium too, Mandy thought. She knew that lack of calcium could sometimes cause the uterus to fail to contract.

Jimmy held Zoe still while she slipped a catheter into the vein and gave a small dose of the calcium gluconate. Then she drew up the oxytocin that would restart Zoe's contractions. With Jimmy cuddling the tired husky, Mandy slid the needle into the muscle. It had been a very long day, she thought. Not that she resented being asked at all. She would see it through until Zoe's whelping was finished, but she would be glad to get to bed, once all the pups were safely delivered.

Zoe was still panting when they settled her in one of Animal Ark's larger kennels. 'We'll need to give her time again,' Mandy explained to Jimmy. 'I've only given her a tiny dose. The injection will help her uterus contract, but she may still prefer to give birth without us watching her every second.' Zoe wouldn't be left alone, but they did need to give her some space. As they left the kennel room, both she and Jimmy paused for a moment, peering round the door. Zoe was already lying down. Her tail lifted, and her flank began to bulge as she started to strain again in earnest.

'Would you mind if I went into the cottage and put the kettle on?' Mandy asked a couple of minutes later. Zoe seemed to have settled into the labour. She would be safe for a short while with Jimmy. 'I'll come back as soon as I've made tea.'

Even if Zoe did have her second pup, it could still take a while for the rest of the litter to put in an appearance. She watched Jimmy's face closely. If he was at all unsure, she wouldn't leave him, but he seemed happy to be left alone for a few minutes. 'You do what you need to,' he told her. 'I know it's been a long day. I'm really glad you're with me.' He reached out and squeezed her fingers, then turned back to watch Zoe from the doorway. Mandy watched for a moment, then crept out and made her way into the cottage kitchen.

Helen's car drew up, just as she had put the kettle on. Mandy felt a tiny wave of guilt. She had forgotten to call with an update. If she wasn't going to operate, Helen could have stayed in bed.

The door opened, and Helen walked in. Despite the lateness of the hour, her hair was neatly tied back, and her uniform was immaculate. 'Is she still here?' she asked. Her eyes were sparkling with excitement.

'They're in the kennel room,' Mandy said. 'Jimmy's with her. I've just given her oxytocin. There's probably not going to be a caesar.' She gave an apologetic smile. 'Sorry I woke you.'

But Helen looked wide awake. She shook her head. 'Zoe's giving birth at Animal Ark?' she said. 'I wouldn't miss it for the world!'

Mandy grinned in spite of her exhaustion. Even in the early hours of the morning, Helen brought her enthusiasm to work. 'You could go out and see how they're getting on,' she suggested. 'I'll just finish the tea.' She got a third mug out of the cupboard and lined it up with the others on the bench.

Mandy poured three mugs of tea and was just adding the milk, when Helen rushed in. There was panic in her eyes.

'Is something wrong?' Mandy dropped the milk carton on the counter.

Helen seemed breathless. 'I'm not sure,' she said. 'Zoe was licking herself and I thought there was another pup on the way, but she kind of shuddered and stopped. I think there was blood, but she licked it away. Could you check? I don't like the look of her.'

Mandy's knees felt weak. She staggered after Helen as she rushed back out to the kennel room. Helen flicked the light switch and the room was flooded with light. To Mandy's horror the bed behind Zoe was bright red with blood.

'I'll get theatre set up.' Helen didn't pause for a second.

'What is it?' Jimmy's eyes were stretched wide.

Mandy felt a sick churning, but she made her voice as calm as she could. 'She shouldn't be bleeding,' she said. 'We're going to have to open her up.'

She was glad of Helen's whirlwind efficiency as she stood over Zoe a few minutes later in theatre. Helen had set everything out in record time. Now Zoe was spread-eagled on the operating table, prepped and ready to go. Mandy took a breath as she lifted her scalpel. There shouldn't have been blood. Something was seriously wrong. Laying her left hand on the skin at the front of the abdomen, she drew the blade along the length of the midline, cutting through the skin. She dissected down to the white line that joined the abdominal muscles together, then clipped through it. Finally, she slid her scissors into the tiny gap and slid them along to open the wound.

The uterus filled the abdomen. It was a frightening purplish-blue colour, instead of healthy pink. Mandy felt the blood drain from her face, but she took a grip on herself. She lengthened the incision further, gently pulling the muscle aside, so she could look at the whole of the womb. There were the four bulges: four good-sized pups. They were all far forward, still high in the abdomen. But Mandy's eyes were fixed further back. Where the body of the womb should be, there was an ugly blue lump. She would have to get the uterus clear of the abdomen to see it properly.

Mandy's hands were trembling. She took a deep breath and stood back. She needed them to be steady. Moving forward again, with infinite care, she set swabs round the wound, then worked to externalise the diseased womb. Finally, it was out, and she could see the dilation below the lump where the first pup must have been lying, but there was no way Zoe could have given birth to any more of the puppies. A large tumour had blocked their way out. It was a miracle she'd had even one.

Feeling sicker than ever, Mandy thought back to the ultrasound.

Why didn't it show up then? It must have grown really *fast!*

She turned her attention back to the four bulges above the grotesque mass. She must spay Zoe, but she had to get the pups out first. The oxytocin she had given had contracted the muscle of the uterus. Without a way out, there was every chance that the placentas of the remaining puppies would be damaged.

She opened up the first of the bulges and drew out the tiny body. Even if the puppy was fine, it would be anaesthetised; it might not breathe straight away. Handing it to Helen, she reached her fingers in and grasped the hind feet of the second puppy. It took a moment of tugging, but she worked it towards the hole. The uterus was beginning to tear; it was so thin and friable. It wouldn't matter, she thought in desperation. She was going to remove it anyway. The puppy's tongue was blue. Removing the amniotic sac from the little face, Mandy cleared the airway, then handed on the little creature to Helen. Next pup. Her hands were shaking. She should have called Rachel. There was no way she could call Jimmy in to help. She and Helen would just have to manage. Third pup. This one too looked alarmingly blue. Fourth.

She checked Zoe's abdomen. No bleeding. It would be fine for a minute. Laying a clean drape over the wound, she took the third and fourth puppies back from Helen. Helen was working desperately, rubbing the first two pups, holding them, trying to drain any fluid from the tiny lungs. Mandy grabbed a towel and started to rub.

There was no movement.

A minute passed. Two. Three. The tiny tongues were still blue. Though pups three and four were unresponsive,

Mandy's ears strained, hoping for the tiniest noise from Helen's pups. They worked away, side by side, hoping against hope that there would be movement, that the little chests would begin to lift, that one of the tiny mouths would open. *Just let them live. Oh please let them live.*

The moment never came. She would have to get on or Zoe would be at risk too. She bit her lip as she handed the tiny bodies to Helen. Helen would work with them as she monitored Zoe's anaesthetic. There was still hope.

Mandy removed the drape from Zoe's abdomen, feeling sick. The tumour was huge and the uterus was torn. There was no way she could save it.

She began to tie off the cervix and ovaries, her actions mechanical.

I'll have to send the lump off for pathology.

It was smooth and round and looked benign, but she needed to be certain it wasn't cancerous. She checked the rest of the abdomen and the lymph nodes for further lumps. They were clean. The stitching up was always the longest part of a caesarean. Usually the sounds of squealing puppies lightened the room, but this time there was a dreary silence. The click of the anaesthetic valve was the only noise as Zoe breathed in and out.

Half an hour later, Mandy stepped back. A neat line of stitches ran the length of Zoe's abdomen. Mandy leaned on the white-tiled wall. She had never felt so drained. She looked to Helen, but Helen only shook her head, her mouth crumpled. None of the puppies had made it.

Zoe had lost an awful lot of blood too. It would be a while until she was out of the woods. The wall was cold, and Mandy leaned the back of her neck on the tiles, closing her eyes. When she opened them again, the awful scene was still there. Helen was cleaning Zoe's skin. Zoe was breathing at least.

Helen sent a tentative smile in Mandy's direction. 'It wasn't your fault,' she said. 'No-one could have predicted that.'

Mandy swallowed, then pressed her teeth tightly together. Even if Helen was right, it was still awful. *The puppies are dead.* She was going to have to tell Jimmy. How was she going to tell him? She'd given bad news before, but this – it was Zoe. It was *Jimmy.* Taking a deep breath, she went to Zoe's head. The membranes of her gums were paler than they should be. She lifted her eyes to the monitor. Oxygen levels were stable.

She straightened up. 'I need to go and talk to Jimmy,' she told Helen.

Helen looked up, another soft smile crossing her face. 'No problem,' she said. 'I'll finish up here. You can give me a hand to get her into a kennel when you can. She's staying in, I take it?'

'She'll have to,' Mandy replied. 'And we should X-ray her chest to make sure there's no spread up there.' Her bones felt weary. Normally after a caesarean, the patient would go home straight away, but with the tumour and the blood loss, Zoe would stay here. They'd have to watch the puppy too. Zoe might not be up to feeding it.

There was no way of putting it off. She was going to have to tell Jimmy. Feeling as if her feet were straining through thickening cement, she made her way back through to the waiting room. Jimmy was sitting in one of the chairs, cradling the puppy. He started to his feet as soon as he saw Mandy. His eyes widened, his alarm clear.

'Mandy?' His voice was hollow.

Taking a deep breath, Mandy steadied herself. 'I'm really sorry.' It was hard to get the words out. She struggled on. 'There was a tumour in Zoe's uterus. It was stopping the pups from coming out. I had to spay her.' She shut her mouth with a snap. The lump in her throat was so huge that she couldn't talk.

'The puppies?' Jimmy's voice came out in a kind of strangled gasp. Mandy shook her head. She could feel her jaw working as she pushed her teeth together hard. Jimmy looked down at the fluffy white and grey bundle in his hands and very, very carefully placed it back into the box on top of the warming mat. 'What kind of tumour?' How huge Jimmy's eyes were when he was afraid. For a moment, Mandy felt almost detached. 'Is Zoe okay?'

He needs to know. Get a grip.

'She's lost a lot of blood. I don't know what kind of tumour it was. We'll get it tested.' The adrenaline that carried her through surgery was wearing off. Mandy's whole body was shivery. She could hardly bear to look at Jimmy. He hadn't moved a muscle. He was standing there: little boy lost. His arms hung at his sides, his hands were clasping into fists, the knuckles white.

For a moment, he squeezed his eyes shut, then opened them again. 'I'll have to call the twins,' he said. He sounded as exhausted as she felt. 'I told them Zoe was going into labour. They'll be waiting to hear.' He pulled the phone from his pocket, then stood there staring at the screen. His eyes were dry.

'I'll leave you alone to call,' Mandy said, watching his face. Should she stay? She didn't know.

But he managed a smile. 'Thank you.' His voice was grateful. She didn't deserve it. Mandy dug her fingernails into the palms of her hands. For a moment she couldn't move. Then finding her feet, she spun round and walked through the nearest door.

It was the room with the X-ray developer. There was no other door. She would have to wait in here until he was finished. Knees weak, she sat down in front of the computer. The image of Zoe's abdomen was still there on the screen, four skeletons, beautifully clear. They looked awfully high up in the abdomen, Mandy thought. She moved her head back. She had been so intent on the puppies: on measuring their skulls. Now she looked at the bigger picture. She hoped there was nothing, but when she looked, the outline was there. There was a round shape where there should have been nothing. The tumour. That was why the puppies were so high in the abdomen. Mandy felt herself go cold.

'I'm so sorry, Abi. No, there's nothing Mandy could have done. She's upset too.' Jimmy's voice came through the open door. Mandy looked again at the X-ray. She should have noticed, but she hadn't. She had given Zoe the oxytocin. There had been no way out for the pups. She had killed them. There was roaring in her ears.

Chapter Nineteen

Through the partly open doorway, she could still hear Jimmy's voice. Mandy checked the image again. The tumour was obvious. How could she have missed it? Jimmy's phone call was ending. Mandy could hear him saying his farewells. 'Zoe will be fine. She's in good hands.' Bile rose in her throat. Her hands were shaking. Knees as well. Somehow, she made it to her feet. She was going to have to face him.

There were tears in Jimmy's eyes. He held his arms out to her and she moved towards him. For him it was a moment of shared pain: no fault perceived. Her actions were automatic. Her head fell onto his broad shoulder. He smelled so good. When he felt her trembling, he held her more tightly. 'It's not your fault,' he said, '. . . not your fault.' His voice was a murmur: a lullaby. Close as she was, it was as if there was a physical barrier between them.

He doesn't know.

'Come into the cottage,' he said. 'I'll make you some tea.'

I killed the puppies.

He led her inside, his hands gentle, sat her down at the familiar table.

Will Zoe die? She's with Helen: safer that way. Her hands were shaking.

'I'm sorry,' he put a mug of tea in front of her, reached out and stroked her hair. 'I know it's not a good time, but the twins are worried about Zoe. Could they please come and see her as soon as it's safe?'

Mandy put her hands round the mug. It was warm, but she couldn't drink it. The very thought made her feel sick.

'Of course, they can come whenever you want.' She owed them far more than that.

What if Zoe dies?

'I should go back out . . . Helen . . .' Her chair scraped across the floor as she pushed it out. She heard Jimmy's voice. Registered what he said as if through fog. 'I'll call them back. Let them know.' She fled.

Helen had carried Zoe into a kennel. The living puppy in its box had been put in beside its mum. Zoe's head lifted. Despite her exhaustion, she was looking into the box, her maternal instincts kicking in.

'She's doing well,' Helen told Mandy. 'She's awfully pale, though.'

Between licks of her pup, the husky was panting. Fluids ran into the catheter in her leg. Would the children be frightened, Mandy wondered?

'You did your best.' Helen was still sympathetic.

Tears formed in Mandy's eyes. She didn't deserve Helen's compassion. She walked back through into the room with the computer and sat down in front of the screen. The tumour was still there, so clear now she knew what to look for. She closed her eyes, thinking back. She had been so intent on the puppies and the pelvis. Zoe had already had a puppy, ergo the cervix was open. Mandy had felt secure. It was safe to give oxytocin if the cervix was dilated and the puppies weren't too big. Nine hundred and ninety-nine times out of a thousand, it would be fine just to check the puppies. Not this time.

There were footsteps outside the door. It swung open and Adam came in. 'Helen said she thought you were in here,' he said, his voice light. 'I've just had the most awful foaling at Drysdale. First of the season.' His gaze fell on the screen. 'Ooh! Puppies. Are they Zoe's?' he said, then frowned and bent to study the image more closely. 'What on earth is that?' His finger traced round the outline of the tumour.

For a moment, Mandy couldn't speak. She swallowed. Finally, she managed to form the words. 'It's a tumour.' Her voice was flat. 'Zoe's puppies. Zoe's tumour.'

Adam put his hand on her shoulder. 'Poor Zoe,' he said. 'Is she all right? Does Jimmy know?'

Mandy shook her head. There was throbbing behind her eyes and she was beginning to shake again. 'I didn't see the tumour,' she said. It was as if she was disconnected from her body. The words began to pour from her. 'I didn't see the tumour. She'd already had her first puppy. I measured the skulls and checked the pelvis. I gave her oxytocin.' Dad's hand was on her shoulder still. For a long moment, he said nothing, though his fingers were squeezing, trying to reassure.

'And then?' His voice remained calm, though it seemed to Mandy that he was making an effort.

'Then she started to bleed and I opened her up and found the tumour. The puppies died.' She stopped, pressing her teeth together.

The hand on her shoulder was still there. 'Zoe?'

'I spayed her. She lost a lot of blood. She's in the kennels.'

'Do you want me to go and check her?'

How practical he was. He always had been. Her parents had always been able to make everything better, but this time there was no way back.

'I have to tell Jimmy.' She wanted to cry, but there were no tears.

'Doesn't he know?' Adam asked. There was no censure in the words. It was just a question.

'He knows I had to spay Zoe and the puppies are dead. He doesn't know I missed the tumour on the X-ray.' Mandy could feel herself drooping. How easy it would be to let Dad take over, but she couldn't. This was something she had to do herself.

Dad squeezed her shoulder again. 'Better let him know, love. Be honest, but don't beat yourself up too much. It's a bizarre case. I've never seen anything like it. Lots of vets wouldn't even have done an X-ray if one pup had already arrived.'

'I need to X-ray Zoe's chest,' said Mandy.

'Leave that to me.' He gripped her shoulder one last time. 'You go and speak to Jimmy,' he said.

* * *

Jimmy was sitting in the waiting room, peering through the window into the darkness. He turned to see who was coming and stretched out his hand when he saw it was Mandy. It was obvious he'd been crying. 'The twins are on their way,' he said. 'They'll be here in twenty minutes.'

Mandy took his hand, then let it fall. Her legs felt stiff. 'There's something I've got to tell you.' Her voice was steadier than she had expected.

His eyes filled with alarm. 'Is Zoe all right?'

She sat down beside him, searching for words. She couldn't look at his face. 'It's not that. Dad's looking at her, I think she's okay. There's something else.'

Despite not looking at him, she could see him on the edge of her vision. He was gazing at her, his head on one side. Some of the tension had retreated, but he still looked worried. 'What then?'

Her fingers were trembling. She knitted them together. 'I was looking at the X-ray again.' He was looking at her still. She was going to have to look at him. She pressed her fingers together until the tips were white and then lifted her head. 'The tumour was there,' she said. Her breath was uneven, but she had to go on. 'I missed it. If I'd seen it, I wouldn't have given her oxytocin. If I'd operated straight away, the puppies might have made it.'

There it was. It was out. The muscles in his jaw were working. The reddened eyes were confused only for a moment. She saw it hit home. He swallowed, took a deep, shaky breath and pressed his lips together.

He was very still. As if it was a huge effort, he nodded once. The silence stretched out. 'Thanks for telling me,' he said eventually. His mouth quivered for a moment, but he rallied. He reached out again with his hand, unravelling her fingers, twining them in his. He managed a pained smile.

'I'm so sorry,' she whispered. The words were inadequate, but she said them anyway.

'It's not your fault,' he said. 'I know you did your best. It could have happened to anyone.'

Did he really believe that? she wondered. Could it have happened to anyone? Dad had seen the tumour as soon as he'd looked at the X-ray. Her gaze wandered. Outside the window, a pair of car headlights came up the lane. In a moment, the twins would be here.

'Would you mind if I talk to the twins alone?' Jimmy's fingers gripped hers. His voice was urgent. 'I . . . I won't tell them what you just told me, if you don't mind.'

'I don't mind.' It was his decision: his children. 'Tell them whatever you think is best.' It was hard to get the words out. Adam had come out into the waiting room. He walked across with a tactful smile. 'Zoe's comfortable, and her puppy looks happy and healthy.' He must have heard the end of their conversation, because he spoke directly to Jimmy. 'I can take you and the twins through, if that's okay.'

Again, Mandy felt the relief that her father's presence carried. How wonderful he was. Adam turned his kind gaze to her. 'Helen's been speaking to Mum,' he told her. She's awake. Go into the kitchen. I'll be in as soon as we've finished up.'

Outside the window, the car had stopped. The lights

had gone out. The driver's door opened and Dan Jones climbed out. His face was grave.

Jimmy gripped Mandy's fingers one last time, then let go. Mandy could hardly feel her feet as she stood up and walked the familiar steps across the waiting room. She opened the door that led to the cottage and stepped through.

For a moment, it felt as if normality had clicked back into place. Sky rushed towards her, her whole body wagging in ecstasy. Emily was standing beside the kettle waiting for it to boil. Mandy bent to hug Sky. The familiar solidity of her slim body comforted Mandy and she buried her face in the soft fur, breathing in the wonderful sweet smell of Sky's coat. After a moment, Mandy stood up. Mum had the same reassuring look that Dad had given her.

'I thought we'd have some hot chocolate,' she said. She smiled as of old, bustling over to the cupboard, pulling out mugs and chocolate powder, finding biscuits. 'Come and sit down.' She rounded the table and pulled out Mandy's chair. Mandy was reminded again of her childhood. Mum and Dad had always been there when things had gone wrong. She sat down, still unable to speak as Emily opened the fridge, added cream to the steaming mugs.

'Did Jimmy take it okay?' Emily had made hot chocolate for herself as well. She put the drinks on the table and sat down opposite Mandy, her gaze steady. There was no blame in her eyes: only compassion. Mandy nodded, not trusting herself to speak just yet. She felt a prickling in her eyes. Her vision blurred. A tear fell from her eye creating a dark smudge on the green scrub top that she was still wearing. How proud she had been to wear these clothes. They were the outward badge of her education: of her competence to treat animals. *First do no harm.* The ancient phrase was drummed into them at veterinary college.

'Oh, Mandy.' Her mum had reached her hand across the table and placed it over hers. Her thumb moved backwards and forwards, stroking softly. 'I know how hard it is. It happens to us all.'

She sat for a moment, deep in her own thoughts, then her eyes sought Mandy's with a sad smile. 'You remember Jean Knox?' she asked. There was a wistful look on her face that Mandy hadn't seen before.

Of course, she remembered. Jean had been the receptionist at Animal Ark before Mandy had gone to vet school. She could barely remember the time before Jean had arrived.

'Before Jean worked for us, she had a dog called Trixie,' Emily went on. 'She was a lovely thing, a crossbreed with the most wonderful expressive eyes. Jean loved her so much. I'd known her since she was a tiny puppy.' Mum paused and looked down at her mug for a moment, then looked up. 'Well, she came in when she was four years old with a tiny mark on her skin. Just a little hairless lump on her leg.' She stopped again and swallowed hard. Her eyes wandered up to the ceiling as if searching for comfort and she sighed, before looking back at Mandy. 'I told Jean it didn't look sinister. I said she should just keep an eye on it. She came back a couple of months later because it had grown.' Emily put her hands round her mug as if seeking comfort. Her cheek twitched, and she gave the tiniest shake of her head. 'It was such a busy night,' she said. There was a distant look in her eyes. 'I looked at it again. I was sure it was something benign. A histiocytoma, I thought. Told her it would go away if she gave it time. Of course, I should have taken a biopsy, but I didn't.'

Mandy could imagine the scene so clearly. She'd seen plenty of histiocytomas herself. Benign tumours that looked alarming but would just disappear on their own after a few months, no harm done. She couldn't take her eyes off her mum. She had known Jean for years. There had never been a mention of any pets. She had been very fond of some of the patients, but Mandy had assumed she wasn't one for having animals of her own.

'It was a mast cell tumour.' Emily's voice was so quiet that Mandy had to strain to hear. 'By the time I removed it, it had spread. Trixie just faded away. Your dad put her to sleep eventually. I could hardly bring myself to face Jean.' Mum's thumb had stopped moving on Mandy's hand. There was so much pain in her eyes, but she managed a smile. 'I was amazed when she applied to be our receptionist. I'd always thought she must blame me. She never, ever mentioned it. She was far too good to me. You must remember how kind she was.'

Mandy nodded. Jean had always been lovely to everyone, human or animal.

'She never got another pet.' Tears in her mum's eyes. She lifted a hand to brush them away. 'I always wondered whether it was because she couldn't face it after Trixie.'

Mandy gazed across the table, still clinging to her mum's hand. Emily was a wonderful vet. She always had been.

'It's just how it is, being a vet.' Emily's smile was tight. 'Mostly it's a great job, but when it goes wrong, it's the worst thing in the world.'

Adam joined them after a while. 'Jimmy and the twins have gone,' he said, pulling out a seat and sitting down. 'Zoe's doing well and so is her puppy. The X-ray of her chest is clear. Helen's with her for now.' He smiled across the table at Mandy and sighed. 'Sometimes I think this must be the hardest job in the world,' he said, and Emily nodded up at him as he echoed her words.

There was something in that, Mandy thought. Lots of people went to work every day and the worst thing that might happen was that someone would be angry. Losing huge amounts of money or breaking important equipment was bad. But responsibility over life and death? That was different.

'I've seen how much you've learned.' Her dad was gazing at her, just as Mum had. 'Animals trust you. They always have. You've worked so hard and now you're one of the best vets I've worked with. You've saved so many lives already.'

There was a huge lump in Mandy's throat. She might not believe it, but she could see from Adam's face that he did. Despite the awful events of the evening, he thought she was a good vet.

He gave a strangled laugh when he saw her expression.

'We all make mistakes,' he went on. 'Even your mum.' He sent a wry glance towards Emily, who almost managed a smile, but shook her head instead. Adam put an elbow on the table and leaned forward. 'I know you probably don't feel sleepy,' he said, 'but it's really late and I know you were up at the crack of dawn.'

Mandy glanced up at the clock on the wall. Sure enough, it was four a.m. It was tomorrow already. 'I want you to go up to bed and get some rest,' Adam told her. His voice was firm. 'You too,' he said to Emily. 'Helen's going to look after Zoe tonight. I'll give Rachel a call first thing.'

Mandy dropped into the familiar single bed a few minutes later. It was beginning to get light outside. Her window was open and she could hear birds calling to one another. Her face felt hot and she turned over, trying to find a cool part of her pillow. She had expected to cry, but no tears had come. She felt empty, as if there was nothing left in the world to feel. She wondered about the twins. How had they taken it? Would they be worried about their mum? They must have been frightened, seeing Zoe all connected up to her drip, listless after her operation. They had been hoping for so much. Jimmy too. Now it was all awful. Would they ever forgive her?

She lay awake, unblinking eyes on the ceiling. She had to be up in three hours. Despite her pain, she was exhausted and, by degrees, she drifted into a troubled sleep.

Chapter Twenty

She was woken at seven by the phone. There was a brief moment of wondering who would call at this hour, then last night's events crashed into her brain. It must be Jimmy. She reached for the phone on the bedside with a hand that was not altogether steady.

'Hello?' Her voice came out in a kind of croak.

'Good morning.' Confusion hit. It was a woman's voice: crisp and rather strident. 'Sorry to call so early, but I need to confirm your inspection this morning.'

A wrong number at seven in the morning? Mandy wanted to scream. She was gathering herself to reply when the voice boomed into her ear again. 'Can I just check that you are Amanda Hope of Hope Meadows, please?'

Mandy pulled the mobile phone away from her ear for a moment. Frowning, she checked the screen. It was an unknown number. She put the receiver back to her ear. 'Yes,' she said. 'I am. Amanda Hope.' She paused, still trying to gather her thoughts. 'Sorry, who are you?'

This time the voice had a tone of exaggerated patience. 'I'm Clarissa Tarley from the Walmey Foundation. It's about the grant application.'

'Grant . . . ?' Mandy wondered for a moment whether she had entered some kind of parallel universe.

'We're coming out this morning at eight a.m. to inspect your premises. Sorry if there has been any confusion. We've been dealing with your secretary, Nicole. Can I confirm you'll be ready to go ahead this morning? We won't be back in the area this year unfortunately, so this will be the only chance we have to inspect you.'

Inspect her? For a moment, Mandy had an image of a strict school inspector checking behind her ears to see whether she was clean. And her *secretary*? What on earth had Nicole been up to? She lifted a hand to her forehead and pressed hard, trying to dispel the knot of pain that was forming. 'Eight o'clock this morning,' she repeated. 'Okay.'

'Lovely.' The voice was relentlessly upbeat. Mandy gritted her teeth. It wasn't lovely at all.

The moment the woman had gone, Mandy dialled Nicole.

'Hello?' Nicole's voice was sweet in contrast with Clarissa Tarley's.

'Nicole, I've just had a very strange phone call about some grant application. The woman said she'd spoken to you?'

There was a gasp on the other end of the phone. 'Oh my goodness!' Nicole sounded almost as shocked as Mandy felt. 'Was it the Walmey Foundation?' she asked. 'I'm really sorry, Mandy. I only sent the forms in last week. I didn't think anything would happen so quickly.'

'But what is it?' Mandy tried to keep her voice patient, but it was an uphill struggle. Her head was pounding.

'It's for the Walmey Foundation Memorial Grant,' Nicole explained. 'They offer annual funding for rescue centres in rural communities. I called them two weeks ago, they sent me a form and I filled it in. I wasn't really expecting to hear anything. It's only supposed to cover centres that look after small animals, but I thought I'd try anyway . . .' Her voice trailed off.

'Well, they're coming at eight this morning.' Mandy's head hurt. She squeezed her eyes shut. Why had Nicole not told her for goodness' sake? A grant was a great idea, but there was no way she could do it in time. Gran and Grandad wouldn't be in until ten and she was exhausted.

'Oh my god! I'll come straight over,' Nicole spoke again, her voice breathless. 'I don't have to be at college this morning till ten thirty.' She put the phone down before Mandy had time to respond.

Despite the looming deadline, once Mandy had thrown on the smartest-looking pair of jeans and shirt she could grab and dragged a brush through her hair, she checked on Zoe before heading over to Hope Meadows. The puppy was doing well, already fluffing out – it would have a luxurious coat when it was fully grown – but the best that could be said about Zoe was that she was stable. Mandy balled her fists in her pockets and ran across the paddock to Hope Meadows, her heart pounding.

Nicole arrived only ten minutes later. Mandy couldn't bring herself to say much to her, but together they cleaned out the litter trays and cages, the food bowls and kennels, and made sure all the dogs had a chance to run outside in the early morning sunshine.

The cupboard in reception was in a state. Mandy had rifled through everything two days ago when she had been searching for a form about rabbit adoption after a rather hurried phone call from a breeder. She had meant to sort it out, but it had slipped her mind.

To her surprise, everything else seemed in remarkably good order. When she commented on it, Nicole sent her a shy glance. 'I have been trying to tidy up a bit,' she admitted. 'Ever since I sent the application.'

A memory swung into Mandy's head. So that was why Nicole had asked about stationery and checklists. If only she had explained. They could have sorted everything out between them. Now wasn't the time to say anything. She glanced around the cat room. Everything looked tidy. She checked the time. It was almost eight. She dashed back through to reception just in time to see a car draw up outside. Two people, a tall man and a rather stout woman climbed out. The woman was clutching a clipboard.

To the left of the car, a movement caught her eye. Robin and Holly were making their way towards the newcomers, their ears pricked, looking delighted. Mandy was proud of their friendliness, but her breath caught when she saw how much loose fur there was on Robin's rump. There had been no time for grooming. She hadn't even fed them yet. The empty hay net hung in the field shelter. She could only hope that their water trough was clean.

Having greeted the donkeys, the strangers turned and

made their way to the door. Mandy rushed to meet them. She pulled open the door and ushered them inside.

'Welcome to Hope Meadows,' she said, hoping her voice didn't sound too breathless.

The man looked even taller close up. He smiled as he shook hands with both Mandy and Nicole. 'Good morning,' he said. 'I'm Anthony Mearns and this is Clarissa Tarley, who spoke to you earlier.' He gestured to the window, to where the donkeys were still looking over the fence. 'Lovely welcome from your donkeys,' he said.

Clarissa Tarley was not at all as Mandy had imagined her from the voice on the phone. She was shorter than Mandy had expected, with dark curly hair and friendly eyes that smiled at the world from behind an enormous pair of glasses. She grinned as she reached out a hand and Mandy felt herself beginning to relax. 'Shall we see the dog kennels first?' she suggested. Though her voice was as brisk as it had been on the phone, it was less intimidating coming from that jolly, rounded frame.

'Absolutely! This way.' Mandy managed to grin back at both Anthony and Clarissa. 'We're quite full just now,' she added over her shoulder. She was thinking fast as she walked. She would introduce the dogs one at a time, she thought. Tablet and Hattie should go first. They were both very placid. She would leave Brutus the Labrador till last. That way he would have plenty of time to get used to the sound and scent of the visitors. If she was really lucky, he wouldn't bark.

She pushed the door. Already, her mind was moving ahead to the rest of the visit. They would look at the small furries and then Frank the owl. The cats could go last. She would get the kittens out, she thought. Show her feeding regime. Mumma was so much better now.

The door into the kennel room was always a little stiff. Mandy gave it a brisk shove, then went through and held it open. Nicole passed, followed by Clarissa, then Anthony, bending slightly so he didn't bump his head. Mandy took a step backwards to allow space for him. Her heel caught on something. Nicole had left a broom leaning against the wall. The weight of her foot brought the broom handle upright and it hit her head. She flailed for a moment, trying to regain her balance, but then with all the grace of a toad on a tightrope, she crashed over backwards. The broom fell alongside her and she landed in a tangled heap, upsetting an empty metal bowl. It clattered across the floor, then rolled to a stop at the feet of Clarissa Tarley.

To Mandy's relief, Clarissa looked more concerned than judgemental, but the noise set Brutus barking and in an instant, all the other dogs joined in. Anthony jumped at the racket, but rallying, he leaned forwards. 'Are you all right?' he gasped. Mandy began to struggle to her feet and he offered his hand to help her up.

'I'm really sorry.' Mandy's face was burning. She bent down to lift the brush. The racket from the dogs was awful. Even Hattie was yapping madly. Resisting the urge to yell at the frantic dogs, she grabbed the broom. 'Just going to put this away,' she said, though her voice was drowned in the din. Clarissa bent over her clipboard making a note.

Mandy bolted out of the door, opened the cupboard and set the broom inside, then leaned on the wall. Without warning, the events of last night invaded her head. She couldn't do this, she thought. Not without time for preparation. She had been worse than useless with Zoe and now she was messing this up. For a second, she let misery wash over her. Then taking a deep breath, she gave herself a shake. She had left Nicole alone in the kennel with the inspectors and all the dogs going mad. However frustrated she was with Nicole's secrecy, she wasn't being fair. The girl was doing her best. Closing the cupboard door, she squared her shoulders and marched back in.

They had managed to calm some of the dogs, but Brutus was hopelessly rattled. He kept up a low growling throughout the inspection of the dog room. Mandy hoped for the best, but wherever they went in the rescue centre, the animals seemed unsettled. When they went through to see the small animals, the guinea pigs and rabbits were hiding. Even when she fetched salad, something that normally brought them running, none of them appeared. Frank too kept well back and even shrieked his alarm while the inspectors were peering into his cage. She should have kept them further back, Mandy thought, holding back a sigh as Clarissa made yet another note on her pad.

The visit to the cat room was better, although Mandy realised she'd left the broken scales out.

Well that *looks professional* . . .

She'd had a message to say the new ones had come in, but she hadn't had time for another trip to York yet.

To Mandy's amazement, Nicole became surprisingly chatty.

'This is Myler and Jasper and Button,' she explained,

leaning down and taking Button from the cage and handing her to Clarissa. 'Their mum's called Mumma.' Mandy cringed. She had meant to rename Mumma, but somehow it had stuck.

'How lovely.' Anthony reached over to tickle the kitten behind her ear and Button began to purr loudly.

'Mandy's a wonderful vet,' Nicole went on. 'Mumma's so lucky she ended up here.' She crouched on the edge of the kennel and stroked the older cat's head. Mumma closed her eyes, leaning into Nicole's touch. Nicole looked up and smiled. 'Mandy and I have been giving her kittens milk. Mumma really wasn't well when she came in, but Mandy's made her better.'

Clarissa was making another note on her clipboard. She looked up and beamed at Nicole. 'That's great,' she said. She glanced at her watch. 'Is there somewhere we can chat?' she asked. Mandy felt a fresh wave of nerves. She wished they could have stayed in the peaceful cat room.

The question and answer session was awful. It wasn't that the questions were difficult. On a normal day they'd have been easy, but the stresses of last night had caught up. Mandy stumbled over the figures, failed to be specific when they asked her about neutering, and completely forgot to mention the specialist course in rehabilitation of wild birds she had attended. Nor did she tell them about her behavioural expertise.

Throughout the session, she itched to go and sort Brutus out. He was still barking now and then, but every time she was about to make her excuses, Clarissa fired another question her way. Nicole finally went to him. Anthony looked relieved and Mandy kicked herself. She should have sent Nicole in the first place.

She wanted to collapse on the floor when the lengthy session finally drew to a halt. Her shoulders drooped as Clarissa stood up. Anthony sent Mandy what seemed to be a rueful smile as he shook her hand.

'That's all for today.' Mandy was unable to read Clarissa's face as she too held out her hand. 'You'll hear from us in due course.' The woman sent her a smile, but it didn't reach her eyes. Mandy had the fleeting impression that the inspector couldn't wait to escape. A terrible smell met them as they made their way to the door. Mandy pulled the door towards her, hoping the fresh May air would mask the odour. Plastering on a smile, she ushered the inspectors outside, stood for a moment to ensure they had really left, then rushed back inside, wishing she could hold her nose.

'What is that awful stink?' she asked Nicole.

Nicole paused for a moment. 'It was Sky,' she admitted, looking worried. 'I'm afraid she made a mess in her bed. I think I managed to clear it up without them noticing.'

Mandy looked around for Sky. A wave of guilt washed through her as she saw her beloved collie skulking in the corner. 'Come here, Sky,' she called and was relieved when Sky ran towards her with a flick of her tail. The collie's back was hunched and her head was down as if she was making herself as small as possible. Mandy knelt down, but Sky still looked scared. 'I'm sorry,' Mandy said. When she opened her arms, Sky rushed into them. Mandy hugged the collie to her. She must have been really upset to have made a mess inside. No doubt, she had picked up on

Mandy's own nerves. Mandy could only hope that Nicole was right and Clarissa and Anthony hadn't noticed. It would be awful if they thought she couldn't even train her own dog.

Nicole was standing watching. Her face was downcast. 'I'm going to have to go,' she told Mandy. 'School,' she added, as if feeling she had to offer an explanation.

'Thanks for coming.' Mandy looked down at Sky again. The collie still looked upset. No wonder, Mandy thought. Everyone in the building had picked up on her awful mood. She should have pulled herself together.

'I'm so sorry,' Nicole said. 'About the inspection. I should have asked first.' Her voice sounded small as she pulled open the door.

Mandy closed her eyes for a moment. Nicole had been so good. She had charmed the inspectors in the cat kennels, calmed Brutus down and cleaned up Sky's mess without a word. But they wouldn't have had those problems in the first place if Mandy had been warned and prepared. What if they didn't get the funding? This might have been Hope Meadows' only chance. 'Yes, you should,' she said, before she could help it.

With a stricken look, Nicole darted out through the open door and rushed away. Mandy pushed herself upright and headed after her, but by the time she got outside, Nicole had jumped onto her bike and peddled away at top speed.

Mandy was glad when lunchtime came round. She hadn't been able to face breakfast. Gran had spent ages calming

Brutus down, but Frank the owl had remained agitated. He hooted at random intervals and jumped every time Mandy tried to check on him. Even her patients at morning surgery seemed stressed. Mandy knew it was her carrying her agitation around that was the problem. Nicole's wounded look had stayed with her all morning. Mandy had tried to ring, but there had been no reply. Last, but not least, Emily had received a phone call asking her if she was available tomorrow. The hospital had a cancellation and could fit her in. It was good news, but Emily was naturally on edge.

Zoe looked a little better when Mandy checked her just before lunch, though her gums were still pale. She would take the husky up to her bedroom tonight, she decided. Helen couldn't stay in the clinic all the time and Zoe needed someone with her. She tried calling Jimmy, but her call went straight to message. She'd have to try again later.

The phone in the hall rang as she bit into her second piece of cheese on toast. She was glad when Adam stood up and walked through into the hall to answer it. 'Animal Ark.' She heard his voice through the door. What would it be? She didn't feel up to much.

'How are you feeling?' Emily's voice broke through her thoughts.

Mandy had to swallow her mouthful of cheese and wash it down with a sip of coffee before she could answer. 'I'm quite tired,' she admitted. It was, perhaps, the understatement of the year.

Emily sent her a sympathetic smile. The illness and impending tests hadn't dented her ability to read between the lines. 'I'm sure everything seems overwhelming,' she reached out and patted Mandy's hand, 'but give it a few days. It will get better.'

Mandy managed to smile back across the table, though she didn't agree. The puppies were dead. Nothing could ever make that better.

Out in the hall, Mandy heard the phone go down. Adam opened the door. 'That was Mrs Patchett,' he said. Mandy could picture Mrs Patchett's perfectly coiffured ash-blonde hair and her chilly eyes. She always asked for Mandy these days, ever since Mandy had performed a successful caesarean on her deerhound Isla. It hadn't stopped her being difficult, though. 'Isla had a litter two days ago,' Adam told her. 'She asked if you'd go out and check them, please.'

Mandy put down the mug she had just lifted. Her hands were shaking. There was no way she could go out and see a litter of puppies just now. Adam had sounded as if he was offering her a treat, but what if something went wrong? *If she missed something with Isla . . .*

With an effort, she lifted her gaze to meet her dad's. 'Please, Dad, could you get it?' she asked. 'Just this once . . .' she trailed off, feeling sick.

Emily sent her a sympathetic look, but Adam looked surprised. 'Of course I can,' he said. For a moment, she thought he was going to say something else, but he glanced at Emily, then back at Mandy. With a worried look, he made his way to the clinic door and disappeared.

Emily stood up and put the kettle on. 'Have you finished your coffee?' she asked. 'I'm going to make another cup.'

Five minutes later, she had made the drinks and asked Mandy to carry them through into the sitting room. Sunlight was filtering in through the window, warming the air. They sat down together on the sofa.

'Talk to me,' Emily urged.

Sky had followed them through. She lay down at Mandy's feet with a sigh. Mandy was glad that her beloved collie was feeling more relaxed, though she wished she could find some of that comfort herself. 'It's Zoe,' she said. 'And Jimmy. I'm going to have to talk to him later.' She paused for a moment, deep in thought. 'He'll probably be lovely about it all,' she said.

'And that makes it feel worse, doesn't it?' Emily said. She leaned towards Mandy until their shoulders were touching.

Mandy nodded. She couldn't help but feel it would be easier if Jimmy could shout and rage at her. Wouldn't it be better in the open? Didn't she deserve it?

'And how did the inspection go?' Mum asked. 'I know it was difficult, but was it just that you weren't prepared?'

Mandy groaned. 'It couldn't have gone much worse,' she said. 'I tripped over a broom Nicole had left out, and set all the dogs off barking, and . . . oh it was just a mess. I was so cold to her afterwards as well.' The last part was worst, she thought.

'Well, that's not like you,' Emily said confidently. Her shoulder was still against Mandy's.

'I know.' Mandy let her head fall forward. 'I wanted to clarify but she dashed off so fast. I was annoyed with her about the lack of warning, but she's great with the animals. I've tried to call, but I can't get through.'

'She's probably busy at school,' Emily pointed out. 'She'll be fine if you just apologise. She looks up to you so much.'

Mandy felt even more guilty as Emily spoke. It was true, Nicole did look up to her. What kind of role model had she been this morning? While she was still trying to think of a response, her phone rang. She pulled it out of her pocket.

'It's James,' she told her mum.

Emily patted her knee. 'Good,' she replied. 'If anyone can help, he can.'

'Why don't you come over?' James was asking her. Despite her better intentions, Mandy had found herself pouring out her problems to him. 'Come this afternoon, stay overnight. It sounds like you could do with a break.'

For a moment, the idea of James and his lovely flat in York shone in her mind like a ruby in sunlight, but then reality returned. 'I really can't,' she said. 'I'll have to stay here and look after Zoe.'

Though he sounded disappointed, Mandy could tell that he understood completely. It was her responsibility to look after Zoe now. 'Give me a call back,' he urged her. 'Let me know how it's going in a day or two. Maybe I can come to you at the weekend.'

Mandy heaved a sigh as she shoved the mobile back in her pocket. She walked back through to the sitting room. Emily turned to smile at her as she came in.

'How's James?' she asked.

'He's well.' Mandy fought to keep the despondency out of her voice, but it sounded flat, even to her. 'He asked me to stay over.'

'And did you accept?' Emily was gazing at her, eyebrows raised.

'I couldn't,' Mandy said. 'I have to stay here and look after Zoe. She needs someone with her.'

Emily's eyes opened wide. 'I can do that,' she said. Mandy looked at her mum. Emily really did look a lot better. The dark rings round her eyes had all but disappeared. 'Please let me,' Emily urged. 'I'm not doing any vet work. Zoe and her puppy can come in here and sit with me. It's not like she'll be any trouble. I often wake in the night. She'll be company. And you'll be back tomorrow before I have to go for my tests. Really, I'd like to.'

Mandy's resolve crumbled. 'Are you sure?' she asked. 'It wouldn't be too much for you? I guess I could pick up the new cat scales whilst I'm there.'

'That's settled then,' Emily beamed.

By three o'clock, she was halfway to York. As she began the long descent down onto the plain, her phone rang. There was a layby just ahead. She pulled into it and slammed on the brakes.

It was Jimmy. Mandy felt her heart leap into her mouth. She'd wanted to catch him before leaving, to check that he was okay, that he wouldn't mind if she went, but she hadn't had the chance. She had tried to call twice before she set off, but he hadn't replied.

'Hi.' He sounded as if he was making an effort to be cheerful. 'How are you? And how's Zoe?'

She should be with the husky, Mandy thought, filling up with shame. Jimmy had asked after her own health first, even when he was worried about his pet. She should be happy, but instead, she felt cold. 'I'm okay,' she said. 'Zoe's not too bad. Still a bit weak, but she's feeding the pup well.'

'Great.' She could hear the intensity of the relief in Jimmy's voice. 'Can I come and see you all? I have to go out later, but I've half an hour.' His voice was filled with certainty. He was sure she'd be there.

Mandy let her breath out slowly. 'I'm actually on my way to York,' she admitted. 'James asked me, and Mum thought I should go. Mum's looking after Zoe, she's expecting you to call.' She had rehearsed what she was going to say. Back then it had seemed fine. Now it felt awful. She'd abandoned Zoe, without even checking if it was okay with Jimmy first. There was a long silence on the line.

'Okay,' Jimmy said. 'Thanks. I'll give your mum a call.'

There was another silence while Mandy tried to think what she should say. 'I can come back if you like.' She put her hand on the gearstick. She would turn round and go back. She really shouldn't have left in the first place. 'I'll come back,' she repeated.

'No, don't do that. You'll miss me anyway if you're halfway to York.' Jimmy's voice was light, but was it real, or was he faking it to hide the hurt? 'As I said, I have to go out soon.'

Mandy's eyes wandered across the road. There were cows in the field opposite. How contented they looked with their calves beside them. She seemed to have spent so much time lately wishing she could rewind her decisions. She should have waited and seen him before heading to York.

It's okay,' Jimmy's voice was patient. 'You should go to James. It will be good for you to spend some time with him.' There was a moment's pause. 'I'll give your mum a call. It's quite okay. I know it must have been really difficult for you.' His voice had become muffled as if he was finding it hard to speak. Mandy wanted to reach out and hug him, but he was miles away.

'I really am sorry,' she said. 'I tried to call. If I'd known you only had a short time . . .' she trailed off.

'Not your fault,' he said. 'I should have called you earlier.'

Mandy felt a momentary urge to get out of the car and howl. She hadn't in any way meant to suggest he was to blame for not phoning. One of the cows across the road had walked to the bottom of the field and was gazing across at Mandy. She sought for something to say that would make it right, but her mind was empty. 'See you soon,' she said finally. Maybe she could see him tomorrow. He would probably visit Zoe every day until she was ready to go home.

'Yes.' He sounded sad. 'Bye then.'

'Bye,' Mandy whispered. The line went dead.

Chapter Twenty-One

Mandy dashed to Andersen's and picked up the order of cat scales. At least that was something she'd achieved, something that would improve things.

As she was leaving, she caught sight of a new multi-parameter monitor that she knew Helen was hankering after. Putting her scales on the floor at her feet, she stopped to examine it. She had just worked out how the blood-pressure attachment worked, when a loud voice caught her ear.

'We could do with at least five, don't you think?'

Mandy froze. She would know that voice anywhere. She stood very still, hoping to go unnoticed, but then a deeper voice, even more familiar, but equally unwelcome said, 'Mands?'

Mandy dug her fingernails into the palms of her hands as she swung round. There stood a blue-eyed, curly-haired man, wearing a smart shirt and looking like he had stepped out of a menswear catalogue. At his side was a petite woman, in figure-hugging jeans and a cornflower blue silk blouse that looked great against her long glossy black hair: Simon Webster and Samantha Leigh. Mandy hadn't seen Simon since the day she had split up with him last summer.

Samantha was clinging to Simon's arm as if signalling her possession.

Mandy had worked with Simon and Samantha in Leeds before her return to Welford. Within weeks of Mandy's departure, Samantha and Simon had become an item. Simon and Mandy had planned to open a clinic, but when Mandy left, Simon seemed simply to shift Samantha into the place Mandy had vacated. Mandy had heard that the two of them had opened their practice in Leeds at the end of last year.

She couldn't think of two people she wanted to see less right now. Even Abi and Max would be better, she thought to herself, wryly. *They must be growing on me!*

'Hello.' Though she tried her best, it was impossible to find much enthusiasm. Simon's hand was now patting Samantha's clinging one. He was wearing a smug smile, as if running into Mandy was exactly what he had planned.

'How are you? How are things in sleepy Welford?' Simon asked. 'Still saving your animals one by one?' Though his expression was bland, to Mandy the undertone of condescension was distinct. When they had been together, she'd hoped Simon would learn to love Welford as she did, but he had always regarded it as a backwater.

'Yes, I am. Things are fine, thanks.' Even as she said it, Mandy felt defensive. She found herself wanting to list all the things that were going well but she blanked.

Okay, so things could be better right *now . . .*

'We're here to buy some Shor-Line kennels,' Samantha said. Mandy tried to remind herself that Samantha couldn't have known how galling her words would be to Mandy.

Shor-Line offered complimentary custom design as standard. They were stainless steel and easy to clean, with catches that didn't break every other day. Simon and Samantha were running a practice, not a rescue centre, but the contrast rankled.

'That's great,' Mandy managed.

'We've just taken on some new premises in York as a branch practice.' It was Simon's turn to speak. How proud he looked as he stood there, with his hand over Samantha's. 'Sam's dental work is going so well in Leeds that we thought we'd strike while the iron is hot, so to speak.'

Mandy felt like she had been hit in the stomach. Location had been one of the biggest factors in hers and Simon's breakup. She'd wanted to be in Welford and he'd wanted to stay in Leeds. Mandy had suggested York as a compromise at the time, but Simon had refused. Now he was coming here with Samantha?

None of that matters now, she told herself. Things had worked out for the best and her life was good. She just wished she could present it better to the shiny happy couple . . .

'Not just my dental work!' Samantha was smiling up at Simon with sickening sweetness. 'What about your prosthetics referrals?' She turned her eyes to Mandy. 'We had Ava Moon in last month. Little Foo-Foo was in danger of losing her foot, but Simon gave her a new one.'

Mandy blinked at them, taken aback and nonplussed at the same time. Soul singer Ava Moon? Grammy Award-winning celebrity dog lover Ava Moon? She was rarely seen without her Chihuahua, Foo-Foo. Had they really gone to Simon for treatment?

Simon was speaking again, addressing Samantha. 'Well, I may have fixed Foo-Foo's leg, but I think Ava was just as impressed when you offered to straighten her teeth.' He turned to Mandy. 'Are you thinking of buying one of those?' he asked, pointing to the monitor Mandy had been looking at. 'We've got a couple. They are really useful.'

'That's good to know,' Mandy said, with some effort. She felt sick. Here she was, with a rescue centre that couldn't make ends meet, a country veterinary practice under immense pressure and an increasingly complicated relationship. Meanwhile Simon and Samantha seemed to have life sorted. Doubt started to well up inside her. Maybe Simon had been right all along? Maybe Hope Meadows had been a fool's venture from the beginning? After all, a city practice still did good work . . . Her head was starting to spin.

'Mandy, are you okay?' Samantha put a manicured hand on her arm and leaned towards her. 'You look really tired.'

Mandy burned red hot with humiliation. Then, she spotted a sparkle on Samantha's hand: a slim golden ring with a diamond on it.

They're engaged!

The burning feeling got worse. Why should everything be so simple and easy for Simon? Why did his business run perfectly and make loads of money and get celebrity clients? Why did he get to have a partner who came with no strings attached?

'I'm fine.' Mandy tried to get a grip.

This isn't like me. I love my life!

But under the pitying glances of Samantha and Simon it was hard to remember that.

Just then, her phone buzzed. It was James, no doubt wondering where she'd got to.

'I'm afraid I have to dash,' Mandy said, picking up the cat scales and practically running out of the warehouse.

Once Mandy was inside James's clean and bright flat, she couldn't help but feel some of her worries falling away. Sky, too, seemed happy to be here. She lay in the middle of the floor snuggled up with Seamus and Lily.

James was sitting opposite her in his favourite chair. He had faded almost to nothing after Paul's death, but now she noticed his face had filled out again. A real smile flickered across Mandy's face. It was so good to see the old James coming back.

'So do you think Zoe will be okay?' James asked. Mandy had found herself pouring out all her worries again. Now that she was here, bundled up in a blanket and clutching a steaming cup of tea, things didn't look quite so impossible.

'Probably.' Mandy sighed. 'She's lost a lot of blood. It's making her weak, but she should recover eventually.' Mandy knew it was true, though in the early hours, she was plagued by doubt. 'She'll never have puppies again, though. Jimmy wanted to breed a whole sled team.'

'Maybe he can run a two-dog team,' James said. He smiled gently, his eyes sympathetic. 'Whatever happened to the pups,' he reminded her, 'the tumour had to be removed. Zoe would have been spayed whatever happened.' That was true, Mandy thought. She could have been the best surgeon in the world and she couldn't have saved Zoe's womb. Despite that, her guilt remained. 'Is the puppy a boy or girl?' James asked. 'Maybe he or she could have a litter one day.'

'It's a girl,' Mandy replied. In her more optimistic moments, she imagined Zoe recovering fully and the pup grown. She remembered all the names on Abi's list and sighed.

'Jimmy called me on the way over,' she admitted. 'I'd called earlier, but he didn't pick up. I think he was upset I'd gone off to York. I should have been there.'

'Well, it's understandable if he is upset, but he'll forgive you.' James was matter-of-fact. 'If I were you, I'd give him some space to grieve.' James stood up and went across to put the kettle back on.

'There's no chance Abi and Max'll forgive me, though.' Mandy watched as James gathered together the makings for another cup of tea. 'I'm sure I'll always be a puppy killer to them now.'

James raised his eyebrows. 'I'm sure they don't think that at all. Of course, they'll be upset, but pets dying is a part of life.' He studied her. 'It's not like you to be so negative,' he pointed out, his voice gentle.

Mandy sighed again. 'Things are awful at the moment,' she admitted. 'Mum's really not been well. She's due for some tests tomorrow.'

James handed Mandy another cup of tea, sat down and leaned forward. 'What tests?'

'I'm not sure exactly,' Mandy replied. 'Neurology ones. They're definitely going to do an MRI. I don't really know what they're looking for.' For a moment, she was wracked with guilt yet again. She should have asked more. Mum would tell her tomorrow, but what if . . . ? Mandy shoved the thought to the back of her mind. Mum would be fine. She always was.

'And how is Frank getting on?' James had been delighted when Mandy had told him they were calling the owl Frank. 'It suits him,' he had said. Even down the phone, Mandy had been able to hear his grin.

'He was pretty wound up today,' Mandy admitted. 'The first thing I managed to do during the inspection was fall over a broom Nicole had left in the dog kennel. I was sprawled on the floor, every dog in the place was baying, and before long, the whole rescue centre joined in. Frank was screeching like something had his tail feathers. There's no chance whatsoever those people're going to give me funding.' She paused to sip her tea. 'And as if that wasn't enough, I've managed to upset Nicole,' she added. 'I got cross with her. I just felt so frustrated. Everything just keeps getting worse . . .'

James leaned forward. 'I can see why you're upset. But the inspectors won't blame you for your little broom dance,' he said. 'And Nicole should have told you what she was up to before it came down to inspectors at dawn.' He put down his tea and stood up again.

'I've something for you to try,' he said. He opened the fridge and pulled out a plate of savoury pastries. 'I'll just put them in the oven,' he said.

Half an hour later, he handed Mandy a plate. The pastries were delicious, crisp and light, flavoured with cheese and tomato, olive and roasted red peppers. 'We're having an Italian week in the café,' he said. 'We've all kinds of biscuits too. We've had Raj do the food – he has amazing stuff from all round the world. Sherrie and I have been doing themed weeks in the shop. The customers love it.'

Mandy smiled at him and let out a sigh of genuine relief. He seemed happy. And things were going well with the café. No wonder he had a more rounded look to him. 'I'm glad to hear that Raj's made himself useful.' She managed a smile.

James laughed. 'All I need now,' he said, 'is for a pigeon to collide with a wine truck and I'll be set for life.'

Mandy had to set out early in the morning, so as to be back before Mum had to go to hospital. The trip had been worth it, she thought. James always made everything seem better.

Dad was going with Mum to the hospital. He gave strict instructions for Mandy to call him if anything came in that she wasn't happy with, but he made it plain he expected her to manage. His faith steadied her. Zoe wasn't better, but she wasn't any worse either. Jimmy had been a little quiet last night, Helen told her, but hadn't seemed angry at all.

Christine Harford called from Natural England, but she didn't have any good news. 'I've done my best,' she said, 'but I've spoken to the council and Westbow Holdings.

Both said all the surveys were done and nothing was found. We're still waiting on copies but I've no reason not to believe the council. Unless you can give us proof there are red squirrels, we can't take it any further.'

Mandy toyed with the idea of telling her about the discussion with Sam Western in the Fox and Goose, and what Harriet had told her about wining and dining people from the council. What if he had made 'donations' to get the council to say there was a survey when there wasn't?

But she had no proof. She thanked Christine and put the phone down with a horrible feeling that there was nothing more she could do. She had too much on already. Nobody from the village was going to help. They were all wound up about the factory. What a pity Sam Western had taken Jimmy's camera down. It would need an army to track anything down in the wood with their bare eyes.

Mandy bolted down a sandwich for lunch and then slipped into the residential unit to visit Zoe. Helen was already there, looking concerned. Zoe barely lifted her head as Mandy came in.

'She's not improving,' Helen murmured.

Mandy checked Zoe's wound. 'She's healing well. She's just still really anaemic.' She was hoping against hope that the husky would turn the corner soon.

'At least this little one is okay,' said Helen, giving the pup a quick stroke. 'She's got a full belly and she seems happy.'

As if on cue, the pup gave a little mewl. Mandy and Helen both laughed.

★ ★ ★

Emily arrived home from hospital as Mandy finished her afternoon surgery. Mandy saw the car pull up outside and dashed through to the cottage.

Emily looked tired, but relieved, as Adam helped her indoors.

'How was it?' Mandy asked.

'Fine,' said Emily. 'They did all sorts of tests, but we won't have the results for a little while.'

'Well done, Mum.' Mandy knew Emily had struggled to admit to herself that something might be wrong. She was so used to taking care of everyone else that it had been hard to accept that she needed to be the patient now.

Emily smiled. 'Thanks, love.'

'She was very good,' said Adam. 'In fact, she was so good that she deserves this.' He pulled a lollipop out of his coat pocket and handed it to Emily.

Emily and Mandy laughed. Mandy felt a rush of love for her dad, who was making sure her mum had fun, even though his own worry was etched all over his face.

They took Emily through to the kitchen and settled her on a chair whilst Mandy and Adam made dinner between them. Then, dispensing with their normal protocols, they took trays through to the sitting room and ate in front of the TV.

Mandy left her parents watching a nature documentary about penguins to go and do the evening surgery. It was quiet and there was just one visit afterwards, to a pony with laminitis. It wasn't a complicated case. She gave the pony pain relief and instructed the owners to make sure he didn't get too much grass.

The road was quiet as Mandy drove back. The sun was setting over Black Tor. It really was very beautiful. Mandy was more certain than ever after Harriet's visit that Sam Western had not carried out the wildlife survey. Not that it got her any further forward, but her anger was rising.

She drove into Welford and turned onto Walton Road. She was almost home. She turned onto Main Street, then swung right onto the lane that led up to Animal Ark and slammed on her brakes. A bulldozer without any lights was blocking the lane. There was no way past. She sat there for a moment, but there was no movement. What were they doing here? Had they taken a wrong turn? Or . . .

Mandy peered through the gloom, her heart beginning to race. Beyond the gateway on the track that led to the woods, past Liz and Sam Butler's bungalow, there were more shapes looming. She made out another bulldozer, a huge lorry and a JCB. None of them were showing any headlights.

It was Westbow. It must be. But why were they here so late? They couldn't be about to start digging now . . . *right*?

An image of the tiny red-furred squirrel curled up in Abi and Max's cardboard box flashed through Mandy's mind. Abandoning her car in the middle of the road, she leaped out and ran up the track, waving her arms. The vehicles made no sign that they had seen her. The lead bulldozer was trundling onwards through the curved wood-land track.

Mandy sprinted across the field to cut off the corner, then took a flying leap, vaulting over the dry-stone wall that bordered the path. Rushing forwards, she stood in front of the lead bulldozer with her hands raised.

'Stop!' Her heart was in her mouth as the huge vehicle rolled towards her. She waved her hands and yelled as loud as she could.

'STOP!'

Chapter Twenty-Two

The bulldozer ground to a halt. Mandy bent forwards and put her hands on her knees, trying to catch her breath. Her knees were shaking. The door of the bulldozer swung open and a man climbed out onto the track. He put his fists on his hips. 'What's going on?' he demanded.

Mandy straightened up and stared straight at him. 'There are wild animals on this land. It's illegal to go ahead without permission,' she gasped.

The driver pursed his lips. Without a word, he climbed back up into his cab, reached under the dashboard, pulled out a wad of papers, then climbed back down. He held them out. 'I've got a copy of the permit here,' he said. Mandy took the papers and squinted at them in the dim light, but she knew it didn't matter that they had a permit. The question was whether the procedures had been followed *before* it was issued.

Until I see that wildlife survey with my own eyes, I won't let this happen, she thought.

Then suddenly, something caught her eye – the name Marissa Bowie. And there was a telephone number and e-mail address right beside it.

Mandy pulled out her own phone and took a photo of the paper, and as she did so another figure loomed out of the darkness, striding up the track: Sam Western, Mandy realised. His back was ramrod straight, his face filled with fury. Mandy could see the whites of his eyes. 'I might have known it would be you.' He ground out the words. 'You're trespassing on my land. Move out of the way,' he pointed, 'right now.'

He reminded Mandy of a growling Rottweiler, the way he stood four-square in the centre of the track, but there was no way she could back down. She handed the permit back calmly. 'It's you who are breaking the law.' She kept her voice quiet so he had to strain to listen to her.

The bulldozer driver was watching. The other drivers had joined him. Sam glanced back at them, and Mandy thought he was half infuriated and half embarrassed at having to deal with her in front of the builders. 'You trespassed on my land before with your stupid camera,' he spat. 'I told you if I caught you, I'd call the police. I will if you don't shift yourself right now.'

Mandy stood on the track, her feet apart. She was holding herself very straight, gripping on to her temper. 'There's an endangered species living here.' The words were clear on the evening air. 'I will not let you destroy their habitat.'

Sam Western took a step towards Mandy. She stood her ground, but a shiver ran through her. On the evening air, there came the sound of a door opening. A light went on over the doorway of the nearby bungalow and Liz Butler stepped out onto the back doorstep. She was wearing a jaunty beret and a red shirt. Her Bernese Mountain Dog Emma was beside her.

It only took a few moments for them to reach the lead bulldozer. 'What's going on?' she asked, craning her neck to peer up at the huge vehicle in the twilight. She walked a few paces further up the track and looked from Sam to Mandy, then back again. Emma stood beside her, seemingly unworried that her evening walk had been diverted.

'They're trying to clear the woodland,' Mandy began, but Sam spoke louder.

'There's a trespasser on my land,' he said, his voice emphatic. 'She's trespassing.' He glared at Mandy. 'I'm going to call the police.'

'But it's just Mandy.' Liz sounded confused. 'What's going on?'

Mandy spoke, still keeping her voice calm. 'I believe there are red squirrels living in the woods,' she said. 'If there are, it's illegal for Mr Western to build on the land or destroy the habitat.'

Sam took another step towards her. 'There are no squirrels.' He was almost yelling.

Liz frowned and shook her head. 'There probably are,' she said. 'We see them in the garden. They steal peanuts from the bird feeders.'

Mandy felt her jaw drop. Liz had said it with such matter-of-factness. She could have no idea how much it meant to Mandy to hear it – or how foolish Mandy was feeling for not asking the woman who lived right next door to the site if she'd seen the squirrels too. Mandy tried to reel in her surprise and turned to Sam, raising an eyebrow.

Sam folded his arms. He thrust his head forward, his eyes bulging as if he was about to explode. 'Red squirrels next door doesn't mean anything and she is still trespassing,' he spat. 'I have a permit to build here and you are obstructing. I'm calling the police.' Turning his back on Mandy, he pulled a mobile from his pocket and dialled.

'Fine.' Mandy shrugged and thrust her hands in her pockets.

Liz gave her a sideways look of sympathy. 'Do you want me to stay with you?' she asked.

Mandy shook her head.

'I'll be fine.'

Liz looked from Mandy to Sam and then shrugged and gave Emma's lead a gentle tug.

'Well, I'll give you my phone number,' she said. 'And I'll be just over there if you need me.' She nodded towards her bungalow, and then typed her number into Mandy's phone. Sam shot her a look of irritation, but Mandy gave a grateful smile as the enormous dog got to its feet and bounded back along the track.

It took twenty minutes for the police car to arrive. By the time it came, the lane was in darkness. The driver swung into the gateway and stopped. The headlights shone into the gloom, lighting up the bulldozer and Sam and Mandy, who were still facing one another in the lane. One of the drivers lit a cigarette. The rest were leaning against the track of the bulldozer.

Sergeant Jones climbed out of the car, accompanied by

another officer Mandy didn't recognise. They walked up the track, their faces in shadow. Before they even had time to reach the drivers, Sam Western began speaking.

'Good evening, officers. Thanks for coming. This young woman,' he sneered as he indicated Mandy, 'is trespassing on my land. You!' he pointed to the driver of the bulldozer. 'Give me those papers.' He held out his hand.

The driver pushed himself upright, marched over and wordlessly handed the sheaf of papers to Sam.

Sam held out the paper at Sergeant Jones. 'I have permission to build on this land,' he announced. 'I want to continue. Please do your job and remove her.'

To his credit, Dan Jones made no move, other than to take the papers. 'What's your version, Miss Hope?' He looked at Mandy. His tone was merely interested. He was not taking sides until he'd heard what she had to say.

'I think Mr Western is trying to break the law,' she said. 'He should have had a wildlife survey done. I have reason to believe he didn't get one.'

It was a stretch. Despite what Harriet had told her, despite his discussion with Mandy in the Fox and Goose, she had no proof that Sam had not had the survey done. Not being able to find evidence it existed was not proof that it didn't.

'You have the permission there.' Sam's tone was sneering. 'No survey, no permission. Simple as that.'

'I know you have planning permission,' Mandy said, 'but can you show us papers for the survey itself? I've tried to see them. Nobody's been able to find them. That's all I want. Proof the survey was done.'

Dan Jones turned to Sam, his eyebrows raised. 'What about it, Mr Western?' he asked. His tone seemed deliberately unprovocative. Mandy couldn't help but be impressed by the way he was handling the situation. 'Can you produce that for us?'

'I don't have to show you anything.' Sam's voice was louder, more threatening than ever. Mandy saw Sergeant Jones's colleague straightening up. 'I have followed the legal processes. Everything has been done to the letter.'

'Why are you bringing your workmen up here at this time of night? None of them were showing any lights,' Mandy objected. 'Why would you do that if everything is above board as you say?'

Sam drew his chin back, his mouth a disparaging line. 'This was the only time they were available,' he snapped.

For the first time in the exchange, Mandy came close to laughing. 'You could only get workers who work in the middle of the night?' she said. She turned to the police officers. 'When I asked Mr Western about this matter a few days ago, he offered me money for my rescue centre,' she stated, keeping her voice factual, 'and I understand he's been socialising with members of the council in a restaurant in Walton. Now he's saying he's done a survey, but can't produce any evidence.'

'Okay.' Sergeant Jones had been watching Mandy's face as she spoke. He turned to Mr Western. 'Miss Hope has made some allegations against you and you've made some about her,' he said. 'If Miss Hope's main concern is that there's an endangered species living here, and you cannot produce the wildlife survey, then we should allow the correct authorities . . .' his gaze flickered to Mandy, and she filled in the blank smoothly.

'The National Wildlife Crime Unit.'

'. . . onto the land to make certain everything's in order. If you *can* provide the papers to me, then you have permission to go ahead straight away. If Miss Hope doesn't find any evidence, you can go ahead with your work on Sunday. Does that seem an acceptable compromise?'

He looked first to Sam, who nodded, though he looked as though he was struggling to hold back his rage.

'Miss Hope?' Sergeant Jones had been calm throughout. Mandy was very grateful to him.

'Thank you,' she said.

It took her only two minutes to drive home. The lights in the cottage were off. Her parents must be in bed.

Sky greeted her as she came in the door and Mandy sank down for a cuddle, taking comfort from the collie's warmth and solidity. She had to make a plan for the morning, there was nothing for it but to search the forest by hand for signs of the squirrels – but how could she do it? Everyone would be in bed. Pulling out her phone she shot off messages to Gran and Grandad, to Rachel and Helen, James and Susan. Lifting her phone one last time, she dialled Marissa Bowie's number. It went straight to voicemail, so Mandy left a message, pouring out everything about the red squirrels and her investigations and all her doubts about Sam Western and his interactions with the council. Perhaps she was wasting her time and Ms Bowie was hand-in-glove with Sam. Perhaps she knew exactly what was going on. But if not, Mandy wanted her to know.

Bone weary, Mandy stood up after she'd made the call. There was nothing more she wanted than to go to bed, but she really must check on Zoe. Would Mum have taken her upstairs? She didn't want to disturb them if so. She went out to the kennel in the clinic where Zoe was being looked after during the day, but the cage was empty. Wandering back into the cottage, she walked up the stairs and to her relief, Adam met her on the landing.

'Good! You're home,' he said. 'Is everything okay?' His face looked rumpled, his hair greyer than usual in the dim light.

'Do you have Zoe?' Mandy asked.

'Yes.' Even Dad's voice sounded tired. 'Can you have her? I've got to go out early.' Between them they lifted Zoe to her feet and supported her as she made her way into Mandy's bedroom. She flopped into the bed that Mandy had set out. Would she be better at home? Mandy wondered. But she didn't want to send her home when she was still so weak. Mandy set the puppy down beside her and the tiny creature snuggled in under Zoe's flank and went to sleep.

Mandy thought for a moment about telling Adam about the squirrel hunt, but he looked worn out. The last thing he needed was any additional worry. Maybe Mum could look after Zoe again tomorrow, while she went out to search? 'Night, Dad,' she said.

'Night, Mandy.' With a half-salute, he stumbled back into the bedroom.

★ ★ ★

It was already getting light by four thirty. Mandy knew she had to get Hope Meadows organised before she could go out, so she opened up and began the feed rounds early. But to her amazement and delight, there was a knock on the glass door and Gran and Grandad appeared, only a few minutes after her. 'I got your message,' Gran announced. 'We came as soon as it was light. We've sent messages to a few people as well. Hopefully they'll come.'

'The more the merrier.' Mandy hugged her, then Grandad.

'I thought I could stay here and finish off,' Grandad told her. 'That way you and your Gran can go and make a start looking for those squirrels. What do you think?'

'That sounds great,' Mandy confessed. She really didn't want to leave the animals she'd rescued uncared-for, while she went out to find others, no matter how right the cause.

It was beautiful as Mandy and her gran walked down the lane as the light dawned. They were bundled up in thick coats and gloves. Even though it was spring, they needed them in the early morning chill. The floor of the valley was swathed in mist. Trees stood clear of the white blanket, drinking in the first rays of the sun. The woodland itself seemed tranquil as it dozed in the golden light. The thought of bulldozers crashing through the ancient trees made Mandy more determined than ever to find the red squirrels that lived in their mossy grey branches.

They started off the hunt alone, treading slowly and

carefully along the path, phones at the ready to capture any evidence of squirrel activity.

Twigs cracked behind them and Mandy jumped, expecting Sam Western and his men. But it was just Rachel and her fiancé, Brandon Gill.

'Thanks for coming,' Mandy whispered. She directed them to another part of the land to begin their search.

A few minutes later, Susan Collins arrived with a very serious-looking little Jack. He was walking with his finger pressed to his lips the entire time and Mandy had to stifle a giggle. After Susan and Jack came Helen and Seb. To Mandy's delight, Mr Chadwick turned up too, then Mrs Jackson, who lived just up the road from Gran and Grandad. Then James arrived, then Raj.

'James called me,' Raj whispered to Mandy. 'I wanted to give something back for all the help you've given Frank.' She was touched that he'd come.

James had brought a tripod and camera. 'In case you need to set up a stakeout,' he murmured with a grin.

Despite their numbers, everyone seemed determined to search quietly, even as the sun rose and the faint rumble of road traffic from the main village started up. Bev and Gary Parsons arrived at ten, carrying an extremely welcome gift of filled bread rolls and hot flasks of coffee. Gathered together, the group chatted quietly. Mandy listened to the half-whispered conversations. They were filled with optimism.

Mandy was standing on the edge of the wood with James when a car drew up and stopped at the end of the track. A woman climbed out. She had iron grey hair, short and neatly styled, and was wearing a smart blue jacket. She walked up the path. Mr Chadwick was standing closest to the gate and she stopped to speak to him. 'Is Amanda Hope here?' she asked. 'I need to talk to her. I was told at the surgery I could find her here.'

Mr Chadwick smiled, charming as ever. 'She's over there,' he said, pointing. 'But we're trying to keep our voices down, I'm afraid. We're looking for red squirrels, you see.'

'Ah, so I have heard,' said the lady, lowering her voice.

Marissa Bowie! Mandy steeled herself for another show-down like the one she'd had with Sam, but her nerves faded as the woman approached: slightly shy, but with a lovely smile, and real warmth in her serious blue eyes. 'Hello,' she whispered, holding out her hand. 'I'm Marissa Bowie. You left a message.'

'I did.'

'And who is this?' Marissa was looking from Mandy to James.

'This is my friend James,' she replied.

'Pleased to meet you, James.'

For a moment, Mandy didn't know how to begin. Marissa Bowie seemed nothing like Sam Western, but she might still have come to try to persuade them to call off their hunt. Before she could find her voice, Marissa spoke. 'I came straight away. I had no idea there were any problems with the wildlife survey. Do you really think there might be red squirrels?' She was staring at Mandy, and there was a light of excitement in her eyes as she glanced up at the trees that reminded Mandy of Abi and Max when they'd looked at the little creature in its cardboard home.

Could we be so lucky? she wondered. *Could Sam Western's business partner be an animal lover?*

'I do.' Mandy said. 'James and I saw one of them.' She stopped. She wasn't going to go into the details of where they had seen the baby squirrel. 'Liz Butler, who lives there,' Mandy pointed to the bungalow, 'she's seen them too. They come into her garden.'

Marissa looked at the bungalow, then at the group of searchers setting off back into the woods. She looked sad. 'It was my idea to start a new venture in Welford,' she said. 'My father left me a furniture business over near Ripon when he passed away three years ago.' She looked down at her feet for a moment, then sighed as she raised her eyes again. 'I've been looking for somewhere to expand. I met Sam Western through my brother-in-law. He had some land, he said, which was no use for farming. I hadn't even been here until today. Sam's been handling everything . . .' She stopped and looked around again, taking in the venerable trees and the beauty of the valley around them. 'I'm really sorry,' she said, shaking her head. 'I should have come, but I had no idea there was a problem.'

She broke off, her eyes arrested by something over Mandy's shoulder. Footsteps sounded on the track. 'Mandy?' She turned. It was Susan Collins. Her dark hair was tied back in a band. Beside her, Jack was gazing up earnestly, his huge brown eyes serious, his finger still firmly on his lips. 'I think we've found something,' Susan said. 'It looks like a nest, but there was a flash of brown fur. Can you come and have a look?'

She led them along a narrow track, then stopped in a

clearing. 'Up there,' she said, pointing her finger at the tallest of the fir trees. Mandy, James and Marissa peered up into the branches. There, close to the trunk of the tree was a round nest-like structure built of twigs.

'It does look like a drey,' James whispered.

'It does,' Mandy murmured. She moved closer, her eyes on the ground. A moment later, she swooped to pick something up from the ground. 'Look,' she said, holding up a small woody object.

'What is it?' Susan frowned.

'It's the centre of a pine cone that's been chewed,' Mandy announced softly. 'Lots of animals eat the seeds, but only squirrels leave the middle like this.'

'So what should we do?' Marissa asked. She too was gazing up into the tree as if hoping for a miracle.

'We need to try to get some evidence,' James said. He held out his camera to Mandy. 'I'll get it set up.'

Mandy knew they might have to wait quite a while before they were sure if the drey was occupied. James set up his tripod with the camera focussed on the rounded cluster of twigs that was close to invisible near the trunk of a sturdy Norwegian spruce. Susan and Marissa went back to gather the rest of the group. It was important they weren't disturbed.

James and Mandy sat down on the grass. Mandy leaned her head against a tree trunk. They would have to sit very still. It was oddly peaceful. A rabbit lolloped out of the undergrowth, hopped across the clearing and disappeared. A large black beetle walked right up James's arm, then turned and marched back down again. Mandy's feet had gone numb by the time the flash of red fur came. Mandy stiffened. She had to be still. She caught her breath as the squirrel appeared and stood for a moment on the branch. It was so close she could see the tufts of fur on its ears and the brightness of the intense black eyes. It paused a moment longer, then scampered head first down the tree.

'Did you get it?' she whispered to James a minute later.

He was fiddling with his camera, lost in concentration. He unscrewed it from its tripod, then grinned as he handed it to her. 'There you go,' he said.

It was the most wonderful picture. He had caught the squirrel as it stood on the branch. Its reddish-brown fur, white chest and tufty ears were crystal clear. 'That's wonderful,' Mandy breathed. Reaching out her arms, she hugged James. Pulling out her mobile, she made a call to the police and asked to be put through to the National Wildlife Crime Unit. She would go right to the top, she thought. She wanted to make the strongest case possible before Sam Western could interfere any more.

If she had felt the triumph of discovery when she saw the photo, she couldn't help but feel a bit sad as they walked back and saw Marissa standing with all the lovely people of Welford who'd turned out to help them. The squirrels would be saved, but the factory would no longer go ahead. The business would have provided useful jobs for the village.

But Marissa seemed satisfied when they showed her the photograph. 'It is sad about the factory,' she said, 'but there's no way we can build here now.' She looked at Mandy's downcast face. 'Don't worry,' she said. 'I'm sure we can find somewhere else.'

Mandy wished she could share Marissa's optimism. Sam Western owned so much of the land round Welford. It wasn't likely she'd find anywhere, no matter how good her intentions. 'Do you think the police will tell Sam?' Mandy asked.

Marissa squared her shoulders. 'They might well,' she said, 'but don't you worry about it. I'll be speaking to him myself. I want to know whether he did the survey or not, but if he didn't . . .' Mandy smiled at Marissa in surprise. She was physically small, but suddenly Mandy didn't envy Sam one bit. She wouldn't want to be in his shoes if Ms Bowie found out he hadn't been dealing fairly with her money.

They had to wait some time for the police to arrive. The officers followed her into the wood and she showed them the drey. James showed them his photograph. 'Don't worry,' they told Mandy. 'We'll take it from here.'

Bev Parsons had invited all the searchers to come to the Fox and Goose after the search. One by one, they set off down the road. Finally, only Mandy, James and Liz Butler were left.

'I'm so glad you got your proof,' Liz said. 'I love having the squirrels in the garden.' She grinned.

'Are you going to the Fox and Goose?' Mandy asked. Much as she would like to go herself, she needed to get back to Animal Ark. She would check on Zoe, and then she was going to call Jimmy, she decided. Even if he was angry, she had to see him. Without him, today's victory had seemed hollow. Maybe, if Zoe was a bit better, he could take her home.

'I was just going to take Emma out.' Liz grinned. 'She's got way too much energy. Would you like to come or are you joining the others?'

Mandy sighed. If only she could take some of Emma's energy and give it to Zoe. Something stirred in the back of her mind. They had a kit back at Animal Ark for doing blood transfusions. Helen had shown her the collection bag a couple of months ago. She had never used one before, but she knew the theory.

'Liz?' She paused. It was a lot to ask. Concentrate on Zoe, Mandy told herself. She looked Liz right in the eye. 'There was something I was wondering.'

'What is it?' Liz was smiling at her.

'I've a really ill dog in the clinic that needs blood. Is there any chance I . . . we . . . could take some from Emma?'

'You mean like a transfusion?' Liz had her head on one side. She looked interested.

'Just like that, yes. We'd have to do a test to check she's a suitable donor, but it would really help.' Mandy's eyes were on Liz's face. She willed her to say yes.

'I didn't know dogs could give blood.' Liz seemed to be considering. 'I hope someone would do it for us, if Emma was ill,' she said after only a moment. She smiled. 'So, if it'll help the other dog, then yes of course.' Mandy could have hugged her.

Chapter Twenty-Three

Her fingers were shaking as she slid the catheter into the vein on Emma's neck. Despite her nervousness, she hit the vessel on the first attempt. Liz was intent on keeping Emma steady, but James sent Mandy a look of delight as the dark red fluid began to flow into the collection bag.

'We have to tilt the bag every fifteen seconds to mix it,' she told James. He did as she said. Emma was doing really well, Mandy thought. The huge dog was lying wonderfully still. Liz was stroking the silky black fur on Emma's ear. The Mountain Dog's huge frame was relaxed as the life-saving blood flowed.

We're so lucky Emma's blood is suitable.

The bag was almost filled. It had taken just under fifteen minutes. Without disconnecting it, Mandy slid it onto the scales. She looked up. 'That's it now,' she told James. Keeping one hand on the catheter, she pointed James to a clamp. With deft fingers, he applied it to the tubing through which the blood had flowed. It took only a few moments to remove the catheter and put pressure on

Emma's vein. She heaved a sigh of relief. It really couldn't have gone any better. 'Thank you so much,' she told Liz when she had applied a dressing to the area. 'She's been so good.'

'She really has.' Liz looked rightly proud. 'She used to hate the vet's, but I think she's been better recently with your help. She loves popping in for treats.' Between the three of them, they managed to lift the blanket Emma was lying on and lowered her to the floor.

'I'll get her something to eat and drink in a few minutes,' Mandy promised, having looked Emma over. 'You can wait here, if that's okay.' She would need to recheck the big dog before Liz took her home, but for now she was itching to get the precious blood to Zoe.

She set up the drip for Zoe. She had often given fluids, but never blood. The canine blood bank had a website with all kinds of information. Mandy had followed the instructions for cross-matching to the letter. With all that had gone before, and with everything at stake, she had wanted to make everything as safe as she possibly could.

'So what now?' James asked.

'We wait.' Mandy told him.

'Shall I go and make a cup of coffee?' James offered. 'Maybe a sandwich?' Taking her eyes off Zoe for a moment, Mandy glanced up at him. 'I heard your stomach rumbling.' James shrugged, pulling a comical face. It was true, she was hungry, Mandy realised. They hadn't had anything since Bev's rolls and even then, Mandy had been too worked up to eat much.

'That would be lovely,' Mandy admitted. 'I can go, though.'

'Thanks, but no thanks.' James was firm. 'You're the miracle worker here.'

Mandy opened her mouth to object, but James was already halfway to the door.

'Thanks, James,' she called after him. When he got back, she would need to check on Emma but for now, she was going to monitor Zoe.

The husky seemed sleepy as the blood dripped into her vein. Mandy was glad she was getting some rest. She would call Jimmy she thought, and let him know what she was doing. Maybe he'd come. She hadn't seen him for two days. Since catching her on the way to James's on Thursday evening, he'd called the Animal Ark number when he wanted to visit. Each time he'd been in, Mandy had been out on a call. But when she dialled his number now, the phone went straight to voicemail.

Mandy didn't want to leave him a message about the transfusion. 'Hi Jimmy, can you give me a call,' she said. Almost as soon as the words were out of her mouth, she wanted to call them back. What if he thought something bad had happened to Zoe? 'I've found a way to hopefully speed up Zoe's recovery, so we can talk about that when you're free . . .' she trailed off as guilt threatened to overwhelm her again.

Zoe should just be recovering from a normal birth and nursing her puppies. If I'd done the right thing . . .

'We found the squirrels,' she said, keeping her voice bright. 'The factory won't be built here after all. Can you tell the twins that if they hadn't shown me their baby squirrel, we'd never have been able to save them?' She ground to a halt. Was there anything else? Nothing came. 'Call me back,' she said again. 'Please.'

She put the phone down. Surely, he would call soon. She really wanted to speak to him. Helen had assured her he wasn't avoiding her. James had advised her to give him space to grieve. But she wanted to hear it from him. She needed to know whether he could find it in his heart to forgive her for the awful mistake she'd made.

The phone in her pocket vibrated a few minutes later, just after Liz had left with Emma. Mandy had checked the big dog thoroughly before announcing her good to go. With a surge of hope that Jimmy was calling, she checked Zoe's drip before she allowed herself to reply. The blood was running in well. Zoe was fast asleep, but she already seemed to be breathing more easily. Happy that she was ready to update him, she pulled the phone out. Her shoulders fell when she looked at the screen. It was Peter Warry.

'Hello Mr Warry.' She tried to keep the disappointment out of her voice. Whatever her problems, Hope Meadows came first.

'Oh, call me Peter, please.' The voice came down the line loud and clear. 'I know it's short notice,' he said, 'but I was wondering if there was any chance I could come and pick up Holly and Robin today?'

Mandy glanced at Zoe. She was still fast asleep, and more than half the blood transfusion was done. She stood up. Zoe gave a tiny snore. She'd be fine on her own for a few minutes, Mandy thought. Opening the door, she closed it softly and made her way out to the paddock. Robin pricked up his ears and trotted towards her. Holly followed. They both looked really well. There was no reason why Peter shouldn't come and fetch them today. 'Of course you can collect them,' she said. Holly put her head over the gate and nuzzled Mandy's arm. Mandy lifted her hand and ran her fingers down the silky soft fur of the little jenny's muzzle.

'In about an hour?' he said.

'That would be fine.'

Giving Robin a brief pat so that he didn't feel left out, Mandy went inside to search for James. She found him in the kitchen talking to Emily and Adam.

Adam looked up at her with a grin. 'I hear you've been quite the heroine this morning, saving even more of Welford's wildlife,' he teased. 'Just as well you came back from Leeds. Otherwise there'd be no animals left.'

Mandy managed a smile, though her mind was still on the donkeys. She knew they were going to a good home, but it would be odd to see them go.

'James said you're giving Zoe a blood transfusion?' Emily was sitting at the table. James was obviously making sand-wiches for everyone. 'How's it going? I've never actually used the kit myself.'

'I think it's going fine,' Mandy replied. 'I'll need to check her again in a few minutes.' This wasn't what she'd come in to talk about. 'Peter Warry just called,' she said, before anyone could start a new topic. 'He's coming in an hour for Holly and Robin.'

'That's great news, well done, darling.' Emily sounded delighted.

James smiled at her. 'Will you have a sandwich?' he asked. 'Have you time?'

Mandy glanced at the clock on the wall then returned his grin. 'Just the one,' she said, 'then I need to recheck Zoe before I get the donkeys ready. She would give them one last quick groom before sending them off.

'Can I come out with you to check on Zoe?' Adam offered. He too seemed very interested to see how the husky would respond.

'Course you can,' Mandy replied. Pulling out a chair, she sat down and took one of James's thickly sliced cheese sandwiches and wolfed it down. She hadn't realised just how hungry she was.

Adam and Mandy rushed out to check on Zoe as soon as they'd finished eating. James went to make a start on Holly and Robin. For the first time since the operation, the husky looked completely at ease when they peered into her kennel. The blood bag was empty. Adam lifted the catch of the kennel door. As it swung open, Zoe stood up, shook herself and stretched, then made as if to bound out of the cage. Adam only just caught her in time.

'I think she's feeling better,' he said with a laugh.

Mandy felt almost faint with relief. She had been so worried that Zoe might never return to normal.

'So, will you take her round to Jimmy's, once you're finished with the donkeys?' Adam asked.

For a moment, Mandy didn't know what to say. It hadn't been long since she'd called Jimmy. She really wanted to speak to him before going round. Though he hadn't said he blamed her at any point for her awful mistake, she wasn't sure of her reception.

'I called him earlier,' she said. 'I'm waiting for him to call back.'

Adam was still clinging to the rebounding Zoe. He frowned as he looked up at Mandy. 'But can't you just take her round?' he asked. 'He doesn't blame you, does he? You made a mistake, but it could have happened to anyone.'

He sounded so sure of himself, yet Mandy couldn't dismiss it so easily. She didn't know if Jimmy was angry with her. She wouldn't blame him if he was. She sighed. 'I think he's upset that I went to York and I left Zoe behind.'

Adam had finally wrangled Zoe back into the kennel. He straightened with a frown. 'But she was with us!' he said. 'You needed space,' he paused, '. . . and James,' he added. It was true, Mandy thought. James was a huge part of her life. She needed his help sometimes.

'And has he really not spoken to you since?' Adam frowned. 'Helen didn't say anything.'

Mandy shook her head. 'He hasn't been in touch with me,' she said, 'though to be fair, I haven't called him either until today.'

'Well if you won't take her home, I will,' Adam said. Zoe had gone from trying to escape to licking her new puppy, nuzzling the tiny animal with her nose as she encouraged it to drink. 'There's nothing wrong with her. She doesn't need to be here. I'm going out anyway to check on a calf at Upper Welford Hall. I'll drop her off on the way.'

For a moment, Mandy thought about arguing, but it

would be safer for Zoe and her puppy at home, now she was so much better. There was no way Mum could look after her, and Mandy had to go out to get Holly and Robin ready. 'Thanks, Dad,' she said. She would give Jimmy a call later, she thought. Even if he was angry, she had to face him sooner or later.

James already had Holly and Robin tied up. He was halfway through brushing Robin. For the last time, Mandy picked up the dandy brush to make a start on Holly. The little jenny's winter undercoat was almost gone. Her fur was smooth and healthy-looking. Both donkeys were looking very smart.

There came a shout from the lane as they were finishing up. 'Hello!' Mandy smiled when she saw Susan Collins and her son Jack making their way towards the paddock. Susan was holding Jack's hand, but she let it go as they neared the fence and Jack rushed on ahead, stopping short of the donkeys as he had been taught, but talking to them vociferously.

'Hello Robin. Hello Holly. I've got carrots, how are you today?' he said in a sing-song voice. Mandy found herself smiling. He was so good with them. Holly and Robin loved him too.

'Holly and Robin are getting ready to go to their new home,' Mandy told him.

Jack's face fell very slightly, but he nodded once, his eyes serious. 'Mummy told me they'd be going away,' he said. 'She says we can visit them, though.'

Susan turned back towards them with a smile. 'That's right,' she said, reaching out a hand to ruffle Jack's hair. 'Are they really going today?' she asked, looking at Mandy.

'Yes,' Mandy confirmed. 'In about half an hour, in fact.'

'I'm glad we came, in that case,' Susan said. She watched as Jack pulled out some pieces of carrot and handed them through the fence on the flat of his hand. 'He really does love coming here,' she told Mandy. 'And it's good for him. He's come on so much since we've been visiting.'

'It's lovely to have him.' Mandy walked over and opened the gate. She held out a hand to Jack and he took it readily. If only she had found things this easy with Abi and Max, she thought. Somehow, with Susan there, she and Jack had become used to one another.

'Will you help me with their feet?' she asked, looking down at Jack, whose eyes met hers squarely. He looked delighted.

'Yes please,' he said. He rushed over to the grooming box and lifted out the hoof pick and waved it proudly. Together, they lifted each of Holly's feet in turn, then moved over to do Robin's. Just as they were finishing, there came the sound of wheels on gravel and Peter Warry's trailer drove up to the gate.

'I think we should go,' Susan said. Despite her smile, Mandy could see sadness in her eyes. She too would be sorry to see the two donkeys go.

'Shall I give you a lift?' James offered. 'I'll need to get off as well.' He turned to Mandy and held out his arms. 'Look after yourself,' he said, hugging her tightly.

'Thanks, Mandy, see you soon.' Susan and Jack waved.

'Bye, Holly and Robin,' Jack called. 'I'll visit you soon.' Mandy stood with Holly and Robin as the three of them walked away and Peter Warry climbed out of his lorry.

'Just saying goodbye?' Mr Warry nodded at Susan, Jack and James as they disappeared round the corner of the cottage. He opened the gate and walked over to stand beside Holly, letting her get used to him before reaching out a hand to stroke the soft fur under her ear. 'They're looking marvellous,' he said, taking a step back to look at the two donkeys better. He smiled at Mandy. 'Thanks so much for letting me have them,' he said. 'I know they're going to be a big hit.'

'I've really enjoyed having them here,' Mandy said. 'I've not had that much experience with donkeys before. They really are characters, aren't they?' She reached out a hand and pulled the end of the rope that was holding Holly to the post. The knot came undone and Holly moved towards her. She was so different from the frightened foal Mandy had rescued six months earlier from a suburban garden. Neither of them had liked being handled. She and Seb Conway had almost lifted them into the trailer. Now they walked up the ramp and into Peter Warry's truck without a moment's hesitation. She tied them up in the lorry, patted them both, then walked back down the ramp and turned to take one last look. Holly was already tugging on a hay bag that Peter Warry had brought, but Robin was gazing over his shoulder as if taking one last glance at Mandy and the field where he and Holly had been for so many months.

Between them, Peter Warry and Mandy lifted up the

ramp. Peter held out his hand. 'Thanks, Mandy,' he said. 'I'll take very good care of them.'

'I'm sure you will.' Although she felt a pang at their leaving, that was the most important thing. They were going to a wonderful new home.

'Do come and see us, any time you're over our way,' Peter Warry told her as he climbed the stairs up into the cab.

'I will,' Mandy promised. The truck started with a roar. Peter Warry stuck a hand out of the window to salute as he set off down the road. Mandy stood and watched until the lorry was out of sight.

She walked back towards the rescue centre. There was something she had to do. She picked up the phone and dialled Nicole's number.

Nicole picked up after a couple of rings, sounding nervous. 'Hello?'

'Hi Nicole, it's Mandy,' she paused for a moment, trying to find the right words. 'I'm ringing to apologise to you. I was wrong to snap. There were a lot of things going on that had nothing to do with you and I'm sorry I took it out on you.'

'No, that's okay, Mandy.' Nicole's voice sounded a little wobbly. 'You're so busy and you always have so much on your plate, helping all the animals. I mean Animal Ark *and* Hope Meadows, and I know you've been worrying about the squirrels too. I was just trying to help, but I should have told you.'

'It's fine, honestly,' Mandy said, feeling her heart fill with warmth for her young helper. 'There will be other ways of fundraising, not to worry.'

'Oh yes, I've already looked up a few more grants actually . . .' Nicole started to chatter enthusiastically about her online research. Mandy felt her spirits rise. Her grumpiness hadn't put Nicole off trying again. She really was wonderful.

After she and Nicole hung up, Mandy opened the lid of her laptop, keyed in the password and opened her e-mails. There was one from Jimmy at the top of the screen. Her heart thudded as she saw it. Had he sent her a message when Adam had taken Zoe back? Why wouldn't he just call? The time sent was only a few minutes earlier. Her heart pulsed in her throat as she opened the message. Inside there was a link to an old article in the *Westmorland Gazette*, and a brief message.

I wanted you to see this before we spoke again, it read. *I want you to know you're not alone.*

J

Mandy frowned, but the link looked genuine. She clicked on it and a page opened up.

'Cub Scouts at Risk,' read the headline. There was a picture of some boys in uniform standing in a snowy field with cloud-covered mountains in the background. Why on earth had Jimmy sent it? she wondered. Leaning forward in her chair, she began to read.

'Rescue services were scrambled yesterday when fifteen cub scouts failed to return from a walking trip across Loughrigg Fell,' Mandy read. 'The boys became lost when conditions worsened. The mother of one of the boys expressed her gratitude to the brave volunteers and their team of dogs, who located the group in a hollow near to the summit. Two of the boys were suffering from hypothermia.'

Had Jimmy been part of the rescue team? Did he mean she should be proud of what had happened with the squirrels?

She read on. 'The boys have been taken to hospital,' she read, 'where all are making a good recovery.' There was a list of the names of the handlers and their dogs. She checked through it once, then again. Jimmy's name was not amongst them. She was still no wiser about why he'd sent it. There was some advice about checking the weather, adequate preparation and not going out where conditions were deteriorating. Mandy's eyes came to a standstill on the final line of the piece. She read it carefully. 'Park Ranger, Mr J. Marsh was leading the group at the time of the incident. Investigations are ongoing.'

Mandy felt as if her heart had missed a beat. She read the final line again. Jimmy had been in charge of the group when they'd got lost. That was why he'd sent the link. He had made an awful mistake too and some children had almost died. What had the investigation uncovered? she wondered.

He did understand. She pulled her phone out of her pocket and dialled his number.

'I read your article,' she told him. Her heard was racing.

'Can you come over?' he asked.

'Yes,' she said. 'Oh, yes please.' Shoving her phone back in her pocket, she shut down the computer and rushed outside.

He was waiting for her with open arms at the door of Mistletoe Cottage. Mandy had never made it across the garden so quickly. She rushed into his arms and he bent his head and kissed her. How wonderful he smelled. She had been so afraid that he would never understand, but he had done all along. She buried her face in his shoulder. It felt like home.

'Come on in,' he said, when they finally pulled apart. 'It feels properly like home again, now Zoe's back.' He had tears in his eyes. 'Simba's over the moon. Your dad told me about the blood transfusion. I'll have to get a present for Liz Butler and Emma.' He led her inside and into the sitting room. Zoe was there, in her bed, curled around the tiny pup. She looked up when Mandy and Jimmy came in, but didn't move out of the bed. Beside her, Simba was sitting watching the pair as if utterly entranced. 'He's been like that ever since Zoe came home,' Jimmy told her. He sat her down on the sofa and took his place beside her. 'Your dad told me something else,' he said. 'He said you were worried I wouldn't forgive you for what happened to Zoe.' He paused for a moment, gathering his thoughts. 'I was upset, of course I was, but I never thought it was your fault. It was just one of those awful things.' He paused again. On the far side of the room, Simba gave up on her inspection and lay down close to Zoe with a sigh. 'I'm sorry I didn't get in touch,' Jimmy said. 'You sounded so upset when I called you and you were on your way to see James. I thought you needed a bit of space.'

Mandy felt a laugh rising in her throat, which turned to a sob. The past few days had been so full, but she had missed him all the time. Jimmy put his arm around her again and held her tightly. She rested her forehead on his shoulder for a moment, then pulled herself together. 'So, what about you?' she asked. 'You and the scouts. You were investigated?' She stopped, wondering if the memory would be too painful, but Jimmy looked only resigned.

'I should never have taken them that day,' he said with a shake of his head. 'It looked so beautiful. I thought the weather forecast must be wrong. The fog came down and one of the boys slipped down a scree slope and hurt himself. We had to follow, then we couldn't find our way back.' He sighed. 'I've never forgiven myself,' he admitted, reaching out for Mandy's hand as if looking for comfort. 'We could all have died that day because I wasn't careful enough. I'll never, ever take that kind of risk again.' There was pain in his eyes. 'So, I do understand how it feels, at least a little bit.' He drew in a rather shaky breath as he rubbed her hand with his thumb. 'And I'm so sorry you thought I blamed you. It really didn't cross my mind.'

Mandy held his hand tightly. He was always so practical and careful. It was hard to imagine him making such an error, yet he had. 'And the twins?' It all came back to them, she thought. 'Will they be able to forgive me?' She couldn't blame them if they didn't, but a feeling of helplessness ran through her. It would be awful if they really couldn't.

It was as if a dark shadow crossed Jimmy's face. 'They're still terribly upset,' he admitted. 'What with Belle expecting a baby too, they're a bit fragile at the moment. It'll probably take them a while to get over it.'

Despite having his warm hand still in hers, despite the relief of being back together, Mandy felt sadness wash over her. She had felt like he was pushing her before. She'd wanted more time, but not like this. 'We'll give them as much space as they need,' she said. All she could do was hope that in time, they'd learn she wasn't a monster.

Chapter Twenty-Four

'Hello, is that Mandy, please?'

It was a child's voice on the phone. Mandy looked out of the window. Though it had been a few days, the paddock still looked empty without Holly and Robin. She frowned. The voice was familiar. 'Speaking. Who is this?' she asked.

'It's Abi.' She sounded upset, and Mandy's stomach twisted.

So much for giving the twins a lot of space, she thought, though she couldn't think why Abi would be calling her – did she have a question about Zoe? Weren't the twins with Belle and Dan at the moment? She thought Jimmy had said something about them going to the circus, hoping it would take their minds off the puppies and Belle's baby.

'Is everything okay?' she asked.

'Not really.' Abi's voice was hesitant. Mandy bit her lip. She wanted to press her, but she knew it would be better to wait and listen. 'We're with Mum,' Abi began again after a few moments. 'She brought us to the circus. Max and me.' Mandy could hear noise and voices in the background. Were they still there? 'There's an elephant,' she said. 'We thought it would be just clowns and acrobats and stuff, but there's an elephant and . . . and it doesn't look well.' Another pause. 'Mum thinks so too,' she added.

At the mention of an elephant, Mandy's eyebrows shot up and her mind started working furiously. She had spent some time at university working with a zoo vet, but it was a long time ago. 'Can you tell me what you saw?' she asked Abi. 'In what way does it look ill?'

'It was awfully thin.' Abi seemed on surer ground now she knew Mandy believed her. 'And it looked sad. It made me sad just to see it. Please, Mandy, will you please come and look at it for us?' The final words came out in a breathless rush.

'I'll come right away,' Mandy said. She made her voice as reassuring as she could. 'Where is it?' She jotted down the location Abi told her. It was on the far side of Walton. 'All right, I'm on my way. I'm glad you called me,' she added.

She felt a small tremor run through her body as she put the phone down. For Abi's sake, she had tried to sound confident, but just hearing about a sick circus elephant was distressing, and she knew so little about the animals. Finding out what was wrong would be a major challenge. Still, she would have more idea than Abi and Max, or even Belle, she reminded herself. And if she didn't know, she would find someone who did.

She called Seb Conway as she was leaving. From what Abi had said, it sounded like a welfare issue, even if a rather oversized one. Seb had the authority that would allow them to do whatever was necessary. He answered on the first ring and agreed to come. She felt a little calmer as she set out. Seb hadn't sounded at all phased by the idea of being called out to see an elephant. Between them, they would manage.

It was a very traditional-looking circus, Mandy thought as she drew up in the field beside the big top. The huge tent was brightly coloured in red and white stripes. Bunting fluttered from every rope. Crowds of people were pouring from the entrance. She located Seb near the fence that divided the parking area from the field where the tents and lorries stood.

'Everything okay?' he asked.

'Apart from that I've never treated an elephant in my life?' She grinned.

Seb grimaced, though his eyes were amused. 'Apart from that!'

'Well, in that case,' Mandy said, 'everything is absolutely great.' Side by side, they made their way towards the entrance.

Abi and Max were standing with Belle beside one of the enormous wooden pegs that held the guy ropes down.

'Hello,' Mandy said to Abi and Max, then smiled at Belle. They had never spoken before, and it felt distinctly odd to be meeting Jimmy's ex-wife at the circus, with her children and an elephant. She was a beautician, Mandy knew, and she had once been worried that Belle would be terribly glamorous, and she would feel out of place in her wellies, jeans and sensible jumpers.

But though Belle was well dressed and glowing from her pregnancy, she otherwise looked quite normal. Mandy noticed that she had long nails – probably stick-on – that'd been painted in circus-style red and white stripes.

'I don't think we've met.' Belle smiled at Mandy. 'Abi and Max were so worried. Thanks so much for coming.'

'I just hope I can help,' Mandy said. 'Can you tell me more about the elephant?'

Belle looked troubled. 'Poor thing,' she said. 'It only came out for the big finale, but it really didn't look as if it wanted to be there.'

Abi's mouth was turned down. 'It's not fair,' she said, 'making it work when it's not feeling well.' She sounded fierce.

'It was really thin.' It was Max's turn to speak. 'Will you be able to make it better?' He and Abi were both gazing up at her.

Mandy's heart swelled. She'd expected that they would have no faith in her after Zoe, yet both of them were regarding her with trust, as if Max's question was only a formality.

'I'll do my best,' she said.

The ticket office stood to the right of the entrance under a huge sign that proclaimed it to be Courtney's Travelling Circus. An older woman sat behind the glass, her hair piled up on her head with a tiny glittery hat perched on top. She reached out and opened the window with a smile as Mandy and Seb approached.

'Tickets for tomorrow night?' she offered. 'Extra-long showing for Saturday evening. Last night available.'

'Sorry.' Seb was invariably polite, Mandy thought. 'I'm afraid we're not looking for tickets. We've had a report about the welfare of your elephant. We'd like to have a look at him, please. Is it possible to speak to the owner?'

The grin had disappeared from the woman's face and for a moment, Mandy thought she would refuse. Seb stood there in his uniform, a picture of immovable patience. Mandy almost wanted to laugh. With a sigh, the woman stood up. 'Just wait here a moment,' she said and disappeared.

She turned round. Belle and the twins had followed, and all their eyes were fixed on Mandy. Mandy felt uneasy. If the owner kicked off, it might not be a pretty sight. 'They probably won't be too happy to see us,' she murmured to Belle. 'It's probably better if you all go home and wait.' She had kept her voice low, but Abi overheard.

'We can't go home,' she objected, her eyes beseeching. 'I want to see if the elephant's okay.'

'We have to see how he gets on,' Max added. He reached out and took his mum's hand.

Belle looked worried. 'Do you really think they might be angry?' she asked Mandy.

Mandy looked down at Abi and Max and they gazed back at her. No wonder they wanted to stay, she thought. They were worried. She rubbed her chin, then crouched down. She held out a hand to each of them and after only a moment's pause, both Abi and Max reached out their hands to her. She held on tightly as she spoke. 'I know

284

how much you want to see how the elephant is,' she said. 'But Seb and I need to speak to his owner on our own. He'll probably be upset when we tell him his elephant isn't well.' To her amazement, the two sets of green eyes were regarding her with respect. 'I think it would be better for you to go home for now,' she went on, 'but I promise you both,' she looked straight into Abi's eyes, then Max's, 'that I'll call you as soon as I know anything. And if there's anything you can do to help, I will let you know.' Taking a deep breath, she straightened.

Slowly the twins nodded.

Belle was smiling. 'Thank you,' she mouthed.

Mandy watched as the twins and Belle trailed away across the field. She was glad they'd called her, but relieved they were going. If things turned nasty, it was better they didn't see.

The owner was younger than Mandy had expected. For some reason, she had imagined a wizened old man, but the person who strode towards them was as tall as Mandy herself and only a little older. He came to a standstill and held out his hand. 'I'm Mike Courtney,' he said. 'I under-stand you've received a report about Ganesh.' There was no anger in his voice. If anything, he looked nervous. He cleared his throat as he shook hands with Mandy and then Seb.

'If Ganesh is your elephant,' Seb replied, 'then yes. Is it possible for us to see him or her, please?'

Mike Courtney inclined his head very slightly, then turned and indicated that they should follow him. 'This way,' he said.

He led them round the side of the big top. The field was crammed with all kinds of caravans and lorries. It must be a huge task for them to move every few days, Mandy thought. Close to the edge of the grass, in the shade of a tall hedgerow stood a long, white painted trailer. A line of small windows ran along the top edge. There were large double doors in the side, which stood open. Inside, a row of bars blocked the elephant from escaping. They stood back for a moment to inspect it from a distance. It didn't look very high, Mandy thought. Not for something as large as an elephant. Nor was it any wider than a normal lorry, though it was long.

They walked closer and climbed up onto a round step that had been placed outside the door. Despite the windows and the large opening, it was near dark in the furthest corner of the trailer. Mike Courtney stepped down. 'I'll let you in,' he said. He opened a small door at the front of the trailer and led them inside. Although it was small, the trailer was very clean. Fresh water stood in a deep container. There was a rack filled with healthy-looking hay and a large bowl containing cabbage, lettuce and apples as well as a bucket filled with pellets. Ganesh stood in the far corner. He didn't move as Seb reached down and picked up one of the lettuces. It looked fresh. 'We've been trying to tempt him,' Mr Courtney explained, 'but he just isn't hungry.'

'How is he to handle?' Mandy asked. She didn't want to approach if it would distress the poor creature. Even in the dim light of the trailer she could see that Ganesh was, as Max had said, terribly thin. His ribs were standing out under the grooved grey skin. The bones of his face were prominent too. Elephants were highly social animals, Mandy knew. She wondered what was going through Ganesh's mind as he stood there with his head drooping.

'He's very well behaved actually. He's always been very friendly.' Mandy found herself looking at Mr Courtney. She had worried he would be defensive, but as he gazed at the elephant, he looked only sad and rather helpless.

A wave of irritation rose inside her. 'Has a vet looked at him?' she asked. Feeling sorry was all very well, but why hadn't he called someone?

'We did try,' Mr Courtney replied. He cleared his throat again. 'None of them would come. They all said they didn't know anything about elephants.' He gave a tiny shake of his head. 'We even tried to rehome him. Before he went off his food, I mean. I inherited the show from my dad,' he said. He walked over and laid his hand on Ganesh's shoulder. For the first time, the elephant moved, reaching round with his trunk, but after a moment, he let it fall and his head drooped again. Mr Courtney stayed where he was, as if he didn't want to remove his hand. 'I thought at first that we could just keep him, but that was six years ago. It causes no end of complaints that we have him at all, but I have tried to do the best I can.' As he finished speaking, he looked almost as depressed as Ganesh. He probably had done his best, Mandy thought. Her burst of anger had dispersed almost as fast as it had risen.

Mandy had never examined an elephant before. With Mike Courtney's guidance, she crossed the trailer. Ganesh's skin was smoother and firmer than she had expected. His small eyes were sunken and they gazed dully into the distance. He reached out his trunk to her, exploring for a moment. The end of it was dry. Should it be moist like a dog or a cow? Mandy didn't know.

He was very still, she thought. After his brief exploration, he didn't move again. Worst of all, there was a horrible smell, which seemed to linger around his head. On Mike Courtney's prompting, Ganesh opened his mouth. Though it was too dark to see clearly, the stench rolled over her. There was something very wrong. 'I think he might have an infected tooth,' she said after a moment. The big elephant closed his mouth and the awful smell diminished a little. Mandy reached out her hand and stroked Ganesh's trunk. He didn't object, but he showed no sign that he enjoyed it either. He really did seem very sorry for himself. With a last glance, Mandy walked back over to Seb and together, they climbed back down and onto the grass. Mike Courtney stayed behind. Mandy glanced back as she climbed down and he had his arms stretched round as if trying to hug his oversized charge.

'So, what do you think?' Seb asked as soon they were out of earshot.

'I think we need an elephant expert,' Mandy replied with a frown. She looked across the now empty field thinking as hard as she could.

'Didn't you say the man with the llama at the show had a friend who ran a safari park?' Seb asked.

'He did.' Mandy's mind went back to the day of the show and Polly Cormac. She surely must know of a vet who was used to treating zoo animals. 'Give me a minute,' she said to Seb, 'I'll just give Peter a call and see if I can get the number.'

'Tony Simons, elephant expert extraordinaire is on his way,' she announced to Seb a few minutes later, then she added with a sigh, 'unfortunately he won't be here for at least an hour.'

She half expected Seb to say he couldn't wait that long, but he just shrugged. 'Well, it's not as if I've got anything better to do,' he said with a grin.

When Mike Courtney heard help was on its way, he seemed more grateful than ever.

'I really do appreciate it,' he said. 'Like I said before, Dad left me the circus. He loved his animals, my dad. I did too, but I could see the world was changing. There used to be sea lions and tigers as well as horses and dogs. We've rehomed all of them, but I couldn't find anyone to take Ganesh. He's lovely and quiet, but he's a bull elephant. Nobody could find space.' He sighed, his thoughts obviously filled with memories. 'I thought he'd see his days out with us, but I hadn't realised just how long they can live. He's only twenty-five . . .' he trailed off, his face miserable. 'I'll pay for the vet's fees,' he said a few moments later, 'but I don't know what we'll do afterwards. If I could stay here with him, I would, but we have to go.'

Mandy felt her sympathy for him grow. She couldn't take Ganesh either. He could hardly live in the paddock at Hope Meadows. 'We'll ask Mr Simons if he can think of anything when he comes,' she said. She found herself hoping that perhaps Polly Cormac might know of someone, but it was a very long shot.

Mandy was relieved when the ticket office woman re-appeared to say that Tony Simons had arrived. He was a very tall, thin man with a grey beanie hat sitting on top of his black hair. In a procession, they walked back round and climbed up into Ganesh's trailer. Mandy listened as Tony asked Mike all kinds of questions about how long it had been since Ganesh had begun to go off his food, how much he was drinking and whether his faeces had changed.

Unlike Mandy, there was no hesitation in his examination. The thermometer seemed tiny against the huge body. He listened to the enormous chest with his stethoscope. Looking round, he pulled the earpieces from his ears and held them out to Mandy. She slipped them into her own ears and stood listening to the slow beat of the elephant's heart. 'Good and strong,' he assured her. Finally, he made his way to Ganesh's head. He peered into the elephant's mouth using a head torch. It reminded Mandy of her session with Bill the shire horse when she had examined his teeth in the autumn. 'We'll have to sedate him before we can do any proper work,' Tony said. 'But he has an impacted molar. It looks infected. No wonder he's not keen to eat, poor lad.'

'Will you be able to do that here?' Mandy asked. She was trying to imagine laying out the massive body on the grass. There would be no way to restrain Ganesh if he started to thrash about.

'No.' Tony smiled. 'I'll have to give Polly a call to see if she can give us a hand. She has a special enclosure she'll hopefully let us use. What about afterwards, though? He can't come back here.' He looked around as if hoping someone would present him with a solution.

'I'm afraid I don't have any answers to that,' Mandy admitted. This was going to be the hardest part, she thought. 'Do you think Polly might know anyone?' she asked.

Tony looked worried. 'I don't know,' he said. 'I can ask, but it isn't easy to rehome bull elephants.'

It was a tense wait while Tony was on the phone to Polly Cormac. Mike Courtney seemed particularly edgy, shuffling his feet and clearing his throat so often that Mandy wanted to put her fingers in her ears. Tony returned with a huge smile. 'Polly's going to help,' he told them. 'Not just with the operation, but she'll find a place for him as well.'

It was a wonderful moment. Mandy wished she could call and tell the twins what was happening, but it would have to wait for later.

'Right,' Tony's voice brought her back to earth. 'Polly can't take him till tomorrow, and I really would like him to eat something before his trip.' For a horrible moment, Mandy wondered if he was going to suggest they try to force-feed Ganesh, but Tony laughed when she asked. 'No,' he explained. 'I want to give him some pain relief. I'm pretty sure he'll eat by himself.'

Mandy watched Tony again as he prepared Ganesh for his injection. With Mike's encouragement, the big elephant lay down on his side. 'We inject into the triceps muscle,' Tony told her, showing her the area on the outside of Ganesh's front leg. 'Elephants get abscesses really easily, so we need to clean it thoroughly.' He gave the area a good scrub, then disinfected it as if for an operation. Ganesh needed several injections. 'Just as well he's quiet,' Tony said. He shook hands with them all once he was finished. 'Make sure he's got plenty of fresh food and water overnight,' he told Mike. He looked round at them all with his wide grin. 'And I'll see you all in the morning,' he said.

Remembering her promise to the twins, Mandy called them as soon as she was home. Belle answered. 'I'll put you on to Abi,' she said.

Mandy could hear speaking in the background, then Abi's voice, sounding breathless. 'Is the elephant going to be okay?' she gasped.

She sounds like a younger me!

'I think he is,' Mandy replied. She found herself smiling as she spoke. 'His name is Ganesh. He's got bad toothache at the moment, but we called an elephant vet and he's given him some medicine that will help. We've also found a new home for him at a safari park. He's going there tomorrow to have his tooth out.'

'What will happen then? Can he stay there? He won't have to go back to the circus, will he?' Abi still sounded worried.

Mandy wished she could reach through the phone to give her a hug. 'He can stay there for the rest of his life,' she said.

There was a pause on the phone. She could hear voices

again: Max's then Belle's. Then Abi spoke again. 'Max wants to know if we can come with you when you move Ganesh tomorrow,' she said. 'Can we do that? *Please!*'

Mandy wanted to laugh. She and James would have wanted the same thing all those years ago.

'I think we'll need to check with your mum,' Mandy replied after a moment. She hoped Belle didn't feel she was being put on the spot.

'Will you ask her then, please? I'll put the phone on speaker,' Abi said.

'It's fine as far as I'm concerned,' Belle said, once Mandy had explained. 'But actually, they're with Jimmy tomorrow, so he'll have to have the final word.'

'Well, in that case,' Mandy said, 'I'll call and ask him.'

A burst of cheering down the phone. Jimmy would say yes, she thought, and they knew it. Abi and Max had him wrapped around their little fingers. She found herself grinning as she ended the call. For once, it felt wonderful to be on the same side.

Chapter Twenty-Five

The sun had just appeared over the horizon as Jimmy and the twins drove into the parking space at Animal Ark. Jimmy yawned and then apologised. Abi and Max were wide awake. All three of them were dressed in jeans and boots, as was Mandy.

'Will we able to stroke the elephant?' Max asked as they walked out to her car.

'His name is Ganesh,' Abi reminded him. Her tone was so serious that Mandy wanted to laugh. She opened the rear door and Abi scrambled in.

'Well, will we be able to stroke Ganesh then?' Max looked up at Mandy, his green eyes filled with hope.

Mandy smiled. 'I can't guarantee it, but I'll see what I can do,' she said. 'You'll have to be very, very quiet, though,' she went on as Max climbed in. They put their seat belts on as soon as they got in. Mandy climbed into the driver's seat.

As she had hoped, they arrived at the circus a few minutes before Polly was due. Mike Courtney was already up and waiting, smartly dressed and wide awake. He strode towards them.

'Morning!'

'Morning, Mr Courtney. How is he doing?' Mandy asked.

Mike Courtney looked pleased. 'Pretty good, actually.' He crouched down to talk to the twins with a smile. 'And who are you?'

'I'm Abi and this is my brother Max. We've come to see Ganesh,' Abi replied. 'Mummy brought us to see your circus yesterday, but we were worried about him,' she continued.

Mandy wondered for a moment whether Mr Courtney might be annoyed if he thought they had been the ones to report him, but his smile only widened.

'Well, then I have to say thank you to you both.' He looked first at Max, then Abi. 'I couldn't find a new home for him and now Mandy here,' he glanced up at her, then back to the twins, 'she's found him one.' With a final grin, he stood up again and reached out a hand to Jimmy. 'Good to meet you,' he said. When they had shaken hands, he looked down again at Abi and Max. 'So, let's go and see Ganesh!'

Abi and Max were almost jumping up and down.

'You will remember you need to be really quiet,' Jimmy cautioned. 'When the new trailer comes, Ganesh needs to be really calm and he'll only manage it if you can too.'

Abi and Max immediately quieted. Mandy glanced at Jimmy, who was smiling down at the twins. Catching her eye, he reached out and squeezed her hand for the briefest moment. His touch warmed her. They followed round to Ganesh's trailer in silence.

The double doors in the side of the trailer were open still and the platform that Ganesh would step on when they moved him was in place. Abi and Max climbed up to look in through the bars that spanned the doorway. Mandy was amazed by the change in Ganesh. She had almost been afraid to hope that he would eat, but even as they watched, he pulled some hay from the rack with his trunk, put it in his mouth and began to chew. His eyes had brightened and were no longer sunken. The anxious look was gone.

'He looks much better,' Max whispered, gazing at Mandy with shining eyes.

As if he had heard, Ganesh turned from his hay rack, walked over to greet them and reached through the bars with his trunk. Beside Mandy, Max's eyes were on stalks. Abi gasped with delight as the elephant delicately touched her hair, but then remembering she had to be quiet, she looked up at Mandy with huge eyes. Mandy grinned at her. Reassured, Abi put her hand out to touch the rough grey skin.

'Isn't he lovely?' Max whispered as he too reached out a hand. He sighed as if it was almost too wonderful to bear.

Ganesh turned his attention to Mandy's hand. The end of his trunk was moist where yesterday it had been dry.

Even Mike Courtney seemed entranced. 'He's just like his old self,' he said. 'He's eaten and drunk plenty. It's like a miracle.'

The sound of a lorry approaching heralded Polly's arrival. To Mandy's amazement, the extra-wide van came complete with two police cars, one in front and one following.

The policeman in the front car opened his door and got out. Mandy recognised Dan Jones, Belle's husband. She wondered for a moment whether it would be awkward when he and Jimmy were together, but the two men greeted one another courteously.

'Good to see you,' Dan said with a polite nod. 'Belle said the twins were hoping to come along.'

Abi and Max rushed over, looking up at Dan with excitement. 'We got to stroke Ganesh,' Abi said.

'His trunk's amazing,' Max added.

Dan grinned down at them. 'I'm glad to hear it,' he said. He squeezed both Abi and Max on their shoulders, then turned as Polly Cormac came towards them. She was dressed in frayed jeans and a patched sweater, but her blue eyes were filled with warmth. She stopped in front of them, putting her hands on her hips.

'Hello there, Ganesh. How's he doing?' she asked, looking from Mike to Mandy.

'He's eaten well,' Mike said.

Mandy nodded. 'He seems much better,' she said.

'That's good.' Polly gave an approving nod of her head. 'Right then,' she declared. 'We'd better get on.'

Mandy was amazed by the purpose-built truck Polly owned. The interior was temperature controlled and there was a camera inside to monitor how the elephant was doing. Ganesh was used to travelling, but this time he would be going in style. Mike Courtney helped them load the huge animal into the new trailer. Ganesh was very obedient and followed Mike straight in.

Of course, he's done this hundreds of times, thought Mandy.

Though he was obviously pleased for Ganesh, there was sadness in Mike's eyes as he closed the trailer doors.

'Are you okay?' Mandy asked him.

Mike lifted one shoulder in a half-shrug. 'I'll miss him,' he admitted with a sigh. 'He was my old dad's favourite, but it's great that he's going to a better life. Thank you so much for everything you've done.' He wrung Mandy's hand as well as Polly's. He rubbed Max's hair and patted Abi on the shoulder. 'Maybe you'll come and see us again, next time we're in town.'

The procession set off towards the safari park. Dan's police car was in the lead, then Ganesh in his truck with Polly driving. The second police car tucked itself in behind the trailer. Last of all came Mandy's RAV4 with Jimmy, Abi and Max. They had to drive very slowly on the narrow country roads. It took almost double the usual time for them to reach Welford. They passed the oak tree that marked the village boundary, and in a few moments, they passed through the centre of the village. Mandy was amazed to see a few people lining the road. Susan and Jack Collins, Harriet Fallon with her triplets, and Mandy's own grandparents as well as several others.

'Looks like news has spread!' said Mandy, waving at them all.

'Who was that with Susan?' Jimmy asked, once they were past.

'Harriet Fallon,' Mandy told him. 'She was the one who told me about Sam Western and all the councillors meeting.'

The Fox and Goose caught her eye as they passed. Mandy felt a shiver run through her, remembering her awful discussion with Sam and all the Animal Ark clients who had been angry.

Jimmy turned to look out of the window as if wondering what she'd seen, then turned back. 'Are you all right?' he asked.

Mandy sighed. 'Mostly,' she said. 'It's great that we found the squirrels, but lots of other people were angry. They wanted the factory to go ahead. They thought I was interfering.'

Jimmy looked suitably outraged. Mandy caught his expression from the corner of her eye and felt her heart lift. 'You did the right thing,' he said. 'It'll all be forgotten in a few weeks. They'll come round.'

Mandy found herself smiling. It was lovely to have Jimmy there to reassure her.

'Were people angry with you about the squirrels?' Max's voice piped up from the back. In the mirror, she could see his earnest eyes looking at her.

'I'm afraid they were,' she said. 'It wasn't really the squirrels they were angry about, though. They were hoping the new factory would bring some jobs to Welford.'

'But it wasn't *your* fault there were squirrels where they wanted to build the factory.' Abi sounded almost as affronted as Jimmy.

'And you saved our squirrel,' Max said.

'For the second time!' added Abi. Jimmy looked at Mandy as if wondering whether she would object to this version of events, but Mandy just smiled at him.

It took quite a while to reach the safari park. They had to drive very slowly, but they finally arrived. Jimmy looked round as they drove past the open entrance gates. 'Polly told us to follow them,' Mandy said. 'We're going in through a back entrance rather than the way that visitors normally go.'

'Oh. Okay, good.' Jimmy turned in his seat to face Abi and Max, his face serious. 'When we get out,' he warned them, looking at first one, then the other, 'we're all going to have to be very quiet. Ganesh is used to travelling, but his old owner isn't here. I expect he'll be scared. It's very important we don't do anything to upset him. If either of you gets noisy, you'll have to sit in the car until the unloading's finished. Understand?' He gazed at them both in turn and they looked back at him and nodded.

'Yes, Dad,' Max said.

'Of course.' Abi agreed.

Jimmy smiled as if satisfied. 'Good,' he said.

'Are you looking forward to seeing where he's going to live?' Mandy asked.

They both nodded, their faces solemn. They were obviously taking Jimmy very seriously. He must be very proud of them, she thought.

'It doesn't look very nice.' Max was obviously trying to keep the disappointment out of his voice, but he didn't quite manage it. The trailer had come to a standstill outside a smallish enclosure surrounded by a high fence. There was nothing in the pen, though beyond it there was a huge building that looked a bit like a modern cattle shed. It had a gently sloping roof and wooden slatted sides.

Polly Cormac strode towards them. 'Glad to see you got here safely,' she said. 'He had a good journey. We're going to unload him now. Tony's arrived too,' she added.

'Is he going to live in there?' Abi asked Polly, pointing at the shed.

'No, he isn't.' Polly smiled. 'This is where Tony is going to take Ganesh's bad tooth out. His enclosure is over there.' Mandy looked over to where she was pointing. There was a large grassy area filled with trees and bushes. Tyres hung from the trees on ropes. It looked lovely. Polly was speaking again. 'We're going to take him inside,' she explained, 'then Tony'll anaesthetise him, then take his tooth out. There's a viewing area. Do you want to watch?'

There was a collective intake of breath from Abi and Max. Mandy felt quite breathless herself. It would be fascinating to see Tony at work. Working with Ganesh was very different from anything she did, even with her 'large' animal work.

'That would be wonderful,' Jimmy said, 'wouldn't it, you two?' His eyes were sparkling. He was just as excited as they were, Mandy thought.

'Well then, if you can stay back for the moment, we'll take him inside. Tony will get him sedated and then someone will come to fetch you once it's safe,' Polly told them. She nodded as if satisfied. With a quick grin, she left them standing beside the car and began to unlock the heavy metal gates of the pen. Another two park wardens appeared. Between them, they opened up the gates and bolted them to the sides of the trailer. It all looked very sturdy, Mandy thought. Polly did a final check that everything was secure, then between them, they opened the large side door of the truck. Mandy, Jimmy and the twins stood and watched as Ganesh slowly appeared, first his trunk, as if feeling his way, then his head and then he was making his way down the ramp with a warden at each side.

He stopped halfway down, then reached out with his trunk to examine the bars at the side of the ramp. The wardens stood at his elbows. How still they were, Mandy thought. She half expected them to urge him, but they let the huge creature explore. When he began to move his feet again, they moved with him. There was no hurry. It was as if they had all the time in the world. Once he was in the pen, they closed the big gates behind him. Without haste, they opened the huge sliding door that led into the shed. Step by slow step, they guided the elephant inside and then the door slid closed.

The viewing room was painted blue. The walls on either side went most of the way up to the roof, but straight ahead there was a chest-high wall. Beyond it, there was a brightly lit area. Mandy walked to the viewing wall and looked over. Ganesh lay asleep on the ground. There were even more people around him than there had been earlier. She watched as they began to ready Ganesh for his operation. Tony directed one of the helpers to pull open his bottom jaw, while another held his head in place. Another still was handed a flat metal hook to hold the side of Ganesh's mouth out of the way.

Mandy looked round to see how the twins were. Though she and Jimmy were tall enough to look over the wall easily, Abi and Max were having to scrabble upwards. Even standing on their toes, they could only just see over.

'I'll lift you so you can see,' Jimmy promised, 'but I can only manage one at a time. Abi, you were first on the trampoline last week, so now it's Max's turn.'

Abi made no objection. She seemed to have taken Jimmy's instructions about being quiet very seriously indeed. Mandy smiled at her. To her surprise, after a moment's hesitation, Abi came over and looked straight up. 'Mandy,' she said. 'Please could you lift me, so I can see too?'

Mandy felt a glow of happiness rising inside her. Only a few days ago, she had been worried that Abi and Max would never forgive her, and here they were all together. Not only that, but Abi trusted her enough to ask for help. 'Of course I will,' she replied. She lifted Abi and joined Jimmy and Max and they looked over the wall in a row. Mandy risked a glance across at Jimmy as Tony wielded the largest dental drill she had ever seen. Jimmy grinned at her, nodding towards Abi, who was clinging to Mandy's neck, utterly engrossed. Mandy grinned back. Maybe everything was going to work out after all.

Chapter Twenty-Six

'So that's it then?' Helen had been there when Mandy's phone rang, and Mandy had made no attempt to stop her overhearing.

Mandy couldn't wipe the grin from her face. She had hoped for good news, and now here it was. 'Plaster, heating, plumbing, electrics, all complete!' Wildacre was finished at last. She glanced at the clock. It was almost lunchtime. 'Can you manage without me for a few minutes?' she asked. 'I'll be back before afternoon surgery. I've got my mobile.'

'Of course we can.' Helen's smile was almost as wide as Mandy's. She knew how long Mandy had been waiting for this moment. 'Lucy,' she called to her beloved flatcoat retriever. 'I'll just pop Lucy out and then I'm all yours,' she said.

Mandy was still beaming as she walked up the garden path to her new home fifteen minutes later. There had been wildflowers growing all the way up the lane. There were flowers in the garden too, tall blue irises and vibrant garden pinks. Butterflies fluttered on a patch of round-headed allium flowers. It was still half wild, but so different from the mossy dereliction of a few months ago.

She pushed open the newly painted front door and stepped inside. The hallway was bright and welcoming. The Yorkshire stone floor had been scrubbed. The plaster was smooth under the cream paint. She flicked the light switch. The bulb came on and she flicked it off again. It still felt like a miracle that everything was ready and working. She started in the sitting room with its rosy brick fireplace, then made her way back to the little bathroom at the back of the house, all tiled in white. Upstairs, both bedrooms were perfect. She had bought a double bed for the master bedroom and two singles for the smaller room in case of visitors.

My own home!

She made her way back down to the kitchen. She would have lunch here today, she decided. She had brought up a few things already. There was soup in the cupboard and the scrubbed oak table and chairs were good as new. She pulled her phone out of her pocket. She wanted to share this moment with Jimmy.

She glanced round the kitchen twenty minutes later when she heard his car arriving. There was a pan of soup bubbling on the fully functioning stove. She had asked Jimmy to bring rolls and butter. She had been out in the garden and had cut a few flowers. They stood in a washed-out coffee jar in the middle of the table. The sun was shining in at the window. Everything was perfect.

He was standing on the doorstep when she opened the door, wearing a light blue shirt with the sleeves rolled up and open at the neck. He was getting quite tanned, she thought. No wonder when he worked outside every day. In each hand he held a blue plastic bag, but as soon as he saw her, he dropped them on the step, opened his arms and wrapped them around her. Fresh air and the scent of flowers mingled with his aftershave. His stubble felt rough against her cheek as she held him tight against her body.

'Congratulations,' he whispered.

She sighed as they pulled apart. 'Come in,' she said. 'The soup's ready.'

He lifted the bags again and walked inside, putting them on the table in the kitchen. 'Smells good,' he said, sniffing appreciatively.

He pulled out a bag of mini-baguettes, put them on the oven shelf then straightened with a smile. 'I brought a housewarming cake,' he said. He reached into the second of the blue bags. It was a delicious-looking chocolate cake and he set it on the table next to some butter and a chunk of cheese. Bags emptied, he walked towards her. 'Going to take me on the grand tour?' he asked.

Mandy went from room to room again. It was even better with Jimmy there to admire the clean walls, the new-painted window frames and even the carpets. He took her in his arms as they arrived back in the kitchen. 'It's lovely,' he said. 'Almost as lovely as you.' He paused for a moment as his eyes roved the room, taking in the beautifully painted cupboards and the bubbling soup on the stove. 'There's just one problem.'

Mandy stiffened. He still had his arms around her, but

she leaned away slightly to look at him. Was there really something wrong? 'What is it?' she asked.

Jimmy grinned. He looked almost sheepish. 'Well,' he said, 'I'd planned to ask you to move into Mistletoe Cottage with me until this place was ready.' He glanced round the kitchen again. 'And now,' he said, 'it seems I've left it too late. I must remember not to drag my heels next time.'

Mandy felt the flutter of butterflies in her stomach. He'd wanted her to move in with him? That would have been wonderful.

It could still be, she thought. 'Maybe . . . one day, not tomorrow, but if you want to, in the future . . . you could move in here instead,' she suggested. 'You know, there's a spare room I haven't really touched yet, so there'd be room for Abi and Max, if you did. They could decorate it however they like. And there's more room for the dogs,' she added, with a slightly nervous grin.

Jimmy looked at her, his face serious at first, then breaking into a warm smile that lit up his eyes. 'I'll have to check with Abi and Max,' he said, 'but so long as they're happy, I'd love to.'

Mandy wrapped her arms even more tightly round his waist. She could feel his slow, steady heart, beating against hers. It had been a long time since she had felt this happy.

They sat down at the table to eat. The crusty rolls and cheese were perfect with the tomato soup she'd prepared.

'Abi and Max would love this,' Jimmy told her. 'Tomato soup's one of their favourite things.'

Mandy smiled, surprised to find it was quite easy to imagine the twins sitting at the Wildacre kitchen table, playing with the dogs. She paused with her spoon halfway to her mouth. 'How are they?' she asked. She hadn't seen them since they had watched Ganesh having his tooth taken out, just over a week ago. 'No nightmares about enormous dental drills or anything?'

Jimmy laughed. 'Luckily no,' he said.

'He's doing well by the way. Ganesh, I mean,' Mandy said. Polly Cormac had called to say the elephant had settled in well and was eating again without having to have painkillers.

'That's great,' he said, 'and the twins are fine.' He paused for a moment with his eyes on her. He looked pleased, she thought. It was lovely to be able to talk about Abi and Max and for them both to feel completely relaxed.

They finished lunch, then parted at the front door with a kiss.

'I'll call you tomorrow,' Jimmy said. 'When would be a good time?'

'I'm going to release Frank in the evening,' Mandy told him. 'Would you like to come? James is coming over with Raj.' She was looking forward to setting the owl free. He appeared to have made a full recovery. She had removed the stitches and had been watching him closely for the past two days. It would be lovely to see him fly out in the open.

Jimmy sighed. 'I'm afraid I've a group coming for an evening ramble,' he said, 'but good luck. I'll try to catch you before you go.' He waved as he drove off and a few minutes later, Mandy set off back to Animal Ark.

* * *

Adam and Mandy tackled the early afternoon surgery together. Though Mandy had been working harder than ever since Emily had been taken ill, she was still nervous that something would go wrong after her awful mistake with Zoe. Adam had been very patient with her, encouraging her to take things on alone, but she still felt more confident when he was there.

She hadn't told him about Wildacre yet. She wanted to tell her mum and dad together. She had sworn Helen to secrecy, hugging the secret to herself. If they finished early, it would be the ideal opportunity, she thought.

Adam came to her, just as the last client closed the door. 'All done?' he said.

'Yes,' Mandy replied. She took a deep breath. 'Dad, I've something to tell you and Mum. Have you got time?'

Adam stood very still for a moment. 'Yes,' he said, 'but actually I wanted you to come in for a cup of tea. There's something we need to discuss. All of us together.' Mandy felt her breathing quicken. What did they want to talk about? Though they often sat down together, it was rare for Dad to ask like this. Was it bad or good? She tried to read his expression, but there was nothing in his face to indicate. There was a pulse beating in her throat.

'What is it? Is it about Mum?'

'Come into the house and we'll talk there,' he told her, and set off for the door. There was nothing Mandy could do but follow.

She was startled to find not only Mum, but Gran and Grandad sitting around the table in the kitchen. There was a cake on the table and cups and saucers and her heart slowed a little. It couldn't be anything desperately urgent if there had been time to prepare cake and tea.

Grandad smiled up at her. She could see from his expression that he didn't know what was coming either, but he seemed happy enough. He patted the seat beside him. 'You come and sit here, love,' he said. Gran lifted the teapot and began to pour the tea.

Mandy sat down beside her grandfather and Adam took the chair beside Emily. It was hard to take her eyes off her parents. It had to be something important for them to gather everyone like this. All the colours in the kitchen suddenly seemed too bright: the blue of Emily's favourite mug, the orange glaze on the pots hanging above the stove.

Mum looked across the table straight at Mandy, then glanced at Gran and Grandad. 'I've some news I want to tell you all,' she said. She smiled, glancing down at her tea, then back up. 'You all know I've not been well for a while. Now I have a diagnosis.'

Mandy's heart was racing again. She pushed her shoulders back and breathed slowly in and out. She needed to be calm for Emily's sake.

'Apparently, I have multiple sclerosis,' Emily said. She paused to look around. There was a small gasp from Gran. Mandy's fingers were shaking. Grandad reached out a hand and grasped her hand under the table. 'I can see you're all shocked,' Emily went on, 'but I've known for a few days and it's actually a relief to know what's happening.'

How can it be a relief?

Mandy tried to think of what she knew about multiple sclerosis, but her mind was blank and fuzzy. All she could think was why was this happening to Mum? She had always been the healthy one: the one who looked after everyone else and would admit no weakness. She wanted to speak, but how? She couldn't think of a single reassuring thing to say.

Emily sent a gentle smile across the table to Mandy, as if offering comfort. This was the wrong way round, Mandy thought. She should be the one offering support. 'I know it's a shock,' Emily said, 'but I've read a lot in the last few days. It's not as bad as I thought when they first told me. They think I have what's called the relapsing remitting form, so with treatment, I might be almost as good as new for quite a while. I've looked it up and most people who have it live almost as long as those without.'

Under the table, Grandad gripped Mandy's hand more tightly. His touch was reassuring. Was Emily just making light of things? she wondered. Mandy knew so little about MS that she couldn't tell. 'I've seen a specialist and have an MS nurse,' Emily went on. 'They say that for now I can continue to work a bit. But they also said I had to try to sleep at regular times, so I won't be able to do on-call. I also don't want you two . . .' she glanced from Adam to Mandy, '. . . to find yourselves overloaded every time I'm feeling under the weather. We've discussed it . . .' She reached for Adam's hand and he smiled, 'and we want to take on a new vet. I'll become practice manager. I might continue to help out a bit. They seem to have no idea how fast it'll progress, but whatever happens, we want to plan ahead.' She stopped speaking and gazed round the table as if waiting for questions. Mandy still couldn't think of anything to say. Neither, it seemed, could Gran and Grandad.

'Is that okay with you, Mandy?' Dad was still gripping Emily's hand. 'A new vet and your mum as practice manager.'

'Of course it is,' Mandy said. How could her mum be taking this so calmly? she thought. She had known her mum was resilient, but if she, Mandy, felt so frightened, how come Mum was so serene? She was sure it wasn't an act. Mum really seemed to be taking it in her stride.

'Would anyone like some more tea?' Emily looked round the table.

Grandad pushed his cup towards her. 'I'll have another cup, please,' he said.

'And please do have some cake,' Emily said. 'I know it's a lot to take in, but I want to try to carry on as normal for as long as I can.' Was that it? Mandy wondered. Well, if Mum wanted to pretend everything could be normal, Mandy would just have to do her best.

Gran nodded, finding her smile. 'I'll have a small piece, please,' she said.

Adam frowned as if remembering something. He looked across at Mandy, his head on one side. 'You said you'd something to tell me and Mum,' he said. 'Is it something you can share with all of us?'

Somehow, Mandy found a smile. 'I found out this morning that Wildacre is finished,' she said.

Emily clapped her hands together. 'So is it all ready for you to move in?' she asked.

'Not quite,' Mandy said. 'There's still some furniture to

come, but it is just about there.' She paused for a moment, feeling sad, trying to hide it. 'There's no rush now, though.'

'What do you mean?' Adam asked.

'Well, I'll be staying here of course,' Mandy said. 'I came back to help you. I can't move out just now when you need me the most.'

Emily frowned and shook her head. 'No,' she said. 'You can't think that way. You've been working so hard. You deserve your own space . . .' she trailed off, turning her eyes to Adam as if appealing to him.

Adam shook his head, his face worried. 'You can still move in,' he said. 'We'll manage.'

Mandy opened her mouth to say she absolutely couldn't, but Adam gave her a warning look.

'We can talk more about it later,' he said.

Mandy reached out and picked up her tea. It was no more than lukewarm, but she tossed it back. She didn't feel remotely hungry, but she took a piece of Emily's cake.

She wouldn't argue the point now, but surely it wasn't right for her to move out, at least not before they had a new vet. Was it?

Chapter Twenty-Seven

Mandy slept badly, waking up several times in the night and feeling each time a rush of foreboding about her mum's illness. She had spent the evening reading about it on the Internet. It was true what Emily had said; she might remain well for a long time, but there could be awful consequences too. Images kept flashing into Mandy's head: Emily in a wheelchair, or Emily struggling to see. There would be a lot to do, to make sure Emily could stay independent if any of that happened. Mandy found herself looking at Animal Ark and Hope Meadows with new eyes, planning handrails and wheelchair ramps that probably should have been put in anyway. But how could they be, when there was barely enough money in Hope Meadows to cover the feed and bedding, and now they needed to pay a new vet as well? Whining, Sky crawled into bed with Mandy. She hugged the collie close, knowing she needed to rest for now.

Morning surgery and then two calls had passed in a kind of melancholy haze. At lunchtime, she went out to Hope Meadows. She tried to push yesterday's lunch at Wildacre to the back of her mind. Adam seemed to think she'd be moving out on schedule, but Mandy wasn't sure he was right on this one.

She had found reassurance in her animals. Sky was a concerned little shadow. Hattie and Tablet, the two cross-breed rescue dogs seemed to know something was wrong. Every time she got them out, they clung to her, begging for attention. Even the rabbits had been extra friendly. Mumma's kittens were now so well grown that they no longer needed milk, but they loved nuzzling Mandy's face and snuggling up to her.

Mandy texted James about Frank's release. She needed to tell him the news about Emily, so she asked him to come to Hope Meadows first. Then, they would meet Raj up near Mr Chadwick's house. Mandy had decided they should release Frank there. It was close to the place he'd been injured, but not too near the bad corner where Raj had come off the road. Mandy would watch Frank carefully as they released him. He had been flying inside for a few days now. It wasn't the same as if he had really been able to spread his wings, but she felt certain he would manage.

James messaged back saying that was fine. She was looking forward to seeing him. He seemed so happy these days.

She was in the paddock working with Brutus the Labrador, when a van drew up. To her delight, Brutus sat down and looked up at her. She smiled as she reached in her pocket for a treat. When he'd first come to Hope Meadows, he would have barked madly. 'Come on then,' she said to him as they set off across paddock. Raj climbed out of the van, slamming the door behind him.

'Hello,' she called out. Why would Raj have come so early? she wondered. They weren't due to release Frank until the evening. Had he misunderstood? Raj was picking his way across the paddock and seemed intent on looking at his feet. Did he look nervous? She couldn't decide. Beside her, Brutus was becoming almost frantic, trying to wriggle his bottom into the ground to show how willing he was to sit. Mandy looked down. 'You are a really good boy,' she told him and slipped him another chew.

Raj came to a standstill in front of them. 'Who's this?' he asked, nodding towards Brutus, who was still behaving perfectly.

Mandy smiled. 'This is Brutus,' she said. 'He used to go crazy with any kind of distraction, but now he seems only to have eyes for me and my pocket full of goodies.' Brutus wagged his tail, then for the first time, looked over at Raj. 'I think we should take him inside. Otherwise I'll have to give him another treat. Don't want him ending up the size of a house.'

Raj laughed. 'Is that a problem you often have?' he asked.

'Not really,' Mandy said. 'I save all his food for the day and use it for training. It works really well for most Labradors.' They walked back across the paddock together. Brutus trotted at Mandy's side, looking up at her.

'He seems very well trained,' Raj said.

Mandy felt very proud as Brutus trotted into his kennel, without even glancing at the other dogs, and lay down on his bed. He was so different from the crazy, growling bundle that had arrived only a few weeks earlier.

'Would you like a coffee?' she asked Raj as they walked back through to reception. He still hadn't told her why he'd come.

'I don't really have time,' he said. She got the same impression of nerves that she'd had when he first arrived. 'I wanted to ask you something,' he said. He pulled himself up straight and took a deep breath. 'I'd like to invite James out for a meal,' he said. 'Only it's not long since he lost Paul. I just   Well, I just wondered what you thought?'

Mandy couldn't help but be astonished, and then rather flattered that Raj had come to ask her. She also couldn't help looking at Raj slightly differently. She'd never considered him as boyfriend material. But he was a nice man, quite attractive, and an animal lover.

'I know it's difficult,' he said, shuffling his feet. 'I probably shouldn't have come. I'd just made a delivery up the road.'

'No, I'm glad you came,' Mandy reassured him. 'It's difficult to know how to act when someone's been bereaved, I know.' It was hard enough for her as James's friend. Harder still if Raj was hoping for something more.

She turned his question over in her head. James did seem to have been happier recently. Was it possible he liked Raj too? He hadn't mentioned anything, but they'd obviously seen each other a few times since Frank's accident. And had Raj really come to the squirrel hunt for Mandy's sake, or had he come to spend time with James? Either answer was pleasing, she realised.

She would give a lot to see James happy. It had been almost unbearable to see her friend in so much pain. But she had to be honest. 'I don't really have any idea what he'll say.' She paused, thinking. 'I don't see why you shouldn't ask, though. I don't think he'll be upset. He has dated a little since Paul died, but I'm not sure what he's ready for yet. Does that help?'

Raj smiled and let out a sigh of relief. 'Thank you so much,' he said. 'Good, yes. Thank you! I really like James, you know? The last thing I want is to upset him.'

Mandy watched him as he marched out, his shoulders back and his head held high. She found herself grinning, wondering with amusement whether he would have been quite so interested in Frank, had James not been part of the package. Then again, he'd been distraught when they first found him in the lane. If he really did love animals as much as he seemed to, it would stand him in good stead with James.

Mandy put Raj's question firmly out of her mind when James arrived at Animal Ark that evening. She had to tell him about Mum.

'What's wrong?' James said, the minute he saw her.

Mandy gave him a small smile. 'You always know when something's the matter, don't you?'

James became very still when she told him. He loved Emily dearly, Mandy knew, but despite his obvious upset, he was able to talk to her calmly.

'One of Mum's friends was diagnosed ten years ago,' he told her. 'She's still quite well, though I know she feels terribly tired a lot of the time.' They were sitting in the comfortable chairs where she usually chatted to potential owners.

'I'm just so frightened for her,' Mandy admitted. She pushed her lips together. So many times this afternoon, she had felt tears approaching, but she'd had to hide them.

'I know. And I know that feeling well.' James leaned over to take Mandy's hand.

Of course he does, after what he had to watch Paul go through.

'How did you handle it?' Mandy asked. 'I don't want her to know how scared I am.'

'You just always have to think what she needs,' James said. 'Like at work, when you just have to stay calm and give the animal what they need in that moment. That's what you have to do with Emily. Extra stress and fear won't help her. You just being yourself, as normal as possible, is what she needs.'

He's right.

Mandy nodded. 'Thanks, James.' She looked at her watch. 'We should be getting on.'

'Okay, we can talk more in the car if you'd like.' James pushed himself to the edge of the chair and stood up.

It didn't take them long to get Frank ready. They wrapped him in a blanket to move him into the cage he would travel in. Between them, they lifted it out to the car. Frank stood on his perch, fluffing his brown feathers. He twisted his neck to gaze all around as if drinking everything in with his big, dark eyes.

* * *

'I feel like a selfish person,' Mandy said as James climbed into the car beside her. 'I can't say this to anyone else, but after Mum said she was ill, I found myself wondering how it would feel if she was in a wheelchair. It should have been all about her, but I couldn't stop thinking about how it'd affect me.' She put the car in gear and pulled away slowly. She didn't want Frank to be shaken any more than she could help.

James reached over and squeezed her shoulder. 'I think it's quite normal,' he said with a sad smile. 'I used to do the same when Paul was ill. I'd find myself wondering how it would be when he was in hospital or worse, when he had died. Then I felt awful because I should only have been thinking about him. But illness doesn't only affect the person who's ill. It affects those around them too. You've said you don't want to move into Wildacre until they've sorted out a new vet. That doesn't sound like the action of someone selfish to me.'

Mandy blinked away the tears that had formed in her eyes. James was always so honest with her. If he said he thought it was normal, he was probably right. She found herself thinking about Raj. He too had been very thoughtful. Would he ask James out tonight? For a moment, she wondered about asking James what he would say, but Raj had come to her in confidence.

'How do you think Frank will feel when we let him out?' James asked a moment later, sounding determinedly cheerful. Mandy was glad of the change of subject.

✶ ✶ ✶

Raj was waiting for them in his van outside Mr Chadwick's house.

'You managed to find it okay then?' James asked, smiling at Raj. He certainly looked happy, Mandy noticed. She wondered what Raj had decided. He could hardly ask James out there and then with Mandy in tow. They walked round to the back of Mandy's car.

'So how's he been?' Raj asked. He peered through the back windscreen, trying to get a glimpse of Frank.

'Great,' she said. 'He's been raring to go the past few days, but I had to be sure he was strong enough.' She lifted the back door of the car and watched with amusement as James and Raj made a rush to carry the cage between them. 'We should get him well clear of the road,' she told them.

Frank clung to his perch as Raj and James manoeuvred his cage up and over a stile. He stretched himself up into a tall, thin posture and the long feathers at the base of his bill lifted. He was scared, Mandy realised. 'Poor Frankie,' she murmured. 'Not long now.'

The field they had climbed into was gently sloping. Further down the hill, there was a small area of woodland. A few cattle stood looking at them from the far side of the fence that ran down the side of the pasture. A stream flowed out from a pipe that ran under the road, its water burbling softly down the hill.

'What a lovely place,' breathed Raj as they set the cage down. He grinned. 'Lucky Frank,' he said.

Frank seemed to have calmed, now the cage had stopped moving. He surveyed the surrounding land with his feathers fluffed back out. The sun was about to set. Mandy reached down and opened the cage door. Frank paused for only a second. Then his eyes fixed on something and he flapped his wings. Lurching from his perch, he cleared the cage. A moment later, he was swooping across the empty field and over towards the woodland.

'Goodbye, Frank,' James said. His voice was wistful. They stood there for a few minutes more, watching as the sun dipped over the horizon, but Frank didn't reappear.

'Well that's that then,' said Raj. He too sounded sad.

Mandy glanced from Raj to James and back, and a flicker of mischief passed through her mind.

'Do you two mind taking charge of getting the cage back over the wall? Thanks,' Mandy said with a grin at Raj, who looked rather startled. James too looked surprised. Mandy wanted to laugh. Normally, she would be the last person to ask someone else to do the heavy lifting. Despite his confusion, James bent willingly enough to help Raj lift the cage.

Mandy was up and over the stile in a moment and walking, at what she hoped was a fast but non-suspicious pace, away from the two men. Hopefully she'd be out of earshot in a few steps. If Raj wanted to take advantage of the sunset, and the beautiful hillside, it was up to him.

She was crossing the road on the way back to her car when she saw Mr Chadwick coming towards her. He waved a hand. Even in the twilight, she could see he was grinning.

'I thought it was your car,' he said. 'What brings you up here?'

Mandy reached the car and leaned on the bonnet. Perhaps

James and Raj would be a few minutes yet, she thought. 'We just came over to release an owl I'd had in the centre,' she explained. 'He was injured on a road near here, but we patched him up. I thought he'd like it up here.' She glanced back towards the wall. Muted voices sounded from the far side. 'James and Raj are just bringing the cage,' she explained.

To her surprise, when she looked back at him, Mr Chadwick looked worried. 'That's a pity,' he said. Mandy frowned. 'Oh, I don't mean it's a pity he's better.' Mr Chadwick shook his head. 'I just mean this might not be the best place for him now.'

Mandy's heart sank. *Why on earth not?*

She'd met people who objected to certain species of wildlife being nearby, but Mr Chadwick hadn't struck her as one of those types. And besides, who could object to a lovely tawny owl?

Mr Chadwick was grinning now. 'You see, Marissa Bowie was looking for somewhere to build her factory,' he said. 'We got talking and I offered her the house and the grounds. All this here. She didn't want to work with Sam Western any more, so she and I are going into business together.'

Mandy stared at him, trying to keep her jaw from hitting the ground. 'You're volunteering your home for the factory?'

Mr Chadwick grinned at her. 'I am indeed,' he assured her. 'We'll be going through all the proper channels of course, but after all the years I've lived here, I'm pretty sure there are no endangered species. It is a pity about your owl, though,' he said.

Mandy turned a little to look back over to the field where they had released Frank. The moon was rising in the clear sky. It looked huge as it hung low over the hills. 'It shouldn't be a problem,' she said. 'He's a tawny owl. They're very adaptable, unlike the squirrels. If he doesn't like the noise from the building work or from the factory, he'll just move and find a new hunting ground.'

Mr Chadwick looked relieved. 'That's good,' he said. 'Marissa Bowie seems lovely,' he said. 'And I really wanted to make sure Welford still got its factory. All the people who were hoping for jobs will still be close enough.' He looked round at the scattered houses that made up the hamlet. 'And the neighbours here are far enough away that we won't disturb them.'

'But where are you going to live?' Mandy asked. For a split second, she wondered if he was going to say he was moving in with Marissa Bowie. It had been a strange few days. Almost nothing would surprise her, but if he had any more than business plans with Ms Bowie, he wasn't letting on. 'I've bought a small flat in the middle of Welford,' he said. 'It's been lovely getting to know your Gran and Grandad and they've introduced me to so many people. I want to be down in the village so I can see more of them all.'

Mandy heard a scuffling noise and looked round. Frank's cage was perched on top of the wall. James appeared and began to manoeuvre himself past it. Then Raj appeared. He seemed to be grinning.

'I'll let you go,' Mr Chadwick said as James climbed down. Once on the road, James reached back up to take the weight of the cage as Raj worked his way over. If Mr Chadwick was wondering why Mandy wasn't helping, he didn't say anything. He patted her on the shoulder as if very pleased to have told her his news, then headed back down the path towards his front door.

James seemed breathless as they got back into the car to drive back to Animal Ark. He and Raj had said their good-byes in a civil tone. Mandy couldn't tell for certain what had happened, though Raj looked happy. She put the car into gear, took off the handbrake and set off down the hill. She would wait, she thought. They were almost halfway home before James spoke.

'Raj asked me out,' he said.

'Wow, he did?' Mandy did her best to sound nonchalant. They rounded a corner and she reached out a hand to change gear, keeping her eyes on the road ahead.

'I didn't know what to say.' James sounded almost bewil-dered. 'He said his brother was starting a restaurant in a country hotel halfway between York and Bakewell. He wants me to go with him to the opening night.' He stopped.

'Well, that sounds lovely,' Mandy said. The headlights lit up the road ahead with its high walls and grassy verges. 'What did you say?' she asked. Though her eyes were on the road, her attention was all on James.

'I said yes,' he said. His voice was strangely distant. There was a long pause. 'Do you think it's too soon?' he asked.

Mandy risked a glance over at him. Though he looked

troubled, there was also something about the set of his shoulders that told her he was determined to do the right thing. 'James, you've dated before now,' she pointed out.

'Yes, but this is different.' He sounded nervous.

'Because you actually like him?'

'Yes.' This time there was no hesitation.

'Well, in that case, I think you need to go with your feelings,' Mandy said, her voice calm. 'If you like Raj, then go along and see what happens. I don't think Paul would mind.'

When she glanced around again, James was looking straight forward at the road ahead. He turned and caught her glance and smiled, though she could see unshed tears glittering in his eyes. 'I trust your judgement,' he said. 'Thank you.' Despite the tears, his voice was steady.

Chapter Twenty-Eight

'I'll ask Nicole if she can do an extra day.' Mandy put down her hot chocolate and bent to write it on her list. A barely touched plate of biscuits lay on the kitchen table between her and Adam. They had set aside some time to work out how they were going to juggle Mum's work between them, but it wasn't proving easy.

'We could work out a way of paying her,' Adam offered.

Mandy shook her head, her mouth set. 'We agreed we'd keep costs strictly separate,' she reminded him. With Emily out of action at Animal Ark, the business would already be under pressure. She lifted her mug and took another sip. 'Seb knows not to send any more animals my way at the moment. And for now, I won't accept any new rescues. We'll send them to Walton or York as we used to.'

'And if you need to . . .' Adam raised his eyebrows.

Despite her good intentions, Mandy let out a sigh. 'If I need to, I'll ask Seb if he can help find places for the animals that are already here.'

Adam reached out and squeezed her hand. 'It's good it'll be summer soon,' he said. Summer had always been quieter than spring at Animal Ark. Hope Meadows would have been entering its busiest time as they went into the holidays, but there was nothing Mandy could do. She couldn't afford to pay for extra help and she had to put all her efforts into her vet work for now. It wasn't just the additional work she was worried about. If Emily saw that they were under pressure, Mandy wasn't sure she would be able to resist. Mandy didn't want her mum to feel guilty that she couldn't help.

'So is there anything else?' Mandy lifted her mug and drained the last of the hot chocolate. The allocated hour was almost over and she had a call waiting.

'There is something actually,' her dad told her. Mandy settled back into the chair to hear what he had to say. 'It's about the night work. We're going to employ a telephone answering service. They'll take the calls when one of us is out. We should have done it years ago. That way, when it's your night off, you'll be properly off.'

'Sounds like a good idea,' Mandy said. She had grown up with the overnight telephones. Even when the Royal College had begun to allow on-call vets to take calls on their mobiles, Emily and Adam had preferred to field any contact themselves so the working vet wasn't disturbed when they were with an animal. It had been best for the clients to speak to someone they knew, but it was tiring.

'So . . .' Adam continued, 'I've been talking to your mum. We both definitely want you to move into Wildacre.'

Mandy looked at him. 'When do we begin with the service?' she asked.

'Tonight.' Adam sounded pleased. 'I called them yesterday and it's already set up.'

'That's good.' Mandy spoke slowly. Half of her wanted to move out. The other half was sure she should stay and help.

'You've worked so hard with Wildacre,' Adam told her. 'You deserve to enjoy it. And it is only ten minutes away.' He gazed at her, his eyes willing her to agree.

Mandy bit her lip. 'Are you sure, Dad? Really sure? You've thought through everything Mum might need?'

'I have. It's an order, love. You need to make your own life.'

Mandy's eyes filled with tears and she got up and threw her arms around Adam. He reeled, and then laughed.

'We'll be all right, Mandy. I promise.'

Jimmy called her just before lunchtime when she was driving homewards. She pulled the car into the side, then rang him back. 'Would you like to come over?' he asked.

'I'm just on my way home with a blood sample,' she said, 'then I'll be there.' She would put the blood in the fridge and send it off later, she thought. It would be lovely to have lunch with Jimmy. She put the car in gear and set off down the lane.

Jimmy and Simba met her at the door when she arrived at Mistletoe Cottage twenty minutes later. Both seemed equally delighted. Simba bounded round the garden with Sky. Jimmy opened his arms and they hugged. 'How's Zoe?' Mandy asked when they finally pulled apart. The husky had been doing well since coming home, as had her pup.

Each time Mandy visited, the puppy was a little bigger. She was now nearly two weeks old. 'She's great,' Jimmy said. 'Come and see.'

They walked together through into the sitting room. Zoe stood up slowly and stretched then licked Mandy's hand. Mandy reached out to stroke her but Zoe turned away, intent on her puppy. It was no longer as tiny and helpless as it had been. Mandy knelt down to take a closer look. 'Her eyes are open,' she gasped.

'They are,' Jimmy grinned.

Mandy lifted the puppy for a cuddle. The fuzzy brown fur was soft over the chunky little body. The white patches above her eyes gave the puppy a comical look. She nuzzled Mandy, the rounded little muzzle tickling under Mandy's chin. 'She's so sweet,' Mandy said.

Zoe hadn't taken her eyes off her puppy. 'You can have her back now,' Mandy assured the attentive husky. She laid the tiny bundle back in the bed. Zoe lay down too and before long, the puppy was suckling contentedly.

'Lunch is in the oven,' Jimmy said.

Mandy stood up, brushing dog hair from her knees. 'I'll come and give you a hand,' she said. Together they walked through into the kitchen.

'So how's your mum?' Jimmy looked over his shoulder as he opened the oven door.

'She seems a bit better,' Mandy said. 'They've started her on some steroids. Dad and I had a big chat this morning. About how it's all going to work.'

Jimmy pulled a tray from the oven with two baguettes, which were filled with melting brie. 'That's good,' he said, setting the food on the side. 'Shall we take these through?' he asked.

'Yes please.' It would be lovely to be with Zoe and her puppy while they ate.

'So how was your discussion?' Jimmy said, once they were sitting on the sofa. 'When will you get a new vet?'

'Dad's not sure.' Mandy lifted the sandwich. 'The new graduates'll be out soon. Mum and Dad are still trying to decide whether they want someone just out of university or whether it'd be better to have someone with experience.'

'And how about Hope Meadows?' Jimmy asked.

Mandy took a mouthful of the baguette, chewed it carefully and swallowed before she replied. 'We're scaling it back for now,' she said, trying not to sigh. 'I'll keep the animals I have, but we won't take any more till things are settled.' She couldn't help but feel sad.

Jimmy seemed to know how she was feeling. He reached out a hand and laid it on her knee. 'I know it's difficult,' he said, gently, 'but you're right to put your family first. You're doing a wonderful job with all the rescues you have just now. Once you've got your new vet, Hope Meadows'll get back to normal.' His hand was warm and reassuring. 'Actually I might be able to help you with your scaling back,' he said. 'Well assuming you agree, of course.'

'How's that?' Mandy asked. Over in the corner, the puppy had finished suckling. It stood up, staggered a few steps, then flopped down with a sigh, fast asleep.

'Belle and I have been talking.' Jimmy's eyes were also on the puppy. 'We were wondering if we could adopt two of Mumma's kittens for Abi and Max. They'd live here with me. Belle and I thought if they had pets of their own, it might help when the new baby arrives.' He looked at Mandy, raised his eyebrows and smiled. 'What do you think?' he said. 'I know it'll be a houseful, but that way they'll grow up with the puppy.'

Mandy threw open her arms and gave him a hug, almost sending her lunch flying. 'That's a lovely idea,' she said.

She let him go and he laughed. 'Glad you don't mind the idea of having even more animals around,' he said with a grin.

'Was that ever in doubt?' Mandy leaned over and pushed him with her shoulder.

'Not really,' Jimmy admitted.

Just then, his phone buzzed on the table in front of him and lit up with a text message. He read it and let out a short laugh. 'Oh yes, that's right,' he told her. 'The twins reminded me they have a question for you.'

'Oh yes?' Probably about Ganesh, she thought. Every time she'd seen Jimmy since their trip to the safari park, there had been messages and questions.

'They've decided on a name for the puppy,' Jimmy said. 'What do you think of Emma?'

Mandy smiled. Liz Butler would be delighted when she told her. 'That's a lovely idea,' she said. She reached out her hand for one of the slices of cake. Jimmy had warmed it through. It smelled wonderful. She took a bite.

'There's something else,' Jimmy said. He lifted his own plate.

Mandy chewed her mouthful. The icing was just as delicious as it looked. Jimmy seemed to be waiting for a reply. She swallowed, washing the food down with a swig of coffee. 'What?' she asked.

His eyes were on her face. 'They want to give her another name as well,' he said. 'But I said I'd have to ask you first. Would it be okay if we call her Emma Amanda?'

For a moment, Mandy thought she had misheard. Even if the twins had forgiven her for Zoe's lost puppies, Jimmy knew the awful truth. Would he really not mind? She looked into his eyes and he looked back, his gaze steady.

'Are you sure?' she said. She could feel tears prickling behind her eyes.

'I'm sure.' He took the plate from her hand, set it on the table and pulled her into his arms for a kiss. 'I don't know anyone who deserves it more,' he said.

Mandy was almost late back for afternoon surgery. She made it down the road by the skin of her teeth. Mrs Davey was waiting patiently with her hamster cage on her lap. 'Come on in,' Mandy gasped.

'Roo Dhanjal popped in a few minutes ago,' Helen told her an hour later when the waiting room was finally empty. The hamster had been followed by a vomiting cat, a dog with sore ears, a puppy vaccination and two parakeets that were moulting excessively. It had been an interesting afternoon.

'How is Roo?' Mandy asked. She hadn't seen Roo since the day Emily had collapsed, she realised. She must pop over and visit sometime.

'She's fine,' Helen said. 'She had some fantastic news,

though. The factory is going ahead after all. Mr Chadwick's offered Marissa Bowie his house.' Helen sounded so thrilled that Mandy didn't have the heart to say she already knew and had forgotten to tell everyone.

'That's great news,' she said.

A movement at the door caught her eye. Tango was standing outside, staring in. With an audible sigh, Helen stood up and went to open it. The aged ginger cat stalked in. He waited for Helen to close the door, then followed her to the reception desk.

'So how did Roo know?' Mandy asked.

Tango sat on the floor, looking up at Helen. For a moment, Mandy thought Helen was going to ignore him, but he was gazing at her. 'What?' Helen said, sending the cat a glare. 'I've work to do,' she said, 'and you'll only want to get down as soon as you're up.' Tango put his head on one side, then opened his mouth in a silent meow. He looked so sad that Mandy wanted to laugh. Helen growled. 'Oh, for goodness' sake,' she said, reaching down and lifting him up onto the desk. 'Just for a minute. What was it you said again?' she asked Mandy.

'I asked how Roo knew,' Mandy said.

Helen frowned, trying to remember. 'Well Roo had it from Gemma.' Mandy could picture Gemma Moss, standing behind her post-office counter, gossiping away. 'And Gemma got it from Mrs Jackson and Mrs Jackson got it from your gran,' Helen laughed. 'Something like that anyway.'

'I'll have to go and see Gemma,' Mandy said.

'Why?' Helen's eyes were wide. 'Do you need more details?' Helen asked.

It was Mandy's turn to laugh. 'No,' she said. 'I need to send off the blood sample from this morning.'

Collecting the blood sample from the fridge, she called to Sky. 'I'll be back soon,' she told Helen, waving the package to show her.

'See you.'

It was a very beautiful day, Mandy thought as she tramped down the lane. The hedgerows were filled with flowers. A warm spring breeze fluttered the leaves. The air smelled fresh as if it had rushed down from the high moors. Sky was enjoying herself. She trotted ahead, her nose to the ground, exploring everything in their path.

'Hello Mandy, did you hear the news about the factory?' Mandy turned. It was Sally Benster. She was looking a little bashful and nervous.

'I have,' Mandy assured her.

'Isn't it wonderful?' Sally said.

'It is.'

Sally bent down, stroked Sky's head twice, then stood up. 'Mandy, I'm sorry I gave you a hard time about the squirrels. I know you were only trying to do the right thing and I should have respected that.'

Mandy was surprised and touched by her frank apology. 'That's okay,' she said. 'I know why the factory is important. I'm just so pleased it's all worked out.'

Sally departed with a smile.

★   ★   ★

'Hello Mandy, have you heard the news?' Gemma Moss in the post office looked delighted as well. She was wearing a blue flowery summer dress.

'Isn't it great?' Mandy said.

'I hear we have you to thank.' Gemma beamed across the counter. 'If you hadn't got everyone together . . . I knew it would all come right in the end,' she said. She held out a hand, took Mandy's parcel and weighed it. 'Three pounds forty, please.'

Mandy handed over the money and made her way back to the door.

'Come on, Sky,' she said. She had just passed the church when a green Range Rover roared up the lane and slowed to turn onto the road that led to Upper Welford Hall. It was Sam Western. Mandy was sure he had seen her, but he kept his eyes on the road and drove past with a face like thunder. Once he had passed, she couldn't suppress a grin. She would have to face him soon enough on the farm. For now he seemed to be the only person in the village who wasn't sharing in the general jubilation. Her faith in Welford was well and truly restored.

Chapter Twenty-Nine

'Mandy.' Adam's voice echoed up the stairs. Mandy was lying on her bed texting Jimmy. It was almost lunchtime and the shared Saturday morning shift was nearly over. She let her head fall back onto the pillow for a moment. Jimmy had just suggested a walk by the river, but from the urgency in her dad's voice, there was more work to do before she would be free. Pushing herself off the bed, she cantered downstairs.

'Sorry.' Adam smiled at her, his eyes apologetic. 'I was just on my way to a foaling, but there's another urgent call, I'm afraid.'

'Not a problem, Dad.' Mandy found her smile without difficulty.

'It's a lambing ewe.' Adam frowned. 'Must be a really late one,' he said. 'It's Mr Thomas's at Ainthrop. Daffodil. He says you've seen her before?'

Mandy's mind went back to her meeting with Mr Thomas at the show. He'd said then that Daffodil was expecting. 'She's a Portland,' Mandy explained. 'They lamb year round.'

'Do they really?' Adam looked fascinated. 'I never knew that.' He turned and made his way through into the kitchen.

Mandy followed. He stopped at the door and turned to her, rubbing his chin. 'Will you be okay with that?' he asked.

Had he noticed she'd been avoiding obstetrics, Mandy wondered? She still felt jittery after Zoe. What if the ewe needed a caesar? Then again, she'd done loads of lambings this spring and she hadn't had a single operation. There was every chance it would be something straightforward. She pulled her shoulders back. 'I think so,' she said.

Adam reached out a hand and laid it on her upper arm for a moment. His touch was reassuring. 'You'll be fine,' he said. 'You're a great vet. You've been so much help lately. Mum and I are very proud of you.' His hand was still on her arm as he studied her face. 'Don't start second guessing everything,' he said. 'Zoe's case was vanishingly rare. Nobody could have predicted it.'

'I'll be fine,' Mandy said. She would have to be. Dad was going to a foaling and that was even more difficult.

A few minutes later, she was alone in the car with Sky. 'It'll be fine,' she told the collie. She glanced in the rear-view mirror. Sky was sitting in the back seat, looking forwards out of the windscreen. The road to Ainthrop was worth watching, Mandy thought. The midday sun soared high over the fell tops. The first time Mandy had visited Ainthrop, the trees had been bare against the horizon. Now their reaching branches were clothed in the lime green tones of early summer.

She glanced in the mirror again. 'It'll just be a lambing, like all the lambings in spring,' she informed Sky. 'Even if I have to do a caesarean, it'll be fine. I've seen lots of them with Mum and Dad. I even did one once when I was at university.' *That was more than three years ago.* She pushed the thought from her mind. It would be okay. It had to be okay because there was no other option. What would people think if they could see her telling her worries to Sky? she thought. She managed a wry grin. Sky was a great listener.

She dropped down from the high tops into a small dip that was almost a valley. The white paint of the tiny small-holding stood out from the surrounding fields. Mandy stopped the car outside and turned off the engine. Despite her chat with Sky, her hands were shaking. She reached for the door handle and pulled it firmly towards her.

'Miss Hope. I was hoping it would be you.' Mr Thomas looked dashing as ever in his Harris Tweed as he rushed up the front path to meet her.

He's anxious, Mandy thought.

She opened the boot and pulled on her waterproof trousers and the short green calving overall that would keep her dry and clean. Last, she pulled out a pair of long waterproof gloves, a pair of lambing ropes and some lubricant.

'Daffodil's in the shed,' he told her. 'She's in a pen this time,' he added. The last time Mandy had visited Daffodil, she and Mr Thomas had spent over an hour trying to catch the wily ewe. He trotted ahead, round the side of the house and into the small yard. He slid open the door to the old-fashioned byre that Mandy remembered so well from her previous visit. 'The others are all outside,' Mr Thomas told her as he waved her through. 'It's just Daffodil today.' He followed her inside. 'Her waters broke an hour ago,' Mr Thomas said. 'I've been waiting for something to happen, but every time I come out, she just looks at me.'

Despite her nerves, the sight of Daffodil standing in the deep straw of the low barn steadied Mandy. The little ewe needed her help. She walked across to the smaller penned area and climbed over the wooden fence. Daffodil stamped a foot as she approached, but it was the work of a moment to capture the neat head.

Mr Thomas climbed into the pen behind Mandy.

'Can you help me lay her down?' Mandy asked. Between them, they lay the small body down on the clean straw. Mandy picked up the bottle of lubricant and squeezed some out onto her right hand. She knelt down. This was the moment of truth, she thought.

Lifting Daffodil's short tail, she inserted her fingers into the birth canal. She had half hoped to find at least a foot there, but there was nothing. She pushed her hand a little further inside. There was still nothing. Had Mr Thomas been mistaken about the waters breaking? she wondered. She edged her fingers in right to the cervix, and there it was, a tiny twitching nose. She breathed in, then let her breath out slowly.

The lamb was alive at least. Her fingers explored further. Around the nose, instead of being wide open, the cervix was still half closed. She felt around some more. The band was tight and thick. There was no way the lamb would come through.

She thought back to a conversation she'd had with Adam, back at the beginning when she was just starting out. 'If the cervix isn't open, we used to try and stretch it,' he'd said. 'But there's a high risk of damage. If the owner's willing, it's better to operate.' She felt round the obstruction again. She couldn't even get her fingers past to explore the size of the lamb. The little nose twitched again.

Mandy pulled her hand out and straightened up. Mr Thomas was gazing at her. His eyes were brimming with confidence. Mandy wished she shared his certainty. 'How's she getting on?' he asked.

Mandy squared her shoulders. 'I'm afraid Daffodil's cervix hasn't opened properly,' she began. 'The lamb's alive, but it won't come out.'

'So what do you recommend?' Mr Thomas was watching her carefully, waiting for her to tell him what she was going to do. Mandy met his gaze. She had to keep her fears under control or she would be no good to anyone.

'We could wait,' she said. She shuffled her knees. She seemed to be kneeling on something hard under the straw. 'The cervix might open more, or it might not.'

'I see.' He nodded. 'And if not, the lamb might die.' Mr Thomas caught on fast, Mandy thought.

'That's right,' she confirmed. She took a deep breath. 'The other possibility is a caesarean,' she said. She ignored the tremor in her stomach. The words were out there now. If Mr Thomas wanted to go ahead, she would have to do the operation.

'Well then,' Mr Thomas was smiling, as if it was the easiest thing in the world. 'If that's what she needs, then please do go ahead. What will you need?'

'Daffodil can stand up for the moment,' Mandy told him. She got up from her knees and helped Mr Thomas to his feet. 'I could do with some kind of table for my kit, and two or three buckets of warm water,' Mandy told him.

She climbed back over the railings and made her way back to her car. Opening the boot, she picked out her surgical kit, clippers, antiseptic scrub and suture material. What else might she need? Her hands were shaking. She gripped her fingers, then loosened them again. Local anaesthetic. Antibiotic injection. Gloves.

Mandy walked back from the car on knees that didn't feel quite steady. This would be her first caesarean since Zoe, her first ever on a sheep. Her dad's voice echoed in her head. *'You're a great vet.'*

Mum and Dad had been so wonderful. She remembered Mum's story about Jean's dog Trixie. It must have been awful, but Mum was a brilliant vet. Her fantastic mum, who could no longer do the work she loved. She had to do this. Mum and Dad had never needed her more.

Mr Thomas greeted her at the barn door. 'I've brought you a bale of straw as a table, will that do?' He seemed so calm and confident in her ability.

And I have to live up to that.

'That's great,' she answered. A bale would be perfect. Not too big in the tiny pen, not too tall when she would be operating on her knees. They climbed back into the pen together and Mr Thomas steadied Daffodil as Mandy set out her kit. Drape first to cover the hay. Sterile pack and scalpel blade. Surgical gloves. She checked and double-checked in her mind. Did she have everything?

She turned to Daffodil. The little ewe had finally lain down. As Mandy watched, she lifted her tail and her flank bulged. As she strained, she let out an anguished bleat of pain.

Mr Thomas held her still and Mandy put a hand on the woolly rump. 'We'll have it out of there in a few minutes. It'll all be fine,' she murmured, hardly knowing if she was speaking to Daffodil or herself.

With efficient movements, she clipped away the thick wool, then washed the skin clean. Lastly, she put in the local anaesthetic and gave one final scrub.

This was it. There was no going back.

'Hold her tight for me,' Mandy said to Mr Thomas. He shuffled closer on his knees and redoubled his grip.

She lifted up the scalpel handle and slid the blade into place. The scrubbed skin of Daffodil's flank was soft and rounded. Mandy's hand was steady as she cut. Through the skin, through the muscle and she was into the abdomen. She could see the shiny pink surface of the uterus. Inside, there was movement. The lamb was still alive.

Mandy reached her hand inside the sheep's belly. Through the uterine wall, she could feel the lamb. She grasped the hind leg and wielded her scalpel again, running the blade across the surface of the womb with featherlight fingers. She had to get this right. If she cut too deep, the lamb would be injured. If she didn't cut far enough, the uterus would tear. The incision needed to be as long as the hind leg, from hock to hoof.

A moment later she was through. Keeping the uterus clear of the abdomen, Mandy took hold of the tiny leg.

Reaching in, she felt the second back leg. Holding them together, she lifted the lamb and it slid into view: hips, chest, shoulders and finally, the head.

She cleared the airway, then laid the lamb down on the clean straw and began to rub its back. Then the little chest jerked as it took its first breath and then another. Lifting its head, the newborn lamb shook its head, ears flapping noisily. Eyes wide, it gazed around then shook its head again.

Mandy could have watched all day, but she had to return to the task in hand. She turned back to the ewe. There was a second lamb. She had felt another foot. Reaching inside, she found the foot again. She found a second and then a blunt little nose. This lamb was coming out headfirst. She gripped both forelimbs in her right hand and the head in her left. Holding her breath, she pulled steadily.

Mr Thomas gasped. 'Another one?'

A moment later, the second lamb had been born. She laid the second small frame gently onto the straw and heaved a sigh of relief. This lamb was alive as well. Lamb number one was already starting to make wobbly efforts to rise. Both were healthy.

Mandy washed her hands, then checked the uterus again, but there were no more lambs. It was time to close up. She sutured the uterine wall, then the muscle and skin. Long before the last stitch was in place, both lambs were on their feet. Lamb number two seemed particularly fascinated with what was going on.

'I think he's trying to climb back in,' Mr Thomas said with a grin.

'I don't blame him,' Mandy replied. 'I'm sure it was warmer in there.'

She finished the final layer and straightened. It was hard work bending forwards and the muscles round her abdomen were aching. Putting her hands on her hips, she stretched, then pulled herself slowly to her feet. 'She can get up now,' she told Mr Thomas and he released the ewe.

It took only a moment for Daffodil to rise and inspect her lambs. They were still unsteady in the deep straw, but Daffodil went to first one and then the other, sniffing them. Then she started to lick. She seemed completely oblivious to Mandy as she gave the low grumbling nicker that ewes only ever made when they saw their newborn lambs. It was a wonderful sound.

Mr Thomas was still only halfway to his feet. Mandy found she had tears on her face, but she wiped them away and he made no comment as she offered him her hand. 'I think she's healthier than me,' he joked when he finally made it to his feet. He patted her on the shoulder. 'You've done a wonderful job.'

She helped Mr Thomas climb back out of the pen. Daffodil was doing amazingly well. The wound on her side was a row of neat stitches. Her attention was all on her lambs. They were already reaching under her, searching unsteadily for the source of the milk that would sustain them over the coming weeks.

'Will you have a cup of tea this time?' Mr Thomas had finally stopped stamping the feeling back into his toes and he leaned on the gate beside her. 'You were too busy the last time you were here. Say you have time today. Please?'

He was so earnest. Was he lonely, she wondered, up here with just his sheep for company? Her lunch with Jimmy could wait a little longer, she thought. She could stay and celebrate the arrival of Daffodil's lambs over tea.

Mandy smiled. 'That would be lovely.'

As well as tea, Mr Thomas had plied her with teacakes and cheese around the small pine table in his spotless kitchen. To top it off, he had slipped a jar of homemade jam into her hand as she stood up to leave. 'I make it myself,' he'd assured her. 'It's very good.'

'Thank you so much,' she said.

'It's me that should thank you,' he said. 'Will you take another look at her before you go?'

Mandy couldn't resist. 'I'd love to,' she said.

They strolled across the yard to the byre. Daffodil and her lambs were standing in the centre of the strawed area. Daffodil turned her head, glared at them as they came in and stamped her foot.

'She's always been spirited,' Mr Thomas said, looking at Daffodil fondly.

Mandy wanted to laugh. Despite having had an operation under an hour ago, Daffodil was no longer oblivious to their presence. She looked like she would fight Mandy to the death if she tried to get anywhere near the lambs now. The two youngsters were also doing well. They stood close to their mother's flank, staring at Mandy from wide eyes. Their reddish-brown wool had been licked dry. Daffodil stamped her foot again.

346

'We'd better leave her to it,' Mandy murmured.

'I think you're right.' He patted her shoulder again as they made their way round to the car.

Halfway home, Mandy pulled into a layby and stopped. She felt like she needed a minute to herself before plunging back into the chaos of Animal Ark. She pushed the door open and climbed out. The cool breeze lifted her hair, sending a tiny shiver down her spine. She breathed deeply, lifted her hands into the air and stretched her shoulders. It was a beautiful day. In front of her, the road meandered across the moorland through short-cropped grass and springing heather. Clumps of cottongrass bent their heads as the wind flitted over the austere landscape. In the distance, she could see the craggy summit of Askwith Tor. In winter storms the moor was bleak, but now it was gentled by the late spring sunshine and the enormous cerulean sky. A bee buzzed across the tarmac to land on a dandelion at Mandy's feet, then bumbled away in search of another flower.

I did it. Everything's going to be all right.

Chapter Thirty

Mandy turned into the lane that led to Animal Ark. It was almost time for dinner, she thought. Not that she was hungry; Mr Thomas had seen to that. Dad was on duty this evening, but it was too late to go to Jimmy's. The animals in Hope Meadows needed to be fed and cleaned out.

Nicole would be there. Mandy tried to figure out how she was going to ask her if she could work more. Not that she had much doubt that Nicole would say yes. She was so enthusiastic that it was difficult to keep her away, but Mandy couldn't afford to pay her anything. She should have been more organised with trying to get funding. It always seemed to get put to the bottom of the list. Still, looking on the bright side, she was very lucky to have Nicole. She was so good with the animals. Even the difficult Brutus responded well to her gentle patience.

Mandy pulled into the parking area beside the house and made her way round to the rescue centre. She paused on the flagstone path to take in the moment. The sweet trilling song of a wren sounded from the orchard. In the distance, she could hear the low drone of a tractor. The air was beginning to cool, but it carried the sweet scent of moorland flowers.

Her eyes wandered from the soaring fellside to Hope Meadows itself. She loved the wonderful building, which blended so beautifully into the landscape with its stone walls and wooden beams. Her heart still lifted every time she walked through the door. Even if they were scaling back, it would be waiting when everything was more settled. For now, Hattie and Tablet and Brutus and Mumma still needed her help. Jimmy would be taking the kittens soon and Holly and Robin were already established in their new home.

The door was unlocked. Nicole must already be here, she thought. She pushed it open and was hit by a wave of chatter. Jimmy was there, talking to Mum and Dad. Helen and Seb were with Rachel. Gran and Grandad too. As she walked in, silence fell and a row of beaming faces turned to greet her.

Before she could open her mouth, Nicole rushed across the room. She stopped right in front of Mandy, red faced and grinning. 'We got the funding,' she cried. 'They called earlier. I wanted to give you a nice surprise this time so I called everyone and they all came and . . . and . . .' She trailed off, breathless. Mandy wanted to laugh. Nicole usually didn't say much at all. Now she was almost gabbling with excitement. 'You've to call them back as soon as you can,' Nicole went on. 'Can you do it now, please? It's so amazing I can hardly believe it. It won't be true until you say so.' She thrust the phone into Mandy's hand. 'Do phone now. Please.'

Mandy took the phone, hardly knowing what to think. Could it really be true? She felt as if she was floating. Had Nicole pulled it off after all, despite the awful inspection?

Surely not . . . we were terrible!

'Walmey Foundation, Clarissa speaking.' The voice on the phone was as brisk as ever.

'Hello.' Mandy had to work to get the words out. 'It's Mandy Hope from Hope Meadows here. Nicole Woodall asked me to call you.'

The faces of her family and friends in front of her reflected her own hope and terror. She hoped she was managing to sound casual and not like her heart was in her mouth.

'Mandy! Thank you for calling back.' Clarissa sounded as if she was smiling. 'As Nicole probably told you, we want to offer you one of this year's awards. You're still within the first twelve months of opening, so Hope Meadows is eligible for the maximum payment.'

Mandy found she was holding her breath. The figure Clarissa mentioned took her breath away altogether. She had to double-check that she'd heard.

'Thank you,' she stammered when she was finally certain she wasn't dreaming. Nicole looked like she was about to burst with tension, so Mandy gave everyone a quick thumbs up. The room exploded into silent celebration. Nicole jumped up and down, her parents and grandparents hugged and Jimmy punched the air. Mandy turned away, stifling a grin and trying to concentrate on what Clarissa had just said. The donation was more than enough to cover all her costs. She could pay Nicole. If necessary, she could even hire someone else. 'Thank you so much,' she said again.

'Congratulations.' Clarissa sounded pleased. Mandy wondered what it must feel like to give such life-changing news. 'We were very impressed with you and with Hope Meadows.'

'Were you really?' The words burst from Mandy before she had time to think. She let her head fall back against the wall. ' I mean, I thought the visit had been a disaster,' she stammered. 'With the brush and all the barking and . . .' Her face reddened again as she remembered falling over. Every single animal in the place had been wound up. That the inspectors had seen beyond that was a miracle.

Clarissa sounded amused. 'I could see you were nervous,' she said. 'I felt so sorry for you, but it was obvious how much you care. You're doing a great job for the animals and for the surrounding area.'

For the first time in ages, Mandy felt tongue-tied. Hope Meadows hadn't even been open a year. She'd had so many setbacks. In Autumn last year, she had been attacked by Stuart Mortimore, the troubled nephew of the previous owner of Wildacre, who had believed the cottage to be rightfully his. Over the past few weeks she had angered the locals when the building of the factory had come under threat. Only this morning, she had been facing the likelihood that she might not be able to take any new rescues. It was amazing to be told that the inspectors had seen the good she was doing and were able to solve the crisis. 'Thank you so much,' she said finally. 'And can you pass my thanks on to Anthony? It really does mean so much to me.'

Clarissa laughed. 'I can tell,' she said. 'Lovely to be able to help. Thanks for calling.' She hung up and Mandy turned back around.

'We got the funding!'

The silent celebration erupted into noise and Mandy ran to Nicole and hugged her.

'How would you like to become an official member of staff?' she asked. 'I can pay you and everything.' She grinned at Nicole's delighted expression.

Nicole let out a whoop and thrust her small fist into the air, then realising everybody's eyes were on her, she lowered her arm and flushed. 'Thank you, Mandy,' she said.

Helen stepped forward and patted Nicole on the back. 'Brilliant,' she said.

'Woohoo!' Seb reached out to shake Nicole's hand. 'Good for you, Nicole!'

Jimmy came over and wrapped her arms round Mandy. 'Well done,' he whispered. 'There's nobody who deserves it more.'

Mandy smiled at them all as they gathered round, congratulating her and Nicole.

'I think a toast is called for,' Adam called out. He handed Mandy a glass of fizzy grape juice. 'To Mandy, Nicole and Hope Meadows,' he said.

Mandy raised her glass and all around her, her family and friends toasted Hope Meadows. Jimmy's arm was tight around her waist. Whatever was coming her way, she could face it with them all.

★ ★ ★

'Is that the last?' Adam asked as Mandy staggered into the kitchen at Wildacre. She dumped the box on the kitchen table. It contained the new kettle Susan Collins had bought her as a housewarming present and a set of mugs. She would unpack it shortly and then she could have her first official hot chocolate in her very own home.

'It is,' she said. Turning round, she opened her arms and gave him a hug. 'Thanks so much for all your help,' she said.

'I wouldn't have missed it for the world,' he said. 'It's not every day your daughter leaves home for the second time.'

Mandy laughed. 'Glad to be rid of me?' she asked.

Adam grinned. 'Of course,' he said. There was a twinkle in his eye, 'though I'm not sure what I'll do next time I need someone to whip your mother into shape.'

'Did someone mention me?' Emily walked into the kitchen, sending a teasing glare at Adam. She turned to smile at Mandy. 'The bedroom looks lovely with that new throw you've bought,' she said. Mandy regarded her with a feeling of optimism. There was colour in Mum's cheeks and the black circles that had surrounded her eyes for months had begun to fade. She had taken the doctor's advice seriously. She was going to bed at a regular time each night and was very strict about doing too much. The MS nurse was even talking about starting an exercise routine.

'Thanks to you as well, Mum,' Mandy reached out her arms and wrapped them round Emily. She was going to miss them, she thought, even though they were only ten minutes down the road and they would still be working together.

'Don't forget to visit!' Her dad waggled his eyebrows up and down.

Emily shook her head and frowned at him. 'Poor Mandy,' she said. 'I don't know how she puts up with us.'

Mandy laughed. 'It really has been tough.'

Adam glanced at his watch. 'I'm afraid we're going to have to get off,' he said. He looked at Mandy, his face suddenly serious. 'Have a lovely evening,' he said. 'If you need anything, you know where we are.'

Mandy hugged him again. 'Love you,' she said, then turned to wrap her arms around her mum. 'Both of you.' Emily kissed her on the cheek.

They made their way to the front door. It was a wonderfully still afternoon. The graceful trees that lined the track were motionless. Beyond them, the valley slumbered in golden sunlight. The half-wild flowerbeds were alive with buzzing bees and brightly patterned butterflies.

Sky rushed outside when Mandy had opened the door. She too seemed to be enjoying the garden as she rustled through the undergrowth. She stopped to sniff at a delicate rose bush that was thriving on the edge of the lawn.

Wildacre in the spring is the most amazing place ever!

'It really is a beautiful place.' Emily echoed what Mandy was thinking. 'I wasn't sure what to think when you bought it. It was so run down. Now, it's perfect.' She sighed. 'Bye love, and good luck with everything,' she said. Together, she and Adam made their way down the front path and climbed into the Land Rover.

'See you in the morning.' Mandy waved, then stood at the door watching as the car wound its way down the track. In the distance, the church clock began to chime the hour. Apart from Sky, she was alone.

She ought to go inside, she thought. The kettle was waiting to be unpacked and there were a hundred other things to do. Instead, she leaned against the doorjamb. A breath of wind caressed her warm cheeks. The scent of freshly cut grass greeted her like an old friend. Down in the valley bottom, a silage harvester criss-crossed the field. The air was so still that she could hear the drone of the tractor's engine.

Across the valley, another movement caught her eye. A brightly coloured Jeep traversed the dale, then slowed to turn into the long drive that led up to Wildacre.

She watched as it meandered up the track. It drew to a halt beside the cottage. There was a scampering rush and a joyous bark from Sky as Simba and Zoe careered round the corner. Sauntering behind them with a puppy in his arms, came Jimmy. 'I think you can go down now,' he said, looking down at the miniature husky. He grinned as Wildrun Emma Amanda reached up and licked his cheek. He set the squirming little form down on the grass. For a moment she explored, but then let out the tiniest whimper. As if on elastic, Zoe came rushing back. She lay down and the little one made her way round to feed. With a contented sigh, Zoe half closed her eyes as Emma began to suckle.

★   ★   ★

'Well that's all right then.' Jimmy's green eyes were smiling as he walked over and put his arm around Mandy's shoulders. She stood for a moment, enjoying his closeness. Then she turned and wrapped her arms properly round his waist. He gazed at her for a long moment, as if drinking her in, then bent his head and kissed her. His mouth was sweet and gentle yet passionate, leaving her reeling. She laid her head on his shoulder. Close together like this, she could feel that his heart was beating against hers. He smelled of leather and grass and of the shower gel he used every morning. She breathed him in, feeling unbelievably lucky that she could call this wonderful, handsome man her boyfriend. And then, quite unexpectedly, he lifted her as if she weighed almost nothing and carried her into the house. Setting her down in the kitchen, he bent and kissed her again. Then he took a step back, took both of her hands in his and smiled at her as if he would never stop. 'Welcome home, Mandy Hope,' he said.

Summer at Hope Meadows
Lucy Daniels

Newly qualified vet Mandy Hope is leaving Leeds – and her boyfriend Simon – to return to the Yorkshire village she grew up in, where she'll help out with animals of all shapes and sizes in her parents' surgery.

But it's not all plain sailing: Mandy clashes with gruff local Jimmy Marsh, and some of the villagers won't accept a new vet. Meanwhile, Simon is determined that Mandy will rejoin him back in the city.

When tragedy strikes for her best friend James Hunter, and some neglected animals are discovered on a nearby farm, Mandy must prove herself. When it comes to being there for her friends – and protecting animals in need – she's prepared to do whatever it takes . . .

HODDER

Christmas at Mistletoe Cottage
Lucy Daniels

Christmas has arrived in the little village of Welford. The scent of hot roasted chestnuts is in the air, and a layer of frost sparkles on the ground.

This year, vet Mandy Hope is looking forward to the holidays. Her animal rescue centre, Hope Meadows, is up and running – and she's finally going on a date with Jimmy Marsh, owner of the local outward bound centre.

The advent of winter sees all sorts of animals cross Mandy's path, from goats named Rudolph to baby donkeys – and even a pair of reindeer! But when a mysterious local starts causing trouble, Mandy's plans for the centre come under threat. She must call on Jimmy and her fellow villagers to put a stop to the stranger's antics and ensure that Hope Meadows' first Christmas is one to remember.

HODDER

Snowflakes over Moon Cottage
Lucy Daniels

It's Christmas-time in the little Yorkshire village of
Welford, and the first snowflakes are just starting to fall.

As far as Susan Collins is concerned, this Christmas is all
about quality time with her family, especially her son Jack.
After a string of terrible dates, she's given up on love.
And with the class of schoolchildren she teaches making
regular trips to local animal rescue centre Hope Meadows,
Susan's certainly got plenty to keep her busy.

That is, until she meets handsome children's author
Douglas Macleod. He might be the opposite of Susan's
usual type, but an undeniable spark soon lights up
between them. But then Michael Chalk, Jack's father,
turns up on the scene and Susan finds herself torn
between the two men.

With snow settling on the ground and the big day fast
approaching, who will Susan and Jack be choosing to
spend Christmas at Moon Cottage with this year?

HODDER